D1341588

J. B. Priestley

Lost Empires

GREAT NORTHERN

First published in Great Britain by
William Heinemann Ltd 1965

This edition published 2018 by:
Great Northern Books
PO Box 1380, Bradford, West Yorkshire, BD5 5FB
www.greatnorthernbooks.co.uk

© J. B. Priestley 1965

Copyright details unless otherwise stated:
Lost Empires: © J. B. Priestley
A First Word: © Tom Priestley
Variety was his Spice of Life: © Michael Nelson
My Friend Priestley – the Word-Wielding Magician © Barry Cryer
My Own 'Lost Empires' and a Storyteller Supreme © Roy Hudd

Every effort has been made to acknowledge correctly and contact the
copyright holders of material in this book. Great Northern Books Ltd
apologizes for any unintentional errors or omissions, which should be
notified to the publisher.

All rights reserved. No part of this book may be reproduced in any
form or by any means without permission in writing from the
publisher, except by a reviewer who may quote brief passages in a
review.

ISBN:
2018 Paperback edition: 978-1-912101-96-2
2018 Hardback edition: 978-1-912101-95-5

Design by David Burrill

CIP Data
A catalogue for this book is available from the British Library

For more information contact
the J. B. Priestley Society at *www.jbpriestley-society.com*

J. B. Priestley was born in Bradford in 1894. He was educated locally and later worked as a junior clerk in a wool office. After serving in the army throughout the First World War he went to Trinity Hall, Cambridge before setting up in London as a critic and renowned essayist. He won great acclaim and success with his novel *The Good Companions*, 1929. This and his next novel *Angel Pavement*, 1930, earned him an international reputation. Other notable novels include *Bright Day, Lost Empires* and *The Image Men*.

In 1932 he began a new career as a dramatist with *Dangerous Corner*, and went on to write many other well-known plays such as *Time and the Conways, Johnson Over Jordan, Laburnum Grove, An Inspector Calls, When We Are Married, Eden End, The Linden Tree* and *A Severed Head* which he wrote with Iris Murdoch. His plays have been translated and performed all over the world and many have been filmed.

In the 1930s Priestley became increasingly concerned about social justice. *English Journey*, published in 1934, was a seminal account of his travels through England. During the Second World War his regular Sunday night radio *Postscripts* attracted audiences of up to 14 million. Priestley shored up confidence and presented a vision of a better world to come.

In 1958 he became a founder member of The Campaign for Nuclear Disarmament and later in life represented the UK at two UNESCO conferences.

Among his other important books are *Literature and Western Man*, a survey of Western literature over the past 500 years, his memoir *Margin Released*, and *Journey Down A Rainbow* which he wrote with his third wife, the archaeologist Jacquetta Hawkes. J. B. Priestley refused both a knighthood and a peerage but accepted the Order of Merit in 1977. He died in 1984. His ashes were buried near Hubberholme Church in the Yorkshire Dales.

Contents

A First Word
Tom Priestley

Superficially there might seem to be connections between *Lost Empires* and *The Good Companions*; they are both stories of groups of entertainers touring theatres around the country, but here the similarity ends. The Good Companions of the title are a Concert Party, a community of performers working and living together. The Lost Empires are inhabited by individual acts competing for the public's attention in the earlier days of the Music Hall. These acts may be brilliant on stage, but could be weak and self-indulgent off stage. Into this strange world comes a young ambitious painter, and his story is retold by the old maestro. Although a coming of age tale as well – shades of my father's 1946 novel, *Bright Day* – it evokes the lost times, places and characters of the Music Hall, and of course my father loved the Music Hall, feeling that at its best it represented the native talent of the performers. He especially liked the comedians, men, for they were mostly men, who were naturally funny with the added gift of establishing a warm bond with the audience.

But there is a tenuous connection between *The Good Companions* and *Lost Empires*. When the book came out in 1965, it soon attracted the attention of Hollywood, and attempts were made to adapt it for the screen by none other than Victor Saville, who had directed the 1933 film version of *The Good Companions*. Sadly it never came off; sadly too for me because my father had put my name forward as editor. However eventually it was taken for television by Granada, after my father's death in 1984, and I remember being invited up to Manchester to meet some of the cast and crew for publicity photos. What a fine cast skilfully bringing to life the wonderful characters of the book - Brian Glover well chosen to play the comic Tommy Beamish; Olivier in a cameo role as the tragic Harry G. Burrard; John Castle as the irascible yet brilliant Nick Ollanton, and of course a young Colin Firth as the hero of the piece, whose story is so vividly imagined. The magic on the stage created magic in the book. My father enjoyed the rather basic conjuring tricks he would perform for us children, but *Lost Empires* was the best trick of all.

Variety was his Spice of Life
Michael Nelson

J. B. Priestley's interest in music halls and variety theatres dated from his early years in Bradford when he indulged in all the cultural delights – highbrow, middlebrow and lowbrow – which his native city offered. Indeed, he was as much at home in its four theatres as he was in St George's Hall, to which, as he recalled in *Margin Released*, 'the Halle Orchestra came regularly and Nikisch brought the London Symphony'. Yet, ironically, it was as a result of a visit to the Leeds Empire one evening in 1913 that started him off as a paid writer. One of the turns consisted of three young Americans, Hedges Brothers and Jacobsen, and their act encouraged Priestley to write what he called 'a topical skit, an imaginary interview called *Secrets of the Ragtime King'*. He sent it to a popular weekly, *London Opinion*, whose editor accepted it, printed it, and paid the delighted contributor one whole guinea. 'That guinea (wrote Priestley) must not be despised; it could have bought twenty-one cloth-bound masterpieces or nearly four pounds of good tobacco, or a week's holiday'. Moreover the budding author was not just a patron of the stage: he was something of a performer himself. One of his biographers tells us that 'commonly regarded as a baritone, what Priestley's voice lacked in quality he made up in volume with the result that sentimental ballads suffered but comic songs flourished'. And we know that he was an amateur pianist who played chamber music for pleasure – as he recounts in one of the pieces in his delightful collection of short essays called *Delight*.

Given Priestley's abiding interest in popular stage entertainment (particularly 'Clowning') and the special feeling he had for the period just before the First World War it is no wonder that one of his last major novels should feature both that time and the variety theatres which flourished in it. The setting of *Lost Empires* has its poignancy as well as its remembrances, for at the end of the book's main narrative a great and terrible war breaks out and Priestley's world is never quite the same again.

Is this his finest novel? Opinion seems to be divided between it and *Angel Pavement*. The argument need not be pursued: rather, *Lost Empires* should surely be assessed on its own merits. And these are considerable, for it conjures up, with a rare richness, a brightly-lit world of glitter and enchantment but with undertones of corruption, incipient madness, murder, suicide, violence and raw sexuality such as are found in no other of the author's novels. Throw in a sub-plot about women's suffrage and a case of perverting the course of justice and it is difficult to see what else Priestley could have included to make the story work.

While it has not spawned nearly as many adaptations as *The Good Companions* there is a sufficient number to indicate the novel's suitability for translation into other forms. Victor Saville, who had directed the first film version of *The Good Companions*, acquired the film and television rights but over a period of 20 years failed to exploit them. Eventually, in 1985, the Cambridge Theatre Company, in association with the Birmingham Repertory Theatre, presented a musical version in an adaptation by the experienced Leeds-born writers Keith Waterhouse and Willis Hall, and with music by Denis King. It was an ingenious production and a gallant, if only partially successful, attempt to capture the essence of a crowded novel. There is evidence that the touring production (with a non-star cast) was not a commercial success and it never reached the Old Vic in London, for which it was intended.

About the same time Granada Television, having scored a great success with its versions of *The Jewel in the Crown* and *Brideshead Revisited*, announced a multi-million pound, eight-hour production of an adaptation by Ian Curteis. This was screened in 1986, two years after Priestley's death and subsequently issued on DVD. Directed by Alan Grint it is a sumptuous production which is generally faithful to the novel. The cast is a large and interesting one. Colin Firth, then relatively unknown but now at the top of his profession, plays the young hero Richard Herncastle; John Castle is wonderfully sardonic as his uncle, Nick Ollerton; and no less than Laurence Olivier appears as the washed-up comedian Harry Burrard. This is a role with echoes of Archie Rice in John Osborne's *The Entertainer*, which Olivier memorably created on the stage. The supporting cast includes Beatie Edney, Carmen du Sautoy, Gillian Bevan, Alfred Marks and Pamela Stephenson. The production was not as successful as its famous predecessors but remains eminently watchable in its three-disc DVD format. Interestingly, when the television production was screened in the United States each episode was introduced by Alistair Cooke.

In 1994, for the Priestley Centenary, BBC Manchester broadcast a three-part radio adaptation by Bert Coules. It was re-broadcast on the BBC's digital radio channel in 2007 and again in 2008. Given the length and complexity of the original this can only be regarded as a somewhat 'filleted' version, in which whole sequences are omitted. It has its merits, nevertheless: Tom Baker, for example, is suitably brusque and brutal as Ollerton, one of Priestley's most memorable characterisations; and Brigit Forsyth (fondly remembered from the comedy series *Whatever Happened to the Likely Lads*) is coolly enticing as the *femme fatale*, Julie Blane. (The final episode carries a 'health warning' about some of the 'ripe' dialogue). A special point of interest is that the story's theatrical background is given some authenticity by the location recording in the Oldham Coliseum before an audience of local people.

The original novel, which was warmly received when it was first published and has been subsequently praised by Priestley's biographers, remains a fitting testimony to the author's love of the old variety theatres and to the artists who trod the boards, to his delight, in those far off days of his Bradford youth.

Michael Nelson is one of the founding members of The J. B. Priestley Society and is an expert on the stage, radio and screen adaptations of Priestley's work.

My Friend Priestley –
the Word-Wielding Magician
Barry Cryer

Like Dickens, JB's books are character driven. You get the impression that they're so strong, they grab hold of the plot themselves and run with it.

Lost Empires epitomises his love of performance and performers – from *The Good Companions* onwards, there are constant references to music hall and its legitimate twin and this concentration on the live art, would seem to make his work perfect for adaptation. But while his characters leap off the page, they rarely seem to leap off the screen with the same force. TV and film versions of *The Good Companions*, were pale reflections of the original, as was the stage musical, written by two brilliant Americans, Jonny Mercer and Andre Previn, who nevertheless, failed to capture the sheer vitality.

Lost Empires itself, was adapted for television, featuring Laurence Olivier, no less, but, yet again, the basic energy was lacking. Why would this be?

You would imagine a man whose books were crowded with a cast of three dimensional characters would translate naturally to screen and stage, but I think therein lies the answer to JB's genius. They were born on the page and they live there. I once compared his books to an armchair, in which you recline and are reluctant to leave. A lame image, but then again, I'm no Priestley.

Just a devoted fan and I once paused to analyse his appeal for me. We were both born in Yorkshire and I think this combination of wary scepticism, but with a love of life, struck a chord with me.

The man himself, embodied this – I still remember the overtly gruff exterior, belied by the twinkle in the eyes.

He had grown up with music hall legends like Little Tich and Dan Leno and I shared with him a memory of meeting an old man in Leeds, who had been a stage hand when the Fred Karno Company visited the city. He remembered that the leading comedian, though brilliant, was not generally liked and would, on occasion, miss a performance, due to loss of voice. This was ironic, as his name was Chaplin. His understudy, on the other hand, who could replicate all of Charlie's stunts and falls, was popular with the Company. His name was Laurel.

We often talked of comedians and the subject would always arouse his enthusiasm. He was a fan of Monty Python and was annoyed it was not being shown in the Midlands, due to some quirky BBC networking. If it was shown, it would be late at night, after show jumping. He told me he would have liked to have seen John Cleese 'have a go' at *When We are Married*. John as Ormonroyd? The mind boggles.

Our first contact was on the phone. I was working with Graham Chapman at the time, from the aforementioned Monty Python, and he averred that I was a bore on the subject of Priestley and why didn't I ring him? This seemed ridiculous – you can't just ring an idol and anyway, how would I acquire the number?

Then I remembered Wendy at Yorkshire Television who had worked on a documentary about the great man. I rang her and casually asked if she had his number. She had. This had suddenly become simple. It was alarming. Emboldened after a good lunch, I took a deep breath and dialled the number. A woman answered, who I assumed was a secretary or assistant, it was actually a cleaner, 'is Mr Priestley in?' Silence. A click. 'Hello?'

'My name's Barry Cryer.' 'Is it indeed.' He then revealed he had heard me on the wireless and I floated on a pink cloud, but quickly fell to earth. What could I say that wouldn't alarm him? 'My mate and I... er... would like to have tea with you.' 'Who's your mate?' 'Graham Chapman.' Before I could say any more, he was on the subject of Monty Python. 'Monday at three and I'll have you know, I'm giving up my walk.'

The pieces were falling into place. It seemed pre-ordained. That Sunday I was going to see the gang in the Python stage show at the Belgrade Theatre in Coventry, not a million miles from Alveston, near Stratford-on-Avon, where the Priestleys lived. I stayed over and we booked a car for the Monday. John Cleese heard about the jaunt and joined us.

Thus began a friendship that lasted for the remaining years of his life. We stayed for three hours and he and Graham swapped views on pipe tobacco and then his wife Jacquetta, emerged from behind a bookcase and joined us. She had been eavesdropping, in case it was *This is Your Life* or some similar set-up.

Enough of the background – *Lost Empires* has been variously described as 'as full of surprises as a Crystal Palace firework show', 'a recreation of a vanished age, alive and alike in its language and its insights' and 'a novel so outstanding that, far from being unable to put it down, one wants it to stretch out for days.'

Once again, the master is preoccupied with time. So often, in his books, a chance meeting triggers memories and a backward journey into long gone years. In an uncharacteristic prologue, JB, as himself, claims to have met Richard Herncastle, the main protagonist in *Lost Empires* and heard from him, his adventures as a magician's assistant in variety theatre. This semblance of reality launches us into a panoramic voyage around the country and along the way, the interplay between the various acts on the bills, politics and even a murder.

I can't imagine any other novelist keeping the plates spinning with such skill. I read this on a train and nearly missed my stop. Priestley himself, at times, seems a word-wielding magician, with a dash of hypnotism thrown in. Once in his grasp, he never lets you go, but you're a happy captive.

If you've read this before, embark on a return journey. If you haven't, I envy you.

My Own 'Lost Empires'
and a Storyteller Supreme
Roy Hudd

My introduction to JB was in Croydon where my Gran, who brought me up, used to take me every Tuesday to the first house at the Croydon Empire. Sadly, now another lost Empire.

Our Empire was a Variety theatre which, by the early fifties, in an attempt to attract audiences who'd rather stay at home was reduced to presenting tatty nude shows *'Strip Strip Hooray'* and *'Fanny Get Your Fun'* and 'daring' plays like *'Tobacco Road'* and *'No Orchids for Miss Blandish'*. When these types of shows were in town Gran wouldn't take me. 'I'm not sitting in a theatre with a lot of dirty old men,' she would say.

I missed my visits to a live show, so one week when the Empire's top of the bill was, *'Jane of the Daily Mirror – with Fritzi her dachshund,'* my gran took me to the 'legit' Grand Theatre Croydon instead to see a play. I wasn't sure about this at all. No band, no dancers, no jugglers, no ventriloquists with naughty boy dummies, no funny ladies, no trilby hat wearing comedians, no over the top drag acts and no dogs, monkeys or educated horses. Just a pianist playing tunes I'd never heard before and then a curtain silently rose to disclose half a dozen assorted middle aged ordinary people in old fashioned clothes. They talked in what was to me an alien accent but still made me laugh - a bit. Then suddenly bursting into the sitting room of this strange collection of uptight characters was someone I liked – a jolly, loud and drunken man who began to cause chaos with a camera on a tripod. It was like an elephant had arrived in the room. Every time he appeared, always a little bit more worse for wear, I sat up and hugged myself. He was the funniest photographer I'd seen since the classic Sid Field sketch. As we left the theatre Gran asked how I'd enjoyed *When We Are Married* – for the play was of course Priestley's. I could only talk about Henry Ormonroyd, the drunken photographer and how, if ever I went on the stage, I'd like to be him. Some sixty odd years later I was Henry for six months at the Garrick Theatre on Charing Cross Road. I almost got him right.

When I first read *Lost Empires* the world of Richard Herncastle and Uncle Nick had all but disappeared, yet it was a world I did know something about. I came into show business in the late fifties and all the characters and events JB chronicled had hardly changed since the nineteen tens where he set the novel. There were still a few vast Palaces of Variety where magicians with big spectacular acts were 'full bottom' - their names were the bottom line on the posters across the full width but in slightly smaller type than the main attraction. The main acts always had their names across the top of the posters – the headliner. A lot of the magicians I met were, like Uncle Nick, more interested in the devising and the construction of tricks rather than trying to curry favour with the audience. Some still wouldn't allow anyone to watch from the wings while their 'miracles' were being performed.

There were family members involved with the variety acts – usually young ones who really would rather have been at university than being involved in an old-fashioned and dying art form. Like Ricarlo in Priestley's novel there were performers who chased big girls and landladies - and caught them - for mutual satisfaction. There were one or two Harry G. Burrards. Dead eyed, old style, music hall comedians long past their sell by dates who always blamed the punters for their lack of success and were on the edge of doing something terrible to themselves. There were still ageing lads desperately trying to look younger. A favourite comic of mine would walk up and down Charing Cross Road wearing a corset and the world's worst toupee with the glue running down his forehead. There were brilliantly inventive, genuinely funny people who too had dark thoughts behind their loveable exteriors. There were certainly those who drank too much. Priestley himself wrote about one, Jimmy Learmouth, who he described as, 'one of the best comedians I ever saw.' Jimmy Learmouth died at thirty - of booze.

In my time one brilliant comic was such a lush that he had to be locked in his dressing room, to keep him out of the ever present pub that always seemed to be just outside so many stage doors. He once surprised the stage manager who unlocked his dressing room to escort him to the stage only to find him stoned. He had slipped a pound note under the door asking the call boy to get him a bottle of scotch and a packet of drinking straws. The lad returned with the necessary and the comic instructed him, from inside his locked dressing room, to take the cork out of the bottle and put a drinking straw in. He then drank the entire contents through the straw - through the keyhole.

There were former West End actors and actresses who were forced, because of their unreliability, to play small parts in comical sketches. I did pantomime with one who assured me we could get a free pass into the local cinema if we said we were from the theatre. We tried it and the cinema manager said, 'Prove it!' Without a word the West End artiste pulled the collar of his shirt away from his neck. Inside the collar were the unmistakable signs of old greasepaint. We enjoyed the film.

There were agents who smiled at those who made them a few bob and ignored those who didn't. They were always on the lookout for new suppliers of ten percents and often had performers on their books they hadn't even seen. A pal of mine did a terrific act with his wife and after one performance a very famous agent pushed his way into their dressing room and asked, 'Have you got an agent?' 'Yes thanks,' they said. 'Who?' he asked. 'You!' they replied. One agent I knew was trying to find dwarfs for a pantomime. Just a couple turned up for the audition. He told me 'You just can't get 'em you know. Not since the free orange juice!'

It's said that if you write a novel it should always be about something you know. How well JB knew the world of theatre! Not only the 'magic of the playhouse' but, as he says, in this salute to the theatre of the people, 'the playhouse has always seemed to me very pale and thin compared with the warmer and deeper magic of the music hall.' He brings us all that magic and lots of stark, dark truths as well. He so obviously loved comedians. Just read his descriptions of those comic giants Harry Tate, Little Tich, Grock and Chaplin in his book *Particular Pleasures*. Oh for a time machine.

I've so enjoyed reading for the umpteenth time *Lost Empires*. It is, of course, my very favourite of his novels. Perhaps the subject matter has something to do with it, but it's not just that - like all the performers he writes so accurately about, Priestley is timeless. He was a storyteller supreme, a master of his craft with little gems of observation tucked away on every page, such as the description of the Ballroom in the Winter Gardens, Blackpool; or his describing Nancy's legs as 'ravishing and witty!' I hadn't a clue what 'witty' legs were till I met my wife. She has them and I think that's why I fell in love with her.

Thank you Mr Priestley for putting pen to paper.

J. B. Priestley

Lost Empires

Being Richard Herncastle's account
of his life on the variety stage
from November 1913 to August 1914
together with a Prologue and Epilogue.

GREAT NORTHERN

First published in Great Britain by
William Heinemann Ltd 1965

This edition published 2018 by:

Great Northern Books
PO Box 1380, Bradford,
West Yorkshire, BD5 5FB
www.greatnorthernbooks.co.uk

© J. B. Priestley 1965

Every effort has been made to
acknowledge correctly and contact the
copyright holders of material in this book.
Great Northern Books Ltd apologizes for
any unintentional errors or omissions,
which should be notified to the publisher.

All rights reserved. No part of this book
may be reproduced in any form or by any
means without permission in writing from
the publisher, except by a reviewer who
may quote brief passages in a review.

To A. D. Peters from an Old Client,
an Old Friend, after forty years

Author's Note

I have taken an obvious liberty with music-hall history by taking imaginary performers, often at definite dates too, into real variety theatres in real cities and towns. Apart from a few very well-known performers who are mentioned, all the others, together with all the characters not on the stage, are entirely imaginary. With the exception of those noted above, there are no references to actual persons. I beg the reader to accept my assurance here.

J.B.P.

Contents

Prologue
by J.B.P.

I was staying at Askrigg in Wensleydale, where I had gone to ramble and to do some painting. It was late September, not a good time except in a lucky year, for cold dark rain was already driving down the dale. I had not been up there more than a couple of hours before I learnt that Richard Herncastle, the watercolour painter, was now living in Askrigg, in a house made out of two farm cottages, above the village, just off the road to Reeth and Swaledale. He was not on the telephone yet, but they told me at the pub I would find him in – he was now almost crippled by arthritis – so after dinner I walked up there, to find, much to my relief, two long low windows shining through the rain and darkness.

Herncastle was no stranger or I would have not dropped in on him so casually. In the later 1930s I had called on him twice in his studio at Grassington, and each time I had bought several of his watercolours of the Dales. All are good, and two of them, triumphant glimpses of the limestone country in Upper Wharfedale, exquisite in their broadly washed tones, seem to me masterpieces. Indeed, for this North-country landscape, Herncastle at his best is at least the equal of any water-colourist we have had since John Sell Cotman. I admired the work and liked the man, so whatever the years might have done to him, I was looking forward to meeting him again. On the way up there I was trying to work out his age, and concluded that he must be in his early seventies.

After a longish wait and some fumbling behind the door, it was opened by a man I would never have recognized as Herncastle if I had not known he was there. He had been a rather handsome upstanding fellow even when nearing his fifties; now he had shrunk, was bent, and had grown a beard.

'Herncastle,' I said, 'you remember me – Priestley?'

'Why of course. Come in, come in.'

While I was taking off my raincoat, I told him how I came to be in Askrigg and had heard he was living in this house; then I followed him along a passage into a long, low-ceilinged room, filled with pictures, prints, books; and we settled ourselves in front of a wood fire.

'I'm here on my own just now,' he said. 'My wife's staying in London with our married daughter, and the woman who comes in to look after me goes home at five. And this damned arthritis slows me down. Half the time I go fumbling around like a man of ninety.'

'How about work?'

'Off and on. Sometimes I know what I'm doing with a brush, sometimes I don't. And then I'm hard to live with – best left alone.' He gave me a grin then, and I noticed what I ought to have remembered about him, that he had eyes of an unusually clear blue, not pale as such eyes often are, in the North German and Scandinavian style, but at least as deep as cerulean. It crossed my mind then – and this is important because of what follows these introductory remarks – that in his youth he must have been uncommonly good-looking.

During the next half hour or so we drank a little whisky, smoked our pipes, and in an elderly rumbling fashion exchanged news of what we were doing or trying to do. One thing pleased him. A publisher I knew was doing a book on his work, with a dozen big colour plates and thirty to forty black-and-white reproductions, and some young man I did not know had nearly finished a biographical and critical text for it. But they needed an appreciative Introduction, and already both Herncastle and the publisher had discussed the possibility of asking me to do it.

'Now I'll admit it, J.B.,' he said, shouting a bit, like a good Yorkshireman, to cover his shyness, 'I've got you here and now I'm rushing you – eh? Dirty work.'

'No, I'd be very glad to do it. I've wanted a chance to say what I feel about your work. So that's settled. By the way, have you been doing some writing yourself?' I pointed to the near end of a long work-table. There were notebooks and a lot of odd sheets on it, and a tape recorder and quite a pile of spools.

He looked embarrassed, cleared his throat, then said nothing, so that I was about to change the subject when at last he did reply.

'You imagine I've always been a painter, don't you?'

'No, I don't,' I said slowly, trying to remember. 'I have a vague idea that before the First War you were doing office work in the wool trade, just as I was. It must have been something you said at Grassington.'

Now he grinned and pointed his pipestem at me. 'I was for a bit. At the West Bruddersford Spinners. But after that, and before I joined up in the war, I was on the variety stage-'

'Good God!-'

'I thought that'ud shake you. Well, I was. Toured all over. And that's where the writing comes in. Have you noticed the way the past comes curving back to you, as if you weren't getting further and further away from it but coming nearer to some of it?' He stared anxiously at me.

'I have, though I've also noticed that it doesn't seem to happen to everybody–'

'That's right, that's right; Oh – I'm glad to hear you say that. To tell you the truth, I was beginning to wonder if there were something peculiar about me. For instance, my wife doesn't feel it. You'd think a woman might, but she doesn't. The past is dead and done with – except for a few romantic-sentimental bits – as far as she's concerned. She doesn't suddenly *taste* it the way I do. Well, I've talked so much, the last year or two, about that time when I was in Variety, she insisted I must get it down in writing – or if I didn't feel I could write, then I'd better talk it into that tape recorder. So that's what I've been up to.'

'And how's it going?'

'I've about given it up. It's a proper bloody mess. I'm trying to do what I can't do. Some of it comes out right, just as it happened – now and again I've surprised myself – but then I lose it again or botch it up.' Slowly and rather shakily he began to put some more wood on the fire, and took the opportunity of talking to me without looking at me. 'If we're in for a few wet days – and I fancy we are – perhaps you wouldn't mind, just to pass the time, reading what I've written and taking this recorder and these spools to listen to what I've talked into 'em. Or is that asking too much?'

It wasn't. And the dale was lost in the rain day after day. I listened to his recordings, afterwards sending them to a stenographer; I read what he had written, including many pages of fragmentary notes, about which I closely questioned him, making my own notes; and we spent four afternoons and evenings filling the gaps in his narrative. The result is what follows in this book. It is Richard Herncastle's story, not mine. If there are passages here and there that sound more like me than like him, that is because in these places I had to enlarge upon what he had found hard to express at all; but in every instance he agreed with what I had finally set down. (We corresponded at some length, of course, after I had left Askrigg.) Fortunately, our temperaments and outlooks are not dissimilar, in spite of some obvious superficial differences. It was left to me to organize and translate this untidy mass of experience, remembered after half a century, into a fairly smooth autobiographical narrative. I admit that some of the writing is not his but mine, whether it is bridging the original gaps or attempting to capture certain heightened moments; but, I must say again, it is not my story but his – being a first-person account of an early passage in the life of Richard Herncastle, CBE, ARA, RWS, watercolour painter but onetime assistant to an illusionist on the variety stage.

Book One

1

To explain how my Uncle Nick asked me to join him, I have to go back to my mother's funeral. This was late in October 1913. It was a raw day up at North Top cemetery, with not much light about; we looked like a lot of figures in an old wood engraving. It was a land of Christmas gone mad, because so many of the other mourners were ancient relatives I never saw except at Christmas, great-aunts with huge clicking sets of false teeth and accents so broad, with so many dialect words, they might have been talking a foreign language. I remember I felt nothing but the cold and a vague sense of depression. My mother had died after four months in the Infirmary, worn almost to a skeleton by the cancer that had been eating her alive, and after seeing her so often like that, only wanting to be released, I had no feeling left for her death and burial. But I was not enjoying myself, as the ancient relatives soon began to do after the coffin had vanished and they had dried their eyes. My Aunt Mary, mother's only sister, was providing the ham and tongue and tea with a drop of rum in it; and I was wondering how soon I could escape from the rattle and chatter. Then I saw Uncle Nick, who had hardly spoken a word and had been looking disgusted, get up and beckon me to follow him out. I muttered something to Aunt Mary, and then went after him.

'You don't want to stay with that lot, do you, lad?' He was climbing into the longest and thickest overcoat I had ever seen.

'No, I don't, Uncle Nick. I was wondering how to get away.'

'You come with me. I want to talk to you anyhow.' He jammed on his head something rarely seen in the provinces in those days – a black trilby. 'We'll run down to the Great Northern. I need a drink. And one wouldn't do you any harm, lad.'

It was only the middle of the afternoon, but bars were open all day then. I liked the idea of sitting in the Great Northern having a drink with Uncle Nick, especially at that time of day when I ought to have been staring at a ledger in the West Bruddersford Spinners' office. I followed him eagerly into his motor-car, which was all new and shining and, he explained proudly, had just been delivered to him from France. It was the third car he had owned, and he said he could drive it, even though it was new, as well as any chauffeur. On the way down to the

Great Northern he was busy dodging the trams and the big horse-drawn drays, so he hardly spoke. But once inside the bar, leathery but cosy, and empty except for two wool men arguing about merinos and crossbreds and getting sozzled, he was a different man, easy and relaxed.

The oldish waiter recognized him at once. 'Mr Ollanton, isn't it? Not on here this week, are you? No, I thought not.'

'Manchester,' said Uncle Nick. 'And I won't have to be too long starting to motor back there. So let's have a bottle of *Pol Roger sec* in an ice bucket, sharp as you can.' He turned to me. 'Never drink anything except champagne. It's not showing off. I like champagne, and it likes me. If and when I can't afford champagne, I'll drink nothing. Care for a cigar, lad?'

'No, thanks, Uncle Nick. I'll stick to my pipe, if you don't mind.'

I watched him cut and then light his cigar, which he did slowly and carefully, with a sort of precision that was very characteristic of him, I realized. Not that I knew him very well, though he was my mother's only brother. I hadn't seen much of him before he went on the stage, chiefly because he and my father didn't like each other; and then for the last ten years he had been touring in variety, not only in this country but also in America and on the Continent, for his Indian Magician act, not depending on language, could be played anywhere. After my father died, when I was fifteen, I had seen him several times as *Ganga Dun*, his stage name and suggested of course by Kipling's *Gunga Din*, because whenever he was appearing in Leeds or Bradford he always sent mother and me passes for the stalls. These were nearly always for the first house, so that when we went round to see him he would be still in his Indian make-up, and I had hardly ever seen him without it. Now I looked hard at him.

He was tallish, thin, and very dark, with a hooked nose and a slight cast in his eyes that gave him a sinister look, which I think he cultivated. His real name was Albert Edward Ollanton, but he had been known as Nick long before he went on the stage; even my mother, who had clung to Albert Edward, had had to let go of them; and to me he had always been Uncle Nick.

When the waiter had poured out the champagne, Uncle Nick said to him, 'Don't go for a minute. Give you a free show. Got a ha'penny, one of you?' I had, and produced it. 'Right, lad, now mark it so you'll know it again. That'll do. Now give it to me.'

30

He put it in his right-hand coat pocket, and then, only a moment later, brought out a small metal box, which he placed carefully on the table between us. 'Now watch.' He opened the metal box and took out of it a match-box, which had several elastic bands round it. When he had taken these off, he opened the match-box and showed us a tiny silk bag, sealed by very small elastic bands. 'Now you open that bag, lad.' I did, and of course inside it was my ha'penny.

'That's clever,' cried the waiter. 'My word, that *is* clever, Mr Ollanton.'

'I've dozens of 'em,' said Uncle Nick. 'Only thing that amuses me nowadays – miniature pocket tricks. But the show's over – and I want to talk to this nephew of mine, so off you pop. We'll take a drink first, though,' he added, to me.

I didn't like the champagne, which seemed to me to have a metallic sort of taste and also stung the inside of my nose, but I pretended to be enjoying it and grinned across at Uncle Nick, who was now staring at me in his saturnine fashion. I don't often come across stage people nowadays, and when I do they look like anybody else; but in 1913 they seemed like specimens of an alien race. The men at least had a curious sallow-shiny look and their eyes were dark-rimmed as if they couldn't get rid of the black on their eyelashes; and this made my uncle all the more Nickish and sinister. It would be too much to say he frightened me – after all, he *was* my uncle – but it was no joke being stared at by him across a table, and I couldn't imagine myself disagreeing sharply with anything he might say.

'Now, Richard lad, I want to know how you stand – what you're doing – what you'd like to be doing. Just tell me straight. No fancy work. And short as you can make it because I haven't all that time.'

'I want to be a painter, Uncle Nick – watercolours mostly. And if my father hadn't died, I was going to the Art School. But as it happened-'

'You're a clerk in an office-'

'Yes, they gave me a job because my father had been cashier there. I'm getting twenty-two-and-six a week now-'

'But you don't like it-'

'I hate it. But what could I do? I've been going to some evening classes at the Art School, and I do some sketching on Saturday afternoons and Sundays-'

'Yes, yes, yes.' Uncle Nick waved his cigar between us. 'Your mother needed the money and you did what you could. You're a decent lad, Richard.'

'You helped too, Uncle Nick.'

'Ah – you knew that, did you? Well, she could have had more, if she'd wanted it, but you know how she was. Now let's see how you stand, Richard. Your mother's gone – you earn twenty-two-and-six pen-pushing – and you've got no girl expecting you to marry her, have you, lad? No? Good! Well, you can have a job with me at five pounds a week.'

'Five pounds a week!' I couldn't believe it. I had never seen myself earning five pounds a week for years and years. It seemed a lot of money then. I knew chaps who lived the life of rollicking men-about-town on far less than five pounds a week. 'But what could I do that would be worth so much?'

Uncle Nick stared at me almost malevolently. 'Don't get wrong ideas. This is business, lad. You'll earn your money, though you'll be free in the daytime to do your painting. I'm paying you exactly what I've been paying the young man whose place you'll take. He's leaving – going into the fish-and-chip trade with his older brother in Sheffield – and that's all right to me because he's such a miserable empty-headed young bugger I could never spend ten minutes talking to him. You might be a bit of company for me. Or am I wrong?' He didn't smile, but just looked hard at me.

'I hope not, Uncle Nick.' I tried to give him a smile. 'But what would I have to do? And could I do it? I don't know anything about conjuring.'

'Don't talk silly, lad. I never said anything about conjuring. You'll be a sort of general assistant. Besides coming on in the act – and that's dead easy – you'll make sure all our stuff gets away and arrives at the next place in good time, you'll take the band calls on Monday mornings to make sure the conductor knows what he's doing, and when I think you're up to it you'll take charge of the other four-'

'Who are they?'

'Who do you think – Alexander's Ragtime Band? Just shut up and listen. I've only got five people in my company – smallest on tour for a big illusionist's act – you don't catch me doing any Great Lafayette circuses. I'm down to a bare minimum. At the moment, first there's Norman Hislop, the one who's leaving and whose job I'm offering you. Then there's Sam and Ben Hayes, father and son. They walk on in the act, but they're really mechanics and keep the gear in trim and help me with anything new I'm working at. Don't forget I was a mechanic before I went on the stage. I pay Sam five a week, and Ben four. Then there's Barney. He's a dwarf – big head, tiny legs – but you've seen him. I pay him four. Then I have to have a girl. They're always changing. The one I have now, a Cockney, is called Cissie Mapes. And she only gets four pounds a week, but as she shares my digs I pay her living expenses. Here, drink up. I'll have to be off in five minutes.' He filled our glasses again, to the brim without spilling a drop, though he did it very quickly. 'Well, Richard lad, what d'you say? Seems to me you've everything to gain and nothing to lose.'

'Except that if I walk out of the West Bruddersford Spinners, they'll never take me back again.'

'Oh – for God's sake!' He looked as disgusted as he sounded.

'No, Uncle Nick, I was only arguing a point-'

'Don't, then. I haven't time. Let's finish these and start moving.' He said no more until we had left the bar. 'What's it to be, then? Yes or No?'

'It's Yes. When do I begin?'

'Next Monday. Newcastle. That'll give you a week with young Hislop showing you what to do. Be at the stage door of the Empire at eleven o'clock. Clear up everything here, of course. Sell the house-'

'It's already mortgaged-'

'All right, all right, just clear everything up so you're not worrying about it. And here's a fiver, and if you can manage it, get yourself another suit, try to look a bit smarter.' He was now climbing into his immense overcoat.

'I was just thinking,' I said as I followed him out to his car. 'You're paying out twenty-two pounds a week in wages – and then there are other expenses and railway fares-'

'Terrible, isn't it?' He turned at the door of his car, knocked some ash off his cigar, and gave me one of his dark mocking looks. 'Specially when you remember I'm only getting a hundred and fifty pounds a week – a hundred and seventy-five next year. See you in Newcastle then, lad.'

After some preliminary gasping and spluttering, when Uncle Nick pretended I wasn't there still watching him, he moved off, and a minute later he had vanished into the mist and smoke of the late October afternoon. I had three large glasses of champagne inside me;

I had just agreed to exchange an office stool and a sensible life in Bruddersford for some unimaginable music-hall hocus-pocus; I was only twenty and had never been away from home except for occasional weeks at the seaside and one visit to London, the year before my father died; and now – and it lasted the remainder of the week – I had that feeling of unreality and emptiness which we know when one familiar world is melting away and the next one has not yet closed round us. However, I had plenty to do the rest of that week, clearing up at the office, arranging what could be done with the house and furniture, and then, having more money to spend than I'd ever had before, buying two ready-made suits – one a dashing Harris tweed and the other a dark blue serge – some fancy shirts, socks, knitted ties, and, most important of all, a fine range of watercolour paints, eight brushes, and three big sketch-books – one of Cox, the other two of Ingres paper – fit to make your mouth water.

Then on Sunday, still half in a dream, I took a train, which didn't seem to want to go there, to Newcastle.

2

Years ago, I think it was in the late 1930s, I saw a film that took me back to that first week I had with Uncle Nick. I can't remember what the film was called or what it was about, but most of it took place in Newcastle, which came out as a night city with square black buildings, a deep black river, high bridges, menacing shadows. I don't say I saw Newcastle exactly like that in 1913, but the general rather sinister effect – which had nothing to do with the people there – was much the same. I was nervous about the job of course, and then, to be at the Empire by eleven on Monday morning, I had to spend Sunday night there. This I did in a cheap hotel, where I couldn't get to sleep for a long time because the place was full of Norwegian sailors, who seemed to be mostly mad drunken giants. And I still had that empty and unreal feeling when I walked through a chilly and sooty morning to find the stage door of the Empire.

Norman Hislop, whose job I was taking over, was waiting outside for me, smoking a cigarette. 'They really mean *No Smoking* backstage here,' he told me, 'so if you want to light up, this is your chance. We've nearly half an hour.' He was tall and thin and dressy – pink shirt and black knitted tie – with a long nose and a slack mouth, the kind that smokes a cigarette as if it were part of a dud conspiracy.

I asked him what happened at a 'band call' and he explained, as if he were about a hundred years old and I were thirteen, that it was a kind of skeleton rehearsal with the orchestra, when you made sure they had the band parts right and the conductor understood the cues. 'Old Nick'll never go near one. You'll have to do it all the time. He hates conductors – never stands 'em a drink like the others do, but if anything goes wrong they know he'll think nothing of reporting 'em to London. So as a rule they don't make any mistakes. After all, he's bottom of the bill, and top of it now and again.'

Here I had better explain that 'bottom of the bill' didn't mean the opposite of 'top', the least important of the eight acts that usually made up a bill, but the act next in importance to the 'top', the star attraction. I already knew this because Uncle Nick himself, the first time I had gone backstage to see him, had been careful to point this out.

People kept on pushing past us, on their way to or from the band call, but I hardly noticed them as Hislop went on talking. 'I don't know what Old Nick's like as an uncle – yes, he told me who you were – but he's a hard sod to work for – and I'll bet you'll soon find that out, even if you are his nephew. I'd be leaving anyhow – I've a chance with my brother I wouldn't miss – but even without that I don't think I'd have stuck it much longer. You can't please him 'cos he doesn't want to be pleased. All he likes is frightening people – a real Old Nick he is. Clever of course – everybody admits that, but everybody's glad too when he isn't there. And that's true even of our little Cissie, who has to sleep with him when he feels like it. And don't try anything there, Herncastle, if you want to keep the job. She might fancy it – with your looks – but just remember she's terrified of him. He has that effect on people.'

'Isn't it just his appearance?' I said. 'That nose of his. That slight dark squint. And perhaps the way he talks.'

'No, it's what's behind the looks and the talk. He doesn't like people. Doesn't want to get on with them. And if they don't like him, so much the better. To hell with them! You'll see.'

I didn't know what to reply to this, so I pretended to be busy with my pipe.

'It's been particularly awkward lately – and that's another reason why I'm glad to be going. I don't know if he's told you how we've been block-booked, having all the same agent. No? Well, come and take a look at this bill.' We went a few yards down the street. He tapped the bill as he talked. 'Look – apart from these two fill-ins, we're all playing the same halls every week, the same six acts. And you might as well get to know who they are. First, there's Tommy Beamish the comedian – top o' the bill-'

'I've seen him. He's very funny.'

'He doesn't amuse me,' said Hislop loftily, 'but he's a great draw. He'll murder 'em up here 'cos he comes from Tyneside. *Ricarlo* – Italian juggler – a good turn and a nice quiet chap but always looking for women. *The Four Colmars* – foreign acrobats, three men and a girl – and wait till you see the girl! Talk about a stunner! Then, *Harry G. Burrard – the Eccentric comedian* – putrid! And the last of us six – *Susie, Nancy, and Three Gentlemen* – nice little song-and-dance turn. Susie's married to one of the three gents, Bob Hodson, and the other two are a pair of puffs, Ambrose and Esmond. Nancy Ellis is Susie's sister – only eighteen – and a scrumptious bit, saucy as the devil in the act, but very quiet off, and don't make any mistake – there's nothing doing there, I've tried. Well, they're all nice and friendly, travelling round together the way we have to, all except one-'

'Uncle Nick?'

'That's right. You'll see. And that's why I said it had been particularly awkward lately. Odd man out, he is, and loves it. Doesn't like the people in front neither. Despises 'em. And not just because they're provincial. He says they're even worse in the West End. And he's played the Coliseum and the Palladium at two-fifty a week, and could have gone back but he wouldn't accept the bookings. He doesn't like London. God knows what he does like! I doubt if he even enjoys Cissie.' He opened his mouth and showed me a yellowish wagging tongue and some bad teeth.

I was tired of him. 'Hadn't we better go in?'

It was different from what it had been backstage when I had gone during a show. Though there were people bustling around, it seemed cold, darkish, sad. I followed Hislop to the side of the stage, where there were no warm lights now, just one big white one. A burly foreigner was shouting at the conductor and stamping a foot to give him the rhythm he wanted. Hislop said that was the oldest and the leader of the Colmar troupe. There was no sign of any stunning girl. After this Colmar had walked away, pulling a face, Hislop introduced me to the stage manager, whose name I've forgotten, and then to the conductor or 'musical director', as most of them liked to be called, a Mr Broadbent, who had a heavy moustache and was fat but out of temper.

'When does your act get some new band parts?' Mr Broadbent shouted up at Hislop. 'It's like trying to read fly-paper down here.'

'I'll tell the boss,' said Hislop, grinning. 'Or *he* will,' he added, pointing to me.

'Well, let's get on with it, let's get on with it,' said Mr Broadbent, scowling down at his score. 'Same business, same opening – first eight bars, gentlemen.'

'Now take notice, Herncastle,' Hislop muttered into my ear. 'You'll be doing it yourself next Monday morning. And Old Nick'll burn you up if anything goes wrong.'

It took about twenty minutes to get everything dead right, but when it was all over I didn't feel too anxious, because I knew that by next Monday I would know exactly how the act went, and, though I might be new, I couldn't believe Hislop could do anything I couldn't do. But what I had to do then, when we were free to go, was to buy him a drink at a little pub round the corner, because he immediately suggested it. The bar there was ringed round with signed photographs of star artistes, and later I discovered there was almost always one of these little pubs not far round the corner from every stage door, always with those signed photographs, and always with a lot of idiotic chat going across the bar counter. One man in there, drinking whisky and with a long bony face huddled into the upturned collar of a tweed overcoat that would have frightened a horse, turned out to be Harry G. Burrard, Eccentric Comedian. But if he was 'nice and friendly' with Hislop, I saw no signs of it.

'Here, I've just remembered,' said Hislop as soon as we had finished the beer I had bought. 'You have to go to the Private Bar of the County, to see your uncle. What's the time – quarter past twelve? You'll just do it. He said half past.' And he explained how I would find the hotel.

There were a lot of men standing around the counter of the Private Bar, but I felt sure Uncle Nick wouldn't be one of them. He was sitting at a table in a far corner, with a bottle of champagne in front of him. Two men and a girl were with him, the girl sitting staring at nothing and the two men poring over some sketches or diagrams.

'Well, here you are, lad,' said Uncle Nick. I felt he was glad – or at least, relieved – to see me, though it was hard to tell. 'My nephew, Richard Herncastle. Miss Cissie Mapes. And this is Sam Hayes, and this is his son, Ben.' They looked almost exactly alike, two wooden-faced long-chinned men, but Sam's moustache was greyish and Ben's was ginger. They gave me an incurious look and a nod, drank some beer, then frowned again at their bits of paper.

'Don't imagine we're just drinking, Richard,' said Uncle Nick. 'We're working. I've an idea for a new effect, not easy as a piece of mechanics. And so far Sam and Ben here don't know what the hell they have to do. So we're busy, lad, and you're no use to us. How did the band call go?'

'All right, Uncle Nick. I'll be able to take it next Monday when I'll know exactly how the act goes.'

'I hope so. I'm expecting better things from you, lad, than I ever got from young Hislop, who's lazy and half-witted. Now I want you in front tonight for the first house – I'll see they pass you in. Sit through the whole show – God help you – and then come to my dressing-room as soon as it's over. And don't forget that Monday's first house consists chiefly of deadheads who get free passes for exhibiting bills, not there to enjoy themselves, they wouldn't know how. It's like a show in a morgue. And that's all till tonight.'

'What about his digs, Nick?' This was from the girl, Cissie Mapes.

'Quite right, Cissie, I was forgetting. Well, you knock off that port-and-lemon, go with him to collect his stuff and show him where he's staying. And if you're both feeling hungry, go and eat – but not at my expense. Don't come back. I'm too busy here.'

We went off like two kids out of school. I guessed Cissie Mapes to be a few years older than I was, about twenty-five or so. She was wearing a big hat with a bright green feather in it, a pinkish coat and a lot of cheap rabbity fur, and plenty of makeup, not so much to improve her looks as to announce that she was on the stage. Her looks weren't bad either in a rather weak style: melting-toffee eyes, not much nose, a loose pouting mouth and a fall-away chin; not unlike the kind of girls that posed then on sentimental coloured picture-postcards. She had a thin little voice, very Cockney, and was half cheeky and half shy and innocent. There was a lot of sex about her – she used her eyes and was a great nudger and tapper and toucher – but it misfired with me; I didn't find her attractive, but on the other hand I rather liked her in a chummy way. We took a taxi, at her suggestion, collected my two bags from that hotel, and then went from the dock region, past the Empire, and finally arrived at some terrace or other of houses that had known better days.

'I got you this room next door to us – see,' said Cissie. 'We're in proper theatre digs as usual, but this woman – Mrs Michael – doesn't let rooms as a rule and she's just doing us a favour like. So you'll have to be careful. She's very respectable. Her husband's captain of a ship – and he's away. So keep sober and don't try anything on.'

'I only drink a glass or two of beer,' I protested. 'And I wouldn't know how to start trying anything on, as you call it.'

She gave me a bright look and a nudge. 'I believe you – thousands wouldn't. Well, don't be a naughty boy here anyhow.' We had now stopped outside the house. 'She says she'll give you some breakfast but nothing else, so you're having supper with us – next door – look. Now you take your bags in, and I'll wait, then we'll get him to drive us to a caffy. You're hungry, aren't you?'

I admitted I was.

'So am I. Nearly always am. So don't be too long. But talk nicely to Mrs Michael. She's doing us a favour.'

Mrs Michael was a small, rather thin, intensely dark woman, probably about forty. My appearance surprised her. 'Why, you're just a lad. And you don't look like a theatrical neither.'

'I've only just started, Mrs Michael.'

'I might have managed a bit of hot supper for you, if I'd known,' she began, still looking surprised.

'No, my uncle will be expecting me next door, and he'll probably have a lot of things to tell me. And if you'll let me have a key, I promise to come in very quietly-'

'I'm a poor sleeper, I'll hear you. Still, you can have a key. And this is your room, and as you can see, it's as neat and clean as a new pin.' And so it was, though it was also cold and cheerless. After telling her I had to go straight out to eat, I had a quick wash, then hurried downstairs. She was waiting there to give me the key. She also gave me a small tight smile, out of some rare store of them.

'You remind me of one of Captain Michael's nephews – mate of a coaster now. You look a sober quiet lad, and I trust you are.'

'Oh I am, Mrs Michael, I am.' And I hurried out.

Cissie and I ordered plaice and chips and sultana pudding in the cafe, which was quite large and had a trio playing *The Count of Luxemburg* and the *Indian Love Lyrics*. At first Cissie was very much on the stage, for the benefit of the people at the nearby tables, but after we started eating she dropped her voice and turned chummy and confidential.

'I like eating in places like this, not too posh, don't you, Dick? I'm going to call you Dick, even though *he* doesn't. Always Richard with him, isn't it? But then I like eating – I'm always ever so hungry – and he doesn't. Just a sandwich or something all day – and that champagne of course – and even at night, even if it's a really nice hot supper – steak and chips or a mixed grill – he doesn't touch half of it. You must know his wife – him being your uncle – what's she like?'

'I only met her once, about four years ago, when she came up to Leeds with him. I didn't like her much. She seemed to be drinking a lot, and she was bad-tempered.'

'She's fat as a pig now, he says.' She giggled. 'He admits he can't endure her. Gives her ten pounds a week to stay away from him – in Brighton. They're as good as separated but that's as far as it goes. No more wives for him, he says.' She looked at me half hopefully, as if I might know better, then when I obviously didn't, she ended with a forlorn little smile and tucked into her pudding.

'If he saw me eating this, he'd throw it across the room,' she went on. He says if I start putting on weight, I'll be out of the act. It's getting down into that pedestal chiefly. You'll see what I mean tonight. All last week in Manchester it was making my behind sore, but for God's sake don't tell him. Dick, promise you won't tell him anything I say – solemn promise.'

'Right, Cissie. I promise.'

She put down her spoon to reach across and squeeze my hand. 'I didn't know what you'd be like, and I was a bit upset when he first told me about you. Not that I'm sorry to be seeing the last of that Norman Hislop. He's just as nasty-minded as he's idle, and he's been rubbing Nick up the wrong way for months now. Let's have coffee, shall we? Miss! Miss! But naturally I was a bit worried – I mean to say, his nephew in the company – perhaps spying on everybody. But you're nice, I can see that, Dick. Nice – and just a little bit naughty – um?'

I grunted something. I had never cared about this nice-but-naughty business, which girls like Cissie at that time worked very hard.

Then over our coffee she looked solemn, and young though I knew what I was in for next. Most women talk about the men they're involved with in one of two quite different ways. Either they sound as if they were animal trainers and had one that talked and brought home some money – all very odd and amusing; or they go to the other extreme, as if they were serving some high priest of a mysterious religion, whose every whim was a commandment from on high; and this of course was poor Cissie on the subject of Uncle Nick. He was no sooner out of one mood, she told me solemnly and proudly, than he was in another; and she never knew what would come next, except he still never ate much and went on drinking champagne; and one day, like today, he'd work all hours with Sam and Ben, never even taking a nap before the show, and the next day perhaps he'd never stir from the fire but just go on reading books; and then sometimes he'd treat her like dirt, till she went and cried her eyes out, and then at other times he'd take her out in his motor-car and be ever so nice and attentive and take her to posh places that were his choice not hers because they always made her feel uncomfortable; and now and again she felt he really loved her, at least in his own peculiar way, and yet half the time he made her feel she was lucky to be still in the act, let alone sharing digs with him. He really was the strangest man she'd ever had anything to do with, and she'd known some peculiar ones in her time.

'Though mind you, Dick,' she said, regarding me earnestly, 'I'm not grumbling. Don't think that. I know I've been lucky. I'm not clever, I'm stupid, and my looks aren't so grand and I'm no Venus Who's-it. Where I'm lucky is having such small bones. My wrist – see. And other places – not on view. I'm just what he needs for the act. You take a good look at that pedestal tonight, you'd never believe I'm in there. He picked me out of a Panto chorus in Brixton – two-ten a week, two shows a day, twelve changes in each show – I used to cry out of sheer bloody weariness, to say nothing of scene-shifters trying to get you into a corner and maul you about with big sweaty hands. That was a great life, I don't think. So I'm not grumbling. I've been lucky, even though I have to take plenty – living with him as I do and everybody knowing it, and some of 'em trying to take advantage, as if I was just a common little tart. One of 'em called me that when I told him to take his hands off me.'

'Who was that?' And when she hesitated, I went on: 'You might as well tell me, Cissie.'

'It was that Harry Burrard – but he was drunk. Anyhow I doubt if he's all there. I never told Nick, who can't stand him anyhow and might have made it an excuse to get him out of the show. And afterwards I felt sorry for the silly old blighter. So don't you tell Nick.'

'What about the other women on the bill? How do you get along with them, Cissie?'

She pulled a face. 'I'm a bit out of luck with this lot. Nobody I could make a true friend of, you might say. Susie Hodson and her sister Nancy are nice, talented too – I think you'll like their turn – but they keep themselves to themselves. Nonie, the girl with the Colmars, the acrobats, is foreign of course, and anyhow she's a little bitch if I ever saw one. Then the only other woman is Julie Blane, who's with Tommy Beamish and lives with him, they say. She used to be legit and pretends to be very haigh-clarss, not on the same earth with me, though she's only playing feed to a comedian, even if he is top of the bill, and has to sleep with him to do that – though I must say she doesn't look as if she sleeps with anybody – downright haggard she looks. And that's the lot in the female department, and I wish Nick was going into Panto for a change, so long as I'm not in the chorus. But it's a good bill, Dick, and I think you'll enjoy most of it, even if it is Monday First House full of fat pubkeepers and their fat wives and the fish-and-chip merchants all on free passes. Well, I'd better see if Nick wants anything. What are you going to do?'

'I didn't get much sleep last night. I'll walk back to Mrs Michael's and try for a nap.'

'And that's all you do try for – remember. Be good now – and if you can't be good, be careful.' Then, as we were going downstairs to the street, she squeezed my arm. 'Nick says you want to be an artist,' though what she actually said was 'a nartist', but I don't propose to cope with Cissie's accent. 'Is that right, Dick?'

'Yes, I want to be a painter.'

'You ought to paint me sometime.'

'I'm not going in for that kind of painting, Cissie. I want to do landscapes in watercolour mostly. But I might try a sketch one day,' I told her, as if from a great height.

'Oh do. I'll bet you're awfully clever. Well, bye-bye till tonight.'

(I did try that sketch, and I still have it when so much, a whole world and more than half a century of time, has gone; and though it's terrible, probably the worst drawing I've ever kept, I've only to give it a glance to see and hear Cissie Mapes again.)

Mrs Michael wasn't about when I got back to her house. I slept until nearly five, waking up feeling cold and wondering for a minute or two where I was. But then when I went downstairs Mrs Michael was there, in the kitchen, sitting over a pot of tea, and she asked me, rather abruptly and severely, if I'd like a cup and some buttered currant loaf. I thanked her very warmly, to show her that I knew this was outside our agreement and that she was doing me a favour, and had two cups of tea and three slices of currant loaf. When I told her I must be off to the Empire for the first house, she shook her head.

'To tell you the truth, Mr Herncastle, I don't care for those places – and neither does Cap'n Michael. It seems to me that when they're not downright stupid, they're vulgar. I'm not against entertainment, I'm fond of our chapel concerts or a nice lantern lecture, but if I'd my way I'd close all your Empires and Palaces tomorrow.' Here was a fanatical glint in her eye that vanished when she looked at me. 'I don't like to think of a quiet decent young man like yourself, Mr Herncastle, earning his living in those places and having to mix with half-naked painted women. In fact it's *wrong*.' She brought this out very fiercely, as if she'd had a quick inward glimpse of me lost in orgies. 'But off you go, then. Off you go–'

I was passed in to the Empire, down to what were grandly called the *fauteuils*, by the house manager himself, magnificent in white tie and tails: 'Nick Ollanton's nephew, eh? Wonderful act – one of the best. Always look forward to it – and a glass or two of champagne – ha ha! If you're going behind after the show, look out for me and I'll take you through the pass door.'

3

It might be the worst house of the week – and indeed most of the people sitting near me looked stupid – but even so it was wonderful in a way to leave the darkening and chilly streets of Newcastle and then find oneself sitting in the fourth row at the Empire. I think the secret of all these music-halls is that while they seemed big – and most of them were – at the same time they seemed warm, cosy, intimate. A lot has been written about the magic of the playhouse, but it has always seemed to me very pale and thin compared with the warmer and deeper magic of the music-hall, which attracted more men than women to itself just because there was something richly feminine about it, belonging half to some vast tolerant mother and half to some bewitching mistress. I don't say I was putting all this into words as I stared about me that night, saw the orchestral players switch on their lights and try their instruments, noticed fat Mr Broadbent, no longer out of temper, bobbing up, first to smile at two people sitting just in front of me and then to tap with his baton, and heard his orchestra, with its desperate strings as usual fighting a losing battle with the woodwind and brass, scurrying through Grieg's *Norwegian Dances*; but I will swear some such thoughts were going through my head. And for the first time since I had promised to join Uncle Nick, instead of feeling confused, dubious, vaguely apprehensive, I felt quite happy about it. I was still going to be a watercolour painter – nothing could shake me about that – but until I could keep myself by painting, the variety stage, at five pounds a week instead of twenty-two-and-six, would be better than any office.

The first turn was a 'fill-in', a pair of trick cyclists, and of course I wasn't interested in them, only in the people I would be travelling with for the next few months. The first of these, the second act on the programme, were the Colmars, three male acrobats and a girl, Hislop's 'stunner', called Nonie. It was one of those acts, which had always rather bored me, in which the men stood on each other's shoulders and chucked the girl around a lot. (I saw one recently, on a TV circus programme, and it seemed just the same, unchanged in a world of bewildering transformations.) Nonie was rather small and seemed quite young, probably still in her teens, but there was nothing undeveloped about her figure. Her legs were magnificent in their tights, and her full breasts made her glittering bodice rise and fall. And the way she held herself and moved, among the three sweating males, suggested she was tremendously conscious of herself as a female. Her sex came over the footlights like a sharp challenge. In those days of long skirts, stays and demure blouses, we had to guess what girls really looked like; but Nonie Colmar (who plays an important part in this story, so I'm not wasting time on her) triumphantly displayed what a well-shaped girl had to offer. I don't think I was any more lustful than most of us were then, but my mouth almost watered at the sight of her.

Next was Harry G. Burrard, Eccentric Comedian, who came rushing on, with the band playing its loudest, waving his arms and hoarsely breaking at once into one of his hell-for-leather idiotic songs. His make-up and costume – a grotesque ginger wig, a white face and red nose, an enormous collar, a bottle-green tunic and peg-top patched pants – left the audience in no doubt that he was a funny man. But this Monday first house offered him only a few distant giggles. Perhaps like me they didn't think him funny. *Diddy-diddy – oodah – oodah – oodah*, he croaked away, still waving his arms; and nobody cared. I don't think I am being influenced by the knowledge of what happened afterwards if I say that, at first, he made me feel embarrassed, and then, as he went on and on without any encouragement, I began to feel sorry for him. I was near enough to see his eyes, and they seemed to me – though of course I might have been deceiving myself – fixed in a kind of despair. I know I felt relieved when he took himself off, with the band at its loudest again, pretending desperately that a little weary clapping was an ovation.

Uncle Nick was next, the last act before the interval. This was the time he preferred, because it meant that the wings were clear of people waiting to go on. The orchestra opened as usual with part of the *Ballet Egyptien*, and then there was the familiar *Ganga Dun* big set, some kind of glittering Indian temple, which Uncle Nick had designed himself. It looked important and showy, but also its structure and glitter helped his act. I watched it now of course with new and keener eyes, reminding myself that I would soon be taking part in it. Sam and Ben Hayes and Norman Hislop, hardly recognizable in Indian make-up and costume, came backing on, and then Barney, the dwarf, also an Indian now, scuttled across the stage with squeals and backward looks of terror; and finally Cissie Mapes, a gauzily clothed Hindoo maiden, arrived to prostrate herself before some advancing figure off-stage. A gong sounded. And there – a tall, commanding, sinister figure – was the Indian magician himself, who announced his arrival by letting loose a vivid green thunderflash. There was no doubt that Uncle Nick was a superb showman. Even the stolid fat deadheads sitting all round me, waiting for death rather than for any entertainment, were not entirely unimpressed. But *Ganga Dun*, intent upon magical feats as if they were part of some religious rite, gave no sign that he was aware of the existence of any audience. Unsmiling, grave, he behaved as if they were not there.

At first, from seemingly empty bowls and vases, handed to him by the Hindoo maiden, he produced bunches of flowers, fruit, coloured silks, gold and silver coins; and then he performed the feat, a genuinely Oriental one, of covering a heap of sand with a cloth once, twice, three times, while a magical plant appeared to grow there. The Hindoo maiden was then carried by the magician's slaves and her rigid body placed across two trestles. *Ganga Dun* regarded her sombrely, made some mysterious passes, then beckoned the slaves to remove the trestles. The Hindoo maiden remained there, now apparently unsupported. A few more passes and she slowly rose about two feet higher. The magician passed – or appeared to pass – hoops round her body, to prove that no wires were holding it up. Another gong, another green flash, and the magician was holding her by the hand as she bowed and smiled. But then an angry rival magician, as tall as *Ganga Dun* and nearly as imposing, wearing a turban, a majestic beard, and stiff long robes that hid his feet, arrived rather slowly and shakily, to challenge the magic power of *Ganga*. This he did not in words – nothing was said throughout the act – but by means of various insulting gestures. *Ganga* soon lost his patience, went nearer, summoned the gong and the green flash again – and then there was no rival magician, only the robes in a heap on the floor. It was a very effective trick, and it would have left me puzzled if I hadn't noticed that it was Barney the dwarf who was wearing the beard and turban, so that I guessed he had been raised two feet or so by stilts or something, and that at the end of the trick he was hiding in the heap of robes. But now a pedestal, about four feet high and very fancy, was brought on to the stage, and a white box was placed on top of it. Cissie as Hindoo maiden climbed into the box, and even while its lid, which faced away from the audience, was still slowly closing, the box was lifted off the pedestal, securely roped, then fastened to a hook let down from the flies. The box remained in mid-air for a few moments. The magician scowled at it; there was a roll on the side-drum: as if in despair he plucked a pistol out of his robes and fired three times at the box, which was then lowered and opened, all its sides falling down, and was plainly seen to be empty. There was a chord from the orchestra; *Ganga Dun*, aware at last of the audience, bowed to it almost negligently: the act was over. I led the rather scattered applause, but did not succeed in bringing back the magician before the curtain to take a final bow. When the lights went up for the interval, I looked around me. The Monday first-house people looked just as stolid as they had done before. Their sense of wonder had not been touched and aroused, because they had none. If my uncle had brought on three elephants and made them disappear, those people would have hardly raised an eyebrow.

The house manager stood me a Bass in the Circle Bar, which was almost empty. 'Wonderful act – one of the best,' he said again. 'I must have seen that girl-in-the-box trick twenty or thirty times and I still don't know how it's done. You do, I suppose – um?'

'Yes, I do. I tried not to sound too grand and condescending. He waited, obviously wanting me to tell him how it was done, but I wasn't having any. So now he frowned.

'You can tell him from me, I noticed he cut three minutes out of the act. Naughty – very naughty! I'm supposed to report him to head office for that, but of course I know he wouldn't do it to a full house. Always gets a wonderful reception with the right house. Great showman – Nick Ollanton – though he can be naughty – very naughty. Staying in front for the next half, I hope? Good! Three very good turns coming on – Ricarlo the juggler – those girls, Susie and Nancy – then Tommy Beamish. You've seen Tommy before, I expect. Wonderful comedian, Tommy – and they worship him up here. He'll have 'em rolling before the week's out. But he may walk through it this first house. He can be a naughty boy too, Tommy. Lovely talent though – lovely. Well, off you go and enjoy yourself. Give 'em a hand if nobody else does.'

Ricarlo was an elegant and graceful though not handsome Italian, probably about forty, who worked in full evening dress, and did most of his juggling, which was superb, with a top hat, a cane, and a cigar, to which he added, after a few minutes, a pair of yellow gloves. Throughout the band played, very softly, the same little tune, one I had never heard before, half gay and half melancholy. And indeed there was something half gay and half melancholy about Ricarlo himself and his act. His movements, so graceful and quick, so beautifully timed, had about them a kind of infectious joy; but his dark and big-boned face, with its ebony stare, seemed carved and dyed in melancholy, the sort of blank sadness that I have since noticed many Latin people seem to be sunk into, behind their noisiness and flash of teeth and eyeballs. As I watched him dreamily – there is something almost hypnotic about this sort of juggling – I felt that there was a man I might come to like. And once again I led such scattered applause as he received.

The front cloth of unbelievable shop windows, before which Ricarlo had appeared so elegantly and incongruously, gave place to a garden scene, first in a greenish moonlight, where two girls and three men began singing softly. This of course was the song-and-dance act of *Susie, Nancy and Three Gentlemen*. When the lights went up I saw that the three men were wearing grey morning dress and grey toppers; and I also saw, with an interest that soon rose to excitement, that Susie and Nancy were quite bewitching creatures. Susie, the taller and older and the one I knew was married, was a ripe brunette.

Nancy, who looked about eighteen, was a blonde with short curly hair, unusual in those days, a saucy look and manner, and legs that were both ravishing and witty. The whole act was out of the usual music-hall run, more like a visitation from musical comedy, and perhaps a trifle too deliberately 'retained'; the dancing, apart from Nancy's, was careful rather than brilliant; the songs were melodious nothings about Orange Girls and Kitty on the Telephone and so on; and no commanding talent was audible or visible; but – and I'll admit my instant infatuation – with the adorable Nancy may have swayed my judgment – the act conveyed something that seemed to vanish from the world not long afterwards, something I never found again in any place of entertainment – a kind of young and innocent gaiety, a bit silly as youth itself can be silly, without any sort of depth in it, any weight of experience, but somehow enchanting and lingering in the memory as an enchantment, so that later, when everything was different, and fragments of the songs returned to my mind, I was at once haunted by a bright lost world that had taken my own youth with it. As for that little Nancy, so pert and saucy and yet somehow so innocent, I began to fall in love with her there and then. And as I clapped until my hands ached, and glared at the fat deadheads who turned their idiot faces my way, I thought how wonderful it was that Uncle Nick had asked me to join him, so that I would see this girl again, and again and again, and would soon go backstage where she existed. But I did not really think of her existing in the corridors, passages and spaces there that I had seen and smelt that morning, but in some unchanging sunlit garden, some perpetual Maytime: I was already touched, barmy.

Luckily for me, Tommy Beamish, topping the bill, came on next. I had seen him before, but not in this particular sketch, in which he was 'supported by Miss Julie Blane and Mr Hubert Courtenay, both well known in the West End Theatre'. He was one of those rare comedians who began to make me laugh as soon as they appeared. He was a born comic, a plumpish man with a round cherubic face, usually decorated with an improbable ginger moustache, and with rather bulging eyes that stared in bewilderment or suddenly blazed in droll indignation. He never bothered with the ordinary comedian's patter, told no funny stories, sang no comic songs. He would lose himself in a labyrinth of misunderstandings and cross purposes, and would go on repeating some commonplace phrase or even one word, with deepening bewilderment or growing indignation, like a creature from some other world baffled by this one, until he had only to make the smallest gesture or mutter half a word to produce another roar of laughter from the nearest stalls to the high distant gallery, lost in the smoke. Like all the great variety artistes, he was able through the projection of his stage personality and his marvellous sense of timing to dominate every kind of audience, keeping them hushed and still when it suited him and then releasing their laughter as if he were pressing a trigger. He was the best comedian I ever saw on the stage – I am not forgetting Chaplin, but he belongs to the screen – and I have not seen his equal these past forty years or so; yet now there must be only a few of us, our memories already hazy, who remember him at all.

The sketch they played that night was simple enough in outline. Mr Hubert Courtenay, an old Shakespearean type of actor who suggested he was really the Doge of Venice or the banished Duke in Arden, was an immensely dignified country gentleman. Miss Julie Blane, though she could not keep the mischief out of her splendid eyes, played with some skill his anxious and delicate-minded daughter. They had sent for a vet for poor little Fido, and in his world of dubious communications and infinite cross purposes, Tommy Beamish had found himself summoned to the house, though he was in fact a plumber. The resulting confusion created the atmosphere in which Tommy was at his best. The indignant Courtenay rolled out words like 'prevaricate' and 'dilatory' and 'callousness', which Tommy repeated in amazement, brought back to taste again, chopped in half and flung the pieces about when he felt himself at bay. His slightest reference to plumbing operations, to his astonishment and then despair, were regarded as outrages by the quivering Miss Blane, whom he followed round the stage, sometimes climbing over the furniture, hoping to make it clear to her that he was not some kind of monster. A decent well-meaning man, only anxious to be helpful and impressed by the gentility of his patrons, he floundered into deeper and deeper misunderstandings, sometimes almost ready to cry and at others leaping to a height of blazing indignation. Even the fat deadheads all round me had to laugh, though they hated doing it. And as for me, I laughed so much and so long that often I lost the sight of Tommy in that curious and disturbing red haze which comes with violent laughter just as it does – so we are told, though I have never experienced it – with sudden and terrible anger.

What with the delectable and tantalizing Nancy and then the

sublime idiocies of Tommy Beamish, I had had as much as I could take and wanted to cool off, so I went out during the final turn, a 'fill-in' trampoline act, caring nothing, like most people then, about the inevitable flickering bioscope that would end the programme. (We never imagined that soon it would help to put an end to Variety itself.) I wandered around for a few minutes, passing the queues now waiting for the second house, my excitement cooling in the Newcastle night air, chilly and sooty like that of most industrial towns then, as if they were really one vast railway station. Then I found the stage door and asked for Uncle Nick's dressing-room.

He was sitting alone, smoking a cigar, still with his make-up on but without his turban. 'Well, Richard, how do you think the act's looking?'

'Better than ever,' I told him. 'Even with that rotten audience.'

'I cut the Magic Ball trick. I can't astonish those blockheads, so why waste one of my cleverest effects? You can watch it tonight from the side – no point in you sitting out front again. I want you to note very carefully from now on everything that young Hislop has to do, and if you can't do it better by the end of the week, then you'll have made a fool of me.' He sounded heavy and grumpy, as if he needed some champagne – there was none in sight – or the applause the second house would give him. 'You stayed on after the interval? No, no, quite right. Get the feel of the whole show. How was Tommy Beamish?'

'Funnier than ever, I thought,' I began enthusiastically, and then checked myself.

Uncle Nick took out his cigar and grunted at it. 'He doesn't like me, and I don't like him. I suppose he's a very successful comedian, but then I don't like comedians. They have to pretend to be even sillier than the people who are watching 'em – and that's saying a lot – and after a time it does something to 'em. Their brains soften, then their characters. Before the week's out, Tommy Beamish often has to be more than half-pissed before he can go on. That Blane woman, who lives with him, has a hell of a time. Here I'm lucky, lad. I haven't to pretend to be sillier than they are but cleverer, and that's all right because I *am* cleverer – though that's not saying much because, as you'll soon find out, most people who come to variety shows are half-witted. I could fool *them* in my sleep. I do my work for about one person out of every two hundred.' There was a rather timid knock, then Cissie Mapes looked in, still a Hindoo maiden.

51

'Where have you been?' And Uncle Nick frowned at her.

'I wanted to mend a skirt, Nick. Why?'

'Because you were late again out of the box—'

'They had it off centre again, like I told you, Nick—'

'Get it right between you this next time, girl, or else—'

'I told them, Nick. It's that Hislop really. Dick'll be better, won't you, Dick? Did you enjoy the show?'

'Most of it, Cissie,' I told her, trying not to appear too matey in case Uncle Nick didn't like it.

'That little Nancy Ellis – um – what about her?'

'Pop off, pop off, girl,' said Uncle Nick sharply. He waited a moment after she left. 'You'd better understand this, Richard. She has to be out of that box – there's a hinged flap on the bottom – and into the pedestal long before the trick lid has closed. It's watching that lid close so slowly, then all the fuss and bustle we have as soon as it is closed, that deceives 'em. Deceived you, didn't it?'

'No,' I replied without thinking, 'because Cissie told me about the pedestal-'

'Why the devil can't she keep her big mouth shut? I know it's only you – and you have to know – but she'll go gassing and blabbing around until that box trick, which I've already refused a thousand for, won't be worth a navvy's fart. How did Barney look as the rival magician?'

'Very good. I recognized him but I doubt if anybody else would. It's a very convincing trick.'

'Glad you think so, Richard.' He took a pull or two at his cigar, then took it out, looked me in the eye, and went on in that particular way, simple and honest and serious, which most men fall into when they are discussing the special techniques of their professions: 'The key device there was the stilt-boots Barney uses, which I had to design and make myself. There's always a key device for every illusion, and it's never the one the clever customers think it is. In the box trick, it's the lid that's still slowly closing when Cissie's already in the pedestal. It makes 'em feel she's lowering herself slowly into the box when in fact she's already out of it. In the levitation effect, the key device isn't the steel bar that raises and lowers her – any fool can work one of them – but the hoops that seem to pass right round her. I'm working now on putting an open doorway on the stage. Somebody comes in on a bicycle, rides across to the doorway at a smart pace, but instead of going through it – vanishes, bicycle and all. The bike is the key device, of course. If I can't make it do what I want it to do, then I'll send the bike through the doorway and the rider will have disappeared. Can you ride a bike, by the way?'

I said I could, but pointed out that I was no Cissie or Barney but was five-foot-ten and weighed nearly twelve stone. He told me he wasn't worried about my size and weight, and then he asked me to find Sam and Ben Hayes for him because he wanted to talk to them about the Magic Ball trick, which would be going back into the act for the second house. After that I could go down into the wings. He'd told the stage manager I would be there.

It was queer watching it all again from the side, feeling now I was part of it. Luckily the atmosphere was quite different from what it had been during the first house. The audience was now large, lively and responsive. The Colmars went very well, and had to take several calls. After the last one, little Nonie, excited and smiling and as if unaware of what she was doing, brushed past me, very close, though she could easily have avoided me, as the three men did. I felt as if sex had just been invented. As I stared after her, somebody muttered close to my ear: 'She's done it to us all, chum. Take no notice.'

'What?' I turned, and saw it was Harry G. Burrard, in the same monstrous make-up and costume, waiting to go on. *'Dee-doo-diddly-oodoo.'* And, waving his arms, he made his noisy entrance.

While he was still churning out his hoarse imbecilities, I found Uncle Nick, now the tall sinister magician again, standing by my side.

'Don't enjoy him, do you, lad?'

'No, I don't.'

'They don't neither, not any more. His day's done. They're silly but not *that* silly – and now the poor bugger knows it.' He moved away, as if to concentrate upon the entrance he would soon make. Behind Burrard's front cloth – 'in one', as they called it – the Indian Temple had been set, and I saw that Hislop, Sam and Ben were now rapidly checking the props there, while Burrard, in a sweat, was frantically grinding out his last verses. Finally he came rushing off, stamped his feet hard to add to the applause, rushed back as if everybody loved him, came off again and would have gone back once more if the stage manager hadn't stopped him. Then he stood near me, while the orchestra went into our *Ballet Egyptien* music, and I could hear him breathing hard. And I could see the terrible despair in his eyes. His day indeed was done.

Though I knew how most of the tricks were worked and I was now watching it from the wings, I found Uncle Nick's act even more impressive than I had done at the first house, seeing it from the front. This was chiefly because of the audience, whose gasps I could hear before the applause. And Uncle Nick himself seemed more adroit and more commanding, a master showman at ease in his own element. It was there and then that I suddenly found myself possessed by a pride in and a loyalty to the act that never left me afterwards, no matter what I might think of my uncle or feel about life on the variety stage.

He was called back several times, and finally he waved each hand negligently and then showed the audience two large bouquets. (They were of course made of artificial flowers that could be closely pressed and then folded into tiny packets, which were released by a spring. A lot of these effects were used at the beginning of the act, and I was glad to learn that Sam and Ben were responsible between them for making sure they were properly folded and that the springs were in good order.) As the curtain came down for the interval, Uncle Nick joined me in the wings and must have noticed that I was looking pleased.

'Went well, didn't it?'

'Wonderful,' I told him. 'Uncle Nick, I promise you here and now I'll do everything I can for the act.'

He took off his turban. 'I hate this dam' thing. All right, Richard my lad, that's a promise. Now you're having your supper with us. Cissie told you, didn't she? Right. Well, I've a man coming to see me so I may be about an hour yet. You can make yourself useful, helping the others to make certain the props are cleared, then you can watch some of the next half, if you haven't had enough of it already, or go and have a drink – or do what you like. But don't expect me to wait supper for you. Be up there before eleven, lad.'

Hislop showed me what he had to do, which wasn't much because Sam and Ben did most of the work, but by the time I was free to return to my place in the wings, Ricarlo was on. I realized of course that at any moment I would see that girl Nancy again, and this time with no footlights (which I hadn't learnt then to call 'floats') between us, but as fellow performers backstage. I waited, half suffocated by excitement, which stayed with me even after I had told myself not to be a fool. And here I want to make the point, which may turn up again in these reminiscences, that I believe this excitement didn't help to create my future relationship with Nancy, but that the relationship, which already existed in some larger time, made itself felt to me, in my immediate narrower time, in the form of this strange excitement: the future was influencing the present. Of course I can't prove this – even though the suffocating feeling was out of all proportion to anything I was conscious of – but it is what I believe.

Then they were there, standing only a few feet away, both Nancy and her sister. They glanced at me, probably wondering who I was, so I nodded and smiled. They gave me a small nod and smile. Soon they were joined by Bob Hodson, Susie's husband, easy to distinguish from the other two 'Gentlemen', Ambrose and Esmond; and there was some whispering between them. When Nancy, still as entrancing as she had seemed on the stage, gave me another look, and I smiled again, there was no answering smile, just a brief contemptuous stare before she turned away. I felt humiliated, then angry. Who the blazes did she think she was? And what lies had Hodson been telling them?

I tried hard not to enjoy their act again, especially Nancy's performance, but it didn't work. It seemed all different, of course, now that I wasn't seeing it from the front, and the magic garden was so much paint and canvas and the moonlight and sunlight were so many colours in the battens, floats and perches. And now of course the delicious Nancy was no longer playing to me but – in every sense, as I remembered that last cold stare – *away* from me, happily bewitching any and every lout sitting in front, gaping at her legs. She came off the stage twice during the act but remained just out of sight of the audience, never even throwing a look in my direction. But even so, and though I still felt angry, the magic, belonging to some innocent Maytime of the world, took hold again, though now instead of expanding with it, as I had done before, I didn't feel happy but sort of *ached* at it, as if already I was feeling shut out.

They were singing and dancing, all five of them, their last number when Tommy Beamish and Company arrived, bringing with them – for they were standing quite close to me – a reek of whisky. This was certainly true of Tommy Beamish and Miss Blane, who were almost at my elbow. Hubert Courtenay, looking like a painted bishop, was out of smelling range. But it was not until Nancy and her sister were taking their final calls, in front of the curtain because the sets were now being changed, that I saw that Tommy Beamish was giving me a belligerent stare.

'You one of the nuts?' he asked.

'I don't think so, Mr Beamish.'

'Want to come on in my sketch?'

'No, of course not—'

'Then why don't you take a walk? We don't have to have you standing there, do we? Not a policeman or fireman, are you?'

'Oh, stop it, Tommy,' said Miss Blane. 'He's probably got a perfectly good reason for being here. Haven't you?' She said this to me, of course, giving me a smile that was also a little appeal for help. Her splendid dark eyes were anxious.

'If I'm in the way I'll move,' I told them both. 'But I've just joined my uncle, Nick Ollanton—'

'One of my favourite colleagues, I don't think,' said Tommy Beamish sourly. 'I wish he'd vanish himself one of these nights—'

'Tommy, please!'

'Oh – put a sock in it. *Tommy, please!*' He lurched away, going nearer to where he would make his entrance. Courtenay, who opened their sketch with a telephone conversation, was now going on.

'I can't stay,' Miss Blane whispered hastily. 'I'm on just after Tommy–'

'I know. I was in front at the first house. I thought Tommy was marvellous. You were good too, Miss Blane.'

'Thank you, but it isn't my kind of acting. What's your name?'

'Dick Herncastle. I'm not a really a pro. I'm trying to be a watercolour painter.'

'You're rather sweet. And you mustn't mind Tommy. He's being rather difficult tonight.' A great roar of laughter reached us from the house. 'There! Listen to them. He's probably feeling better already. I must get ready for my entrance.' Her hand rested on my arm for a moment, then she hurried away.

I didn't stop to watch the sketch. I wasn't in the mood for it, much as I admired Tommy Beamish, for I was feeling half bewildered, half depressed. And it didn't make me feel any better when shouts of laughter seemed to follow me out, until I turned the corner and went down the steps towards the stage door. Cissie Mapes was waiting there, looking rather forlorn. However, she brightened when she saw me, and began chattering at once about the act.

'I can't tell you how glad I am that that Hislop's going. He's never liked me 'cos I showed him right from the start I wasn't having any – you know what I mean. So if he could make it hard for me, in the act, he would – sly an' mean as hell he is. You won't have no trouble with Sam and Ben, they're very reliable. Think about nothing but their work and betting on horses. Barney's different of course, being a dwarf. I had trouble with him one time – though I never told Nick. You'll have to watch him, Dick. He isn't reliable, specially if he's had a few drinks. I don't think he's all there, but you can't blame him – poor little man. There never seem to be any women dwarfs for them. I've seen dozens of men but never a woman. I was on a bill once when there were six of 'em, in one of them knockabout sketches, and you couldn't move for angry little men. Here's Nick. You can tell he's *somebody*, can't you?' And certainly in his immense overcoat, with a white silk scarf and the black trilby a little to one side, he looked impressive – in a rather theatrical style.

Quarter of an hour later we were eating steak-and-kidney pie and welsh rarebit, and drinking champagne, in the back room of their digs, which had signed photographs of variety stars round the walls, too much heavy furniture, and an enormous fire from which it was impossible to escape. When Uncle Nick had lit a cigar and I had brought out my pipe, Cissie, who was hot, flushed and excited, began: 'Now, Dick, you must tell us what you felt, your first day in variety—'

'No, he mustn't,' said Uncle Nick. 'And you get off to bed, girl.'

'Oh – Nick – why?'

'Don't argue. Pop off.'

She got up slowly, her weak pretty face sagging, looking ready to cry, and then without a word hurried out. Uncle Nick filled his glass and poured a little more champagne into mine. Then he gave me a sardonic look. 'I can read you like a book, lad. Poor little Cissie! Brutal old Nick! That's what you're saying to yourself, isn't it?'

'Well, uncle, I must say you did seem a bit hard on her-'

'Let's settle this now, lad. Cissie Mapes has got the best job she's ever had or ever will have. I pay her board and lodging, so the four pounds a week she gets is mostly pocket money. She's in clover. She's just about enough sense to come in out of the rain. When she listens to me, with her mouth wide open, more than half the time she doesn't know what I'm talking about. And I don't keep her on because of what she lets me have upstairs. It'll do but I've had better – much better. The point is, though she looks all right in her Indian costumes, not thin at all, she's actually got very small bones, so she can squeeze herself into half the space the audience thinks she needs. If she couldn't, I'd have her out of the act – sharp. And she wouldn't be staying on upstairs neither. But I must warn you, lad, that when I do want my greens I don't fancy other fellows' leavings. So don't start any messing about there.'

'You don't need to warn me, Uncle Nick. To begin with, I'm not interested–'

'Too early to say that. She hasn't got to work on you yet. And she will. You're a good-looking lad, and she doesn't get enough from me. Besides, they like a bit of sentiment. Oh – she'll be having a try soon. And don't look so disgusted, Richard. Start facing the facts, even when they begin to look nasty. You're thinking I'm a hard man, aren't you?'

'I only said—'

'Well, I *am*. It wasn't easy getting to where I am now. First I had to turn myself into a good mechanic and learn a few tricks. Then I had to persuade that old German, Krausser, who did an Indian illusionist act, called himself *Bimba-Bamba*, to take me on, after I'd repaired one or two things for him, when he was appearing at the Palace, Bruddersford. He looked a nice kind old man, but in fact he turned out to be a slave-driving bastard, and I had three years of it, waiting for the stroke that killed him. Then I'm living on bread and marge and tea in a Clapham basement, working out the new act and wearing out my britches' arse at the agents'. So it's hard coming up. But that's not all. Touring in variety can easily be a very sloppy life. You can come into it a man and end up as a poached egg. And women are ready to do the poaching. We have to have 'em – we're made that way, if we're normal – but they're born softeners and entanglers, and the only way to stop 'em is to be short and brutal with 'em whenever you feel like it.'

'But couldn't you be missing something?'

He regarded me, over his cigar, with a kind of genial contempt. 'You're just out of the egg, lad. I like to use my intelligence and look after myself, and I advise you to do the same. Of course you won't be very popular. You probably know already that I'm not. I don't mean with the public but with our dear *fellow art-eests* – eh?'

'No, they don't seem to like you very much, Uncle Nick.' I could have added that I didn't care for him very much myself in this mood, but I didn't.

'They know I despise 'em, lad. And I think if I was doing anything else on that stage but an illusion act, I'd despise myself. No wonder so many of these comedians drink themselves into the rats. After pretending for years to be even sillier than the halfwits out in front, they hate living with themselves. But I'm cleverer than the public. Also, I'm an honest illusionist. I mean by that, I'm frankly doing it for their amusement, not like these big illusionists in Westminster, Whitehall and the City, expensive bloody hypocrites. But of course most people – and specially if they're English – want to be deceived. They'll meet you more than half way. Now I don't think you've seen this – it's rather neat.'

He brought out a metal tube about three inches long, and into it he jammed what remained of his cigar, together with a lot of ash. Then he fitted a screw cap on to the tube, placed it between us, grinned at me and said: 'Hocus-pocus and Hitchy Koo! Now you can unscrew that cap and find the cigar and the ash.' And of course they weren't there, and when I tipped up the tube a lot of gilded pellets rolled out of it.

'Ashes to gold, lad,' said Uncle Nick complacently, scooping up the pellets.

'I must say I don't see—'

'You won't, lad. I never explain these pocket tricks of mine, though there's no real money in 'em. But a man has to have a hobby – and these pocket tricks are mine.' He emptied his glass and then carefully filled it with what was left of the champagne. Even now I can recall quite clearly his long dark face, not as sallow as usual because of the wine and the heat of the room, which was making me sweat; and I can catch the sudden melancholy of his look as he raised his eyes from the glass, to talk to me. 'Trouble with a man like me – intelligent, not easily taken in, able to see through people – is that he soon gets bored. Everything becomes a bit stale. That's why I'm glad you've joined me, Richard. I can talk to you.'

I nodded and smiled, doing my best, though I didn't feel much like nodding and smiling.

'Yes, I know people by this time. They're mostly a lot of lost animals, who happen to know they were born and that soon they'll die and be forgotten. They know it but they don't want to think about it. That's where the illusions come in – the honest ones like mine, to amuse 'em, and all the big bloody lies still waiting for 'em outside when our show's over.' For a moment or two he stared sombrely not at me but somewhere past me. Then he seemed almost to whisper. 'Last year I played two weeks at the London Coliseum. One night an old Hindoo was brought round to see me. A fellow from the India Office brought him. I had to tell them I'd never been near India. But I said to the old Hindoo – who smiled all the time, never stopped – that if anything was badly wrong in my act, I'd try to get it put right. Well, still smiling, he mentioned one or two things, and I made a note of 'em. Then he talked, smiling away.'

'What about?' I asked, after waiting a moment for my uncle to go on with his tale.

'What about? Bloody horrors, mostly. Smiling all the time too. I'm not easily frightened, but he gave me the cold shivers. Fire, fury and bloody murder everywhere, and he talked about it all as if he was a kid at a magic lantern show.'

'But what—'

'Some other time, lad.' He got up. 'My fault, I know – I shouldn't have started what I wasn't ready to finish. But you'll have to wait. Or give it a permanent miss. Now push off, lad. We've talked enough for one night.'

He meant that *he* had, for I had hardly been allowed to finish one remark. Clearly he was annoyed with himself, and in another minute would be annoyed with me, so off I went. And as I crept up Mrs Michael's stairs, I felt I had arrived at the end of a gigantic crowded day.

4

The following Sunday afternoon, November 2nd 1913, found me on a train going from Newcastle to Edinburgh, our next date. This was no Scotch Express but a slow, stopping train, a typical Sunday afternoon job. We seemed to crawl through the drizzle, not really going anywhere. Uncle Nick and Cissie were doing the journey by car, but I had to take the train that was carrying all our gear. It was an important part of my work to make sure that our stuff – and there was plenty of it, what with the temple set, all the mechanical effects, all the props and costumes – was taken out of one theatre and then safely deposited in the next. I was also more or less responsible for Sam and Ben Hayes and Barney – especially Barney. But I was not worried about him on this afternoon, because I knew that the three of them were in the next carriage playing nap. I had a carriage to myself, the train, which had no corridors, no dining-car, no anything, being almost empty. This seemed a good time to think about things, to take stock, to ask myself a few questions.

I had taken over from Hislop in the act on Thursday, though only for the first house, but then had gone on for both houses on Friday and Saturday. Feeling a fool in the Indian make-up and costume, when I appeared for the first time on the Thursday, I had a few panicky seconds when I reached the illuminated and searching area of the stage, but I soon recovered. Indeed, Cissie and Sam Hayes told me I was better than Hislop, who had always been inclined to be slapdash, whereas I am naturally careful in the way I handle things, as a painter should be. Even Uncle Nick, who didn't like praising anybody, threw me a few words of thanks after the final show on Saturday. Of course the business of getting all our stuff out and away was quite new to me, but Sam and Ben Hayes helped me. They had looked sideways at me at the beginning of the week, chiefly because I was the boss's nephew and might go telling tales, but by the end of the week they had accepted me and volunteered to help with the move to Edinburgh.

Right to the end I was always glad that I had Sam and Ben Hayes working with me, but we never became friends. There are some people who never seem quite real, and Sam and Ben were like that. I couldn't imagine what they were like when they were by themselves. Their build and features were almost identical, and they spoke in exactly the same way, with a strong West Riding accent and hardly moving their lips, as if they might have been ventriloquists. All this, and the stiff way they held themselves, made them seem as if they belonged to some special race of wooden people. They were very conscientious, completely dependable, and, so far as they can be said to have enjoyed anything, I think they enjoyed their work. Outside it they gave all their attention to horse-racing. The only papers I ever saw them reading were racing papers, which they would study slowly and solemnly together, before placing their next bets. When and how they did their betting I never knew, and I never saw them depressed by their losses or elated after a win. There didn't seem to be any *fun* in it for them; they took it all, if anything, even more heavily and seriously than they did their work; and when I came upon them in a pub, as I did occasionally, they would be muttering over their pints to other solemn punters. It was just as if they belonged to some strange religion. I doubt if they would have played cards, as they were doing on that train to Edinburgh, if Barney hadn't insisted on a game of nap.

I can see Barney clearly even now, after more than fifty years. The biggest thing about him was his forehead, enormous and bulging. When only his face was visible, he looked like a peevish philosopher. His arms were not too short and were in fact quite strong, but his legs might have belonged to a three-year-old. He was very nimble and could scuttle around, on and off the stage, on his tiny legs; but he wasn't young, probably about forty (this was Uncle Nick's guess, and he knew him better than I did), and though he pretended to be more energetic than the rest of us, there were odd times when I caught sight of him collapsed in some corner, just a big sad head. It was easy to feel sorry for him, though he resented any sign of it, but not easy to like him. As if to prove that he was a man and not a freak or goblin, he overdid everything in an irritating way. If people were angry and shouting, he wanted to be the angriest and shout the loudest. If they were larking about, he would insist upon making the biggest fool of himself. If things looked bad, he would make them look worse. If he could find a pub where he could stand on a chair and be accepted as one of the company, without any pointing and guffaws, then he would want to stand rounds he could not afford and soon drink more than was good for him, for being so small he couldn't really take very much. It was rather depressing to spend much time with him because he was like a goblin caricature of a man, making you feel what fools we all are.

Luckily for him, perhaps – there is a doubt here because he had had no education and could barely read or write – he had been born and brought up in a fairground, and had spent all his life in one or another kind of show business – fairs, circuses, pantomimes, variety. He was very moody, sometimes sulkily silent for days, sometimes wanting to talk too much, in a jerky and spluttery fashion, not pleasant to listen to; and when in an excitedly reminiscent vein he was apt to boast and tell obvious lies. He always kept quiet and watchful when Uncle Nick was around, not just because Uncle Nick was the boss but also because he was deeply afraid of him, as if he felt Uncle Nick really was a magician. He knew I wasn't, and as I tried to deal with him as if he were just another man and not a freak, he took to me, and insisted – though this was later on — upon going along with me when I went out sketching. He would never try any drawing or painting himself, though I kept on telling him he ought, but was fascinated by what I did. He became, so to speak, part of the sketching act, and though there was little he could do to help me, he fussed around in a self-important manner. If too many children came to look, he would drive them away, like an infuriated gnome. But I am getting too far ahead, for all this was much later.

However, even during this first week in Newcastle, I had made a start, had begun fixing a pattern I followed throughout the tour. If it was fine, I went out with a sketch-book. If it was wet or too cold to sit about, I would go to the local art gallery or ask to see some art books in the Reference Library. The beauty of this job, as I had realized from the first, was that it left me with most of my days free, so that I could keep on with what I really wanted to do. (I was also beginning to save about three pounds out of the five I was being paid every week.) Sprawling in the carriage I had to myself on that slow train to Edinburgh, feeling snug in there out of the afternoon's chill drizzle and with the navy cut in my pipe burning nicely, I thought of all the free days ahead and all the gold sovereigns I would be saving, preferring this cosy rumination to the two Sunday papers I had bought, which seemed to be making some fuss about Winston Churchill and Admiral von Tirpitz. Then we crawled into the station at Berwick-on-Tweed. I opened the carriage door, but then decided against getting out to stretch my legs, re-lit my pipe and, as my reverie had been broken, picked up one of the papers. After a minute or two, hearing the guard's whistle, I looked up to see if I had closed the door. I hadn't, and the train was now creeping out of the station. I had just time to help somebody in, banging the door behind him as the train gathered speed. The carriage seemed to be full of yellow-green-purple tweed overcoat, together with some gasping and wheezing. It was Harry G. Burrard, Eccentric Comedian.

'Thanks, cully,' he said hoarsely. 'Might have had to spend half the bleeding night there. Got out to try to send a wire. An' what a hope I had! Lost me titfer into the bargain.'

'Lost your what?'

'Don't show your ignorance, cully. *Titfer* – otherwise tit-for-tat – otherwise hat. Made special too – West End. Harry G. Burrard has everything made special. That's me, cully — the one and only Harry G. Burrard.' He was now stretched out on the opposite side, with only his too-black dyed hair and his long bony face emerging from that monstrous overcoat. But he pulled out of the nearer pocket an unusually large flask, pigskin and gold, which he offered me. 'How about a little of what you fancy, cully? No? Then excuse me, Sir Marmaduke.' He took a long pull at it, closing his eyes. The smell of whisky seemed to warm the carriage. When he opened his eyes, which were small and almost a yellow ochre, he stared at me rather suspiciously.

'Seen you before somewhere, cully, haven't I?'

'Of course you have. Newcastle Empire. I've just joined Nick Ollanton. As a matter of fact he's my uncle.'

Burrard pulled a face. 'He's a pal, that bugger, I don't think. Told me to me face – where was it? – Manchester? – he didn't want to follow me on the bill and he was going to tell head office. Did he?'

'He's never said anything to me about it, Mr Burrard—'

'Harry to you, cully. Can't blame you if he's your uncle. I've had uncles I wouldn't be seen dead with. One old sod got fifteen years. How d'you like being in variety?'

'It's all right so far.'

'All right? Don't make me laugh. I've had thirty years of it – twenty of 'em at top money – but now I don't recognize it, don't know where the hell I am. Sometimes I think I'm going on in Lapland or somewhere. In the old days I'd play four or five halls a night – London of course – and it took it out of you – but you were on – *bingo bango* – then you were off, on to the next house – and if you were half-pissed, so were they – and you were all pals, having a night out. Now they sit on their hands and hope for death – and so do you. It isn't the same thing, cully. It's another bleeding world. I'm shouting my head off to a lot of strangers. Remind me to show you some of the old programmes. I look at 'em and wonder what happened and where it went all wrong. Twenty-five acts,' he shouted hoarsely, his eyes gleaming, 'and where are they? I'd be on the bill with Dan Leno, Herbert Campbell, Dutch Daly, Albert Chevalier, Jenny Hill and Lottie Collins. There aren't women like that any more. They'd arrest 'em on sight in Brum now. What have we got in this bill – y'know, for a short time? I don't go looking for it any more – your age I was a bleeding stallion – but I like to know there's a nice piece of it handy. Well, where is it with this lot? Ollanton – your uncle – he's got himself fixed up. So has Tommy Beamish, though I'll bet it's all so West End and refined, he doesn't know when it's happening. What's left for you and me, cully? Them song-and-dance sisters are so lah-di-dah they won't give you the time of day. They don't belong in variety anyhow, that lot – they ought to be on the end of a very refined exclusive bloody pier, they ought. And all you got left is that little Frenchie – Nonie – lovely legs, bum and tits – and looks hotter than mustard – and asking for it. Am I right, cully?'

'I'd say you were, Harry, but I don't really know her.'

He took another pull at his flask before replying, then wagged a finger at me. 'Don't waste your time trying there, young fella-me-lad. Tell you what she is – little Nonie – she's Moss's Empire Number One cock-teaser, she is. And if somebody doesn't jump on her soon and put a bun in her oven, she's going to play her little game once too often – you mark my words, cully. Lot of people think I don't notice much. I notice everything. I don't say much, but I don't miss anything. I see things you've no idea of, cully.'

'What, for instance?' I didn't really want to know; I was just making conversation.

He looked very cunning, then leant forward and spoke in a whisper. They're sending people round all the time now. Nobody notices 'em but me. But that's partly why everything's going wrong. These people they're sending round are doing it. On the quiet of course, all on the quiet. I noticed one last night – front row – big black moustache. I can tell 'em at a glance. Here – listen.' He beckoned me closer. 'There's one on this train. He knew I spotted him. They don't like it, of course. Send in a report: *Harry Burrard again – wire instructions*. And they pass the word on, wherever we're going – Edinburgh, Aberdeen, Glasgow: *Give Burrard the bird*. Of course it won't work – the public won't have it – still an old favourite. But give 'em time and it'll work. And then, where am I?' He was shouting now. 'Where am I? Finished, cully, finished! Well up a bleeding gum tree! I wouldn't even get a licence for a boozer. All right, I'm getting excited. But so would you be if you knew half of what I know. Look – when we get to Edinburgh – keep close to me and I'll give you the office. The one that gets off this train – I'll show him to you, no pointing, just a nudge – he'll meet another of 'em who'll be on the platform – you'll see.'

But what I did see, there and then, was that Harry G. Burrard, Eccentric Comedian, was already half barmy. He dropped off to sleep long before we reached Edinburgh, and as soon as the train stopped I hurried out, after giving him a shake, to collect Sam and Ben and then to make sure all our stuff was taken out of the van. By the time everything had been taken care of, it was quite late, and when I finally arrived at the digs, which I was sharing with Uncle Nick and Cissie that week, there was nobody in the place still up except Cissie, who explained where my bedroom was and then brought me my supper from the kitchen.

'Nick went off to bed, properly fed up,' she explained. 'He forgot to bring any champagne. Nothing to drink, so he's been snapping my head off. What's been happening to you, Dick? Did you meet any nice girls on the train?'

'No, I had Harry G. Burrard instead.' And over supper I told her what he had said.

Cissie looked worried. 'D'you think there *are* these people they're sending round?'

'Now, don't you start, Cissie. Of course there aren't. What people? And who's supposed to be sending 'em? No, it's all barmy stuff. He's just quietly going dotty, poor old Burrard.'

She didn't say anything until I'd finished supper. Then when I stood up, she came closer, gripped my arm and whispered: Don't tell Nick – I mean about poor Burrard. He hates him enough already – and has complained about us having to follow him – says he sends them out to the bar – and if Nick knew about this, he'd have Burrard out of the bill before you could say Jack Robinson. I mean, he's not *dangerous*, is he? Just going soft – um?'

I pulled a chair close to what was left of the fire – they didn't pile coal on in Edinburgh as they did in Newcastle – and lit my pipe. Cissie sat on a cushion near the other end of the fender. She gave me a smiling and rather moist glance of approval. I think she had been crying just before I arrived, and now she felt better. 'Y'know, Dick, I can feel cosy with you. They're always talking now about what women want – votes and all that – but one thing most of us want is to feel cosy with somebody—'

The door opened, and she was up in a flash. Uncle Nick was

wearing a scarlet silk dressing-gown; he looked pale and rumpled; there was a glitter of bad temper in his eyes.

'Off to bed, girl – sharp!' Then when she had hurried past him, he gave me a hard look. 'Late, weren't you, lad ?'

'I was as quick as I could be, uncle. There's no hurry in Scotland on Sunday nights, it seems. And I wasn't spinning anything out, not when I was feeling famished.'

'Well, you're here. Get off to bed.'

I might be only twenty and new to everything, but I wasn't having this. It didn't really matter to him when I went to bed, but he was going to be the boss in everything and didn't want me to have any will of my own. But I wasn't another Cissie Mapes. I returned his hard stare.

'Why should I, Uncle Nick? I don't want to go straight to bed when I've only just had my supper. I want to have a smoke and let it settle.'

'Don't forget you have to take that band call in the morning.'

'I'm not forgetting. And after all it's not so late.'

'They think it is here. But finish your pipe if you have to. And don't make a noise upstairs.' He was very curt, and didn't say Good night. I stayed down there only about another ten minutes, mostly on principle. I remembered my mother saying – indeed, almost boasting – that all the Ollantons were self-willed and obstinate. Well, I was half an Ollanton.

5

Next morning I was out of the house by eight o'clock, long before Uncle Nick was visible. I did what I had to do backstage, except for the band call of course, not due to start until about eleven, and then took some time off to look at Edinburgh. It was a raw morning but there was some pale sunlight, here and there brushing the stone with a faint gold; and I walked about the beautiful old city, the first I had ever seen, in an enchantment. Princes Street was still unspoilt then, before the multiple stores had invaded it. I stared up at the Castle and at Calton Hill as if I were in a dream world. For an hour or so I was all painter, wondering how this air and stone, these warm and cold greys, sepias and sudden blacks, could ever be captured by a minimum of line and maximum of broad washes; and I almost forgot I had anything to do with the variety stage, which anyhow seemed utterly remote from this scene. But as I am not writing here about my life as a painter, I will linger no more among those delectable first glimpses but take myself, excited and happy, straight back to the stage door.

It was all a wild confusion on and around the stage, with sets going up and props being unpacked and the stage manager and the electricians shouting at one another and the cleaners banging about in front and the orchestra coming in and tuning up and the performers arriving and greeting each other or trying to attract the attention of the stage manager and the electricians or sorting out their band parts. As I roamed around I told myself I wanted to get to know everybody and be friendly, but I knew that what I really wanted was to see little Nancy Ellis and, failing her, the tantalizing Nonie Colmar and the splendidly dark-eyed, arm-touching Miss Julie Blane. Sex not friendship was the lure.

Here I feel I ought to say something about our sexual feelings in those days before the First War. It will, I hope, save a lot of explanation later. As everybody knows, ever since then, certainly in this country, sex has come more and more out into the open, and at the same time there has obviously been more and more sexual titillation, in stage shows, films, advertising. But what many people, especially public moralists, don't realize is that this has cut both ways. The new freedom, even with all the new titillation thrown in, has released an amount of sexual feeling that was, so to speak, unhealthily dammed up in those days. Because less sex came out, there was all the more of it inside, haunting and tantalizing the imagination. It was all the more mysterious and fascinating. You can say that because the girls in 1913 wore so many clothes, covering them from top to toe, we wondered all the oftener and harder what they would be like without those clothes. There was a kind of stifling excitement about the whole thing that I imagine hardly exists now. I was a fairly normal youth then, neither particularly prudish nor lecherous, but the atmosphere was such – and I think now it was a suffocating and unhealthy atmosphere – that I spent half my mental life prowling uneasily on the edge of sexual discovery and revelation. It made sex much more a delicious thing in itself – Cissie's 'naughty but nice' line, which was very common then – and much less a natural urge to be satisfied within a relationship, than it is now. On the stage, of course, it was all more free-and-easy and the girls showed as much of themselves as they were allowed to do – and as a rule they had uncommonly good figures – but all this was happening within the strict general rules, which made it all the more raffish and exciting. I don't say that when I accepted Uncle Nick's offer to join him, I had sex in mind, but I did very soon find myself infected by a confused sexual excitement, an increasing sense of anticipation, that made hypocritical bosh out of my pretence that I wanted to get to know everybody and be friendly. All I really cared about were the two girls and the woman.

At this band call the acts were taken roughly in the running order of the programme. I was watching Colmar lose his temper again and thump the stage when I found somebody standing very close to me. It was Nonie, now muffled in a long coat and skirt but still somehow suggesting a lot of sex. She had greenish eyes, an absurdity of a nose, and a ripe underlip, which she pushed out at the least provocation. 'My oncle,' she said, smiling, 'always is angry with orchestra.'

'And my uncle won't even come and speak to conductors.'

'Oo is 'e – your oncle?'

I told her who he was and who I was.

'You are afraid of eem?'

I said, truthfully enough, that I wasn't. Why, was she?

She came closer still, so that I could smell her perfume and felt her breast against my arm. She whispered – and I can't bother with her broken English – that I must be very brave because everybody she knew, except perhaps her own uncle, was afraid of Uncle Nick. It was not, I gathered, simply because he was severe and occasionally bad-tempered, which would have been reasonable enough, but because she and a few mysterious others she didn't name really confused him with his act and felt that he might have some sinister magical power. And all the time she was telling me this, she kept as close as she could, and ended by jiggling hot little fingers inside the stiff collar I was wearing. But then she moved quickly away: her uncle had ended his battle with the conductor.

With his monstrous overcoat hanging loose and wearing a tweed cap with its peak raised high above his long, melancholy face, Burrard was staring down at the conductor.

'Now look, Harry old man,' the conductor was saying, 'we could play these numbers of yours in our sleep. So don't worry. And when are you going to get some new numbers?'

'Who told you to say that?' Burrard demanded angrily.

'What do you mean, old man?'

'I'm just asking you a civil question, that's all, a civil question,' Burrard shouted.

'All right, let's get on with it, Harry.' He tapped with his baton. 'Same Entrance and Till Ready.'

When Burrard came off and I moved forward, he stopped me. 'You ought to have waited for me yesterday at the station, cully. I could have shown you if you'd given me a chance. There were three of 'em. There's one outside now. Want to see?'

'No, I'm on next.' And I had to push past him. There was the same grumble there had been at Newcastle about our band parts, and I made up my mind to tell Uncle Nick we ought to replace them – and if possible improve our music. Seeing I was young and green, the conductor, who probably disliked Uncle Nick as much as Uncle Nick was ready to dislike him, took it out of me and several times made me look silly, so that I heard some sniggers both from the orchestra pit and the wings. I was sweating when it was over, so I went down to the stage door, not to leave the theatre but just to cool off. On the stairs I bumped into Bob Hodson, who was hurrying up, afraid that he might be late for his call. 'See if there are any for us, Nancy,' he was shouting over his shoulder. This could only mean she was down there, asking for letters. So I stopped at the cubby-hole, waited until she had been handed several letters, and then enquired rather grandly on behalf of the whole *Ganga Dun* company. And there were in fact two for Uncle Nick, and I took them, though he had never asked me so far to collect his correspondence.

'Good morning, Miss Ellis,' I said, all bright and chummy, though my heart was pounding away.

She looked up from the letter she was reading. It was the first time I had seen her face clearly, without make-up and stage lighting. Her eyes weren't blue but a warm grey. However, it wasn't warm for me. She gave me a cold stare, tilted her nose and chin, and without a word turned away and went up the stairs. I heard a light easy laugh from somebody whose arrival I hadn't noticed.

'Good morning, Mr – what is it? – Herncastle,' Miss Blane said, smiling. 'What have you done to her?'

'That's what I'm wondering, Miss Blane. She snubbed me the other night, but I thought I'd try again.'

'I don't blame you. She's an attractive child. Just a moment.' And she enquired about letters. 'Were you about to run away – to hide your blushes – poor boy? If not, come up to my dressing-room. God! – I'm tired.' She slipped a hand under my arm as we went upstairs. 'We went to a party last night – yes, they have parties even in Edinburgh on Sunday – and poor Tommy's still out. That's why I've come down for this wretched band call. If you'd told me five years ago I'd be creeping down on a Monday morning to tell a music-hall orchestra what to do, I'd have – well, something outrageous. What did you say your name was, my dear?'

'Herncastle—'

'No, I'm not so stupid. Your other name.'

'Richard. Dick.'

'Yes, and you want to be a painter. Now – where am I? Along here, I think. Yes, here we are.'

In the dressing-room I saw her clearly for the first time, as I had just seen Nancy Ellis. I realize now that Julie Blane had run out of luck from the very start because she had been born twenty years too soon. She had nothing of the cow-eyed, dimpled, pink-and-white prettiness still admired, especially on the stage, in 1913, whereas twenty years later, when the Garbos and Hepburns filled the screens (and Julie Blane was dead and forgotten), she might have taken a place beside them. She had a broad if rather low forehead, finely arched eyebrows, wide and delicately padded cheekbones with hollows below them, a slightly curved longish nose, a wide and flexible, thin-lipped mouth. She caught me staring at her in the mirror below which she had been setting out some things.

'Don't stare so hard,' she said, turning round. 'I'm a hundred years old this morning. And I never was pretty.'

'No, you're not pretty—'

'Gallant Dick Herncastle—'

'You're beautiful, Miss Blane.'

'Nonsense! But if you're going to work so hard, flattering me, you might as well call me Julie.'

'I'm not flattering you. I wasn't thinking about pleasing you. In a sense I wasn't considering you at all,' I went on stubbornly. 'I was

71

looking at your face as a kind of object – and then I saw that it was beautiful.'

'A-ha! The artist speaks.'

'Well,' I'm not much of a painter yet. Don't pretend to be. But even so, I *am* a painter – and I see with a painter's eye.'

'And talk like a solemn young goose. Come here.' When I did, she kissed me on the lips but only lightly and briefly. 'Thank you, Dick. We ought to be going down, I suppose. The band hasn't to do much for us – I've only three cues for the conductor – but Tommy insists on just the right tempo for his entrance and he ought to be here to see to it himself. But I felt I couldn't wake him up. Let's go, then, Dick.'

'You also happen to have a beautiful voice,' I said, or almost growled, as we went along the corridor.

'At it again, are you? Well, I do think I have a nice voice, but there isn't much *happen* about it. Training and hard work, Dick dear. For two years I was the pet slave of a wonderful old actress. Now about this girl – Nancy Who's-it – who's snubbing you so fiercely – have you fallen in love with her, poor boy?'

'Not yet. Too soon. But I think I easily might. What's the matter with her? What am I supposed to have done? She doesn't know me.'

'No, of course not. But I think I can put you out of your misery. I fancy it was something your uncle said about their act, which I find rather charming – even though the men are so awful.'

'I do too.'

'Especially your little Nancy. She could go a long way if she wanted to. But she doesn't, her sister told me. It's the sister and her husband – a silly fellow – who are ambitious. Apparently Nancy isn't at all – doesn't even like being on the stage. Odd, isn't it, when she obviously has most of the talent in that act?'

I heard some giggling in a corner when we got down to the stage level. There, capering in front of Nonie, was Barney, our dwarf. His back was turned to me and I didn't call out to him.

'One of your Indian colleagues, isn't he, Dick?' said Julie, sweetly malicious. Then, lowering her voice: 'I keep telling myself that I ought to feel sorry for him, but I can't help thinking he's a horrid little creature. And I always feel that girl's a vicious little thing. But perhaps you find her exciting. I know Tommy rather fancied her at the beginning of the tour. Listen – no, they've not quite finished yet. If you'd like to wait, Dick – and I shan't be long – we might have a drink, something I could more than do with this very minute. Would you like me to tell your hard-hearted little Nancy that the sins of the uncle should not be visited upon the innocent and admiring nephew?'

'No, thank you, Julie. But I should like to wait and have that drink with you.'

As she went on-stage, Bob Hodson came off and marched straight up to me. He was wearing a loosely-cut suit of Harris tweed, the hairy kind that seems to have disappeared but was very popular then with men like Hodson. And, for that matter, he had the kind of looks, seen often on the stage then, that suddenly vanished about fifty years ago: dark curly hair parted in the middle; a square ruddy face, with not much nose but a big chin that he jutted out as far as it would go; he was a sort of romantic sketch in grease paint of a naval officer. And though I couldn't have produced any evidence for my belief, I knew for certain he was an empty man.

'Look here, Ollanton,' he began.

'My name's not Ollanton, it's Herncastle.'

'Well, Herncastle then. You're annoying my sister-in-law, Miss Ellis-'

'Annoying her? All I've done is to say *Good morning* to her. She can get over that, can't she?'

'She doesn't want to speak to you, so don't speak to her.'

'Oh – push off!'

'How would you like a punch on the nose?'

'Try it and see.' And I gave him a hard stare. I was no bruiser, but then neither was he. Besides, I might be young and silly but I wasn't empty.

'Well, just leave her alone in future, Horncastle—'

'Herncastle. You might as well get it right before you call in the police.'

He marched away, trying hard to fill that suit and to show me a grimly determined back. I didn't feel angry with him, an officious ass, but I was furious with Nancy Ellis for running to this idiot with a complaint about me. This was worse than her snubbing tactics. I chased her out of my mind. No more time and attention to be wasted on any thought of silly little Nancy Ellis.

'Well now,' said Julie Blane, 'we'll have that drink. I've been here before – not with Tommy but when I was a real actress on tour – and there's quite a pleasant place where we all used to go, not too far from here.'

On our way, I asked her what Tommy Beamish was really like. 'I think he's a wonderful comedian,' I added. 'I've admired him for years. So I had a shock when he was so rude and bad-tempered – you probably don't remember – but it was my first night backstage—'

'Oh – I remember only too well. You only had a minute of him – I'd several hellish hours. He was angry because that Monday first house was so bad. He thought the Newcastle Empire ought to be sold out for him, even at six-fifteen on Monday. And because he was feeling angry and hurt, he started drinking, which is something he doesn't usually do between performances. Then – what is he really like? Oh dear! What can I say? A lollipop with a fish-hook inside it? Or the other way round. Wormwood with a chocolate centre? Oh – it's too difficult. Ask me sometime when we're sitting quietly with an hour or two to spare. Then, if you feel like it, you can explain that Old Nick uncle of yours, who doesn't seem to me – or to anybody else – exactly a charmer. But I'm assuming now we're going to be friends, Dick. Are we?'

'I'd like it very much,' I told her, not using her bantering tone. 'Even if you weren't you – or say, only half you – I would. I'm feeling rather friendless so far on the variety stage.'

'Bless your heart, so am I, my dear. It's not my kind of world, my kind of acting, and they're not my sort of people. Well then, Dick, we'll be friends as far as we can be. I say that because Tommy can be very demanding and – I must warn you – can easily be very jealous. And the fact that it was an innocent friendship – and – horrors! – I'm nearly old enough to be your mother – wouldn't make him any less jealous. We had an old clown-fiddler – a darling old thing – with us on this bill as far as Manchester, and we became friends – he told me fascinating circus stories by the hour – and Tommy hated it. In fact I believe he rang up the agent and got the old man taken out of our bill. He swore black and blue he hadn't, when I charged him with it – I was furious and threatened to walk out – but even so I think he was lying. Tommy can lie like the devil, though sometimes out of pure kindness. He's a most complicated character, which is probably why he's such a wonderful comedian. And you're right, he is. And I ought to know, after months of him twice-nightly, and never knowing what he's going to do or say next and sometimes completely drying because I want to laugh so much. I've heard of star comics who insist – absolutely *insist*

– on the people playing with them pretending to be overcome. But not Tommy Beamish. It's agony sometimes trying to play this idiotic indignant woman with a straight face.'

We turned into an expensive-looking bar, and there at the counter was old Courtenay, who waved a hand at Julie. He was standing at the edge of a group all dashingly dressed and obviously actors and actresses out of some play on tour. Several of them knew Julie and there were embraces and kisses and cries of 'Darling, darling!' and in a flash the woman I had been with vanished and in her place was a high-voiced excited creature quite strange to me. As I dubiously watched and listened to this transformed Julie, not having been taken into the group yet myself, I had that odd feeling that somebody I knew, somewhere in the place, was staring hard at me. I looked around. Uncle Nick and Cissie was sitting at a small table. And he was staring very hard at me. I went across.

He looked so angry that I felt I had to lie to him. 'Hello, Uncle Nick! Here are two letters for you. Miss Blane told me you might be here.'

'If you've any sense, lad, you'll keep away from Miss Blane. Sit down.' He began reading his letters. Cissie, who looked a bit tawdry in that place and probably knew it, gave me an appealing look, as if asking me to be tactful because Uncle Nick was in one of his moods. I replied with an understanding nod. She sipped her port-and-lemon or whatever it was in a manner so ladylike that she looked idiotic. Uncle Nick pocketed his letters, filled his glass from the half-bottle of champagne, and stared darkly across at the theatrical group.

'Look at 'em. Like a lot of powdered apes. Which is about what they are. Nothing of their own. They aren't anything till somebody tells 'em what to say and what to do. Conceited apes.'

'Nick's quite right,' Cissie told me.

But this didn't help. 'Richard will believe me or he won't, girl. I don't think a testimonial from you will make any difference. But I'm warning you, lad. Keep away from that woman, Blane.'

'But why, uncle? She seems quite sensible and friendly, not like most of the others.'

'You don't have to bother with any of 'em. I don't, do I?'

'No, but I have to see more of them—'

'Not much more. Don't forget I've been years in this business. Now what's she up to?' He was looking at Julie Blane, who was walking towards us carrying a bottle and a glass. I got up, but Uncle Nick didn't move.

'Good morning,' she said to them brightly. Cissie muttered something but if Uncle Nick spoke, I didn't hear him. There was now an angry sparkle in Julie's eye, but she smiled at me as she gave me the glass and the opened bottle of lager. Dick, I promised you a drink so here it is. I've met some old friends, so – if you don't mind—'

'No, of course not. Thank you, Julie.'

She swept away – something that women, especially actresses, could do then with some style – and I sat down and began pouring out the lager.

'So it's Dick and Julie already, is it?' Uncle Nick was obviously angry. 'All right, I'll have to talk straight to you, lad. I knew I'd have to do it sooner or later when I gave you this job. You're a nice-looking lad and so far you know nothing and you've been nowhere. For somebody like that woman, Julie Blane, you're fresh meat to a tiger. I know what I'm talking about when I tell you to keep away from her. If you don't, sooner or later she'll eat you for breakfast.' He stopped to take a drink.

'He's right, Dick, I know he is,' Cissie told me earnestly. 'I'm sure you don't understand yet—'

'That's enough from you, Cissie,' said Uncle Nick sharply. 'In fact I'd do this a lot better without you. Pop off to the *Ladies* or something.'

She got up slowly, with an injured air, and then moved off with a rather pathetic attempt at ladylike dignity.

Uncle Nick, watching her go, said: 'Ever noticed – or are you too young – that girls like Cissie – and above all, tarts – always go for a pee trying to look like duchesses?' He waited a moment and then looked hard at me, half-closing his eyes and almost squinting. But he no longer spoke angrily. 'You think I'm prejudiced against Julie Blane, don't you, lad?'

'Well, uncle, it's beginning to look like it,' I replied rather sulkily.

'I'm narrow-minded and suspicious. I'm just a variety turn and she's been a West End actress. And so on and so forth – eh? Well, let me tell you a few things about Miss Julie Blane. If you knew a bit more, you'd have been asking yourself what the hell she's doing here, playing feed twice-nightly to a comic – rough stuff – and then going back to his digs every night for some even rougher stuff – because I've heard some queer stories about Tommy Beamish's private life.'

'I may not know much,' I mumbled, feeling embarrassed, 'but I have wondered about all that.'

'She was a good actress and began playing leading parts. But then she took to the bottle. And let me say here, lad, there's far less excuse for them than there is for us on the halls. We have to make an immediate effect, all on our own, most of the time with big noisy audiences. Then when we've done it once, we have to sit in our dressing-rooms, just waiting to do it again. That's where weak silly chaps like Tommy Beamish come unstuck. And he hardly picked a temperance reformer when he picked Julie Blane. She was drinking so hard that one night she fell flat on her face on the stage of the Comedy Theatre. Then it was good-bye to the West End. She had to take what she could get, and what she got was Tommy Beamish, twice-nightly on the stage and once-nightly, but with trimmings, on or round the bed.' He gave a contemptuous glance in her direction – and I knew she was still there because I had heard her laugh come ringing out – and then looked at me, darkly triumphant. 'Now do you see what I mean?'

I didn't reply. Suddenly I hated him, not because he'd destroyed some wonderful image of Julie Blane – I hadn't one then and only admired her looks and manner and welcomed her friendliness – but because there seemed something so hard and mean about that triumphant look of his, because he'd enjoyed telling me, without a flicker of compassion, what a mess she'd made of her life and stage career. I felt vaguely there was in him a dark and wicked envy of anybody and anything of finer quality, a hatred, half contemptuous, half envious, of any kind of life more generous and therefore more vulnerable than his own. He was like that Sunday-newspaper public which enjoys nothing better than seeing a reputation clawed down, mutilated, covered with muck. He was all right; he had everything well arranged and nicely under control; if other people couldn't live along the same tight hard line, let 'em suffer.

Something of what I felt must have showed. 'All right, lad, you do see what I mean, but you don't like it and just now you don't like me. I'll have to bear it. But there's one thing.' He produced a card. 'I met a man I know here earlier this morning. I told him about you, and he gave me this for you.' He gave me the card, which admitted me as a temporary member to the Edinburgh Arts Club. 'You might find it useful, might not. Only – don't go there when I might want you, that's all, lad.'

I realized then that although I thought I knew all about people, in fact I didn't understand them at all. Just when I'd turned Uncle Nick into one kind of man, he'd turned himself into somebody quite different. It wouldn't have been easy for him to ask a favour of anybody, but now he'd just done it entirely for my sake. I thanked him in a mumbling and shamefaced fashion, feeling very young.

'You could go along there and have a snack if you wanted to,' he told me.

Cissie came back now, sat down as if we weren't there, and sipped her drink.

'I'd like to, uncle, but I don't think I'll have time. I wanted to pick up a sandwich somewhere, then hurry to the digs for my gear and do a quick sketch or two while it's fine.'

'It may be fine,' said Cissie, still looking away from us, 'but you could easily catch your death of cold.'

'Go on then, lad. Take the opportunity. We may be rehearsing most of next week. But I'll explain about that after the first house. Oh – and see you're there in good time tonight to check everything with Sam and Ben.'

Well, I did some sketching, and then was backstage by quarter to six, a minute or two before Sam and Ben arrived. We had a little trouble with the mechanical part of the levitation effect, which needed oiling, but everything else seemed in good order. When I went up to put on my costume and make-up, which Hislop had taught me how to do in five minutes, I ran slap into Nonie, tripping down with a cloak over her glittering bodice and tights. When I said 'Sorry!', she laughed, pushed her breasts hard against me, wriggled a bit, then dodged under my arms, leaving me feeling excited even though I didn't really care for her.

It was a thin and gloomy house, and, when I stood with Uncle Nick in the wings, while Burrard was desperately waving his arms and shouting his head off, Uncle Nick muttered: 'I can't follow this silly bugger much longer. He'll have to go, contract or no contract.' When he came off, to the faintest rattle of applause, Burrard tried to say something but Uncle Nick told him to shut up and walked away. The band played our opening music as if half of them were reading the evening papers. As I went on, following Sam and Ben, I could hear Uncle Nick complaining to the stage manager. Fortunately there was nothing ingratiating about *Ganga Dun*, very much a haughty, aloof and contemptuous Indian magician, so that Uncle Nick could play him equally well if he was out of temper, except that he was apt then to force the pace of the act and so increase the danger of something going wrong. He knew and I knew that Cissie was slow again dropping out of the box into the pedestal, but the audience didn't – but then they gave little sign of knowing anything. After taking a perfunctory call, Uncle Nick hurried off. I stayed behind with Sam and Ben, though it was their job to make sure everything was ready for the second performance, chiefly to let Uncle Nick take it out of poor Cissie and the management and anybody else before I went up. On the stairs I passed Nancy Ellis, looking hellishly attractive in her stage costume, but it was stony face passing stony face. I didn't have to bother with that one.

Uncle Nick had taken off his robe and turban and was sitting in an old dressing-gown, smoking a cigar he didn't seem to be enjoying. 'I thought you took a band call this morning,' he began at once.

'I did. And the opening music was all right—'

'Perhaps you don't listen—'

'I listen, uncle. I'm more interested in music than you are. I was thinking this morning it's time we had some new band parts and some better music.'

He pointed his cigar at me. 'You're only twenty. You don't know anything. You've only been on the job five minutes. Now you're telling me how to run my act. I've half a mind to tell you to bugger off. Now let's have less of your bloody cheek, lad.'

'All right, Uncle Nick. If you think I'm cheeky, I'm sorry. I'm not trying to be. I like the act. I'm proud of it. I'm ready to do everything I can to help you with it.'

He looked at me rather strangely. I couldn't tell what his look meant because after all he was still half an Indian magician. He flicked the ash off his cigar. 'I believe you, Richard. I don't know why I should, but I do. Now if you've anything to say – spit it out.'

'Look, uncle. You don't take band calls because you don't like musical directors. Well, *they* don't like *you*.'

'I'm not asking 'em to like me, lad. All I ask is that they do their work properly, just as I do mine – the work they're paid to do—'

'Yes, but perhaps they aren't paid very much—'

'I know, I know,' he said irritably. 'Where d'you think I've been these last ten years? They like to be sweetened – a fiver – some drinks and cigars while you tell 'em what a good band they have. And I object to it. On principle I object to it. I've complained more than once both to agents and managements.'

I said nothing for a moment or two, just looked at him. 'I did my best this morning. I'll do my best every Monday morning. I promise you that, uncle. But don't take it out of me if they don't like your attitude. Now what are we going to be rehearsing next week?'

'Ah – I'll show you.' He brought out a number of diagrams, now his eager, simpler and happier self, a creator. 'It's the bike trick, of course. But not with the bike disappearing, just the rider. The effect is – you see a man riding up to this open doorway, then the bike goes through and the man vanishes. And that'll make 'em sit up, except on Monday in Edinburgh. Now this is how it's done.' And he showed me the diagrams, which he had drawn himself to an exact scale. Later, Uncle Nick sold this *Vanishing Cyclist* effect to an American illusionist for, I think, seven thousand five hundred dollars; and, for all I know, somebody somewhere may still be doing the trick; so that even now I don't feel I ought to give away its secret. But it wasn't – as people used to say – 'all done by mirrors'. The doorway and the bit of wall surrounding it were not as simple as they looked; two identical bicycles, built specially to Uncle Nick's orders, were used. And I was told there and then that I would have to be the cyclist.

'I'm not trying to dodge anything, uncle. But remember I'm no lightweight, and while I can ride a bike I'm no trick cyclist either.'

'It has to be you, lad. Cissie would be wrong, and anyhow they'll have seen her in the levitation and the box trick. Sam's too old and stiff, and Ben's not quick enough. Barney is – he can be very sharp when he wants to be – but he'd look wrong. I'd gladly do it myself – I could, easy – but I've got to be diverting their attention with my "Ready – steady – *Go!*" – the first lines I've ever given myself to speak – and then the green flash, otherwise we haven't a chance.'

'I wouldn't have thought we had even then. It seems too cheeky.'

'I know what I'm doing, lad. This is my business, and I'm a master of it. Everything depends on the two seconds – or even a bit less than that – when they think they're staring hard and they aren't. It's all in the split-second timing. Which means we'll be rehearsing most of next week, when I'll have all the equipment I need for the effect. That's what those two letters were about, this morning. Now take another look at these diagrams. Everything's here.' He was proud of his diagrams.

'Of course you understand all this and I don't,' I said, after looking at the diagrams again. 'But from these I can't see why you can't do what you originally intended to do – to make both the rider *and* the bike disappear.'

'I'll tell you why,' he said pleasantly, almost giving me a smile. All his usual impatience and prejudice and arrogance never showed when he began to discuss this kind of problem. The vanishing – as I have it now – still isn't good enough unless there's something to take their eye at once. If, after the green flash, they see that bright new bicycle going through the doorway, their eyes and their attention will have to follow it.

'Mind you, Richard, I'll tell 'em on the programme what to expect – the cyclist vanishing in the doorway while his cycle goes through it. So that's what they'll expect to see – and what they *will* see. And there's nothing original about that, Richard. These twerps are having it done to them all their lives. They see what they're told they'll see.' He was back on the familiar sardonic hard line again.

I risked a gibe. 'You're not exactly one of these big-hearted variety artistes who love their audiences, are you, Uncle Nick? I keep reading about them.'

'So do I, lad.' His tone was very dry. 'I've even met a few – they have the fourpenny gallery singing idiotic choruses.'

'You don't seem even to like yours, Uncle Nick.'

'I've told you before, lad – I despise the silly sods. And don't imagine your Tommy Beamish, the great comic, is any different. Not deep down, where he's all so mixed up he's really half barmy. He earns two hundred and fifty a week showing these people a reflection of themselves in a trick mirror, just looking a bit sillier than they are. He doesn't really like 'em any more than I do. Look at it. These thickheads come crowding into variety theatres to be flattered a bit, to clap or boo or walk out to demonstrate their power, and to forget for a couple of hours all the bloody mess outside. Yes, everything in the papers that they didn't know what to do about – delicate women being forcibly fed, strikes and lock-outs, civil war in Ulster, government scandals about shares, Germany looking more and more dangerous. We're all slithering into a bog, lad. Here, give me those diagrams. They may be about a bit of nonsense, to make twice-nightly rows of twerps gape and clap, but as far as I'm concerned they're a little patch of sanity and reasonableness. Now listen.'

He waited a moment, as if needing a little time to return to his comparatively simple and earnest professional self. 'All right, they'll see what we tell 'em they'll see. But of course it isn't as easy as that. We have to rehearse the trick over and over and over again – and you won't enjoy it, lad – until we get a split-second timing. Everything will be slowed up before the vanishing, so that the minds of the audience will still be moving in slow time when we'll be working unbelievably fast. That's the secret, lad. It's really how I get away with the old box trick, which I wouldn't bother with if I hadn't thought of that slowly closing lid, which makes 'em feel that Cissie's still settling down into the box when she's already out of it and into the pedestal. I've read every book I can find on conjuring and illusionists' effects, all about misdirection, false choices, and the rest of it; but not one of them sees the importance of this slow time in the audience's mind when you're working fast on the stage. It's my speciality, Richard.'

There was a knock, and he frowned, clearly not wanting to be disturbed when he was happily explaining himself. 'All right, all right,' he shouted. 'Come in.'

It was Barney. He was still wearing his enormous turban and dark make-up but no robe, simply his own dwarfish shirt and trousers. Everything about him looked idiotic except his eyes, half blind with fear. I wanted to creep away but Uncle Nick checked me. 'No, lad, you'd better listen to this.' Then he stared at Barney.

'Mis' Ollanton,' Barney began in his jerky spluttery fashion, 'Sam said – you wanted to see me, Mis' Ollanton—'

'Then where have you been? Hanging about the women – trying to turn yourself into a pet dog?'

'No, no, Mis' Ollanton. Jus' been—' But he couldn't think what had been keeping him.

'I've a letter here from an agency in London, Barney.' Uncle Nick snatched up the first that came to hand, then pretended to glance through it. 'Little men aren't in great demand, Barney. More than a dozen of 'em here. Want three pounds ten, some of 'em. Others are available at three pounds and even two pounds ten. I'm paying you four, Barney.'

'Yes, Mis' Ollanton – very good – but I work hard, Mis' Ollanton—' Barney shook his head desperately, put a hand to his forehead, and so removed some of his make-up.

'Don't touch anything now until you've washed that muck off,' said Uncle Nick sharply. 'Now I'm not trying to beat you down a few shillings, Barney. I'm warning you. And this is the last time. You were slow again dropping in the *Rival Magician* effect—'

'Mis' Ollanton, sir, it's them stilt-boots. Sam says—'

'Don't tell me what Sam or anybody says. Go wash your hands and then bring those stilt-boots. But if I find they're all right and it's your carelessness, this is your last warning, Barney. If you're slow again, I'll wire London for another dwarf – that's all it'll take, a wire – and you're out – out.'

After poor Barney had scuttled away, Uncle Nick pointed his cigar at me. 'Don't ever be soft with him because you feel sorry for him. He'll take advantage of it – sharp. He doesn't like us, y'know – hates us – I mean us men. He fancies the women all right, so long as they don't laugh at him – then he hates them worse than he does us.'

The second house wasn't much better than the first, but nothing went wrong during the act. I had supper with Uncle Nick and Cissie and all three of us were rather dreary and went to bed early. It was still fine, though cold, on Tuesday, and I was able to do some sketching just outside the city during the morning. After some dithering I presented that card at the Arts Club and had a late lunch there, sitting next to a gnarled old Scot, who told me that his natural deep love of his native moors and glens had ruined him as a landscape painter, because they were too picturesque and encouraged sloppy bad art. The next day it rained, so in the afternoon I went to the art gallery. There were not many people in there but one of them, a small and rather forlorn figure in that setting, was Nancy Ellis. I took the stony face I showed her along to the watercolour room, which was empty, and not asking to be crowded on a darkish November afternoon. I was peering at some early nineteenth-century ink-and-wash drawings when I heard somebody enter. Then a throat was delicately cleared.

'There's something I want to say to you,' said Nancy Ellis. She was wearing a tweed coat that looked too big for her, and one of those anglers' tweed hats that girls sometimes wore then, with a lot of fair curls escaping from it. She had no makeup on and her face was pale, serious, not trying to look pretty.

'Is there? Well, go on.'

'You needn't sound like that.'

'I'm sorry, but I don't want to be snubbed again—'

'I can't be snubbing you if I've just come up to talk to you,' she said indignantly. 'I call that stupid.'

'So do I. I'm feeling a bit stupid.'

'Well, you were engrossed in the pictures, weren't you? So it's my fault. But I wanted to tell you that I didn't ask Bob – Bob Hodson, my brother-in-law – to talk to you like that. I said something silly to Susie, my sister, and she must have said something to him, and then – well, he's rather like that – always interfering and trying to be important.'

'Did he tell you he'd spoken to me?'

'No. Actually it was Julie Blane. She overheard him. And last night, when she was going along to her dressing-room and I'd just come out of mine – it was after the last show – she stopped me and told me about it – and about you. She's interested in you, isn't she?'

'I doubt it.'

'Oh yes, she is. I can tell. Susie and Bob are always telling me to keep away from her. They don't like her.'

'They don't seem to like anybody—'

'That's the limit, coming from you!'

'Why me?' I was genuinely surprised.

'Well, what about your frightful uncle? He's the one who hates everybody.'

We had raised our voices by this time, and then we noticed there were two other people in the room, a tall thin pair with those pulled-down Edinburgh mouths, who were staring at us with intense disapproval.

'Come on,' I muttered. And as soon as we were out of the room I said that explanations weren't over, they'd hardly begun, and that we ought to find a teashop. She said she didn't know that she ought, that she'd half-promised her sister to do something or other, that it was raining, and kept on showing reluctance right up to the entrance to the teashop, though somehow she found it and I didn't. There, snug in a corner, she took off her floppy hat and shook out her curls, robbing them of the diamond raindrops that I can recall to this day. Over the tea, the scones, the jam, we stopped sparring and began confiding in each other, all ears but even more – all eyes.

Because she insisted that I should explain myself first, I told her how I had come to join Uncle Nick, simply because I could earn more money than I could in an office and so perhaps find it easier to become a professional painter. Then she told me that her parents had been theatrical people, working mostly in musical comedy and concert parties, that her father had died and her mother had married again and had gone to Australia, leaving Susie, five years older than she was, to look after her. She'd been in some kind of act with Susie and Bob for the last two years.

'But they don't like being in variety. And Susie's very ambitious. Bob only thinks he is, but she *really* is. But she wants either to be in musical comedy, if they can find the right parts together, or to run their own concert party. Bob's very keen on that idea. He fancies himself as a great runner of things, though Susie will have to do most of the real work. And she will too. Have you been in front?'

'Yes, on the Monday in Newcastle. It's a very good act.'

'Susie's scrumptious, isn't she?'

'No. I mean – she's all right. But you're the one.'

'Oh – no!' She scowled at me. 'That's silly. You're saying that because you think I'll be pleased. Well, I'm not.'

'I can see that. But I'm not trying to flatter you, I'm telling the truth. You carry that act. I thought you were wonderful.'

And as I looked at that pale resentful face, still not free of its scowl and hardly looking even passably pretty at that moment, I thought – and, I must admit, longingly – of the stage Nancy, so enchantingly gay and saucy, of those ravishing and witty legs, and of that Maytime of painted flats and coloured lights. And suddenly I felt miserable, because I wanted to believe in reality and not in theatrical illusion.

'Why are you looking like that?' she demanded.

'I was wondering which is really you—'

'This is me – the real me. Why are you being so silly? I'm a serious girl – and I believe in serious things. That's not me, capering and larking about, showing my legs and being cheeky. I'm only like that because it's what Susie and Bob want. I'm trying to please them – especially Susie—'

'Not the public?'

'No.' She pulled a face.

'Well, all I can say, Nancy, is that you pleased me – enormously. I think I'm more than half in love with that saucy girl in the act.' And as soon as I had made this fatuous remark, I regretted it.

She looked disgusted. 'I can see we're not going to be friends. Do you want any more tea?'

'Yes, please. By the way, I must be at least two years older than you.'

'What's that got to do with it?' Her look and tone were icy.

'After all, what are you being so serious about?'

'What are you? Legs?'

'Legs come into it, if they're worth looking at. As I told you, I want to be a painter. That's what I take seriously – painting.' I was rather grand about this, as one is at twenty. 'If it had been fine this afternoon, I'd have been out sketching. The art gallery was the next best thing. I know what I'm doing. But what's this great seriousness of yours all about?'

'Life,' she announced with immense solemn pride. And then suddenly and quite unexpectedly she laughed. So I laughed. Then, we both laughed together. Now warm and steamy, the teashop was filling up, but we still had our corner to ourselves.

'Now what about my frightful uncle, as you called him?'

'We're against him,' she declared promptly. 'He started it. He told the agent, who told Bob, that he loathed our act and didn't want it booked on the same bill. He seems to hate everybody. What's the matter with him?'

'At the moment I couldn't begin to explain him,' I told her. 'Before I came into variety – and of course I've only just made a beginning – I used to think I knew about people, but now suddenly everybody seems so contradictory.'

'Including me, I suppose?'

'Well – yes – you too.' I think my tone was rueful.

This brought me something new – a slow sweet smile, arriving from some mysterious feminine depth. 'I bet you never knew anything about people. Perhaps you're just a bit closer to them now, that's all. But if we're ever going to be friends—'

'And I hope we are,' I threw in quickly.

'Well, perhaps, perhaps not. I'm not like Susie and Bob, good old pals with anybody. And we won't even make a start – and I don't count this — unless you understand that this is the real me, not that cheeky fake in the show.' She waited a moment, but this time I kept quiet. 'I must be going. And thank you for the lovely tea.'

That night, after we'd finished at the second house, which gave Uncle Nick a good reception, I changed at once and watched in the wings, on the side I knew she never used, *Susie, Nancy, and Three*

Gentlemen. She left me entranced all over again. It was maddening.

6

The train we took from Edinburgh was very different from the one the Sunday before: it was a corridor train and had a dining-car; and we had a whole coach reserved for us. Uncle Nick and Cissie had gone on by car, and Tommy Beamish and Julie were missing too; but all the rest of us were there. In Edinburgh I had bought a long thick overcoat, nearly as big as Uncle Nick's though not as grand, and a dark grey trilby to match it, so that I rather fancied my appearance. I shared a compartment with Sam and Ben, who stared glumly at Sunday newspapers, and Barney, who was excited and restless and kept popping in and out and talking all kinds of nonsense. There were patches of fog along the line so that at times we only crept along. I was out in the corridor, hoping to catch at least a glimpse of some fine scenery, when I found Nancy at my elbow. She was looking pale and rather tired, but there was something enormously attractive and appealing about her smudged grey eyes.

'Hello! I was wondering if you'd like to be introduced properly to Susie and the others.'

'Yes, please, Nancy. And my name is Herncastle – Richard Herncastle – Dick—'

'I know. Come on.'

I've had warmer welcomes than the one I received in that compartment. Susie, a sharp-featured brunette, was sufficiently polite, but clearly didn't regard me as a great treat. Bob Hodson gave me a nod but no smile, and he returned in three seconds flat to the newspaper he had been reading. But Ambrose and Esmond, the two 'puffs', were friendly and eager to talk. Ambrose favoured blue, Esmond brown, otherwise they looked almost like twins, both with wavy hair, thin and delicate faces, high voices. (But their life lines, now exactly parallel, were soon to rush away from each other, for while Esmond vanished in the mud and ruin of Paschendaele, Ambrose by the middle 1920s was one of the most successful comic actors on the West End stage.) And they spoke so quickly and excitedly, and so often overlapped, that I never really knew which of them was talking.

'Nancy says you don't really want to be on the stage.' This was Susie, and I guessed at once she was not simply making polite conversation. 'You want to be an artist – or something.'

I didn't deny this.

'It's our *life*,' said Susie. 'The Theatre's in our *blood*.' She looked sharply from me to Nancy.

'And every bit of it,' cried Ambrose and Esmond, 'including the box office.'

Bob Hodson looked up from his paper. 'Not funny.' As he looked down again, Ambrose, Esmond and Nancy exchanged bright glances.

'Certainly the box office,' said Susie firmly. 'I'm a pro, not an amateur. And one day I'll be in management.' She gave me a smiling look, opening her eyes, as wide as she could. They were quite unlike Nancy's – a hardish raw umber. 'Nancy feels just as I do, though she pretends not to — as you may have gathered.' Nancy scowled but said nothing. 'Of course I mean the real Theatre, not this awful variety nonsense.'

'Twice-nightly, dear,' cried Ambrose and Esmond. 'Just before or just after the fish-and-chips. And they're so much better *after*.'

'We're all *longing* to get back. Even Nancy – aren't you, darling?'

'No, I'm not.' Nancy looked and sounded mutinous.

'How can you say that? You know very well you hate this twice-nightly touring—'

'Of course I do. But that doesn't mean I'm longing to get back to the Theatre – or some idiotic pier pavilion—'

'All those waves and *crashings*!' This, of course, was either Ambrose or Esmond, perhaps both. 'And always too fine to go in or too wet to turn out. And all the dear kiddies, bang in the centre, wanting to be taken out to wee-wee!'

'Oh – shut up, you two,' said Bob.

'I'm not longing to get back there,' Nancy continued, still scowling a little, 'or to anywhere else, I'm not longing for anything. I wish I was.'

'She has such talent too,' Susie said to me. 'Don't you think so, Mr Herncastle?'

'Yes, I think she's wonderful.' This brought me a special scowl for myself. And I think if we'd been alone I would have kissed her, even if it had meant having my face slapped. I noticed that Ambrose and Esmond, who were quick and intuitive, gave me a look and then exchanged more bright glances.

'What I'd like to know,' said Bob, laying aside his paper, 'is why your uncle is so bloody disagreeable.'

'Now, Bob!' said his wife. But she looked at me inquiringly.

'Well, don't you think he is, Herncastle?'

'Sometimes – yes. But then you see he doesn't enjoy performing – doesn't think of himself as an actor – only enjoys working out new tricks and effects.'

'He's very clever, of course,' Susie admitted.

'Marvellous!' Ambrose and Esmond cried. 'But when we tried to watch him from the wings, he flew into the most terrible rage – absolutely terrified us.'

'Go on,' Nancy said to me. 'You haven't finished yet, have you, Dick?'

'I was only going to say that most people want other people to like them. Well, Uncle Nick doesn't. It's all the same to him if they dislike him.'

'We know that,' said Nancy, falsely sweet. 'Does it run in the family?'

'Stop flirting, dear,' cried Ambrose or Esmond. 'Look – you're making him blush.'

'Oh – don't be stupid.' But she didn't look at them but at me, as if she regretted having asked me into the compartment. However, the next moment the door was violently jerked open, and there was Barney, all grin and jiggling tiny legs. Whenever he opened a door like this, his appearance was startling, at its most dwarfish and freakish.

'Mis' Herncastle, Mis' Herncastle,' Barney began, all excited, pleased with himself, and silly, as I realized at once. 'Nonie wants see you, Nonie wants see you. Nonie's sitting with us, Mis' Herncastle. She sent special message, Mis' Herncastle. Listen, Mis' Herncastle—'

'Oh – push off,' Bob shouted at him.

'Not talking to you.' Barney may have been afraid of Uncle Nick, but he cared nothing for any Bob Hodson.

'I said – *push off*.' And Bob got up, though in fact I was standing between him and Barney.

'What you say, Mis' Herncastle?'

'Well, I don't particularly want to see Nonie, but I'll be coming back in a minute or two. You run along, Barney.'

He went at once.

'Like touring with a bloody circus,' Bob grumbled. 'Do you have to have a freak like that?'

'Bob, don't be so *hard*. He hasn't got two heads or anything.' This was Ambrose or Esmond – perhaps a duet. 'He's just a *little* man. He can't help it, poor thing!'

'That's what I keep telling myself,' said Nancy.

'He can help the way he behaves,' said Susie, looking disgusted. 'The horrible little wretch. One night – where was it? – Liverpool? – he came up behind me and put his arms round my waist – nearly frightened me out of my life.'

'My God! Why didn't you tell me?' This was Bob the dwarf-killer.

'Don't be silly, Bob,' said Nancy. 'We can't be telling you things like that all the time. If he can manage it at all, he's a *toucher* – and not the only one, though he has more excuse, I suppose, poor little mannie.' She looked at me. 'Don't forget your Nonie's waiting for you.'

'She isn't my Nonie. I've hardly spoken to her. This is just some bit of mischief that she and Barney have cooked between them. He's always showing off to make her laugh.'

'Well, now you can show off to make *her* laugh,' said Nancy, picking up a newspaper. She was probably feeling sorry, as I was, that she had invited me into their carriage. She and I didn't seem to be having much luck.

But I went back to discover that Nonie and Barney weren't waiting for me but were now in the compartment next to ours, sitting wide-eyed and open-mouthed listening to Harry Burrard, who was talking rapidly and earnestly, his face glistening with sweat. I didn't want to hear any more about crazy conspiracies, so I hurried next door, asked Sam and Ben if they were going to eat lunch in the dining-car, and when they said they weren't, I went along by myself. I had spoken to Sam and Ben as if I'd been eating for years in dining-cars, but in fact I was feeling rather apprehensive because I had never been in one before. So I was glad to see Ricarlo, the juggler, sitting in there, and I greeted him warmly and immediately took the vacant place opposite to him.

Ricarlo must have been feeling lonely; he began talking at once and hardly stopped throughout the meal. His English was quite fluent but he still had a heavy Italian accent, sprinkling unnecessary vowels as he did salt and pepper on his meat and vegetables. So if he wanted to say, 'These people are no good', what came out was something like 'Deesa peoples is-a no-a good'. At that time I had never listened before to an Italian speaking English, and I was fascinated by his strange rhythm and tone and the half comic, half melancholy effect they had. But though it could be fascinating to listen to, I know it is as boring to read as it is to write this kind of broken English, so I won't attempt even to suggest most of it. But ever since I had first watched him juggling so beautifully, with that gay-sad little tune going on and on, I had wondered about him, finding it impossible to imagine what sort of life an Italian led, moving week after week, month after month, from one Empire to the next, through a succession of gloomy and alien industrial towns. And about these, he was entirely frank: they were to him like places in a long bad dream.

Finding in me a sympathetic listener, he was frank about everything. (Another thing in my favour, I soon discovered, was that unlike almost everybody else on our bill he was ready to admire Uncle Nick not only as a performer but also as a man, perhaps because in their work they were both stern perfectionists.) He had a wife and six children – and he showed me photographs of them – who lived in Lucca, and lived very well too because he sent them half his salary, which I gathered was about sixty pounds a week. He didn't need to assure me, though he did, that with the equivalent in lire of thirty pounds arriving every week, his wife could queen it in Lucca or anywhere else in Italy. And with six children to look after, she had no desire to go touring with him in the dark and cold of Britain. Moreover, he tried if possible to take a three-months' holiday every year, back home and a happy family man again.

Here, at work and on tour, he told me he had two problems on his hands. The first was literally on his hands, for now that he was into his forties he was afraid of losing his dexterity, so that for at least two hours every day he practised his juggling, not only what he included in his act but also possible new variations. At the moment, he told me with enormous gravity, he was trying to add a bottle and a glass to the top hat, cane and cigar: 'Is-a ver' hard-a dees-a bot' an' glass – diff'rent-a feel – diff'rent-a weight.' Then a smile illuminated his dark and big-boned face: 'But I do eet-a soon – in-a Glas-a-gow maybe – you watch-a me in-a Glas-a-gow, my frien' – eh?' I told him I would, having already assured him that his act gave me great pleasure. Then he discussed, with equal gravity, his other problem. His morning practice and his two shows a night still left him with a fair amount of free time, and he spent this time searching – and often vainly, week after week – for the kind of women he could enjoy having. They had to be blonde, plump, willing and amiable though not necessarily passionate, and between the ages of thirty and forty-five. He didn't rule out prostitutes but greatly preferred – and indeed was always looking out for – charming amateurs, on whom he was prepared to spend more money than the prostitutes demanded. So in town after town he went on the hunt, looking into bars and teashops, haunting the main shopping districts, his dark eyes encountering and challenging any promising pair of blue eyes, keeping close to the trail and then, at exactly the right moment, adopting one of many well-tested ruses to get acquainted. Sometimes of course they had seen him on the stage, which made it easier, but if they had not he would often beg them to do him a favour, adding that he was worried about his performance, by accepting a ticket for the show and then telling him afterwards if he had any reason to feel worried – a gambit that hardly ever failed. His richest hunting-grounds were places like Bristol, Plymouth and Portsmouth – he was almost indignant about naval officers' wives, they were so easy – and, to my surprise, he was hopeful about his prospects in Aberdeen, where he promised to report progress. Though a solitary hunter both by inclination and in his technique, he was so pleased by my interest in his hobby that he invited me to accompany him on one or two afternoons, but I got out of that by telling him I would be rehearsing most of the week.

Over coffee and a couple of thin black cigars he brought out, I asked him his opinion of the girls we had with us. Nonie he denounced at once as a little bitch who sooner or later would run herself into trouble; the three men were anxious to get back to Alsace to train another girl for the act; but their contract would keep them here another three months. Nancy he admired, and in twenty years' time she would be just ripe for him but then he would be too fat and old; so he 'talk-a big-a non-a-sense'. Julie Blane did not appeal to him at all, and when I said that I thought she was beautiful, he closed his eyes, struck out his lower lip, wagged his head, in despair at the difference in our tastes. But then he opened his eyes very wide, stared at me a moment or two, and said: 'Hern-a-castle, my frien', I tell-a you som-a-theeng.'

We had, he said, a madman appearing with us. I told him I knew that, having had to listen to poor Burrard. But to my astonishment he waved aside Burrard, whom he hardly knew. No, the madman he had spotted was our star, Tommy Beamish. When I said I couldn't believe this, he plunged excitedly into a defence of his statement, keeping his voice low – for there were still a few people at the other tables – and speaking so fast that I found it hard to follow him. What I gathered was that he had known two other brilliant comedians, one Italian, the other French, who had behaved more or less exactly as Tommy was doing, sometimes – drinking hard and being uproarious, sometimes retreating into silence and bitterness; and both of them had lost their minds. Gesticulating neatly and vividly, wrapping up the whole tragic affair into a parcel for me, he said that he had studied Tommy's behaviour and noted a certain look in his eyes, and now was sadly certain that soon Tommy would go the same way. I still didn't believe him, but I couldn't help being shaken a little by the dark ruin in Ricarlo's gaze. But then, the tragedy over, he flashed a smile at me and insisted that we should drink a little brandy, to celebrate the good talk we'd had.

(Twenty years afterwards, I did some painting in Italy and was largely defeated by its clear light and uncompromising tones. Finding myself not far from Lucca, I paid a visit to the fine old town, wondering what had become of Ricarlo now that he could no longer be juggling. And there, in Lucca, I found him, fat and prosperous, the proprietor of a small hotel and restaurant; and we drank a lot of wine and talked ourselves back into those variety theatres of 1913 and 1914 and the world, half splendid, half silly, that had produced them and then had been blown to bits. An artist in his own way, a devoted family man, once an unwearying hunter of buxom yielding blondes, Ricarlo seems to me one of the most satisfactory figures in these reminiscences. I wish there could have been more of him than there will be – if you see what I mean.)

Uncle Nick knew of no theatrical digs in Aberdeen, so he had given me the address of an hotel there where I should be staying with him and Cissie. When I found this hotel, they had not arrived; but though the light was already going, it was still afternoon. My room, on the top floor, was very clean, very small, very cold, and offered me a brass bedstead, a jug and bowl for washing, three framed stern texts, a narrow pitch-pine wardrobe that looked like an up-ended coffin, and a bad-tempered midget gasfire. But after the late lunch and Ricarlo's brandy, I slept for an hour under my new overcoat. When I woke up it was dark and I couldn't think where I was, and then when I remembered I didn't feel too happy about it. The incandescent gas light belonged to the same bad-tempered-midget series as the fire. So I went downstairs, wondering what to do with myself. But there, round a tea table, were Uncle Nick and Cissie, Tommy Beamish and Julie.

I waited a moment or two at the bottom of the stairs, where I could see them without their noticing me, just to take them in. They made an odd quartet: Uncle Nick so tall and dark and definite, and Tommy Beamish, short and plump, fair and wavering; Cissie, badly over-dressed, with her face a kind of simpering apology for it; and Julie, severely dressed, bored and withdrawn, with those fine bones and slightly hollow cheeks, that beauty before its time. Portraiture was a long way from my line, even then when I was not quite sure what my line would be; but I remember how I wished, as I stared across at them from the shadowy staircase, I could get them down, exactly as they were then, on canvas or paper. There are some queer moments, not associated with anything dramatic or emotional, that seem to come out of a deeper reality, as if they are trying to tell us something we can never really know; and this was one of those moments.

'So here you are, lad,' said Uncle Nick, with an unsmiling nod at me. 'All in order?'

'So far,' I told him, standing there rather awkwardly.

'You'd like some tea, wouldn't you, Dick?' said Cissie, getting up. 'I'll go and ask them for another cup.'

'You can ring, can't you?' Uncle Nick called after her. 'Well, sit there, Richard.' I took a chair next to Cissie's, then looked across the table and smiled at Julie, who didn't return the smile but merely raised her eyebrows about half an inch.

'Tell me, old bean,' said Tommy Beamish, a funny man at once. 'Did you by any chance notice along at the station a man with a face like this?' And immediately he looked like one of those elderly Scots with very long upper lips.

'Yes, he was there, Mr Beamish, looking after your baggage.'

'Ay, ay, ay,' Tommy croaked. 'Then all's well.' He turned to Julie. 'Ye hear that, lassie? All's well. Your beautiful drawing-room's here – quite safe.'

'Well, you save it, Tommy. Until the first house tomorrow.' Julie's tone wasn't exactly contemptuous but it couldn't be said to be warm, sympathetic, womanly.

Another man, not the one who was shaking his head and grinning at her, flashed her a look from the back of Tommy's eyes; and I couldn't help remembering what Ricarlo had said. Cissie returned with the tea-things for me, filled my cup, passed me the scones and jam, all with an affectionate semi-maternal air. Before I joined them she had probably been feeling embarrassed, out of it, and at least I gave her something to do. She alone seemed glad to see me there; the other three gave me the impression of rather resenting my arrival. With Uncle Nick, I must confess, it was hard to tell; I couldn't imagine him giving anybody a warm welcome. Tommy Beamish, I felt, was ready to dislike me, for reasons best known to himself. But why Julie, who was going to be my friend, should be so frosty was a mystery to me. I knew she had to be careful not to arouse Tommy's jealousy, because of course she had told me, but surely this was overdoing it?

After tea I went out for a walk, not that I expected to see anything, just to stretch my legs and get some air. The air was cold and not very clear, but had in it a fine promise of the sea, a kind of richness and wildness. I'd had plenty of seaside holidays, of course, but never before had I been so close to the sea in winter. It was grand. But I wished I had somebody with me, and I wondered where Nancy Ellis was staying and what she was doing.

When I got back I found Uncle Nick sitting in the small and cheerless hotel lounge, brooding over his diagrams.

'Where have you been?' he asked, giving me a suspicious look.

I felt like telling him that he didn't own me. 'A walk. By myself. I wanted some air.'

'Take your overcoat off and sit down a minute, lad. Supper here's at eight. And, by the way, yours'll go on my bill, though you'll have to pay for your own bed and breakfast. Now tonight I'm going out. And so is Beamish. There's a man here called Sir Alec Inverurie, who's a big shareholder in two or three music hall syndicates. I've met him in London, and so has Beamish. He's telephoned to ask us both out to supper at his house. Not the women of course, because his wife'll be there and Sir Alec's very respectable – at least when he's up here in Aberdeen. In London, on his own, he isn't so particular. So I want you to have your supper with Cissie, who isn't too pleased to be left out.

What you do about Miss Blane I don't know and don't care. I guess she'll have to come down because they don't serve anything in the rooms here. In fact they seem to think we're bloody lucky if they serve anything anywhere. It's that kind of place. And you'll soon understand why I prefer to stay in dig's. Anything to say?'

'Not specially, Uncle Nick. I don't suppose Miss Blane's pleased at being left out either—'

'If she doesn't like it, she can lump it, like Cissie,' he said cheerfully and brutally. 'Let me tell you one thing about women, lad. Start giving in to 'em and soon they're asking for the earth, and nag, or sulk if you're not handing it to 'em on a plate. The only way to keep 'em reasonable is not to marry 'em. I've found that out. So has Tommy Beamish, silly as he looks.'

'I don't think he likes me.'

'What the hell does it matter whether he likes you or not? You're talking like a big soft girl, lad. You'll have to toughen yourself up a bit if you're going to live this life. What happened on the train? Talk to anybody?'

'Ricarlo, mostly. We got on very well.'

'He has the right ideas – except for that woman-chasing. He concentrates on his act – and a dam' good act it is, too – and then minds his own business. If I were putting my own show on the road, he's the only one out of all this lot I'd want with me. Beamish is clever and a big draw, but he's too unreliable. He'll come a cropper yet. That song-and-dance act – Susie What's-her-name — is too pretty-pretty and genteel and has no guts – doesn't belong in variety: I didn't want them on the bill. The Colmars aren't bad but they need a girl who isn't throwing her tits and bum at everybody. She'll get herself raped one of these nights. As for that poor bugger Burrard, he ought to be out of the bill now. I've complained twice. He sends 'em out to the bars and they're coming back halfway through my act. No, I'd take Ricarlo, and forget the rest. All right, lad. Make sure you're down just before eight. And don't forget you'll have a long day tomorrow. We start rehearsing this bike effect tomorrow afternoon. And remind the stage manager in the morning that I wrote to him last week, claiming the stage all afternoon.'

When I went down again to the lounge, at a few minutes to eight, to my surprise Julie Blane came down before Cissie did. She was in a bad temper.

'There's nowhere else to go, as Tommy knows damned well,' she began. 'So either I sit by myself, which I loathe, or I have to join you and that awful little tart-'

'I don't think that's a fair description of Cissie—'

'It may not be what she is but it's certainly what she looks like. Anyhow, Tommy shouldn't have gone off like that. I'm *furious*.'

'When you were sitting with him at tea-time, you looked horribly bored—'

'Oh, for God's sake, don't *you* start. *Men!*' she cried in despair, giving me a whiff of whisky. She must have been drinking with Tommy up in their room. '*And* boys! Yes, that's one for you. All the same.'

'Why are we all the same?'

She ignored that. 'Tommy's supposed to be a wild one who doesn't care a damn. But as soon as Sir Alec What's-it crooks a little finger, off he goes, all spruce and obliging.'

'That's nothing to do with me.'

'Who's talking – or thinking – about you, you silly boy? Pooh to you!'

'I must say,' I began with disastrous heaviness, 'for somebody who said only last Monday we ought to become friends—'

'Oh – don't be so pompous and tiresome. You haven't a hope of becoming one of my friends if you start talking like that—'

'You have a lot of friends, I suppose?' That was nasty, and as soon as I'd said it, I wished I hadn't.

But it didn't make her angrier. She gave me a long level look – and I saw again how beautiful her eyes were – and then she said very quietly: 'Say you're sorry, Dick, or I swear I'll never speak to you again. I mean it.'

'Yes, Julie, I *am* sorry. I didn't really know what I was saying. And I wish we hadn't to have Cissie—'

'Well, we do. And here she comes,' she added hastily. 'Why doesn't somebody tell her not to wear such awful clothes?'

We shared the dining-room with three middle-aged men who appeared to be talking business and took no notice of us. I sat between Julie and Cissie, who, instead of sparring as I thought they might do, took turns to bait me, having instantly and mysteriously agreed, for the duration of the meal, to form a feminine alliance.

'Did you talk to your dear little Nancy on the train, Dick?' This was from Julie.

'Just the very thing I was going to ask, Miss Blane,' said Cissie, very much the other lady.

If they had been my own age I would have told them to shut up, there and then, but as it was I felt I couldn't. 'Yes, she introduced me to her sister. But we didn't say very much. Barney interrupted us. Then I spent a long time with Ricarlo in the dining-car.'

But they weren't going to be fobbed off with Barney and Ricarlo. Nancy was the chink through which the arrows and darts could go.

'Little Nancy was telling me, the other day, Miss Mapes, that she'd leave the stage tomorrow if she could. Such a pity – with that nice little talent!'

'They're hoping to get into Panto, I heard,' said Cissie. 'That was weeks ago – they may have fixed it now.'

'Yes of course. And Dick wouldn't like that, would you, Dick? Now – don't blush.'

'I'm not.' And I'm sure I wasn't. Cissie giggled, and I glared at her. 'Now why don't you turn it up, you two?'

'Turn what up, my dear?' Julie inquired smoothly.

'Look – I'll give you the lot. I ran into Nancy Ellis one afternoon last week in the art gallery. We had tea together and seemed to disagree most of the time.'

'Is that why she introduced you to her sister?'

'I didn't like her sister much – and I can't stand that blighter Hodson. I much prefer Ambrose and Esmond.'

'Oo – Dick!' Cissie cried. 'You be careful. Don't forget – you're very good looking.'

'I suppose he is, in a way,' said Julie, looking me over as if she'd never seen me before. 'Though I must say, it hadn't occurred to me before. But of course it doesn't matter what we think, Miss Mapes. The point is, what does his little Nancy think?'

'I'll bet she's got her eye on him all right, Miss Blane.'

'Probably. And I'd say she's a very determined little thing, wouldn't you?'

At this point the old waiter, who might have sat for Raeburn in an earlier incarnation, came to rescue me and to clear the plates.

'I noticed poor Burrard talking his head off to Barney and the Colmar girl,' I began as soon as the waiter had padded away. But they weren't having any.

'If she doesn't like being on the stage,' said Cissie, 'then I expect what she wants is to get married. Don't you think, Miss Blane?'

'Certainly. Probably some man she's met already, though he may not know she has her eye on him. Older than she is, I'd say, considerably older – and with money, of course, lots of it.'

'How about John D. Rockefeller?' I inquired mildly. 'First you say she's got her eye on me. Then you say it must be somebody quite different from me. You don't know what you're saying. So let's change the subject.'

'What about clothes?' said Julie, giving me a look. 'I mean ours – not yours.'

'Well now, Miss Blane, I was going to ask you where you get most of yours.' Cissie sounded genuinely eager. So Julie relented, and they talked fairly seriously about clothes until the meal was over.

'I don't feel like sitting about here,' said Cissie. 'It's so dreary. Dick, couldn't we go out for a little walk?'

As I hesitated, Julie said hastily: 'Yes, why don't you? I'm going to bed – to read. Has anybody anything worth reading?'

Cissie hadn't, of course, but I said I had a few books with me: 'I don't suppose you want to read about the Early English Watercolourists–'

'I certainly don't—'

'But I've a pocket edition of Mason's *At The Villa Rose*—'

'That's much better. I read it two or three years ago, but now I've forgotten what happened. Drop it into my room, like an angel – it's Twelve.'

'And I'll go and get ready, Dick,' said Cissie. 'It's cold out, isn't it?'

We all went up together. Then I left them to climb up to my ice-box, got the *Mason*, and tapped on the door of Room Twelve. It was a big room and there was only one light burning, but it seemed to be very untidy, with clothes all over the place, Tommy's as well as hers, and there was a strong mixed smell of cigarettes and whisky. I gave Julie the book.

'Shut that door a minute, just a minute,' she whispered. Then when I turned, after shutting it very quietly: 'Come here.'

We were standing very close when she smiled and murmured, 'Did I tease him, then? The nice serious boy who hates being teased – um? Well, I'm sorry. You can see how sorry I am.'

My arms went round her without my telling them to; then her arms were around me and she was pressing herself against me; then we were kissing and her mouth opened under mine and her tongue, pointed, almost hard, furiously alive, darted against mine. I had never known such excitement, either in myself or in anybody else, but after a few more moments of it she made a great and almost hysterical effort, freeing herself.

'No, no, no — for Christ's sake – get out – go on – hurry up – go – go.'

I was still swinging between excitement and bewilderment when Cissie, wearing a long coat and an enormous hat that looked ridiculous on her, joined me downstairs. Saying nothing, we walked into the cold night and the smell of the sea.

There were very few people about, and of course none of the traffic that would be there now. Not knowing nor caring where we were going, we went from one side-street to another, from the hard light of the street-lamps to long stretches of shadow, hearing a few footsteps and an occasional raised voice. Cissie, who couldn't walk properly but only teeter along, clung to my arm. And I think that somehow, through much thick cloth, it conveyed to her a sense of the sexual excitement I'd been feeling.

'What happened when you took her that book, Dick?' she asked in a kind of small sad way.

'What d'you think? Nothing.'

'No, not nothing. Still, it couldn't have been very much, the time you were there.' She waited a moment or two. 'She's very attracted to you, she is, though she pretends not to be. But I can tell.'

'Then you know more than I do.'

'Of course I do, you silly. I may be ignorant – I *am* – but there are some things I know about. And don't forget what Nick said about her. You keep your mind on Nancy Ellis, if you have to think about the female sex.'

'It's you women – not me – who won't let the subject drop, Cissie.'

'Yes, Dick, I know. That's how we are.' She didn't sigh exactly – hardly anybody does, outside novels – but she made a vague sort of mournful noise. 'Oh crumbs! Sunday night! I've always hated Sunday nights, ever since I can remember. That's why I was so mad at Nick – going off like that and leaving me alone. I didn't want to go to Sir Alec Thingummy's house – he can keep it – but I didn't want to be left alone in a horrible dreary Scotch hotel – on a Sunday of all nights.'

'You haven't been alone.'

'No, not really – that's right. Thanks to you, Dick dear. And I'm ever so grateful you've come out on this walk. I know you didn't want to, really. I'm fond of you, Dick. Let's go along here.'

We turned towards a terrace, with tall houses on one side and nothing on the other side, where we chose to walk: no houses, only a few trees and a kind of narrow promenade. 'It's nicer here,' Cissie continued, a little brighter than she had been but still rather small and sad. 'And I'll tell you somebody else who's fond of you in his own way, though you'll never believe me, the way he talks to you. Yes, your Uncle Nick.'

'He doesn't show many signs of it.'

'Well, that's him, isn't it? No need to tell *me*. Here, let's sit down a minute. I'm no good at walking. Tired already.'

I hadn't noticed the seat, but she had. 'You'll soon feel cold,' I told her as we sat down. 'And you can't sit close to me with that hat.'

'I'm taking it off.' And I saw that she was busy unpinning it. 'There – see!' She held the hat in her left hand and put her right hand, from which the glove had mysteriously vanished, first on my shoulder and then up to my cheek, as she leaned against me. Dick, I want you to do something for me,' she said softly. 'Just because I'm feeling miserable. Will you? It's nothing to do with making love – don't get wrong ideas – but something quite different. Something I never have. So, Dick, please just hold me close – as if you liked me a lot but didn't want to have me – and just be gentle and kind. Even if it's all pretending – just this once.'

She raised herself a little and put her cheek to mine, and I put an arm round her and rubbed my cheek against hers and then gently kissed her cheek, her trembling eyelids, her lips, which tasted of something I didn't enjoy, just as I didn't enjoy the overdose of scent she'd given herself. Then she was crying, and between sobs and gulps she said anything that came into her head. 'I feel so frightened sometimes – what'll become of me? – He doesn't love me – just wants me when he feels like it – and I love him – not always – I can hate him sometimes – but mostly love him – though what's the use?' There was a good deal more of it before I said we ought to be going back. The left side of my new overcoat stank of that scent of hers for several days.

Once in bed I tried to wipe out the whole day and to read C. J. Holmes's *Notes on the Science of Picture Making*, which I had bought

101

second-hand in Edinburgh for three-and-six. I couldn't read myself to sleep with it because I had to leave my bed to turn the light out. And then of course I began remembering and thinking.

7

If I'd ever had any idea that I wasn't earning the five pounds a week that Uncle Nick paid me, it vanished on that Monday, 10th November 1913, in Aberdeen. By the time we'd done the second show, I was ready to drop. I'd had all the usual fuss in the morning, making sure all our stuff was there, all the business with the stage manager and the carpenter about our Indian Temple set, the effects and props, the lighting plot for the electricians; and then of course there was the band call, a shambles because Tommy Beamish decided to take his hangover down there and then waste everybody's time. I had breakfasted off a pair of kippers at eight, and by half-past one, when I had taken our call and had argued with six people about clearing the stage for us for our afternoon rehearsal, I was hungry again, very thirsty, and out of temper. Finally, leaving Sam and Ben to assemble all we needed for the bike trick, I had a pint and some peculiar sandwiches at a pub that ought to have been round the corner from the stage door but wasn't. When I hurried back, Uncle Nick, still hatted and overcoated, was standing in the middle of the stage, under the hard-working light, looking like an illustration of Guy Boothby's *Doctor Nicola*.

'Where the hell have you been?'

'I dashed out for a quick bite and a drink.'

'Couldn't you have waited?'

'Now look,' I told him angrily, 'I don't know what time you got up, uncle, but I've already been down here about five hours. I'm not grumbling. It's my job. But don't talk to me and look at me as if I'd been sitting around somewhere. I've not been off my feet since eight o'clock this morning.'

'You don't know you're born yet, lad. And next time you want to give me some bloody cheek, just keep your voice down.' He didn't grin because he'd become too much the Indian Magician – but I could tell by his tone that he felt friendlier. 'Now while we're waiting – just try that bike. No, not there, Sam,' he shouted, moving up.

The bicycle was very much lighter and smaller than any machine I'd ridden since I was a kid, and at first I found it hard to manage. I nearly ran into Cissie, who was hanging around offstage, looking forlorn and apprehensive. 'Dick, do be careful,' she whispered, as I stopped and she grabbed the bike. 'You've no idea what he's like when he's working out something new. He's a demon – honest he is. You've just not got to mind. He can't help it.'

As a matter of fact I didn't resent him at all once we began seriously rehearsing the illusion, though I couldn't see how it could possibly work. He was extremely exacting, making us do what we had to do over and over again, long after we thought we were perfect, his idea of perfection being very different from ours. All five of us were involved in it – Sam and Ben Hayes, dependable but inclined to be slow; Cissie and Barney, quicker but apt to be bungling out of sheer nervousness; and I, who found the cycling irksome and irritating; and for four weary afternoons, from Monday to Thursday, he held us, so to speak, at the point of his will, out of an iron self-discipline, never becoming less demanding and exacting, never tampering with his own standard of perfection, no matter how mutinous we might be looking or how tired he might be feeling. I can't go into details without giving away the trick, but my part in it was to approach the open doorway quite slowly on my bicycle and then at a given signal, when Uncle Nick would fire his green flash, turn and race off the stage through a concealed gap in the set; and I had to do this over and over and over again because the other people were making mistakes; so that I often damned and blasted under my breath all this slave-driving; but in fact I couldn't help admiring Uncle Nick because he compelled us by sheer force of will to bring to life what he had first imagined and then had worked out in his diagrams. What had seemed ridiculous on Monday began taking shape on Tuesday and Wednesday, and late on Thursday afternoon it appeared a marvel. I never saw it from the front, of course, but the house manager and the stage manager did, by request, at five on Thursday. And though the stage lighting was not as it would be when the illusion was included in the act, and none of us was wearing costume and make-up, both men were enthusiastic.

The house manager, who had seen none of our rehearsals, came back and cried: 'Marvellous, Mr Ollanton! It's a certain winner. Can't imagine how you do it. Must have it in your act at once.'

'Not possible,' said Uncle Nick. 'Sorry! Can't bring it in until next week – Glasgow. Sorry again! But tell me – as a favour – exactly what you saw.'

'Oh – well – yes. I saw this open doorway brought on and saw you walk through it several times to prove it's all right – just a doorway. Then this young fellow comes riding on towards the doorway, and you said "Ready – steady – go" or something of that sort, you waved your green flash, and I saw the bicycle go through the doorway and your dwarf came running on to catch it – and the young fellow had completely disappeared – where to, God knows! Isn't that right, Mr Ollanton?'

'Quite right. Thanks very much. Must clear now.' And as he moved my way, Uncle Nick gave me a wink. Later, he said, 'You remember what I told you – about their minds moving slowly while we're working fast? Of course the green flash blinds them while the two hinged flaps come out of the wall, and then I'm waving it towards the other side of the doorway where they expect to see the bike coming out – and Cissie's quick enough now but not steady enough, her bike's still wobbling too much – and then of course they see Barney running on to catch it – and the flaps are back before they've had time to notice 'em. They see what they expect to see. But while they've had little time, we've had a lot of time – that's the chief secret. Well, lad, now we can take it easy for a while. And don't forget Sir Alec's party tonight.'

I knew about this party of course – it had been fixed up when Uncle Nick and Tommy Beamish saw Sir Alec on Sunday night – but I hadn't been thinking much about it, chiefly because I'd been too tired after all this trick cycling during the day and then two shows at night. However, I knew that we were going to Sir Alec's as soon as we'd changed after the second performance on Thursday night, that we men weren't expected to wear evening dress, which meant I wouldn't have to hire one, and that everybody wasn't going, Uncle Nick and Tommy Beamish being allowed to choose the guests. Gustav Colmar and Nonie were going; Uncle Nick and Cissie and I; Ricarlo, Nancy, Susie and her husband; and Tommy Beamish of course, Julie and old Courtenay: twelve of us in all. And the first there were Uncle Nick, wearing a high collar, a tie with a ruby pin in it, and a dark suit I'd never seen before, Cissie with too much rouge on and in a heliotrope dress that clashed with her cheeks, and I, in the blue serge suit I had bought for thirty bob.

Looking back at it now, I suppose that Sir Alec Inverurie lived in a substantial villa, just outside the city, but as it was the largest house I had ever been in up to that time, it seemed to me then a vast glittering mansion. Sir Alec himself was a squat elderly man who poked his head forward, so that he seemed rather like a pink and polished turtle. Up to a point he was warmly hospitable, but somehow he never allowed you to forget that he was rich and you weren't and that you were being given a great treat. Lady Inverurie was a large-boned, stiffish sort of woman who wore the same look of faint astonishment throughout the party. She had a widowed sister, Mrs Gregory, who was much younger and plumper, a rosy blonde, and I was not surprised, a little later, to see that Ricarlo had taken her into a corner, where no doubt he was begging her to give him a report on his juggling. Then there were some assorted Aberdonians, and among them two rather pretty girls, Kitty and Phyllis, who were apparently inseparable and laughed a lot, always simultaneously.

After Sir Alec had commanded champagne for him, Uncle Nick entertained the company by showing them some of his pocket tricks, which really were remarkable. I thought they were wasted on most of these people, just because they had no curiosity as to how such things could be done but simply accepted them as entertainment. At the end of this little performance, I found myself sitting on a sofa between Kitty and Phyllis. Not having seen our show – they were being taken the next night, Friday second house – but having been told I was on the stage, they took it for granted I was some sort of comic, so that every time I said anything they screamed with laughter. When I told them that Aberdeen's larger granite buildings photographed better than they really looked, I might have been Tommy Beamish (who had not yet arrived), the way they laughed, always both together like puppets sharing strings, and told me what a scream I was. They were still at it when I looked up and caught sight, among new arrivals, of Nancy Ellis. She was wearing a new dress, emerald green and rather fancy, and had had her hair done in a different older way, with an emerald green bandeau, and she didn't look right and herself at all; yet somehow, perhaps because she had tried so hard and the total effect was wrong, she seemed essentially charming and touching, and my heart went out to her. I made some excuse to the laughing girls, told Nancy she must be as hungry as I was, and took her into the adjoining room, where there were two long tables of splendid cold food.

'Well, now you can start making *me* laugh,' she said, after we had helped ourselves.

'You heard those girls?'

'Everybody must have done.'

'I wasn't being funny, Nancy. They're a pair of idiots. I'm on the stage – so I must be a funny man. That's how their minds work – God knows why!'

'You don't understand about girls, do you, Dick?'

'Probably not.'

'They didn't think you were funny. They just laughed like that to make other people feel they were having a wonderful time with you – to make them feel envious. We deal in envy a lot, we girls. Sometimes I think we're stinkers. Why haven't I seen you roaming round, this week, Dick?'

I told her about the bike trick. 'And we're putting it into the act next week in Glasgow.'

She laughed. 'Dick Herncastle, the old pro. And this is only your third week. I seem to have had years and years of it. And my trouble is, I hate audiences. Even when they're good, I still don't like them. Silly idiots! Where are you staying this week?'

'Oh, *she's* there, is she?' This was after I'd told her about the hotel, and of course she meant Julie Blane not Cissie. 'You want to be careful with that one.' She wasn't entirely serious but not entirely flippant either. The look she gave me was more serious than her tone of voice.

'I've hardly exchanged a word with her since Sunday,' I said. 'We've been busy all day. We don't eat supper at the hotel but have something sent in between the houses. And when we've got back there, I've just crept up to bed, aching with tiredness. But why must I be careful with Miss Blane?'

'Because I think she's desperate, though about what I don't know. And she's very attractive in her own way. Susie and Bob don't think so, but I think they're wrong, though of course she's older than they are and years and years older than you, Dick. And she's *hungry* – for somebody or something. She's been quite nice to me, and she's obviously very experienced and very clever, I mean professionally,

106

but somehow she seems to me a rather frightening person—'

'They're here.' I could see the doorway and she couldn't, and Julie and Tommy Beamish and old Courtenay were just coming in, along with Sir Alec and Lady Inverurie, Uncle Nick and several others. And I must say that Julie and Tommy – and particularly Tommy, who was already more than half tight – immediately began to give that party a lift. I was giving it one myself inside, because, not liking champagne and not seeing any beer, I was drinking Sir Alec's excellent whisky, though taking plenty of water with it.

Then the party really got going. Sir Alec and one of his Tory friends were denouncing Lloyd George, as so many True Blues were then, when Tommy Beamish took over. Somehow, by some magic of his own, looking and sounding like an idiot Lloyd George, he launched into an impassioned nonsense speech about health insurance and sevenpence for fourpence, and mangel-wurzels and wicked peers, and then when he had most of us weak with laughter, he commanded us to fall into line and follow him. This we did, hand in hand, mostly, if we were not too old and stiff for it, jigging along to the tune of *The Galloping Major*, a popular music-hall song then – and *bumpity-bumptity-bumpity-bump* we went up and down stairs and all over the house. I had Nancy's hand in mine, of course, and in spite of that too mature dress she was wearing – though I think her other hand had plucked up its long tight skirt – she seemed to turn at once into the saucy bright-glancing girl she was in the act, and she didn't merely jig along as the rest of us did but improvised all manner of little dancing steps. At the same time, though, when she looked up at me, laughing, she also seemed to be the other Nancy, the one who didn't care about her stage act, but now not critical and dubious, unsure of me, but warm and friendly and trusting. And I don't care if anybody sees me as a young idiot, I can only say that during that romp I felt something I have rarely felt outside the times when my work was going really well, and that is a sensation of pure happiness. Our high spirits together created that great blue bubble, a world unmapped and outside solar space and time, which most of us see so rarely and some people never know at all. Often, during the First War and just afterwards, I looked back at that quarter of an hour, trying to recapture its quality, like a man exiled for ever from a beautiful homeland.

Well, of course we couldn't stay on that level, but it was still a lively party. Uncle Nick surprised me – though I knew he'd had plenty of champagne – by completely abandoning his usual air of sardonic detachment and improvising with Tommy Beamish a very funny conjuring and thought-reading act. Ricarlo juggled with spoons and glasses, rolling an eye, when he could spare one, towards a beaming and probably already weakening Mrs Gregory. Julie Blane and old Courtenay did a kind of duet version of *The Green Eye of the Little Yellow God*, with some interruptions from Tommy Beamish, now in uproarious form. Nancy and her sister and Bob Hodson sang a nonsense trio. Then I seem to remember taking part in an eightsome reel, wondering all the time what I did next. It must have been just after that, when I had left the crowded drawing-room to find a cool drink in the empty dining-room, that I found Julie squeezing my arm.

'Dick, you've got to help me with him—'

'Tommy?'

'Yes. He's in that cloakroom by the front door – completely plastered of course – and he's been trying to take his clothes off after being sick all over them – and I've got to get him out of here before something awful happens – back to the hotel and safe in bed. And you've got to help me, Dick.'

'Of course, Julie. But how do we do it?'

'Sir Alec's chauffeur is waiting outside with the car, to take some people home. So dodge out – don't let anybody see you if you can manage it – and warn him, then make for the cloakroom and give me a hand with Tommy. Oh God – I can't tell you how I hate this – but it's got to be done.'

I had in fact almost to carry him out to the car, which fortunately was a big one, so that when we got him inside, at the back, and he utterly collapsed, we let him lie on the floor while Julie supported his head and shoulders so that he couldn't be badly bumped. We asked no help from the chauffeur, a severe-looking fellow who obviously didn't propose to do anything except run us down to the hotel.

'You're pretty strong, aren't you, Dick?' Julie said anxiously when we were on our way.

And I was in those days; after the war it was different. 'If you're worried about getting him to your room, I think I can manage it, with just a little help.'

I did too, and while Julie, who was feeling shaky, went off to a bathroom, I undressed poor Tommy, who frightened me by beginning to breathe in a peculiar way and then opening his eyes and rolling them around. I got him into his pyjamas and into the double bed.

'Thank you, Dick.' Julie had come back very quietly and spoke softly. 'But he's on the wrong side. We'll have to move him.' And this wasn't difficult because now he was completely out and making snoring noises. 'Would you like a drink?'

'No, thanks, Julie.'

'I need one, in spite of that bad example.' She swallowed some whisky, neat. 'Why are you looking like that?'

'I was thinking about Tommy,' I whispered. We needn't have whispered, but we did. 'What he did to that party. How happy he made me feel. And now – this.'

'Quite – quite, Mr Herncastle. And I have a lot of – *this*.'

Hardly aware of what I was doing, I had moved closer to her and now I had my hands just below her shoulders and squeezed a little. 'I'm terribly sorry, Julie.'

She gave a quick shake to free herself. 'I didn't ask you to be sorry, did I? What do you know about anything? You're only a boy. And stop trying to maul me about. I hate it. You'd better go now.'

'I had, hadn't I? Good night, Miss Blane.'

I went at once, closed the door carefully, and then walked quickly but quietly along the corridor, so quietly that I thought I heard the door being opened behind me, but I never looked back. Next day, Friday, Uncle Nick never asked me what had happened at the party, and when Cissie seemed to want to talk about it, he shut her up. I didn't see Julie either then or on Saturday, but she may have been keeping out of my way as I was out of hers. It was the same with Nancy. We all seemed to play out our week in Aberdeen separate and in a glum silence, all except Ricarlo, for I ran into him on Saturday afternoon with a smiling Mrs Gregory by his side, and in passing he flashed me a huge bright wicked wink.

8

The Glasgow week began badly. In the train from Aberdeen on the Sunday, I had hoped to see at last some fine Highland scenery, but it was curtained off by sheets of rain. We had a corridor again but neither Nancy and her lot nor Ricarlo appeared to be travelling by that train; so my choice of company was restricted to Sam and Ben, who never wanted to talk about anything except racing, Barney, excitable, ridiculous and irritating, the Colmars and Burrard. Once again I saw Burrard talking earnestly to Nonie Colmar and Barney, who were nudging each other and trying not to giggle in his face; but this time I wasn't able to sneak past without Burrard noticing me. He came bouncing out, seized me by the arm, almost dragged me into his compartment, and sternly ordered Nonie and Barney to leave us alone.

'Can't talk sense to a foreign little tart and a midget,' he said when they had gone. 'The brains aren't there. Now you're different, cully. All right – you're young – so you're too easy, too careless – don't use your eyes and ears – but you're not completely bloody ignorant. You know what I'm talking about, don't you, cully?'

'Well, I'm not sure, Mr Burrard—'

'Harry – Harry – how many times have I to tell you? Now listen, cully, and use your loaf. What's it going to be like in Glasgow? How many of 'em'll be there? Give a guess. Three? Four? No, cully, you'd be out. I say six to eight. Might be ten. And you know what they'll be doing 'cos I've already told you and you can't be that bleeding stupid. The word's been passed on and instructions wired – definite instructions: *Give Burrard the bird*. And sooner or later it'll work of course – I'm just one man and they're an organization. But I'm not lying down, y'know, cully – Harry Burrard doesn't lie down to let 'em walk over him – no bloody fear! I heard about Sir Alec, y'know – I tell you, I keep my ears open – and I knew him twenty years ago, but he never came near me – and I'll tell you why.' He glanced wildly towards the door, then leant forward. '*Cos Sir bloody Alec had had his orders*. Not a suggestion, no – *definite orders*. He has to take 'em like the rest.' There was a lot more of this stuff and I had really stopped listening when he got up to open a bag lying on the seat. Then my ears went to work with my eyes. 'And if I catch one right on the job I give it to him – he gets it. *With this.*' And he opened the bag to show me, lying on top of shirts and ties and socks, surprisingly neatly folded and packed, a revolver. 'Loaded, of course. And I know how to use it, cully.' So I wasted the next ten minutes begging him to get rid of the thing, but first he laughed at me and then, losing his temper, told me to clear out.

Well, that wasn't a good beginning, and then we were late running into Glasgow, I had to fuss around making sure of our baggage, it was still raining, the city looked big, dark, strange, and I had a hell of a job in an old cab trying to find the digs, where this time I would be on my own, at the address Cissie had given me. And Monday morning, when it was still dark and wet, was no better, even worse; first seeing our stuff in and helping to sort it out; then giving some new cues to the stage manager and the electricians, because we were now putting in the *Vanishing Cyclist*; then a worse band call than ever because we really needed some new music and hadn't got any and so had to fiddle about with what we had; and then, in the afternoon, just when I needed a rest, finding myself pedalling away on that damned bike again because the trick had to be rehearsed at least a dozen times more before the audience saw it. Uncle Nick swore at everybody; I swore back at him; Sam and Ben turned sulky and sullen; Barney kept disappearing; and Cissie cried. I didn't even go back to my digs again before the first house; it was still raining and there didn't seem time; I had some tea in a cafe where there were too many people all steaming and cross; and then I crawled up to a dressing-room, long before I had to be there, and saw it would be murderously too small for Sam, Ben, Barney and me. So if this was Glasgow, they could keep it.

Then everything was different. This happens so often – though it always seems almost miraculous, as if an unknown sun had risen – that I have never been able to understand how anyone, not suffering from an incurable disease, can fall into utter despair and begin contemplating suicide. I don't know why Glasgow, in the week beginning 17th November 1913, should have decided it must go to a music hall; but our first houses were well filled, our second houses were packed, and they loved us. Our *Vanishing Cyclist* was an immediate success; all Tuesday's papers singled it out and praised it; and every time I went scorching through that hidden gap in the set I could hear the huge gasp go up from the audience, ready to swear they saw me vanish in the doorway. The whole act went magnificently, performance after performance. So did the others. And I was so delighted about this that during the interval at the second house, when I had finished with the stage, I would hastily remove my dusky make-up, which I hated, and get out of the smelly Indian costume, just to go down to watch Ricarlo, look at and listen to Nancy and Susie and their three gentlemen, and then enjoy with the uproarious crowd the wild antics and lunacies of Tommy Beamish and the outraged gentility of Julie and old Courtenay. I had heard that the Glasgow audiences only liked their own, a Harry Lauder or a Neil Kenyon, but it was not true of them that week, when Tommy, who really had a kind of genius at these times, set them bellowing or screaming just as he pleased.

He had to make a very funny exit during the sketch, to examine a bathroom while the fuming father and bewildered daughter wondered what kind of lunatic they were having to endure; and I remember that at the Tuesday second house, as he came rushing off, out of breath, sweating, his eyes gleaming, followed by the huge hard rattle of laughter, he stopped near me to get his breath and to slow down for his next entrance, when he would be quiet and bewildered, a man lost in a strange world.

'Listen to that, old boy,' he panted. 'Just listen to it. Eh?'

'It's tremendous.'

'So it is – so it is. It's what I'm here for. But – I'll tell you something – old boy. It's the cruellest bloody sound in the world – just people laughing like that. Gives me the creeps sometimes. Well – on we go!'

And then as he crept back on to the stage, his face a mask of bewilderment deepening to despair, and the huge hard rattle rose again, I knew what he meant. It wasn't innocent and natural, as the soft laughter between friends could be; there was something fierce and vindictive about it, not coming from a happy people but from those whose bewilderment deepening to despair was not a mask; and I noticed after that, as we played in so many different towns, that the poorer and darker the streets surrounding us, the closer we were to misery, the louder and harder the laughter was.

The one who wasn't doing better but even worse was poor Harry G. Burrard, Eccentric Comedian. As we followed him, we couldn't help noticing this. They didn't want him any more, and voices from the gallery told him so. He was in fact now 'getting the bird' – a strange term for something dreaded and horrible. His *Diddy-diddy-oodah-oodah-oodah*, coming out of a lost gaiety, evenings gone never to return, now made me shudder. He came off muttering curses on his imaginary persecutors, and at the first house on Wednesday he had tried to tell me how many there were, but Uncle Nick told him to shut up and added brutally that their agent was coming to see what was left of his act. I had told Uncle Nick about Burrard's persecution mania and had mentioned the revolver he had shown me on the train, but Uncle Nick said it was all nonsense, that Burrard had always been lazy, refusing to find new material and to change his act while there was still time, and that he, Nick Ollanton, who never stopped working to improve his act, had no patience with or sympathy for the idle ignorant clown. 'We're here to do our best and earn our money, lad, and Burrard doesn't even begin to try. Let him go and serve pints in a third-rate pub. It's all he's fit for. So don't give me any more about Harry Burrard. Forget him.'

Apart from poor Burrard, we were all rising with the tide of packed houses and enthusiastic appreciation. Of course we were not like a theatrical company, which comes to an audience as one unit. We were so many entirely separate and independent acts, but because we were touring together, forming the greater part of one continuing bill, we could respond together to a heart-warming week like this. So for the first time, as far as my very limited experience went, dressing-room doors were left open, except when people were actually dressing, and congratulatory visits were exchanged, together with some drink, or there were smiling encounters along the corridors. There was almost a party atmosphere. Even Uncle Nick, sardonically detached and generally unpopular, perhaps because he was secretly delighted by the immediate success of his *Vanishing Cyclist* and the press notices, allowed himself to receive and even to offer a few compliments and congratulations. Even the musical director, after paying a call between the houses on Tuesday to make some suggestions about our music, was offered a glass of champagne.

After the first house on Tuesday I ran into Julie, both of us wearing costume and make-up of course, though I'd taken off my turban. 'No, Dick,' and she put up a hand to stop me. 'Stay a moment. I'll find it easier to apologize when we're both looking so ridiculous.'

'I'm not looking for apologies,' I told her, stiffly.

'Oh – don't be pompous,' she cried. 'I'd much rather you were angry. But anyhow, I'm sorry, my dear, truly sorry. You came and helped me at once, leaving the party and all those girls. You managed to cope with Tommy, when it would have been far too much for me. Then when I ought to have been thanking you, I had to start spitting and snarling and clawing like a wounded cat.' She waited a moment, just looking at me. 'I behaved very badly, and I really am sorry. There! Well, say something.'

'Let's forget it. Only – just one thing. And I'm not trying to give you a dig. But the next time you give me a man's job to do, as you did last Thursday night, don't tell me when I've done it, that I'm only a boy—'

'Oh – that's what you really hated, is it? But Dick my darling, don't forget I'm thirty-five – yes, *thirty-five* – so I can't help thinking you're a boy – oh, the biggest and brightest and sweetest of all boys – but a boy.' Now she came closer, burying both hands in the Indian robe I was wearing, and whispered: 'Yes, let's forget Thursday, my dear. Remember the Sunday before, when you gave me the book. I didn't quite behave as if you were a boy then, did I? Or have you forgotten?'

'Of course I haven't forgotten, Julie. But one night it's like that – then the next time I'm trying to maul you about – though I'd barely touched you—'

'Richard Herncastle – oh, it's really rather a good name, isn't it? Perhaps one day you may be famous. But what I wanted to say, you sweet idiot, is that you must learn a little about women – just watch for a few signs—'

'When do I get a chance?'

'You'll have to lend me another book, won't you?' She touched my mouth with her finger. 'I must run or Tommy'll be shouting for me. 'Bye, my dear.'

She could leave me like that and I would feel a stifling kind of excitement, not good because it killed everything round it stone dead. But if I just saw her, without exchanging either any bright chat or any whispering and touching, it was quite different. What I felt then, being aware of her beauty and perhaps all the more keenly aware because other people seemed blind to it, was a sort of impersonal admiration, as if she had been a picture, but this always gave way to a feeling of deep compassion, which arose not simply out of what I already knew about her but also out of a conviction, not rational, entirely intuitive, that she was doomed, as if some invisible court had passed its sentence on her. At the same time, even while moved by this compassion, I could still feel there was an element in her that was undependable, tricky, perhaps treacherous. And if all this seems very complicated, I am sorry, but I think that if anything I am simplifying my confusion during this particular period, when Julie and I had only these odd occasional encounters. Finally, there was something else – which some people won't believe, but I can't help that – that just as I knew intuitively there would never be any escape for her, not only into some kind of happiness but even into contentment, as if I could see her hurrying along one wrong road after another, I also knew, though it was all very vague, that sooner or later I would enter into a relationship with her that wouldn't do either of us any good at all.

During the second house on the Wednesday, after I had changed and looked in on Uncle Nick, who was taking it easy and had given me a glass of his champagne, and after I had passed on the stairs Susie, Bob, Ambrose and Esmond, coming up to change, I ran into Nancy. It was the first time we'd had a chance to be alone while she was still in her stage costume; and perhaps – and it flashed through my mind as soon as I saw her – she might still be the saucy girl with the beautiful and witty legs, not the serious disapproving one with the rather pale face and the smudgy reproachful eyes.

'It's my girl in pink,' I shouted, opening my arms.

'Not yours – theirs – anybody's,' she cried. And as I tried to stop her, rather clumsily, on one side, laughing she dodged past me on the other side, the beautiful and witty legs flying upstairs. I charged after her. At the first landing, not hers, she feinted to turn, deceiving me for a moment, and it was not until we reached the second landing that I caught up to her.

'No, Dick, you mustn't,' she cried, still half laughing, as my arms went round her. 'It isn't fair. I hate you. You're a beast.'

'This girl doesn't think so – no, not this one.' And then because she rested against me for one delicious moment, I let my grasp go slack. She tore out of my arms, with a little shriek of triumph; she went with a kind of dancing run along the corridor; and shouting some nonsense I tore after her. But as I said earlier, there was a kind of party atmosphere backstage these nights, with dressing-room doors wide open and people exchanging visits or chatting along the corridors. So there were arms stretched out and cheers for our race. I think it was Ambrose and Esmond who wouldn't allow Nancy to escape, blocking the way, together with the call boy – he was called Edgar, I remember — who must have just brought up food and drink for somebody. And my arms were around Nancy again, and she was laughing while telling me I was a brute, and I was laughing in breathless triumph, and the others were laughing in sympathy, and either Ambrose or Esmond or both of them together was exclaiming, 'Really it's marvellous – we're all so madly gay these nights,' when we heard the shot, which came from a closed dressing-room nearer the stairs. We all stared in that direction and then at one another.

'Who dresses there?' somebody asked.

'Mr Burrard,' said Edgar. As call boy he had the freedom of all dressing-rooms, so he added: 'I'd better go and see, hadn't I?'

He hurried along, and rather uneasily several of us drifted after him. He went in, came out with a face like paper, tried to speak but began retching and then was sick. I hadn't noticed Uncle Nick leaving his dressing-room, which was at the other end of the corridor, but now, still the Indian Magician and tall, imposing, authoritative in his robes, he swept past us, saying, 'Keep away. I'll do this.' Nobody said a word while he was in the dressing-room; we might have been all turned to stone.

'Burrard's dead,' he announced curtly when he came out. 'Shot himself.' He closed the door behind him. 'Keep out. You wouldn't like it. Where's that boy? Never mind. Richard, go down and tell the stage manager. Somebody'll have to ring up the police.'

As I went downstairs, there was a rush to my side and a hand gripped mine. It was Nancy. 'I'm coming with you, Dick. I don't know why. Just to be doing something, I suppose. You don't mind, do you? I don't want to listen to them all talking. Don't talk, Dick, please.' She seemed mostly a small desperate hand.

As soon as we reached the stage level, we could hear Tommy's sketch going uproariously. I left Nancy to go up to the prompt corner to whisper to the stage manager. In the brilliantly illuminated box of the stage, Tommy Beamish, with his improbable ginger moustache and his gleaming but strangely wavering eyes, was crying, 'Immaterial? *Immaterial?*' in a tone of horror and was beginning to climb over the sofa. When I rejoined Nancy, she was crying, and I took her further away from the stage, towards the stairs, and then held her and tried to comfort her.

'It seems so much worse because I couldn't *bear* him—'

'He was out of his mind, Nancy. I warned Uncle Nick — I told him poor Burrard seemed to me quite barmy—'

'But perhaps that was because nobody liked him any more. Perhaps if we'd just pretended, Dick—'

'No, it must have been something else, Nancy. Probably something that attacked his brain.' (And I wasn't far out, I learnt later from the inquest.)

'You won't believe me when I say I don't like this life – but I don't – I don't – I don't—'

'I know – I know – I know–' I said soothingly, holding her a little tighter and rubbing my cheek against her hair.

She didn't move for a few moments, then she pulled away gently, gave me a quick kiss, and said: 'We must go up. Lend me your handkerchief.' Then as we walked towards the stairs: 'Perhaps he could hear us – chasing about and laughing – not caring what happened to *him*. And even now I can't help feeling he was so *awful*. I stopped speaking to him weeks and weeks ago. And somehow that makes it worse. Perhaps we were all happy too soon.'

'I don't believe that, Nancy. And I hope you won't.'

'I don't know what I believe, Dick. I'm all muddled up. If somebody had told me Burrard was leaving us, I'd have been delighted. Now it's horrible – frightening.' I let her move a step ahead of me now, though she was going slowly, drooping a little above that short pink skirt. She went on: 'We none of us wanted him – not even any of those idiots in front – we longed for him to go and leave us. So he did – like that. And perhaps we made him. And perhaps now it'll never be the same.'

And perhaps it wasn't.

Book Two

1

ere were two immediate changes, and, as far as I was concerned,
th were for the better. The first was that we left Glasgow for the
est Riding, my own part of the world – and of course Uncle Nick's
o, but unlike me he had no affection for it, and indeed disliked it.
e said too many people round there were narrow, stupid and
nceited, which may have been his honest opinion. But another
ason may have been that he was always liable to be recognized by
ople who remembered him before he became a variety star and
dn't hesitate to tell him so, some of them calling him Albert Edward
o.) We were playing three consecutive weeks in the West Riding –
st Bradford, then Leeds, then Sheffield, which meant we should
ve no long Sunday train journeys. And I knew Bradford pretty well,
ving been fairly often, and I knew that if the weather was no good
' outdoor sketching – and now, with no more rehearsing, I was free
day – I could go to the Cartwright Memorial Hall or to the Reference
rary in Darley Street to look through some special numbers of *The
dio*. We were all in digs fairly close together and only about ten
nutes' walk from the Empire. I was two doors away from Uncle Nick
d Cissie, and was sharing a sitting-room with Ricarlo, who must
ve known in advance about our landlady, Mrs Sugden, a widow of
out the right age, proportions, colouring, even if at first sight she
emed too grimly businesslike for dalliance. Nancy, Susie and Bob
dson were at the end of the same terrace, and Julie and Tommy
amish (I never did know where old Courtenay hid himself) were not
away. And though it was late November, Monday morning was fine
d clear, without a threat of rain or fog, though cold enough, with a
ter of frost and a sprinkling of snow already on the highest hilltops.
uld see myself doing some sketching, possibly on the moors, and
re was Nancy, not a hundred yards away; and it all seemed
endid, as indeed it was until that damned agent came. But he makes
entrance later.

The second change for the better was the act that replaced poor
rrard's. *Jennings and Johnson, Comedy Duo* – as they called
mselves on the bill – were Americans and had only just arrived in
gland. Bill Jennings and Hank Johnson had married two sisters, now

running a dress shop in Cleveland, Ohio, but were not otherwi
related; nevertheless, they looked, talked, behaved, almost exact
alike both on and off the stage. They were in their late forties or ear
fifties, broadfaced, comfortable, genuinely humorous men who we
always easy, never perturbed, and in a quiet and amiable fashi
didn't seem to give a damn, just as Uncle Nick (who took to them
once) didn't in his own saturnine way. Their act was as much ahe
of its time as poor Burrard's had been behind it. They were
immediately before us, as Burrard had been, so I always knew h
their act was going, and very often it left our audiences, especially
the first houses, more bewildered than amused. I loved it. They p
on hardly any make-up; they wore dark blue suits, winged colla
sober ties; and they looked like a couple of insurance men or ba
cashiers, except for the twinkle in their eyes. They would sing, poke
faced and without any enthusiasm, some quite incongruous dit
(*Every night sitting in the parlour – Ain't love grand?*), exchange so
indolent and nonsensical backchat, and then, wearing bowler hats th
they would take off to toss imaginary flowers out of them, they wou
go slowly and gravely, as if two middle-aged insurance men had go
mad, through the motions of a ballet. They were masters of th
incongruity which, at least in my opinion, added the necessa
condiments and spices to music-hall fare.

Off the stage they existed in an atmosphere of cigars, whisky, c
lechery (they were after Nonie Colmar like a shot), humoro
reminiscence filled with incredibly tall stories. They were alwa
friendly with me but they called me 'Son', and it was only Uncle Ni
out of all the people on the bill, whom they regarded as their eq
and their friend. He too had toured America, on the Orpheum a
Pantages and other circuits, often playing three and even four sho
a day, and this gave the three of them plenty of common grou
Moreover, Uncle Nick was a very good billiards and snooker play
and as they were experts at American Pool, he was able to spend ma
happy afternoons teaching them our English varieties of these cu
and-ball games. The arrival of Jennings and Johnson was a little pi
of luck coming just before I would need one, as we shall see. Their
never failed to amuse me, no matter what I might be feeling; th
companionship helped to keep Uncle Nick in a good temper just wh
I was all too often in a bad temper, as we shall also see. Perhap
they hadn't turned up, Uncle Nick might have bounced me back

my office stool.

The weather staying fine, very cold on the tops but crisp and clear, both on Tuesday and Wednesday of that week in Bradford, I put a slab of pork or veal-and-ham pie (they were very good then in the West Riding) in the knapsack with my painting gear, took trams towards the moors, and did some sketching. It had to be hurried because I soon felt cold; I also felt rather lonely. So on Wednesday, after the second house, I waited for Nancy and insisted upon walking up to the digs with her. I told her what I'd been doing with myself, then went on:

'It's wintry of course now, but there's some wonderful country up there and I wish you'd come and have a look at it with me tomorrow.'

'And what do I do while you're trying to paint? Stand about and freeze?'

'All right, forget it, Nancy. It is cold up there – and you're not used to it, not like our girls—'

'What girls?'

'Never mind. It was just an idea. I happened to remember how I'd been wishing today, all day – but no – sorry I spoke.'

'My goodness! You can be artful when you try, can't you, Dick? Very well, I'll risk it, just to prove I needn't be outdone by *your girls*, if they exist. Where do we go and when do we start?'

We took a train in the middle of the morning to Ilkley and climbed up to Rombalds Moor. It was a late November day in a thousand, with a pale sun visible all the time, no patches of fog anywhere, the moorland tracks quite hard and the grass glittering with frost and the great shapes of the hills firmly drawn in sepia and indigo. Nancy, muffled up in tweeds and wearing her angler's hat, her eyes shining above pink cheeks and an equally pink ridiculous nose, looked comical and enchanting. I felt again what I had felt during that romp at Sir Alec's, that sensation of pure happiness, but this time of course it lasted much longer. And even while I wished we could go on for ever, climbing together into this high empty world ('And I realize now,' Nancy said, 'I haven't been breathing any *real* air for ages and ages,') I felt too, obscurely and far below the level of this conscious wish, that if we only knew more we *could* go on for ever. This exalted state somehow existed permanently; it didn't leave us but we in our blindness and ignorance *turned away from it*.

The few sketches I did were very quick, hardly more than notes that might later guide my memory. I worked as fast as I could so that

Nancy wouldn't feel the cold and get impatient. I told her so and was promptly and sharply told in my turn not to tell her what she knew already. But then when I was hastily putting away my gear after the final sketch, quite unexpectedly, for we hadn't touched each other up to then, she put her arms round my neck and kissed me gently.

'No, no, that's all,' she said. 'It didn't mean what you think. It was just the look on your face, a kind of happy child's look. That's what I wanted to kiss, so don't start imagining things. And let's go. I'm frozen.'

When the colour and much of the light had gone, we came to the village of Hawksworth, no more than a cluster of low stone cottages. There we learnt that a Mrs Wilkinson might provide us with tea, and after a little hesitation, because it was the wrong time of year and she wasn't sure she 'could manage', Mrs Wilkinson, a kind of talking russet apple, did provide us with tea – not in the usual front room, where there was no fire, but in the kitchen, where there was a splendid fire, a settle, and many mysterious gleaming utensils. After we had taken turns with a piece of yellow soap and a bowl in the passage, which had a fine country smell of hens and white-wash, we sat down to an enormous tea while Mrs Wilkinson, after being assured that we had enough, busied herself elsewhere.

'My goodness! I'm being a greedy pig,' said Nancy, who looked entrancing in the lamplight. 'But I love it here. I'd like to come and stay here every summer. Just Mrs Wilkinson and me – though you could call now and again. Say something, Dick. What's the matter? Aren't you enjoying it?'

'Of course. But I suddenly felt I was enjoying it *too* much. As if—' But there I stopped. I didn't want to say any more just then. Nancy looked at me. It was the most intimate and most revealing thing that had ever happened between us. Over and over again, afterwards, I tried to recapture that look, but I never could, though God knows I remembered its existence.

'Are you sure you've had enough?' Mrs Wilkinson was back with us. 'Well, that'll be one-and-two altogether – sevenpence each.' As I paid her, she went on: 'Ah must say you're a right nice-looking young couple. An' Ah think you come from somewhere round here, young man – but she doesn't. Do you, love?'

'No, I don't,' said Nancy, smiling. 'As it happens we're both playing in Bradford this week. We're on the stage.'

'Stage? Well, Ah'd never have thought it.'

'And we don't know what we're doing,' I cried, jumping up.

'Why – what's the matter, Dick?'

'It's nearly five o'clock now and we're miles from anywhere – trains, trams, anything. I've got to be ready to go on before seven.'

'Oh – gosh – yes, of course.' Nancy was now as alarmed as I was. 'Mrs Wilkinson, what can we do?'

'Lad next door can drive you to station in his horse and trap – though it'll cost you half-a-crown. Knows how to charge, that lad. Shall Ah tell him?'

'Yes, please. Get your things, Dick. We must hurry – hurry – hurry—'

The luck stayed with us – it was that kind of day – though I was half-sick with anxiety as we rattled down in the trap to the station – Menston, I think – and kept asking the 'lad', who was years older than I was, to drive faster, faster. Though the air was so cold on our faces, I could feel myself beginning to sweat. And Nancy, knowing what I felt, kept squeezing my hand hard. Now everything depended on there being a train quite soon, for if there weren't, I was done for, but the lovely luck of the day held into the dark. We had only a few minutes to wait for the train. Even then, of course, it seemed to crawl and stop too often. It was half past six when we reached the Midland Station in Bradford, which I knew was about half a mile from the Empire. I told Nancy, who had plenty of time, that I would have to run for it, and when she insisted upon carrying my knapsack and sketchbook, I gave them to her at once and literally began running. Sam, Ben and Barney had already left the dressing-room when I arrived there, sweating and gasping. I did a quick change almost worthy of R. A. Roberts himself (he used to play a whole sketch about Dick Turpin by himself, making incredibly quick changes), and then rushed down to the stage only to discover that Jennings and Johnson – bless them! – were just beginning their ballet routine. And the luck held out longer still, for Uncle Nick, who went down usually in good time, was actually late for once, later in fact than I was. But then the luck, having held out so far, vanished without saying Goodbye.

What happened was that when I had changed after our second show I went along to Uncle Nick's dressing-room, as I often did, and found him smoking a cigar and drinking champagne with a visitor. This was an oldish tubby man, hot and sweaty, who was wearing a collar with wide wings and a polkadot bow tie and a suit of Donegal tweed. And I took an instant dislike to him.

'Joe, this is my nephew, Richard Herncastle,' said Uncle Nick. 'Mr Joe Bosenby – my agent.'

'Well, well, well, well!' cried Bosenby, grabbing my hand and then pumping it as if I'd just taken him off a sinking ship. 'My congratulations, young man!'

'What for?'

'I'll tell you what for. Because you're now working with one of the cleverest artistes – yes, and one of the most successful artistes – in variety today. I've handled 'em all, and I know. Marvellous! You realize it's a privilege, don't you?' Bosenby was one of those fast talkers who ask questions but don't let you answer them. 'Of course you realize it's a privilege.'

'He doesn't, Joe,' said Uncle Nick dryly. 'And anyhow, stop selling me to him.'

'I can't help it, Nick old boy. What a marvellous act! And better than ever – better than ever. That *Vanishing Cyclist* had me beaten tonight – and I've seen 'em all – seen 'em all. And that box trick with the girl – best in the business – marvellous! Well now, Nick – where were we?'

'Just a minute.' Then Uncle Nick looked at me. 'Tell Cissie not to wait, and that I'm having supper with Joe Bosenby. Better walk her up to the digs yourself, lad. By the way, we're losing the girl Cissie says you fancy. They're all going into a panto – where is it, Joe?'

'Theatre Royal, Plymouth. Jimmy Glover's show. Start rehearsing next week. It's little Nancy who's taken your eye, is it, young man? Don't blame you. Clever kid – nice kid. But that's how it is in this business – here today, gone tomorrow. I've booked *The Musical Tiplows* to replace Susie and Nancy. Nice refined act – always goes well. Father and two daughters. And I don't see this young man keeping a sharp lookout for *those* two – eh, Nick?' And Bosenby gave a yelp of a laugh. I could have killed him.

After I had given Cissie Uncle Nick's message, she said: 'What's the matter with you, Dick? I know there's *something*.'

I told her what Bosenby had said. 'And Cissie,' I went on, 'do you mind hanging on until I've spoken to Nancy?'

'No, I don't mind, Dick. But if I was you, I wouldn't say anything to her tonight. I don't think you're in a proper mood. You might say something you'll be sorry for afterwards. If you'll take my advice, you won't say anything to her tonight.'

But of course I didn't take her advice. We never do accept any sensible advice at the very time we need it. Nobody could have stopped me behaving like a young idiot. I waited, a sour vat of anger, bitterness, stupidity, and then caught Nancy on her way up to her dressing-room.

'Oh – Dick, I've been thinking about today. It was so much better than I expected it to be. I'd love to go back there in spring or summer. And when we wouldn't have to hurry away from Mrs Wilkinson's. Why, Dick – what's the matter?'

I hadn't spoken, and the light was bad where we were standing, so how did she know that something was wrong? Ninety-nine out of a hundred of them, nine times out of ten, can do it. But how, with what? Nobody tells us.

'I've just heard that you're leaving – to go into a pantomime,' I began heavily.

'Oh – yes,' she said brightly. 'Plymouth. I'm playing Dandini, and Susie the second principal boy—'

'You sound very pleased about it-'

'Well, in a way I am. Panto's more fun – and you're in a company – and can settle down without having to move on every week – you know.'

And that's another thing I've noticed about most women – that while they can perceive in a flash that something is wrong, that you're in a bad mood, the way they then behave isn't governed by this intuition. Either they ignore it or wilfully defy it. God knows I was determined to be stupid, but even so, if she hadn't sounded so pleased about leaving me for pantomime and Plymouth, I might have been less accusing, less bitter.

'I must say—' and of course I was as heavy as lead '—for somebody who pretends not to like being on the stage, I can't see why panto should be more fun. You'll be showing even more leg every afternoon and evening. You'll—'

'Stop it, Dick.' She was very sharp.

'I also had a silly idea that we were friends—'

'I wish you could hear yourself.'

'I *am* hearing myself. And I know that if *I* were leaving, I'd sound – and feel – sorry, and not be so bloody bright about it—'

'Go and swear at somebody else. Good night.' And she began hurrying up the steps, the lovely legs twinkling at me.

'Oh – good night then – good night,' I shouted after her. 'Good-bye.'

When we think about our youth we are too apt to remember its rushes of wild happiness and to forget its equally sudden and appalling descents into misery. But now that I am remembering everything, I can't forget what I felt, after my idiotic shouting, as I stared at the empty steps. I was like a man weighing a ton on a dead planet.

'You said or did something silly,' Cissie told me as soon as we were outside, 'and now you're really miserable, aren't you – you silly boy?'

'Cold night, isn't it?'

'Yes, it is.' She took my arm and squeezed it. 'Well, if you don't want to talk about it, you needn't, Dick. But I must say, I wish it had been that other one – Julie Blane – who was leaving. You know she's got her eye on you, don't you? Oh – yes – she has. I can tell.'

'Well, I don't know how. I haven't exchanged ten words with her for the past week. So let's not talk about her either. What about Bill Jennings and Hank Johnson?'

'They're all right. Nice fellows in a way. But their hands wander a lot. And if I thought I'd have to sit up late with one of 'em, I'd have both legs in one stocking.'

'Your mind runs on a tramline, Cissie.'

This didn't worry her. 'If you mean what I think you mean – doesn't yours?'

'No, it doesn't.'

'I believe you but thousands wouldn't. I won't believe you, though, if you tell me you haven't been thinking about little Nancy Ellis in bed—'

'Well, I haven't. So turn it up, Cissie.' And it was quite true – I hadn't. It doesn't follow that if I had been mentally undressing Nancy, I would have admitted it to Cissie; but it was the honest truth that I hadn't. And this doesn't mean I wasn't charged up to the eyebrows with sex, because, as I've already suggested, I was. My imagination would heat up round an image of Julie Blane or Nonie, who still occasionally bumped into me, or some girl I would stare at in a teashop. But if I thought about Nancy, she had her clothes on and so had I, and we were arguing, not making love.

And of course if I'd had any sense, I'd have sought her out on the Friday or Saturday and we'd have done some real arguing and then made it up. But I wasn't going to make the first move, and neither was she. What I didn't understand, during those two days, was what it would be like when she really had gone. While she was still close at hand, round any corner, the quarrel was a kind of idiot game I was playing stubbornly; but as soon as she was three hundred miles away, there was a great blank in the pattern of my life, quite impossible to ignore until the whole pattern changed, leaving her out of it, and I changed with it, first in anger, then in despair. And after that, of course, I wasn't quite the same chap.

2

The following Monday, at the Leeds Empire, *The Musical Tiplows* pushed in ahead of me at the band call and were demanding and fussy and time-wasting, and I would have hated them even if they hadn't been there instead of Nancy. I disliked their kind of musical act anyhow; it was an imitation drawing-room performance, with Father at the piano, under a shaded lamp, accompanying the Girls; and everything they played was either hackneyed or dripping with syrup. Mr Tiplow had a lot of silvery hair and a drooping moustache; one Miss Tiplow, who played the 'cello, was long and thin, and the other, who alternated between a fiddle and a flute, was short and fat; and all three somehow suggested a Phiz illustration to Dickens.

'Son,' said Bill Jennings, who must have noticed me scowling at the Tiplows, 'what's wrong with you guys is you can't appreciate genu-wine ree-finement.'

'I'll tell you another thing, son,' Hank Jennings drawled. 'You're looking at two females that even Bill will keep his hands off.'

'Boy, I'm trying to imagine them playing Butte, Montana, on a Saturday night,' said Bill dreamily.

'There's a bar across the street, friends,' said Hank. 'You coming, son? You could ask for plenty of water with it.'

I said I wouldn't risk it, not having had my turn. A few minutes later, Julie Blane came up to me. 'How long are these idiots going to be, Dick? Are you next? Good! Then wait for me, and we'll have drink – um? Lovely.'

We found a quiet corner in the bar, where Jennings and Johnson, with some other people, were drawling away at the counter. 'God knows what Tommy will do to those Tiplows. They were made for him to burlesque. He'll murder them. And you'll be delighted, won't you, Dick my dear?'

'Yes, Julie. So let me know when he puts them into the act.'

'You can't forgive them because they're here and your little Nancy isn't.' When I didn't reply, she went on: 'We exchanged a few words on Saturday night. I gather you've had a row.'

I nodded, and then drank about half of my beer. When I put the glass down I saw that she was giving me a curious speculative sort of look. I waited for her to speak.

'You do realize, don't you, that for sixpence – or, say, a shilling if you're eloquent – you could send her a wire to the Theatre Royal, Plymouth, and probably put an end to your ridiculous quarrel?' And perhaps I ought to add here that in those days everybody in the theatre sent telegrams, hardly ever writing a letter.

'What do I say – that I'm sorry and it's all my fault – when it was she who behaved badly?'

'Yes, of course. Don't you know anything about women?'

'No, not much. We'd had what I thought was a wonderful day out together. I thought we were becoming close friends – to say the least of it. And then, that night, she didn't even pretend to be sorry she was leaving. Something more amusing had turned up – so cheerio – good-bye! All right, that's that. And I'm not sending any apologetic wires or letters. Why should I?'

'But now you're feeling miserable – lonely?' She was serious, and her dark but strangely brilliant look was searching. After I answered her with a shrug, she smiled and said that she needed another whisky, and I told her it was my turn and I went to get it for her.

'Thanks, Dick.' She swallowed most of it, then looked hard at me again. 'She's a nice kid,' she began slowly. 'But though you're feeling miserable, lonely, you're not going to make it up with her? You're sure about that, my dear?'

'Yes, I am, Julie. And now I vote we change the subject. I don't see any point in all this.'

'Don't you?' She gave me a smile, half affectionate, half mocking. Then she turned on her bright manner. 'It's all rather ghastly just now. Tommy's been playing these dates for years, so that while I've no friends in the neighbourhood he's got lots – mostly horrible people – bookies and pub proprietors and their dull fat wives. We're staying at one of their pubs. Where are you this week?'

'Sharing digs with Uncle Nick and Cissie.'

'Doesn't she ever sneak out of his bed and climb into yours? Because I know she adores you, my dear.'

'Uncle Nick's a bit hard with her, so she wants sympathy. But there's no bed work. She doesn't want it, and I'm dam' sure I don't.'

'You must have friends round here.'

'A few, but when they're free – in the evenings – I'm not.'

'But some of them must have places of their own – flats – haven't they?'

'No, they haven't.' I was deliberately unresponsive because I'd suddenly realized what was in her mind. And the trouble was, I wasn't in the right mood for any artful bed-planning. Even there and then, a pub corner on a Monday morning, she still seemed to me the most beautiful woman — indeed, to be honest, the only really beautiful woman – I'd ever known; but I wasn't in the mood for arranging that she should take her clothes off somewhere on Thursday or Friday afternoon. Not even if it could be worked, which I doubted.

'I see. No places of their own.' She raised her eyebrows, which weren't thick but were clearly marked, so good for raising. 'Haven't had much social life so far, have you, Dick dear?'

'Not the kind you'd like, Julie – no. Don't forget that up to a few weeks ago, I was a junior clerk in a spinning mill. You're practically slumming, Miss Blane.'

'Oh – shut up and don't be stupid. I must fly. But tell me this. Do we try to see more of each other – or don't we?'

'Of course we do. But I'll have to leave it to you–'

'I know. And it isn't going to be easy. But I'll see.'

However, as things turned out that week, we did see more of each other, with nobody objecting and without any plotting and planning on her part. This odd business began that very Monday night. After our second show, I was sitting in Uncle Nick's dressing-room while he was removing his make-up and changing – I always did this very quickly but Uncle Nick liked to take it easy, to sip champagne and talk – when the call boy came in and said there was a gentleman at the stage door asking to see *Ganga Dun*, on very urgent business. And this gentleman wasn't trying to sell anything: it was very urgent *private* business. After hesitating a moment, for he didn't welcome visitors, Uncle Nick told the boy to bring him up.

The visitor was a man in his fifties, thin and bearded, not unlike a smaller and dimmer Bernard Shaw. He wore the kind of Jaeger stuff associated then with theosophists, socialists, vegetarians. 'It's extremely kind of you to see me, Mr Dun—'

'My name's Ollanton,' Uncle Nick told him dryly. '*Ganga Dun* is simply a stage name. And if you've come to have a talk about India, I must tell you I've never even been there.'

'Oh – what a pity! Not that I wanted to talk about India. I've never been there either. But I assumed you were Indian. And therefore more likely to give me a sympathetic hearing. Now I'm afraid you may think my request for help quite unreasonable. My name's Foster-Jones – hyphenated – Foster-Jones. Not unfamiliar, I imagine.' He waited expectantly.

'It is to me. What about you, Richard? By the way, this is my nephew, Richard Herncastle. He's the tall young Indian in the act – the vanishing cyclist.'

'How d'you do? You must be extremely clever—'

'No, I'm not, but my uncle is,' I told him. 'And the only Foster-Jones I've heard of is the suffragette – Mrs Foster-Jones—'

'Exactly, exactly. My wife. And it's on her behalf I'm here. Two friends brought me here tonight – I rarely go to music halls – but they felt I needed some distraction. And as soon as I saw your amazing performance, Mr Ollanton, I also saw a faint ray of hope. And that's why I'm here, sir.' He looked appealingly at Uncle Nick.

'Well, go on, Mr Foster-Jones,' said Uncle Nick, pretending not to be curious though I could see that he was. 'What's it all about?'

Foster-Jones looked solemn. 'Mr Ollanton, I hope you believe that women should have the vote.'

'No, I don't. And I often think it ought to be taken away from most men – half-wits, the majority of 'em.'

'Oh dear – oh dear!' Foster-Jones had one of those faces just right for falling. 'Now I don't know what to do. If you're unsympathetic to the cause, I feel I ought not to tell you any more.'

'Please yourself. But you might tell me what you had in mind when you asked to see me.'

Foster-Jones hesitated, as if he didn't know what to say, and then said the one thing that would fix Uncle Nick's attention and interest. 'I wanted you to make my wife disappear.'

'You did, did you?' There was a gleam in Uncle Nick's eye.

'Not on the stage, of course – but actually – in real life – from a meeting, in fact. Oh dear – now I'm telling you too much.'

'You'd better tell us the lot now. Even if we can't do anything for you, we promise to keep what you tell us to ourselves – eh, Richard? Right. Now then, Mr Foster-Jones.'

'My wife Agnes – Agnes Foster-Jones – is one of the leaders of the suffragette movement. She's already suffered two terms of imprisonment – a delicate, highly-strung woman, please remember. She's now *on the run*, as they say – hiding from the police, who would arrest her on sight. Actually—' and now he lowered his voice – 'she's staying with friends, keen sympathizers, not ten miles from here. Now on Sunday, here in Leeds, a big meeting and demonstration have been arranged. And the police of course will be in attendance. Now if my wife could suddenly appear on the platform and make a speech – she's an extremely good speaker – the effect would be sensational. And she's determined to do it. But of course as soon as she'd finished speaking, she'd be arrested at once, either immediately after she left the platform or as she tried to get out of the hall. But if in some way she could disappear after making her speech—' He finished the sentence not with his voice but with his eyes, looking at Uncle Nick like a sick spaniel. 'It suddenly occurred to me, as I watched your extraordinary tricks and illusions tonight, that you might be able to do something. I dare say we could offer you a fee—'

'No, no, no, forget that. It's the problem that interests me. She has to appear on the platform and make a speech – and it must be a short speech, I warn you – and then apparently vanish, to escape arrest. That's it, isn't it? Well, it oughtn't to be too difficult.'

'Goodness gracious me! It really can be done, can it, Mr Ollanton?' Foster-Jones was all eagerness, admiration, excitement.

Uncle Nick enjoyed the admiration but disapproved of the eagerness and excitement. 'Take it easy, now. If I've work to do, so have you. First, I want you to come back here tomorrow at this time, and bring with you a rough plan of the hall showing entrances and exits, and also – this is most important – a more detailed plan of the platform, showing exactly how one can reach it and leave it. You've got that? Right. I also need several photographs of your wife – and at least one of them full-length – together with details of her build – height, weight, and so forth—'

'I think I could tell you now,' Foster-Jones began eagerly.

'Tomorrow, if you don't mind. Will she take orders from you?'

'Well – no, not exactly. We don't believe in that kind of relationship–'

'I do,' said Uncle Nick grimly. 'Well, tell her that I can't undertake to rescue her from the police unless she promises to do exactly what I tell her to do. No argument. No wanting to do this, not wanting to do that. And what I'll ask her to do will be quite simple, quite reasonable. Nothing like what Richard here and the others have to do in my act.'

'No, of course not. I don't think there'll be any difficulty there, Mr Ollanton. My wife can be headstrong – but not in this instance, I'm sure. Is there anything else?'

'Yes. In order to pull this off properly, I may have to take one or two other people into my confidence. You'll have to trust me there, Mr Foster-Jones. But just remember I could run into trouble, helping somebody to avoid arrest, so I'm not likely to risk anybody talking too much, am I? No, no, never mind any thanks. I haven't done anything yet. And I'm hungry and I want my supper. So off you go, and be back here tomorrow night. Richard, see if Cissie's ready.'

When I came back to tell him she was waiting for us – and he had now taken off his make-up and was dressing – he said: 'It's a nuisance, but I can't risk telling Cissie what we're up to. Whatever she promised, she'd never be able to keep it to herself. If we tell her, we might as well have it in the *Yorkshire Evening Post*. So you be careful, lad. If she thinks we're up to something, she'd try worming it out of you when she wouldn't dare to tackle me. So watch it, lad.'

During supper Uncle Nick hardly spoke, while Cissie and I made rude remarks about the Tiplow family, who appeared to have snubbed Cissie when she made a friendly approach to them. But as soon as we had done and Uncle Nick lit a cigar, he told Cissie sharply to pop off to bed. 'You're looking tired, girl, and anyhow I want to have a word with Richard about a possible new effect. So off you go.' And Cissie didn't object chiefly because she never had the slightest interest in the technical side of the act, which always seemed to her a lot of nonsense. She had never seen it from in front and couldn't imagine how it would appear to an audience. But I genuinely enjoyed listening to Uncle Nick discussing his technical problems, before any of them reached the diagram stage when Sam and Ben could be brought in; and this was probably the chief reason why he liked to have me around.

'You don't see Mrs Foster-Jones – who's quite a famous suffragette, by the way – climbing into a trick box after she's left the platform, do you, uncle?'

After producing two superb smoke rings, he said slowly, enjoying himself: 'I did turn it over in my mind. Just as a bloody great lark. But this is too serious, lad.'

'I know it is. If they get their hands on her, they may be forcibly feeding her by the end of next week. And that's not funny, Uncle Nick.'

'Thanks for telling me. I may not care whether she gets the vote or not, but now – you silly young bugger – I'm on her side – and chancing my arm.' He said nothing for a moment or two, silently and happily sorting out his ideas. 'I think misdirection is what we want here, lad. She makes her speech – and she'll have to keep it short – then the police see her leave the platform and close in on her, to make the arrest. Only that won't be Mrs Foster-Jones, the one they see leaving the platform. And they'll be too busy to notice the real one, who'll now look a bit different, of course. This can be worked out nicely so long as there's a central entrance on to the platform, as there usually is in these big halls. And if there are some steps going down from one end of the platform, as there often are, then I can work it beautifully.'

'But it means that somebody will have to impersonate Mrs Foster-Jones. And who's that going to be?'

'I know who it isn't going to be – and that's our Cissie. But apart from that, we can't decide until we know more about Mrs Foster-Jones. And now you can leave it to me, lad. I'll see if there's any better way of doing it. So off you go. And I don't mind telling you, lad, I'm going to enjoy this.'

'I know you are. And I think I am too. 'Night, Uncle Nick.'

Foster-Jones saved me from a lot of misery, that week in Leeds. Nancy had gone, and I was still feeling the loss and the hurt. Sketching outdoors was impossible; the clear cold weather of the week before might have ended in snow – and I have always been fascinated by snowy landscapes – but instead it turned to dark rain and dirty low ceilings of cloud; with Leeds, never a favourite of mine, no treat at all. So in this situation, Foster-Jones was a life-saver.

He arrived in Uncle Nick's dressing-room, on Tuesday night, bringing with him the female half of the two keen sympathizers, who was called Muriel Dirks. She was small but had a large, damply pale face and huge poached eyes. When asked for an opinion she was always helpful and sounded quite cheerful, but somehow she looked all the time as if she was about to cry. However, as soon as Foster-Jones produced the plans of the hall, Uncle Nick ignored both of them and talked to me as if they weren't there.

'You see, lad,' he began triumphantly, 'this is just what I wanted. Look here. Steps going down from each end of the platform to the floor of the hall, with a pass door leading from the auditorium to the artistes' rooms, offices and whatnot, at the back, behind the platform. Now then – look – the platform has a central entrance, between these rows of seats on each side – for choirs, special supporters of meetings – they'll be filling those seats on Sunday, if it's a big meeting.'

'You are, aren't you, Muriel?' said Foster-Jones anxiously.

'Of course we are,' Mrs Dirks began. 'We've already sent out-'

But Uncle Nick wasn't bothering with them, and he cut in brutally: 'Now look, lad. We put up a screen, masking that central entrance. Mrs Foster-Jones, at the end of her speech, when they're cheering her, all excited, exits a bit uncertainly towards the screen, disappears behind it, but then apparently changes her mind, comes out again, hurries along the platform towards the steps, goes down the steps, making for the pass door – there. She'll be hardly through it before the police will have closed in on her. Then Bob's your uncle!'

'Well, he may be,' said Muriel Dirks rather sharply. 'But if the police have got Mrs Foster-Jones—'

'I must say, Mr Ollanton,' said-Foster-Jones hastily, 'I don't quite see–'

'Now just a minute.' Uncle Nick was now acknowledging their existence. 'What d'you take me for? That's not Mrs Foster-Jones who reappears on the platform from behind the screen. The real Mrs Foster-Jones, not looking quite the same as she did on the platform, can be on her way out of the building. Misdirection – that's what we're aiming at. It's the safest way to play this. Give the police something to do. Show 'em a striking dress or coat – something out of the ordinary – and so long as the second woman, who'll be wearing it, isn't too unlike Mrs Foster-Jones – they'll be certain it's her.'

'It's a clever plan, extremely clever,' said Foster-Jones uncertainly. 'But – well, what do you think, Muriel?'

'I must say, I feel rather doubtful. Wouldn't the police have to be very stupid?'

'No, they wouldn't.' Uncle Nick gave her a hard look, then transferred it to Foster-Jones. 'You people are trying to teach me my business. I'm in the Deception Trade, and earn a lot of money at it. The police will see what I want 'em to see – and no more. Not one of 'em will be close to that screen, don't forget. Let's say she's wearing a bright red coat. They see that bright red coat go behind the screen at one end of it and come out, just when they're thinking of making a move, at the other end of it. And they've time to look but not to think. I tell you, it's child's play compared to what we do twice-nightly here – eh, Richard?'

'Yes, uncle, I agree. It is, so long as the other woman's right, and both women know exactly what to do.'

'Hello, are you starting now, lad?' Uncle Nick gave a contemptuous snort. 'Naturally, it's all got to be carefully worked out. Now what about those photographs of your wife, Mr Foster-Jones?'

'I'm afraid what I've got won't be very helpful,' he said apologetically, as he handed over a cabinet head-and-shoulders photograph and several pictures clipped from newspapers. 'She's five-foot five-inches, rather slight build, dark hair going grey-'

'Yes, yes, yes,' Uncle Nick said impatiently. 'But we'll have to do better than this. We have to work at this job, not play at it. A professional effect, planned and worked out to the last detail, not an amateur muddle.' He looked at Foster-Jones, then at Muriel.

'I have a friend who looks vaguely like Agnes Foster-Jones,' said Muriel in a small uneasy voice. 'But I really doubt if she'd be able—'

'So do I,' said Uncle Nick, interrupting her sharply. 'And I think you two had better leave us for half an hour. There's a pub across the street-'

'We're not pub people, I'm afraid, Mr Ollanton,' said Foster-Jones.

'No, I suppose not. Well, go down and wait just inside the stage door until I send for you. Or would you rather give it up? You wouldn't? All right then, just wait downstairs. I don't want you to leave because there may be some things we'll have to settle tonight.' As soon as they'd gone he poured out some champagne for us both – he always kept a bottle in his dressing-room that had a little tap running through the cork – and when we'd taken a drink, he looked inquiringly at me. 'Any ideas, lad?'

'I've one. Julie Blane.'

'Any reason – apart from the fact you'd still like to have her – on the quiet?'

'Yes. She's about the same height and build. She's a clever experienced actress, who'd be ready to do exactly what she's told. And she knows about clothes.'

'I hate to admit it, but you're quite right, lad. But we don't know she'd agree to do it.'

'I think she would. I know she's in sympathy with the suffragettes. And I think it's the sort of trick she'd enjoy playing.'

'No doubt. But if we bring her in, we can't leave Tommy Beamish out. He'd have to be told, and after a few whiskies how's he going to keep his big mouth shut? It's a hell of a risk.'

'It might be less of one if you gave him something to do, brought him into the act, made it a production.' I said this hopefully, trying to forget that Tommy Beamish was unreliable even as a top-of-the-bill pro.

'And if he doesn't know too much. Then he can't spill too much.' Uncle Nick sipped his champagne and looked thoughtful. Then he went on: 'I'll have to rush this through tonight, lad. If Miss Blane's going to do it, she ought to see Mrs Foster-Jones tomorrow – to notice how she looks, how she moves, and to settle the clothes business. I'll ask Foster-Jones if he can provide a car to take her there. I'm not using mine. I'm not going. I'll work out an exact plan for them but I'm not getting up in the morning to go miles from anywhere in the rain. And Tommy's not going. I'll tell him he's too well known. Now give me a good reason why you should go with Miss Blane. No, I'm serious, lad.'

'I'm the artist,' I told him, half grinning, half solemn. 'I'm the one with the trained eye. I'm the one-'

'That'll do, lad. Now I'll see Tommy and Miss Blane and then Foster-Jones and Mrs Who's-it. You pick up Cissie and have your suppers – and keep mine hot, I may be late. And don't forget – not a word to Cissie.'

It was still raining, and Cissie and I ran for a tram, and it was crowded, and then we hurried, not speaking, from the tram-stop to the digs. But as soon as we were facing each other across the supper table, Cissie said rather peevishly: 'I know very well something's happening, so you might as well tell me what it is, Dick. I don't pretend to be clever but I just *know* about some things, just as I'd know at once if Nick was seeing another woman.'

I believe she was right too. Because she didn't concentrate and sharpen it, her mind could be open to anything that might be blowing around. She wouldn't have done badly, I fancy, as a fortune-teller.

'Yes, there *is* something, Cissie, but you wouldn't be interested. He's trying to work out a new trick. That's why he's stayed behind to see two people who might be able to help him.'

'All right. But he could *tell* me, couldn't he, instead of just shutting me up?'

'Now, come on, Cissie. You ought to understand him now better than that. If the trick doesn't work out, he'll feel foolish. And that's about the last thing he wants to feel. He doesn't mind me knowing, but he'd hate *you* to know. He has to appear very grand in your eyes.'

'Yes, that's right enough. You're a very clever boy, Dick. It must run in the family. But I'll tell you something.' She finished a roast potato, and then drank some stout. 'He came right off his high horse one time, not so long since. Where was it? Birmingham – that's where it was. And he'd got the 'flu or something. Terrible high temperature he had. Wouldn't eat a thing. Just drank his champagne. Stayed in bed all day – hardly able to get his breath sometimes – looking awful. But he would go on and get through his act somehow. I begged and begged him not to – but you know him – got a will of iron, he has. But of course I had to look after him day and night – help him dress and undress and even put his make-up on for him. And he was so ashamed and miserable because he wasn't grand and lordly for once – because I had to look after *him* – and he couldn't understand that it was then I really and truly loved him, loved him every minute – never never stopped loving him.'

As she was looking at me so earnestly, I said: 'Yes, Cissie, I can imagine that.'

'No, you can't,' she said rather crossly. 'You're saying that just to say something. You're like your uncle – you'll say anything to me, just to shut me up.' She took the cover off the pudding. 'Oh Christmas! It's baked jam roll – and I can't resist it – and if he finds out I've had some, he'll raise Cain.' So we worked out a baked-jam-roll plot so that she could have some and Uncle Nick wouldn't know.

But by the time he came in, we'd cleared our supper things long ago and Cissie had given me her opinion of about thirty to forty different cities and towns, which she described as if they were people. 'Better get off to bed, lad,' he began at once, cleverly reversing his usual bedtime orders to us. 'You're going out to see those people in the morning. There's a car of sorts, and it'll be calling for you about eleven. So off you go, Cissie. I want my supper. I'm downright hungry for once. Good night, Richard.'

The car that arrived at quarter-past eleven, next morning, was driven – and may have been owned – by a keenly sympathizing young man called Arnold, who had a golden mane of hair and obviously belonged to what was known in the West Riding then as 'The Hatless Brigade'. (But this has to be pronounced in the West Riding fashion to bring out the full bitter flavour.) Sitting in front with Arnold was Foster-Jones, to act as guide. The car was large but had a battered look; it was an open tourer but not open now because the hood, which had been knocked about a bit, was down – or do I mean up? Certainly at the back, where I was, I felt the thing was very much down. It wasn't actually raining but it was an unpleasant morning, chilly and damp and anxious to creep back into night again as soon as it could.

I thought as we went round to pick up Julie at her pub that she'd be furious, what with having to get up and eat some breakfast, and then having to face this dreary cold morning in this dubious car. And I was quite wrong. She was in high spirits, her eyes sparkling below the little fur hat she was wearing. 'I think this is going to be *fun*, don't you, Dick?' she said as soon as she'd tucked herself in beside me. 'Where are we going?'

'I don't know. That's the great secret.'

'Of course. How stupid of me! Well, something's happening and I'm so glad. It was all becoming so boring. How are you, Dick darling? Still sulky? Come closer, I'm cold. Haven't you got any gloves – or don't you bother?'

Arnold and his car, you might say, bounced us out of Leeds; sometimes we were roaring, rattling, hooting along; at other times we exploded a lot but more or less in the same place. It wasn't easy to see out from the back, but we seemed to be going Headingley way and then taking the road to Otley.

'Where I *have* been very stupid, Dick,' said Julie softly during one of the non-exploding stops, 'is not bringing anything to drink. I mean, real booze. It's obviously a day for it, and although these are very sweet people, I'm sure, I have a horrible feeling that a cup of tea – or some new kind of coffee that really isn't coffee – is about as far as they'll go. Did you know that Mr Foster-Jones makes Health Foods? Well, he does, just outside Godalming. He's probably brought a case of date sandwiches and nut cutlets with him, and we'll have some for lunch. So listen – Dick, darling – if I suddenly say I'm feeling sick or faint, just outside a pub, you've got to back me up. Promise now.'

It happened that the car began coughing and then stopped within sight of a small pub at a crossroads. Julie nudged me. 'Oh, I say, Mr Foster-Jones,' I called out. 'Do you mind if we get out for a few minutes? Miss Blane's feeling rather faint – sick—'

'I'm so terribly sorry,' Julie cried.

'Oh dear! If you feel you must, of course,' said Foster-Jones. 'Though we've only about a mile to go now, and I'm sure that Agnes and Muriel Dirks will be able to offer us a good hot herbal drink—'

But we got out and ran, and the next minute Julie was ordering two double whiskies, and as soon as she had downed hers she demanded another double for herself. (And if anybody is interested, the total cost of these three doubles was one shilling and sixpence.) Back in the car, she smiled brilliantly at Foster-Jones, who I thought looked rather pained, and said she was now ready to go anywhere at any speed.

Finally, we turned down a lane and drew up outside two low stone cottages that had been turned into one. Julie exclaimed with pleasure at the sight of everything. Muriel Dirks, whose husband, a schoolmaster, didn't come home for lunch, was laying a table for six. Mrs Foster-Jones and Julie, who appeared to take to each other at once, plunged immediately into the clothes problem, talking hard all the way. I sat where I could watch Mrs Foster-Jones, and surreptitiously attempted a few drawings of her in a small sketchbook I had brought. She was younger than her husband – and, I felt, probably worth ten of him – but of course years older than Julie, twelve at least. She was thinner and frailer and couldn't match Julie's magnificent eyes and the beautiful bone structure of her face, but she wasn't without a certain beauty of her own, born of a sensitiveness to experience, courage and will, and a kind of gaiety, intensely feminine, that I was sure Foster-Jones, virtuous but entirely lacking humour, wouldn't appreciate or begin to understand. It may seem foolish, but as I stared at her I was ready not only to admire but to love Agnes Foster-Jones, and though my tentative sketches were bad, I still have them. Up to that moment I hadn't thought much about the position of women, their demands for more and better education, for some political responsibility and fairer treatment, but just looking at and taking in this woman, so very different from the wild and nasty cartoons of suffragettes in the popular press, converted me at once to the feminism I have held to ever since. The very sight of her, delicate but gay, so frail, so brave, made the average member of a parliament seem an ivory-headed ass. She had been twice in prison, and now any policeman had only to put his meaty hand on her shoulder and she would be in a cell again. Yet she was ready to appear at that meeting on Sunday, and could even laugh as she and Julie tried to solve the clothes problem. I began to feel then, what I have believed ever since, that given equal opportunities women are *better than ordinary men*, only extraordinary men rising to their level – and, after all, most extraordinary men appreciate and enjoy women as few ordinary men do.

During lunch, which was well-meant but not very appetizing or nourishing, I stared across the table at Mrs Foster-Jones and Julie sitting together. They were not unlike two sisters who'd taken two widely separated roads in life. Julie's was the more beautiful face, and though at that time I wasn't conscious of wanting her, the sexual element was there; but I began to feel that Agnes Foster-Jones had the better face, even the wear and tear it showed, the lines and hollows, having a kind of beauty, quite different from Julie's and perhaps more satisfying; and indeed by comparison it brought out – even though Julie was innocently enjoying herself – that trickiness, that vague suggestion of something false in her nature, which I had been aware of in Julie several times before. And I can't help believing — though I don't want to exaggerate this – that even then, behind these thoughts and others only half-formed, was a queer uneasiness not about the future but, so to speak, already washing back from it, a mild foretaste of what would be in its own place and time nothing less than anguish.

As the representative of the master plotter, Uncle Nick, I was asked to approve such plans as the two women had now made. Julie was to buy the most eye-catching long coat that Leeds could offer at a reasonable price. She would also find a hat – and this wouldn't be difficult – that would overshadow most of her face. Mrs Foster-Jones, who said all her clothes were now in a terrible state, anyhow, would wear her oldest travelling coat, pack and bring with her everything she needed, and be ready to leave the city as soon as she had made her speech. Hoping that I wasn't taking too much on myself, I said that I thought both women should be inside the hall, at the back, some time before the meeting began. Both Foster-Jones and Arnold, who turned out to be more sensible than he looked, agreed with this, and then said they would try to locate some small room at the back where the women could wait. 'And if necessary,' said Arnold, grinning, 'I can stick a notice on it saying *Ladies Only*.'

'And that's as far as we go,' I told them. 'We'll have to leave the exact timing and what each of us has to do – every detail – to my uncle, who's very thorough.'

'I'll bet,' said Julie, pulling a face.

'All right, he can be disagreeable,' I told her. 'But if it wasn't for him, Mrs Foster-Jones wouldn't be speaking at that meeting on Sunday.'

'Squashed!' said Julie, as the others fervently agreed with me. 'But oughtn't we to be going, Dick?'

'Yes.' I looked at Foster-Jones. 'Could you be at the Empire about quarter-past eight? I'm going to suggest to Uncle Nick we have a meeting between the houses.'

'Between the houses?' This was Mrs Foster-Jones, who looked and sounded bewildered.

'My dear, he means during the interval between the first performance and the second performance,' said Julie. 'Dick's only been with us a few weeks, but he likes to pretend he's been on the variety stage most of his life. Now we must go. And would you mind stopping a minute at that rather sweet little pub, because I think I left a powder-puff there?' She took an affectionate farewell of Mrs Foster-Jones, thanked Muriel Dirks on behalf of us both for her 'most interesting lunch', and off we went. She had two double whiskies, while I had a quick beer, at the same little pub, and amused herself all the way back by keeping very close to me, and arousing me by various secret little touches, while talking in a loud innocent tone to Foster-

Jones and Arnold in front. The car behaved better than it had done on the way out, but then we had to creep along during the last part of the journey, for a certain amount of fog was joining the December dusk in Leeds.

We held our meeting in Tommy Beamish's dressing-room because it was the largest. Foster-Jones looked bewildered and somewhat apprehensive, as well he might, seeing us all there in our various costumes and make-up. To my astonishment, Jennings and Johnson were there, smoking cigars and drinking Tommy's whisky.

'Don't look like that, son,' said Jennings. 'We're in the act. Ask the Maharajah.'

'Remember, we like women, all kinds, even our wives,' said Johnson.

'And we're cop-haters from way back, son,' said Jennings. 'Maharajah, you're in the chair.'

Uncle Nick looked up from some notes he'd been making and took charge of us, pretending not to love it. I'll start with you, Mr Foster-Jones. Got a notebook? Right. First then – the screen. It ought to open out to about nine feet. It must be at least seven feet high. It mustn't be light, but be careful it's not top-heavy. Better weight it down when it's in position. And let's make sure you know exactly where it goes. Here – look.' And Uncle Nick showed him the plan of the platform. Tommy Beamish yawned and helped himself to his own whisky. Julie closed her eyes. Jennings and Johnson sat twinkling over their cigars.

'That's the screen, then. Now – it's important your wife should be out of the neighbourhood as soon as possible. If she knows anybody in or near Sheffield she can stay with on Sunday night, then I'll drive her there, because we're playing Sheffield next week. If she agrees to this, tell her I'll be waiting in my car, near the artistes' entrance at the back, at nine o'clock.'

'But how will she know it's you, Mr Ollanton? I mean—'

'I know what you mean,' Uncle Nick cut in ruthlessly. 'Just leave that to me. Two more things for you. Make sure the chairman of the meeting announces your wife not much before and not much after five to nine. And make sure – doubly sure – your wife understands she mustn't speak more than – say – three minutes. If she goes on and on, the police'll have time to go round and make for that central entrance, to catch her as she goes off. Then she's for it, and we've all been wasting our time.'

'I do understand that, Mr Ollanton,' Foster-Jones began.

But Uncle Nick cut him short again. 'Finally – you'll have to keep out of all this on Sunday night. Don't try to follow your wife. Don't hope to join her that night. Once they know she's here, you may be spotted and followed. Right? Right. Now how does she find my car? She'll be carefully assisted out of the building by Mr Jennings and Mr Johnson, who can look very respectable, though they aren't. If anybody wants to know, they're two gallant American gentlemen giving their arms to a dithery elderly lady.'

'Man, it would bring tears to your eyes,' said Jennings.

'How about a victrola at the back there,' said Johnson, 'playing *Hearts and Flowers*? Sorry, Chief! Continue.'

'And they know my car, Mr Foster-Jones. And they'll know exactly where to be and what to do. Now, Miss Blane. What do you do?'

'I go there early, wearing the bright coat I'll buy tomorrow, also a hat that hides most of my face. I give the coat to Mrs Foster-Jones. I carry her old coat and hat, and wait behind the screen while she's talking. As soon as she comes behind the screen again, I put on the coat, go out at the other end of the screen, dither a bit and try to imitate her walk and posture, go down towards the platform – and if they aren't still applauding, somebody had better start 'em again, hurry along the platform, go down the steps at the end, make for the near pass door, and hope to find myself arrested. Isn't that it?'

'Except for one thing,' said Uncle Nick, now in his severe rehearsal manner. 'While you and Mrs Foster-Jones are waiting, you must practise that coat swapping – over and over and over again – until you can do it in under three seconds without thinking. The rest of it will be easy for you. You're a good experienced actress. Mrs Foster-Jones isn't and she'll probably be very nervous. And that quick change behind the screen is the key to the whole effect. It's got to look as if she simply walks behind the screen. So don't take any notice if she objects to rehearsing it over and over again. Don't stop until you could do it in two-and-a-half seconds in your sleep.'

'I'll do my best,' Julie told him. 'And I may tell you, I think Mrs Foster-Jones is a darling – and I'll do anything to keep her out of gaol. But what happens to me? I'm not used to arguing with policemen, though I've always thought it might come to that, sooner or later.'

'My nephew, Richard here, looks an innocent lad, and he'll be sitting not far from that door, and he'll go after you—'

'Why can't I do that, Nick?' This was Tommy Beamish, not looking pleased. 'Julie's with me – and—'

'Listen, Tommy.' Uncle Nick wasn't quite so sharp now. 'I've something more important for you to do. It's another key thing. I want you up in the side gallery. And as soon as Miss Blane appears round the screen, I want you to give a shout – 'Here she is. Give her a cheer' – something like that. It's an essential part of the misdirection, and it'll start the cheering and booing and nobody'll be able to think. Now young Richard couldn't do that as well as you could—'

'I should hope not,' said Tommy, still rather sulky. 'Not after all my experience.'

'On the other hand,' Uncle Nick went on smoothly, 'you wouldn't have time to get down, and anyhow you'd better disguise yourself for the gallery part—'

'A dark wig and big teeth,' Tommy began, cheering up at once.

'So young Richard'll have to go after her, and all he's got to do is to identify her.' He looked at me and then at Julie. 'But both of you must waste a bit of time, to keep 'em busy while Mrs Foster-Jones is already on her way.'

'Mr Ollanton,' cried Foster-Jones in a rather shaky voice, 'I really believe we can do it – and I can't tell you how grateful my wife and I—'

'No, save that,' said Uncle Nick. 'We have to work at it yet – you included. We've no time now for any questions. I just heard the call boy. We'll go over it all again on Friday. And remember exactly what you have to do, Mr Foster-Jones. And make certain you've got the right kind of screen and it can't fall down.'

'Our new version of the famous screen scene,' said Julie brightly. 'Let's hope it plays as well as Sheridan's.'

Uncle Nick gave her a small sour smile. 'If it doesn't, some of us will be in a hell of a mess, Miss Blane.'

Julie's returning smile was sweet and false. 'I can see that I will be, I don't know about you. But it's nice – *in a way* — to be working with you, Mr Ollanton.'

Uncle Nick didn't reply; he was now on his way out; and after exchanging glances with Julie, I followed him.

Well, it worked. On Sunday, December 7th, 1913, Mrs Foster-Jones, the notorious suffragette leader, known to be wanted by the police everywhere, made a triumphant appearance on a public platform in

Leeds – and then vanished. At five minutes to nine, there she was, emerging from behind the screen and coming down the central steps to greet the chairman, with the whole place in an uproar, a smiling if frail-looking woman, bareheaded but still wearing a scarlet long coat; and by five past nine there was no trace of her anywhere in the building. Yes, it worked beautifully.

Julie and Mrs Foster-Jones must have practised hard, because from where I was sitting – and I was fairly near the front – it looked as if Mrs Foster-Jones had remained behind the screen just long enough to pick up and pull over her head the hat she was wearing as she appeared again. Julie, never looking up, keeping most of her face hidden by the hat, really did look like Mrs Foster-Jones. Moreover, she had hardly taken more than two or three steps when this huge voice came from the gallery: 'Here she is. Give her a cheer, lads!' and set the place boiling again. And I am not sure if this perfectly-timed stroke, beautifully executed – as they say – by Tommy Beamish, wasn't Uncle Nick's most artful touch in the whole design: nobody had time to observe carefully and to think. As Julie left the platform by the steps at the end the chairman, who had had his instructions, was already appealing for order and beginning to announce the next speaker. I had left my seat before Julie had reached the pass door, but as I reached the aisle leading to it, a policeman and a tall man in a mackintosh went ahead of me. Julie had time to open the door and go through before they caught up with her. I followed the policeman and the tall man, and then found myself in a corridor, where Julie was angrily pulling herself away from an enormous police sergeant.

'What on earth do you think you're doing, man?' she demanded. 'Take your beastly fat hands off me.'

'All right, Mrs Foster-Jones,' said the tall man in the mackintosh, taking charge. 'If you don't give us any trouble, we won't give you any.'

'I don't know what you're talking about,' Julie said. 'Who are you?'

'I'm Detective-Inspector Woods, and I have orders to take you into custody, Mrs Foster-Jones.'

'But don't be silly. I'm not Mrs Foster-Jones.' Now she caught sight of me. 'Oh – hello, Dick!'

'Hello, Julie – what's happening?'

'I don't know – except—'

'Hold it.' The Inspector turned to glare at me. 'You can either clear off *sharp – now –* or come to the station with me.'

'Then I'll come to the station. Though I don't see any point in it.' I'm making myself sound very bold and brassy, but I've no doubt my voice quavered a bit. 'I'm here because I saw Miss Blane hurrying off the platform. And she's a friend of mine. We're on the same variety bill. Last week – Leeds Empire. This week – Sheffield.'

Julie had now taken off her hat. 'And I must say, Inspector, you're not very flattering if you can't tell the difference between me and Mrs Foster-Jones, who's years and years older than I am. My name's Julie Blane. I'm an actress, at present playing in a sketch with Tommy Beamish, the comedian.'

'By gow, you're right an' all,' said the sergeant. 'Saw you the other night. That's who she is, sir.'

'Well, I can see she isn't Mrs Foster-Jones,' the Inspector began slowly. Then a thought hit him hard. 'Go on, you two – sharp—' he shouted. 'See if she's still here. Look in every room. Inquire at the back door. Quick as you can.' As they hurried along the corridor, he stared suspiciously at Julie. 'All right then, you're Miss Julie Blane. But you've still a bit of explaining to do, Miss Blane. Mrs Foster-Jones goes behind that screen, and then you come out, wearing her coat.'

'But I'm not wearing her coat. This is my coat. I bought it last Thursday morning. Look – here's the bill from the shop.' She handed it over but went on talking as the Inspector examined it. 'It does look rather like the coat Mrs Foster-Jones was wearing, except that hers has a high black collar and black cuffs – didn't you notice? I'd come to the meeting, intending to sit on the platform, because I'd heard a rumour Mrs Foster-Jones might appear. Well, of course I was late – I'm always late except in the theatre – and when I got to the top of the steps masked by that screen I heard the applause and Mrs Foster-Jones began speaking, so I stayed where I was. When she came off and hurried past me, I was all dithery – applause always unsettles me – and couldn't decide whether to take a seat on the platform or go. So I wandered on – then some fool in the gallery must have thought I was Mrs Foster-Jones coming back and shouted and other people began shouting and clapping, so then I was in a panic — and hurried through that door, only to be stopped by the sergeant.' She gave the Inspector a rueful little smile. 'If I've been a nuisance, I'm awfully sorry, Inspector. But I couldn't help it if Mrs Foster-Jones's coat looked rather like mine, could I?'

'I don't know. But you'd be ready to give us a signed statement along those lines, would you?'

'Why, of course,' said Julie, raising her eyebrows and opening her eyes until they looked like innocence itself. 'Why not?'

The Inspector took a deep breath and then let it out rather noisily. 'Next time you come here, Miss Blane, I'll see your performance on the stage, where it belongs. I'm dealing with liars all the time – but you take the cake.'

'You don't believe me?' Detective-Inspector Woods wagged a finger in her face: 'You know – and I know – there isn't a word of truth in it. But if you'll say nothing, I'll do nothing. Now get off to Sheffield – or Timbuctoo.' And he went striding along the corridor.

As soon as he'd disappeared, I clasped hold of her and said: 'You were wonderful, Julie. Absolutely perfect. If this has worked – and I'm sure it must have, for Mrs Foster-Jones must be miles away by now – then we owe it all to you.'

Julie closed her eyes. 'Kiss me.'

So we kissed, but soon had to break away because we heard people approaching. It was lucky we did, because one of the people was Tommy Beamish buried within a cap and a huge motoring coat. He liked to look as if he drove the car himself, but actually he had a chauffeur, who also acted as his dresser. (Because he'd already had a long day, this chauffeur, Dixon, hadn't been on duty the night of Sir Alec's party in Aberdeen.) At Uncle Nick's rather pressing request, Tommy, who didn't like me, probably because he knew that Julie did, had reluctantly agreed to give me a lift to Sheffield. My bags were already in the car with theirs, and we set off at once, with Tommy and Julie in the back, talking away about the meeting and how successful the trick had been, while they ate sandwiches and drank whisky, and with me in front beside Dixon, a gloomy and silent man. But Julie, risking Tommy's displeasure, passed me some sandwiches, saying she had more than she wanted, and a metal flask-top – it must have been a very big flask – full of whisky. And as she did this, she managed somehow to draw her hand gently across my cheek.

When we dropped down into Sheffield, I gave Dixon the address that Cissie had given me, for I was sharing digs with her and Uncle Nick again, and I was astounded when he told me he was going to the same address, because Mr Beamish and Miss Blane were staying there. What with her performance at and after the meeting, the kiss, her behaviour in the car, I was now full of Julie, and I couldn't decide whether I was glad or sorry we would be sharing the same roof. Cissie hadn't said anything about them. Did Julie know? Did Tommy Beamish know? When, after much peering and asking and stopping and starting, we arrived finally at a fairly large corner house, I still hadn't decided whether to be glad or sorry, but I had a feeling that I might be in for a most peculiar week.

3

It was certainly a peculiar house. The owner of it, George Wall, had been a skilled steelworker, who had worked for some years in St Petersburg, where he had acquired a Russian wife, and had then returned to Sheffield, had gravely injured a leg through no fault of his own, and out of the compensation he received he had bought this house. His sister, who had been on the stage, had given him the idea of turning the house into theatrical digs. He limped badly, was hardly ever seen except in shirtsleeves, usually rolled up to uncover his very thick muscular arms, smoked black twist in an equally black little pipe, always looked as if he might knock you down but was in fact quite genial and obliging. His wife, Varvara, dark, small, bony, screeched all over the house and was so energetic and tireless that she seemed rather like a shouting insect, some kind of queen ant. She carried what must have been a Russian atmosphere round with her. The house didn't smell like any other place in Sheffield: as soon as you opened the front door, you were somewhere else, probably St Petersburg. She was a good cook and compelled us, by sheer force of will, to try Russian things like cabbage soup and borsch, those tiny meat and fish pasties called *piroshki* and Chicken Kiev, which Julie and I enjoyed even if the others didn't. She was assisted by a fat bursting-out-of-everything 'skivvy', as they called them then, a young woman from one of the small mining towns whose name was Annie, who slept in the next bedroom to mine, at the top of the house, and snored clean through the wall; and also by a mysterious old Russian woman wrapped in a black shawl, who never spoke but stared at us as if we were a pack of imbeciles.

There were no separate servings of meals, not even when we came back after the show. We all had to eat together round a big table in the dining-room. There were two resident boarders in addition to the five of us. One was a quiet elderly widow, who went out to give piano lessons; the other was also elderly but far from quiet – Professor Lancelot Byers, who taught elocution somewhere and gave recitals, not only of short pieces but even gigantic chunks of Dickens. He was full of conventional opinions and platitudes, which he elocuted with enormous dignity, with every vowel, every consonant, perfectly formed, as if he was proclaiming a peace treaty. Julie, Uncle Nick and I were either irritated or bored by him, but Cissie used to listen to him open-mouthed, and Tommy Beamish, his strange eyes glittering with mischief, egged him on, and later, when we had left Sheffield, did a superb burlesque of the Professor Byers manner in a nonsense recitation he introduced into his sketch.

Compelled to spend some time in one another's company, the five of us didn't find it easy. Uncle Nick and Tommy Beamish respected each other as performers and had come together in the Mrs Foster-Jones plot, but they weren't really friendly. Julie disliked Uncle Nick, regarded Cissie with contempt, and had to be careful about me. Poor Cissie was out of her depth all round, but occasionally she scratched back at Julie. Tommy didn't like me, and not simply because he knew that Julie did. I think he resented me partly because I was young and hefty and didn't live under his kind of strain, and also because Julie must have told him that what I wanted was to become a painter, so that to him I wasn't a real 'pro'. I didn't actually return his dislike – even though, under cover of loud professional jocularity, he'd give me a nasty little knock or two – and as yet I wasn't jealous of his hold upon Julie, as I was a little later; but I now took the chance, which I'd never been offered before, of observing him closely and trying to understand the kind of man he was.

As I've already pointed out, Tommy was undoubtedly a superb comic, almost a great one. When he was on the stage he made you feel he was a natural born funny man, who hadn't to have gags invented for him, didn't need any special material, but could create uproarious comedy out of anything and nothing, making you laugh just because he was Tommy Beamish. And superficially he still seemed like this when he was off the stage, a man who couldn't help wildly clowning, even when he was rushing in for a drink or taking his place at the dinner table. (Though like most heavy drinkers, he ate very little.) With his chubby round face, on which experience seemed to have printed nothing, he often suggested a mischievous high-spirited boy. But his curious flickering eyes didn't belong to any such boy. I felt sometimes they looked through a mask at a world that could never be his world. Now it's true that some wonderful clowns – Grock, for instance – always give us the impression that they are innocent and hopeful visitors from some other planet, serious creatures struggling against alien circumstances, defeated by two and two making four. But I didn't feel this about Tommy. The hopeful innocence didn't seem to be there. I began to think there was something desperate and rather sinister about his clowning. He made me feel sometimes that behind that droll mask, through which he glanced so restlessly, was an awful blank desert where he really existed, among bleached bones in a cruel emptiness, without innocence, with hope all gone. And at these times I felt he hated us all, even Julie.

It was tantalizing, almost a torment, being under the same roof with Julie, watched as we were by so many sharp eyes and having no opportunity of spending any time together away from the others. Though I was fascinated by her dark, half-ravaged beauty, which nobody but me seemed to appreciate, I wasn't falling in love with her. If it had been Nancy, I think I would have been happy just being near her. But with Julie it was sheer sexual excitement, which she kept on or near the boil, partly out of feminine mischief because she was bored, but also, as I learnt later, because she herself soon became equally excited. So if we met by chance on the stairs or a landing or had the sitting-room or dining-room to ourselves for a minute or two, we would hastily embrace and kiss; and even when the others were there, Julie would contrive a passing touch, a quick and secret pressure, that would set me on fire. It was a dangerous game that she enjoyed more than I did – at least until she found she was setting herself on fire too.

Moreover, it was bad December weather all that week in Sheffield, leaving me idle and disappointed because I'd hoped to do some sketching in the Peak country, not far away. I did some half-hearted drawing up in my attic room, but it was cheerless up there, and anyhow all this wondering about Julie and wanting her seemed to take the heart and guts out of anything else, a consequence I might have borne in mind if I'd had any sense.

Julie and I had just one afternoon out together, when Tommy had lunched with some of his admirers at a club and came back to sleep it off. Julie had told him she had to do some shopping. We didn't leave the house together, but met at the end of the road, and as it was a dark wettish afternoon we went first to a little cinema, where we entwined our hands and legs as we stared at Bronco Billy Anderson and the Keystone Cops, and then had tea at a neighbouring cafe. Julie was very quiet at first – she was obviously feeling depressed – but finally she began to talk.

'What do you know about me, Dick?'

I told her briefly what Uncle Nick had told me.

'All quite true,' she said. 'I was living with a man – then suddenly I wasn't. He vanished, then married somebody else. He liked drinking, so I drank with him. Then when he wasn't there, I drank for both of us. Then I did the fatal thing. Instead of drinking after work, I drank before it and during it. Then when they had to ring down the curtain on me, everybody knew – and I was out. And not only for the West End but even for any tour worth considering. My only chance – and I'm a good actress, my dear, I really am – was to keep earning reasonably good money, to save a little and try to sober up, then talk somebody into giving me a chance on an Australian or South African tour. After that, if I'd behaved myself, the West End managers might look at me again. The only decent salary, out of which I might save something, was the one I was offered by Tommy Beamish. He was willing to give me a chance because he'd fallen flat on *his* face once and had the curtain rung down on *him*. So, that made two of us. And I can save fifteen pounds every week.'

'Partly, I suppose,' I said pointedly, but not, I hope, nastily, 'because you share his bedroom.'

There was a flash in the darkness of her glance, but she answered me coolly. 'That helps, certainly. But it doesn't make me a tart, Dick my dear. Tommy came to my rescue. I was very grateful. Though, mind you, I can feed him lines when most actresses would dry, give it up as a bad job, tell him he's impossible to work with. I earn my salary twice-nightly, on the stage, far away from that bedroom you dragged into this conversation, you silly boy. Are you jealous?'

'Not yet, but I soon could be.'

'Oh – really? Aren't you taking something for granted?'

'No, I don't think so. And I mentioned the bedroom because I've been thinking about Tommy this week and I was hoping you'd tell me what he's really like.' I waited a moment or two, but when she didn't reply, I went on: 'He's wonderful on the stage, of course, but I'm beginning to feel that off the stage I dislike him as much as he seems to dislike me.'

'That's a kind of envy,' said Julie. 'Just because you're young, strong, good looking. Don't bother about it, my dear.'

'Ricarlo thinks he's mad,' I blurted out.

Julie didn't even blink at this. 'He's mostly a very clever naughty little boy, who can also be very kind and generous. Let's say on four days out of five.'

'What happens on the fifth day?'

'He can be a horror. And you know now why I can't walk out on him. This is my best chance to get back finally to where I belong. But it would be different – it would be much easier – if-' And there she stopped.

'If what?'

She didn't look at me. 'If somebody else was really making love to me,' she said very quietly. And then she did look at me. 'You know, Dick, it would be much better if you didn't keep sharing digs with your uncle and his idiot girl. Why don't you insist upon being on your own?'

'Because they know about digs – and I don't. It's quite simple. Next week we're in Burmanley. I don't know Burmanley – never been there. Uncle Nick and Cissie have lists of addresses.'

'Tommy has too. And I don't know anything about Burmanley either. But we're in Nottingham, aren't we, the week after – Christmas week, that is? All right then. I know some people in Nottingham you could stay with. Will you go there if I can arrange it?'

'Yes, of course, Julie. Let me know in good time, and tell me something about the people, then I can pretend to Uncle Nick and Cissie that I know them. But Burmanley—?'

She laughed. I'm afraid Burmanley will have to be touch-and-go again for us, darling. And that's what it had better be now. We must go, Dick.'

But we hadn't been as clever, under the Wall roof, as we thought we had. I discovered this after lunch on Saturday. It had been a tremendous lunch, with everybody present, ten of us in all – the five of us from the Empire, the two resident boarders, the Walls and the mysterious old Russian woman, who joined us on this special occasion. Annie the maid had a cold and had been sent to bed, so I volunteered to help with the heavy trays from and to the kitchen. Mrs Wall, the small and bony Varvara, who had done most of the cooking, commanded the old Russian woman and her husband George to get on with the washing up, and then took me into a little sitting-room beyond the kitchen, a room I had never seen before. There she poured out some brandy for both of us, lit one of those Russian cigarettes with long paper holders, and after we touched glasses and drank, she stared at me solemnly – she had huge black eyes – across the small table, and then began to talk. She still spoke with a thick Russian accent, and sometimes I missed what she was trying to say, so that I can't pretend to reproduce her speech exactly.

'Deek,' she began. 'I call you Deek because to you I am as mother. You are yong. Nice boy. Good boy, I theenk. So I speak with you as mother. I notice sometheeng. Also Mamushka notice sometheeng. Even my 'usban' George speaks of it. All of us, we see very plain.' There she stopped, produced more smoke, and squinted at me through it.

'I don't understand, Mrs Wall.' And at that moment I really didn't.

'Deek, I speak with you as mother – about loafe—'

'Loaf?' But then I realized she meant love.

'Between man and woman loafe is good. Between girl and boy, like you, loafe is good. Between boy and woman – no real true loafe. It is 'unger for sex, this kind of loafe. All there is between you, Deek, and Mees Blane, is 'unger for sex, animal feeling. No, foolish to deny. We have seen. We have already spoken of it. We *know*. With you, Deek, is because you are yong, strong man. You want girl. You have no girl. With this Mees Blane, it is not the same. She is mature woman, very strong in sex, anyone can see, and she has terrible 'unger.'

'She's got Tommy Beamish,' I muttered.

'Not man for her. I think not man for any woman. I go on Monday – first 'ouse – and I laugh and George he does not stop laughing. Beamish is very fonny comedian. Mees Blane is clever actress – not comedienne – but good for Beamish. On stage, good for him. Off stage – here – no good together, I think. It is all—' And here she almost spat out some Russian term that of course I didn't understand and I think she didn't want me to understand, just bringing it out to satisfy her own feelings. 'Deek, I speak again with you as mother. You have been to bed with this woman?'

'No, I haven't, Mrs Wall,' I replied rather sharply.

'Mind own business – eh? This is what I do all time here. If not, with theatricals, where are we? But you are yong. Nice boy. Good boy. Carry trays. Who else carry trays? Nobody. So I speak with you as mother. You have not been to bed with her. But already she has been to bed with you. She is putting you there in her mind. I have seen it in her eye. She wants you, Deek. Not for loafe – that is not possible between you – but because she has this terrible 'unger. And if you do nothing, then you cannot escape it. This is not nice yong girl – dreaming – Tatiana writing letter to Onegin – but you do not know Pushkin. This is woman – strong in passion. You will know this for first time. Not like yong girls. You will not have known such a woman. It can be madness for nice young man. It happened to my cousin with such an older woman 'ungry with passion. It can be like terrible disease. Not like real true loafe. No 'eart. No soul. No balance – no real understandings. Deek, I speak with you as mother.' She reached across and tapped the back of my hand with her forefinger. 'I am warning. Find nice young girl. No Mees Blane for you, please. Finish now. If you do not finish now, you will be sorry. I am warning.'

'That's right,' said George Wall, limping in at that moment with a towel over his arm. 'Tak' notice of her, lad. An' Ah'll tell yer for why. She's a bit what's-it – psychic – Varvara is, allus 'as bin. But she wouldn't 'ave said owt if she 'adn't taken a bit of a fancy to yer, lad. So yer can bet yer boots she means well. Though if yer onnything like Ah was at your age, ten to one yer won't tak' onny dam' notice.'

'You are idiot, George,' she screeched at him. 'It is serious. I am warning. Go away – wash dishes.'

'Nay, we've done.' He laid a heavy hand on my shoulder. 'She knows what she's talking about, Varvara does, and about this love business, where she comes from – they call a spade a spade – not like us. So just you remember what she's told you.' He gave my shoulder a squeeze. 'An' don't tak' offence, lad. Nowt 'ud bin said if we 'adn't liked yer. But we think yer best o't'lot. An' a word in time—'

'Be quiet. Now it is finished. Deek is good boy – and now he has had warning.'

And it was not so long afterwards, though in other places and when everything seemed so different, that there would suddenly return to my mind, without my wanting to recall it, that stuffy little back sitting-room, with its strange Russian smells, with the darkening Sheffield Saturday afternoon all round it, and with Varvara Wall, all huge black eyes, tapping her warning on the back of my hand. It became in the end my clearest memory of that week. But though in a sense she was only telling me what I knew already, on some obscure level of my mind from which no words came, I forgot her warning until it was too late. When I seemed to feel her tapping my hand again, I was a different Dick Herncastle, lost in a different world of savage joy, bewilderment and anguish.

4

In Burmanley I was sharing digs again with Uncle Nick and Cissie, and of course I never saw them early on Monday morning, when I left for the Empire. Burmanley, a city I'd never seen before, seemed to be mostly gloom, slush, trams, and shop windows decorated – if you can call it that – with tufts of cottonwool, for it was now December 15th, only ten days from Christmas. Our stuff had been safely delivered, but it was chilly and mournful backstage that morning, and both Sam and Ben seemed to have colds. When we could do no more, I took them away to stand them rum-and-coffee, and when I got back the band call had started and nearly everybody was ahead of me. I had hoped to see Julie, but for once old Courtenay was taking their call. Jennings was there but not Johnson, and when Jennings came off and saw me, he grinned and punched me on the chest. 'Son, stay right here,' he said. 'Give yourself a great great time. *The Musical Tiplows* are next – all three of 'em. I'd stay and catch up on some culture, but I'm meeting Hank in the saloon round the corner. So long, son!'

The Tiplows, all three, were more pernickety than ever, and it was nearly half-past twelve before I was free. Then I was surprised to find that Bill Jennings was back, apparently waiting for me to come off. 'Yes, sir, we're holding some kinda meeting back of the saloon,' he said. 'Your uncle said he wanted you there, so I said I'd come and get you, son. House manager's there – name of Carbett – looks like a duke ready for huntin' and fishin'. Also a newspaperman – *Mr Puff* of the *Burmanley Evening Mail*. Also Tommy and Miss Blane. Kinda conference, you might say, son, with the actors buying the drinks,' he continued as we went out. It was always hard to tell whether Bill Jennings was serious or not, but I did gather on our way to the pub that the manager, Carbett, was worried because it looked as if the week's business would be terrible, this being the week before Christmas, and he was anxious to discover if Uncle Nick and Tommy could suggest any publicity stunt that might bring people in, later in the week. And *Mr Puff*, who did the theatrical news and gossip for the evening paper, was there to offer any help he might be able to give. 'And when I left 'em, son,' Bill Jennings concluded, 'the only suggestion – though it's a good one – was *Same Again*.'

When we joined the group in the small back room of the pub – and they had the place to themselves – Uncle Nick was talking. 'Well then, it'll have to be the Indian Box. It seems to be all we've got. I used to use it in the act but then left it out because it wasn't spectacular enough. Oh – Richard – we've still got the Indian Box, haven't we?'

'I've never noticed it,' I began.

'Well, for God's sake, don't tell me we haven't got it.' He glared at me. 'Come on, we must have. It's a fancy Oriental box, about two feet long, one foot high and broad, with a big ornamental key.'

'I've never seen it.' And then, before he could interrupt me again, I added: 'But there's a small packing case about that size that I've never opened because Sam told me we weren't using it.'

'That's all right then, lad. That's it.' He looked round at the others. 'This is how we'll work it. But I warn you I'll need some help all round. Yes, from you, *Mr Puff*, and your paper – and if possible from one of your biggest shops.'

'I'll do my best, Mr Ollanton,' said the journalist, who was a small fat man in a shiny blue suit too small for him. 'But of course it depends on what you have in mind.'

'I've always found the *Evening Mail* very friendly,' said Carbett, the house manager, rather pompously. And he really was trying to look like a sporting landowner, and later I found that with his evening white-tie-and-tails he went to the length of wearing a monocle. 'And I've no doubt if our friend *Mr Puff* likes the idea he'll be able to persuade one of our biggest shops to co-operate with us. Smedley and

Jones, perhaps – eh? But of course it does depend on what you have in mind, Mr Ollanton.'

'Thanks for telling me,' said Uncle Nick dryly. 'All right, this is the effect.' He paused for a moment or two, and I was able to look across at Julie, who held up her glass inquiringly, as if asking me if I wanted a drink. 'You announce tonight that at the special request of some Burmanley friends and admirers, *Ganga Dun* will undertake to read the future. He will place in his Indian Box tonight or tomorrow morning some small sheets of paper on which will be written the *Evening Mail* headlines for Thursday. The box will be locked, corded and sealed in the shop tomorrow. It will remain in the shop window – or in any other prominent place there – until Thursday evening. It will then be taken by a representative of the shop to the Empire on Thursday evening, and will be opened on the stage at the second house and the headlines read out to the audience.'

'Boy, that's a lulu,' cried Hank Johnson.

'But, Mr Ollanton, can you really do this?' asked Carbett.

'If I can't, what the hell am I talking about?' said Uncle Nick, looking disgusted. 'I've done it before. Don't forget, I'm a magician.'

'Is it done by mirrors or electricity, Maestro?' Tommy asked. 'Or are there two boxes?'

'No, there aren't two boxes,' said Uncle Nick coldly. 'And from the time that box leaves me tomorrow, it's never in my possession. And it's locked, corded and sealed, with everybody looking on, in the shop, which then keeps the box on display. The only thing is – I'm not going to be there, because I'm *Ganga Dun*, and I don't propose to wear costume and make-up in the middle of the afternoon. Richard and one or two of you people will have to look after that. Well,' and he looked at the journalist, 'is that good enough for you?'

'It's a bobby-dazzler,' *Mr Puff* exclaimed, getting up. 'I'll telephone the office.'

'Half a minute,' said Tommy. 'What about Alderman Fishface?'

'Alderman Fishblick?'

'All the same. What – you don't know about him,' said Tommy, looking at several of us who obviously didn't know about Alderman Fishblick. 'Explain him, Mr Carbett – spread him out and peg him down.'

Carbett cleared his throat importantly. 'Alderman Fishblick is a local estate agent and a great man on the City Council. Teetotaller, nonsmoker, and dead against theatres and music halls. Music halls especially. Haunts of vice, he says we are. He was denouncing us again, last week—'

'Look here,' the journalist cut in. 'I must get on to the office. Somebody tell me quick where Alderman Fishblick comes into this Indian Box business.' He appealed to Tommy, then to Uncle Nick.

'If you people,' said Uncle Nick, 'will get Alderman Fishblick into one of your headlines on Thursday, I can guarantee that whoever reads those headlines on the stage on Thursday will have to mention Alderman Fishblick.'

'Well, I can't give you as good a guarantee,' the journalist told him, 'but I'll talk to our chaps. I know there's a Council meeting on Thursday morning, and Fishblick nearly always makes a fuss about something. But I must go. I won't telephone, I'll go straight back to the office. Now, Mr Ollanton, can I say you've accepted a challenge to perform your magic Indian Box trick in Burmanley? Right. And you're ready to send the box tomorrow to Smedley and Jones's for them to keep until Thursday? Right. I can get this into the paper tonight. Toodleoo, everybody!' Exit *Mr Puff*.

'I'm working something out for Alderman Fishface myself,' said Tommy. 'It'll be something to do with his estate agency. And I'll want some help, Nick. Like you on that suffragette caper at Leeds. I'll need you and Cissie and young Herncastle. And you Bill, and you Hank.'

'We'll be right in there, man, pitching,' cried Bill.

'So long as it brings pain and sorrow to Alderman Fishblick,' said Hank Johnson solemnly, 'I'm there by your side, Chief. And the drinks are now on me.'

But Uncle Nick told me to go back, unpack the box, make sure the big ornamental key was with it, then take key and box up to his dressing-room. 'We'll have a bite of lunch at the *Crown*,' he added. 'Then I'll make certain the box is all in order before anything comes out in the paper. So off you go, lad.'

At three o'clock on Tuesday afternoon, I was carrying the box, which looked old and very Oriental, into the furniture department (Third Floor) of Smedley and Jones's store. There must have been at least a hundred people there, all that the room could hold when a space had been cleared for us in the middle. I was accompanied – and that is the right term, because it was all done very solemnly – by Tommy and Julie, Jennings and Johnson, who somehow managed to look grave and important, and the manager, Carbett, no longer in his sporting costume and looking rather like an undertaker. Smedley and Jones were represented by the assistant manager, one R. G. Perks, who had called on Uncle Nick at the Empire between the first and second houses, the night before, and who had been nervous then and seemed even more nervous now, as if he thought the box might explode. The Press was represented by *Mr Puff* and several younger and dressier colleagues, looking very cynical, as if they knew how the trick was done, which they certainly didn't. (I had spent some time wondering about it myself.) There was only one person there even more nervous than R. G. Perks, and that was young Richard Herncastle, for I was making my first appearance in public off the stage and without the benefit of Indian costume and make-up.

When we were all ready, R. G. Perks said rather shakily: 'Er. Ladies and er Gentlemen er. On behalf of er Smedley and Jones er glad to welcome you er interesting experiment er now call upon er Mr Carbett er Empire Theatre.'

Carbett told them severely that Burmanley was well known for its sporting spirit and that *Ganga Dun*, now appearing at the Empire in one of the greatest magical acts on the variety stage anywhere, had accepted a challenge to perform here in Burmanley perhaps his most extraordinary feat of magic, and that they would now be addressed by the popular American entertainers, Jennings and Johnson, also on this week's great bill at the Empire.

'Folks,' Bill Jennings began, 'I've been in vaudeville quite a time – not on this side but the other side of the water. And I've seen some great magical and thought-reading acts. But what *Ganga Dun* says he'll do – this beats all. Of course he hasn't done it yet – and maybe he can't do it – what do you say, Hank?'

'I say, Bill – and friends – I say *Ganga Dun's* already finished what he said he'd do. In that box – hold it higher, son, so the folks can see it – in that box, I say, *Ganga Dun* has already placed a sheet or two of paper on which he has written – believe it or not, friends – what will be the headlines of Thursday's *Evening Mail*. Yes, Tommy? Mr Tommy Beamish, folks.'

Uncle Nick hadn't wanted Tommy to speak: he felt that if Tommy started gagging and had everybody laughing, nobody would give me and the box any serious attention. But Tommy insisted, and here he was, standing on a chair: 'Now boys, girls and ratepayers, I think we can't lose. If on Thursday night, second house at the Empire, somebody opens the box, reads out the headlines, and they're all dead right, we've seen something as good as the Indian rope trick. And if they're all wrong, then we have a good laugh at poor old *Ganga Dun* – though I must tell you he isn't poor, he isn't old, and he keeps frightening the life out of me. He's *sin-is-ter* – honestly, he is – he's *sin-is-ter* and *mal-evo-lent*. And he told me yesterday – he speaks English on Mondays – that it isn't done by mirrors or by electricity – so how the blue blazes does he do it? Remember, people, he never sees this box again until it's opened on the Empire stage. And now my distinguished colleague, Lady Macbeth – I beg her pardon, Miss Julie Blane – will tell you all about the box.'

As a matter of fact, Julie, dark, pale-faced, wearing black furs, did look as if she'd just played – or was about to play — Lady Macbeth. She'd told us she couldn't improvise a speech, so Uncle Nick and I between us had written something for her to learn by heart. So now, making full use of her dear and beautifully modulated voice, she made the most effective speech of the afternoon. But I ought to add that during the morning Uncle Nick, with his usual attention to detail, had rehearsed both her and me, her for her timing, me for the locking, cording, sealing, of the box.

'Ladies and Gentlemen, I hope that you can see Mr Herncastle, who is *Ganga Dun's* chief assistant. He will now lock the box. There! And now, with the help of Mr Perks, representing Messrs Smedley and Jones, Mr Herncastle will secure the box with cords. After that they will seal the knots with sealing wax, making use of a signet ring owned by Mr Perks. While they are doing this – and I hope you can all see – I want to explain what will happen to the box. From now until it is opened on the Empire stage on Thursday night, the box will never leave this store, where it will be prominently displayed – in the window to the right of the main door, Mr Perks tells me. I'm sure you have complete confidence in Mr Perks and Messrs Smedley and Jones – I know I have – so that if they tell us on Thursday night that the box has never left the store and that nobody has attempted to open it, we shall believe them. And Mr Perks will be responsible for taking the box straight from here on to the Empire stage. Ganga Dun has sworn that he will not even look at it through the window. Now, there it is, ladies and gentlemen – securely corded and sealed.' There was some applause. 'Mr Perks will now take it down to its place in the window. And that's all, ladies and gentlemen. Until Thursday night, of course. Thank you!'

There was more applause, and then after Perks, carrying the box high above his head, hurried off, people began to move away. 'You were jolly good, Julie,' I told her.

'Thanks, Dick.' She lowered her voice. 'But I wish you'd tell me how he thinks he's going to pull off this trick.'

'I would if I knew. But I don't know. All I do know is that he's done it before – and doesn't think much of it. Perhaps because he didn't invent it himself. Uncle Nick prefers the effects he invents himself.'

'I'll bet he does, knowing your nice kind Uncle Nick. Oh – Tommy wants us. Yes, Tommy dear?'

'Not you, Julie dear. This is for the Ganga Dundians.' He turned to me. 'It's about the Alderman Fishface gag. I've got it all worked out for tomorrow morning. Tonight in my dressing-room I'll explain what everybody has to do. So tell Nick and Sloppy Cis. Right? Not between the shows – I want to take it easy – but after the last house.'

I realize that nowadays, in a different world, the elaborate practical joke we played on Alderman Fishblick, that Wednesday morning in Burmanley, may seem childish, ridiculously unworthy of the care and attention that six or seven adult performers devoted to it. But in its defence there are three things worth mentioning. First, there still existed then a tradition of practical jokes played by stage people, coming down from the days of Toole and Henry Irving, before he became grand and solemn. Secondly, Alderman Fishblick, who really knew nothing about music halls, had repeatedly made public attacks upon them. Thirdly, variety performers like Tommy Beamish and Uncle Nick couldn't help welcoming anything that broke the monotony and boredom of those winter days, when the weather was too bad for golf or for excursions in their new toy, the motor-car. As Uncle Nick told me more than once, especially when he was happily at work on a new illusion, the chief reason why so many variety stars drank too much or got into trouble chasing women too hard, was that they were so bored, after the night's zest and excitement, by these empty days in towns they didn't like. Burmanley was one of them; the weather was bad that week, when it was neither Christmas nor not-Christmas but all cottonwool snowflakes and seedy Santa Clauses; and so we put on a special performance for Alderman Fishblick in his capacity as estate agent. We established our headquarters for the operation, as it might be called now, at a pub not far from where Philips and Fishblick, Estate Agents and Auctioneers, had their offices, so we all knew what was happening in there; and this explains how I can attempt to describe that strange morning from the point of view of poor Fishblick.

So far it had been a dull morning, with some sleet slashing at the windows, and Fishblick, after losing his temper with his secretary, Miss Cleat, and telling the office boy that if he didn't brighten up his ideas he would have to go, didn't know what to do with himself and so began examining the list of properties that Philips and Fishblick had for sale or rent. The chief of these, Hickerston Hall, a white elephant no longer white, had now been empty for over two years, and Fishblick must have been wondering what he could do with it, when a Mr and Mrs Primp were announced, wanting to see him on most urgent business.

'Alderman Fishblick,' said Mr Primp, shaking hands enthusiastically, 'you've probably heard of me – Primp, Tea Merchant, of Mincing Lane. Yes, I'm Primp of Mincing Lane.' He had a straggling beard, eyeglasses, and a high quavering voice. (When Tommy Beamish really took trouble, he could be superb.) Mrs Primp, be-furred and veiled, was both aloof and elegant and looked very rich, Julie having played many such parts.

'Now what about Hickerston Hall?' said Mr Primp. 'I'm thinking of retiring, and yesterday Mrs Primp and I took a look at Hickertson Hall, only from the outside of course, and Mrs Primp fancied it at once – didn't you, dear?'

'I felt something might be done with it,' said Mrs Primp, in a deep contralto that was as rich as her appearance. 'But of course we must look over it.'

'Naturally, naturally, Mrs Primp,' Fishblick told her, trying to keep his excitement out of his voice. 'It's a remarkable property – and it's just possible I might be able to offer you a slight reduction on the asking price—'

Mr Primp waved this aside. 'Primp of Mincing Lane doesn't haggle,' he announced. 'The point is – when can you show us the house? We must return to London tonight, I must warn you, Fishblick.'

'We can go out there now—'

'Impossible. But if you'll call for us at half-past two this afternoon at the Midland Hotel—'

'Of course, Mr Primp. I'll arrange for a car—'

'Meanwhile,' said Mrs Primp, in a tone deeper still, 'you must give us all particulars—'

'Just what I was about to do, Mrs Primp.' Fishblick was so excited he fumbled for a moment or two at his papers. 'Yes, here they are. A very fine property indeed for any man of means—'

'Mr Primp has considerable means, Alderman Fishblick,' said Mrs Primp coldly.

'And I like to do business like this.' And Mr Primp brought his hand down flat on the desk, glaring through his eyeglasses at the startled Fishblick. 'Half-past two at the Midland Hotel, then. And don't keep me waiting. Ask anybody in Mincing Lane about Primp. I don't like any dilly-dallying and shilly-shallying.'

'Yes, Mr Primp. I'm sure you'll find—'

'Good morning to you,' said Mr Primp sharply. 'Come, my dear. No, don't move, Fishblick. You must make your arrangements.'

Fifteen minutes later, while Fishblick was still trying to discover the financial status of Primp of Mincing Lane, Colonel Sloman was announced. He was a tall, dark, imposing-looking man, not unlike a younger Lord Kitchener. He was accompanied by his daughter (Cissie, quietly dressed and with no make-up) and his son, me with a large fair moustache that Uncle Nick had made out of crepe hair while he gave himself a large dark moustache. Incidentally, this Fishblick performance showed me what a good actor Uncle Nick might have been.

'I'm Colonel Sloman, late Chief of Police in Penang. You people are the agents for Hickerston Hall, aren't you? Come, come, my dear sir, either you are or you aren't. If you aren't, say so, I've no time to waste.'

'Yes, we are, Colonel Sloman. You want to look over the house?'

'Of course I want to look over the house. And so do my son and my daughter. We've no intention of buying a house without looking over it. Do you take me for an idiot, man?'

Fishblick, though still feeling rather dazed, made a move round his desk. He was a gingerish, beaky, narrow-mouthed man with eyes not unlike the glass stoppers used in those days for ginger-beer bottles. 'I can take you out there at once, Colonel Sloman—'

'No, you can't. I have an appointment with the Lord Lieutenant – an old friend. Have to be this afternoon. Only time. Call for us at half-past two this afternoon – County Hotel.'

'Oh – dear!' Fishblick was flustered. 'I'm not quite sure—'

'What the devil do you mean, man?' Colonel Sloman thundered. 'If you don't want to sell the property, then say so. *Not quite sure!* Good God – aren't there any real men of business left in this country?'

'It's only a question of *re-arranging* something,' Fishblick began desperately.

'Re-arranging something! Don't talk nonsense, man. I'm seriously interested in this property – and I don't need to tell you, man, that it's obviously been on the market for some time – and if you're at all anxious to sell it, then you will show us over the house this afternoon and will therefore call for us promptly at two-thirty at the County Hotel. I don't care about your arrangements, I have my own. Two-thirty sharp then, at the County. Come along, you two.'

Now in a lather, Fishblick followed us out, trying to explain about his arrangements and re-arrangements, but Uncle Nick refused to listen and waved him away.

It must have been while he was still trying to leave a message for Mr Primp at a Midland Hotel that had never heard of him, that poor Fishblick found himself staring at two extraordinary Americans, who wore unusually large round spectacles and Uncle Sam beards. They wanted to look at Hickerston Hall too, not as a possible private residence, for they lived at Oshkosh close to their main factory, but as a building that might be adapted to the manufacture of their special line of toys.

'Yes, *sir*,' said one of them emphatically, 'Simon and Simon's world-ree-nowned Golliwogs and Teddy Bears.'

'Golliwogs and Teddy Bears?' Fishblick faltered, probably wondering by this time if he were going out of his mind.

'The kiddies' joy in seventeen different countries, sir,' said the other American, staring severely at Fishblick through his enormous spectacles. 'We'd aim to make Hickerston Hall the centre of a noo thriving community.'

'And Simon and Simon are no pikers, sir,' his partner said, staring with equal severity. 'If the place is right, the price will be right – yes, *sir*.'

'So we'll take a look round this afternoon. We'll be waiting for you at the Red Lion – say, at half-past two this afternoon—'

'Only time we have, Alderman. Take it or leave it. If you want to do business with Simon and Simon, you'll be there with an automobile right on the dot at half-past-two.'

They gave the wretched Fishblick no opportunity to cut in. 'Simon and Simon. Total assets five-and-a-half million dollars. Golliwogs and Teddy Bears round the world. See you at halfpast two.'

'Boy,' cried Jennings as they joined us in the pub, 'the poor guy's nuts. When we left him, he didn't know what to say or where to begin.'

'And there'll be hell to pay at tomorrow morning's City Council meeting,' said Johnson. 'He'll rate a headline or I'm Lilian Russell. And mine's a Scotch, Tommy.'

It was decided that the Indian Box should be opened, at the second house on Thursday, not during our act but at the end of Tommy's, after he had taken his call. So then, on we went: Uncle Nick still as *Ganga Dun*, Tommy and Julie, Perks of Smedley and Jones carrying the Indian Box, and I without costume and make-up, back in my best suit. We had a full house, and indeed business had been better ever since we announced the stunt, *Mr Puff* having given us some publicity every evening. Under Uncle Nick's careful direction, we had worked out in advance everything that had to be done on the stage.

Tommy began. 'Ladies, Gentlemen and Friends, this is Mr Perks of Smedley and Jones, and he's here to testify that the Magic Box – there it is – has been in his possession – or Smedley's or Jones's – ever since it was locked, corded and sealed in plain view on Tuesday afternoon, and that *Ganga Dun* has never been near it. That's right, isn't it, Mr Perks?'

After clearing his throat rather desperately, Perks said that it was.

Julie now explained how *Ganga Dun* had accepted the challenge to place in the Box, on Tuesday morning, papers on which would be written headlines appearing in tonight's final edition of the *Evening Mail*. 'If he's done it, I can't imagine how,' she concluded. 'But we do know he hasn't been near the Box since Tuesday morning. I'll now ask Mr Perks and Mr Herncastle, *Ganga Dun's* assistant, to break the seals and untie the cords.'

Perks and I did this, slowly and solemnly. Perks was now breaking into a sweat, and I couldn't help feeling uneasy and anxious, in spite of my confidence in Uncle Nick. If the trick didn't work – and it was still a mystery to me how it could work – Burmanley might begin to throw things at us.

It was now my turn to speak. For the last half hour I had been muttering to myself what I had to say. 'I will now ask *Ganga Dun* to hand me the key, and, to guard against any possible deception, ladies and gentlemen, I will give the key to Mr Perks so that he can open the box.' I went across and bowed gravely to Uncle Nick, who ceremoniously produced the large ornamental key. I held it high as I crossed the stage to Perks. He opened the box and took out of it three pieces of thin paper, which he smoothed out in order to read what was written on them. But Tommy, who wasn't a star for nothing, grabbed them and read out the three headlines. The first was something about Lloyd George, the second about the price of turkeys, and the third, which raised a great yell of laughter, said *Angry Scene at Council Meeting: Alderman Fishblick Again*. As they were still laughing and cheering, Tommy handed the three sheets to Perks, for him to confirm that these were the headlines written on them. Perks nodded vigorously, but couldn't make himself heard. Uncle Nick moved forward a pace or two, to take a bow, and was applauded, but then signalled for the curtain to come down. I could see that he was furious.

'Why the devil did *you* have to interfere?' he demanded of Tommy angrily. 'I'd arranged for this chap Perks to read them out.'

'Much better for me to do it, old boy. He'd never have got that big laugh on Fishface.'

'You look after your laughs, and let me look after my tricks. Most of 'em out there think the headlines weren't on those three sheets, that you were just remembering tonight's headlines.'

'Oh – I don't think so, Nick old boy,' said Tommy airily.

'You don't think at all, that's your trouble,' Uncle Nick growled, and went striding off.

'Now, now, now!' And Tommy hurried after him.

Julie and I went up to our dressing-rooms together, taking our time and keeping close. 'But, Dick darling, how on earth did he do it? I mean, those really *were* the headlines, weren't they? And there they were in the box, and I'm sure little Mr Perks didn't cheat. But how could Nick have known what they'd be, I mean, on Tuesday morning? He can't really tell the -future, can he?'

And I think that if I'd said he could, so long as I'd looked and sounded solemn, she wouldn't have contradicted me. Though no fool, Julie had the deeply feminine desire to defy rationality, logic, evidence, and to welcome any sign of the unpredictable, the marvellous, the miraculous. I have come to believe that this is a good and not a bad thing in woman, helping to prevent us from being imprisoned by our rationality and our theories of cause-and-effect. But I couldn't accept Uncle Nick as a seer, and told her so. 'It's a trick – and one that Uncle Nick has a contempt for – but how it's worked, I don't know yet.'

'I'm madly curious, darling.' She stopped and came closer still. 'Will you promise to tell me as soon as you know?'

'No, Julie, I won't.'

'You wretched boy! The first thing I ever ask you to do for me – and you say *No-oh, Joolie, Ah won't*. Very well, I won't tell you about those people in Nottingham – for next week. You remember?'

'Yes, of course. The people I'm to stay with. But listen, Julie, I made a solemn promise to Uncle Nick never to explain to anybody his tricks and illusions. It's his living, Julie, and mine too just now. Do you want me to break solemn promises?'

She laughed. 'Certainly, so long as you didn't make them to me. All right, darling, I'll forgive you. And here's their name and address.' The folded paper seemed to come out of her waist belt. 'You needn't write to them unless you've decided not to go—'

'Of course I haven't. That's where I'm going.'

'Don't bother writing then. They're expecting you. And I hope you'll be expecting me – unless we're out of luck – some time on Christmas Day. No, darling, come on. Tommy'll be wondering what's become of me.'

When I reached Uncle Nick's dressing-room, he was telling a couple of young reporters to go away. When they had gone and he began changing, he said: 'They even wanted me to tell 'em how it was done. Young twerps! I didn't invent the trick and I don't think much of it, but I'm not making a present of it to the newspapers. Let 'em work it out for themselves. I had to after I first saw it.'

'Julie Blane was asking me to tell her how it was done,' I remarked, with the best casual air I could manage.

'Tommy may have put her up to it. What did you say, lad?'

'That I didn't know how you did it, and that even if I did know, I wouldn't tell her. I'd made a solemn promise, I said.'

'Good for you. Though God knows what she'd worm out of you, if both of you had your pants off. Watch that one, lad. By the way, the management sent this bottle round.' He was now pouring out champagne for us both. 'And it's the least they could do, seeing as how I've been working overtime for 'em. And I hate doing that Box trick. It's too bloody cheeky and it's got no style to it. I wouldn't put my name to it.' He half-emptied his glass, then looked at me. 'Just think carefully, lad, weigh it all up, and then if you can't tell me how it's done, you oughtn't to be working in my act. Take your time.'

I did. He'd finished changing and had tidied up – Uncle Nick was very tidy and he refused to employ a 'dresser', though he could well afford one – before we spoke again. 'Well, lad, what's the verdict?'

'It must be the key, Uncle Nick. There's no other explanation.'

'Quite right. I look at the headlines, write three of 'em on special thin paper. The three sheets are rolled up and inserted into the key. When the key unlocks the box it also shoots out the rolled paper, so by the time the lid's lifted, there are your headlines, waiting inside the box. There's a neat little spring inside the key, a nice job, otherwise the whole bloody thing's childish.' He gave himself some more champagne. 'Keep this to yourself, lad, but I'm just beginning to get an idea – and I've done no work on it yet – for an effect that could really give 'em the creeps. But I'll need another dwarf. However, it'll probably take months to get it right,' he ended, quite happily.

I remember thinking then – and it shows how my mind was working – that the sooner he concentrated on this two-dwarf effect, the better it would be for Julie and me. Perhaps the luck was running our way.

On Saturday I told him and Cissie that I wouldn't be sharing their digs in Nottingham because I'd already arranged to stay with some people I knew there. He didn't care, but Cissie was disappointed. 'Oh – Dick, I did hope we'd all be together for Christmas.'

'Don't start that, girl,' Uncle Nick told her. 'I hate Christmas.'

'Nick, you don't.'

'I do. It's all so stupid.'

'But what about the kiddies?'

'What about the kiddies?' It was brutal mimicry. 'Well, what about 'em? They like Christmas because they get things given. They'd like any other time when they got things given. Middle of April – end of October – any time. The rest of us are just diddled by the shopkeepers, who raise their prices because they're so full of the Christmas spirit of goodwill and peace to all men. I had a Christmas card today – all about old friendship and loving thoughts by the fireside – from the biggest rogue of an agent I've ever had to deal with. No, don't talk to me about Christmas, girl. I'll endure it, but I'm damned if I'll enjoy it. I earn a living by deceiving other people, but I don't have to deceive myself.'

5

I liked the look of Nottingham, which I'd never visited before, and the weather there was better than what we'd had in Sheffield and Burmanley. And Julie's friends, Alfred and Rose Bentwood, gave me the best room I'd had, quite big, with plenty of space around its double bed, well-carpeted and with a fine new gasfire. It was of course their guest room, and, though I insisted upon paying for it, they were really doing me a favour at Julie's request. Before she married, Rose had been on the stage, playing small parts. Alfred Bentwood had a comfortable job with some wholesale tobacconist. They were both about forty, both round and jolly, great theatre-and-party-goers, probably always welcome because they would laugh at anything and laugh nearly as much at nothing. When I first met them, rather late on Sunday night, they laughed so much I thought there must be something odd about my appearance, my fly must be unbuttoned or something; but then I soon realized they laughed like that all the time. They were kind and generous; there was plenty of food and drink in the house, and you could help yourself to anything, day and night; and they were fun to be with for half-an-hour or so, but after that you began to feel there was too much laughing. Julie came out to tea on the Monday – she and Tommy were staying at the *Flying Horse* down in the Poultry – but we'd only opportunity and time for some quick clutching and kissing before I had to leave for the first house.

If this had been an ordinary week, I think I would have enjoyed Nottingham and staying with the Bentwoods. But it was Christmas week, with Christmas Day itself on Thursday (and I apologize for so much always happening on Thursdays in these reminiscences, but that's how it was, so I can't help it), and because it was Christmas week, everything was different and somehow wrong. I suppose I felt we ought not to have been there, at least not until Boxing Day. The audiences were small and were mostly thinking about something else, presents or parties. Uncle Nick especially hated it – though he liked Nottingham in the ordinary way – and cut the *Vanishing Cyclist* out of the act because he said the audiences didn't deserve it. At the second house on Wednesday, Christmas Eve, Tommy was almost rolling drunk but I must admit, for I went down to watch the act, he was also very very funny. As for Jennings and Johnson, they were gently stewed all the week.

However, homeless though we were – and felt – we did our best, and scurried around the crowded shops buying presents. I bought some cigars for Uncle Nick, a scarf for Cissie, some old malt whisky for Jennings and Johnson, and a brooch I couldn't really afford for Julie. I kept thinking about sending a wire to Nancy, at the Theatre Royal, Plymouth, because for some reason or other, and in spite of Julie, I couldn't drive her out of my mind, especially on Wednesday, but in the end I didn't. I also kept wondering what was going to happen on Christmas Day, when of course we wouldn't be playing and the whole town would be shuttered and turned away from us. I knew the Bentwoods were going out for the day, to laugh their heads off with relatives; and up to Christmas Eve Julie hadn't told me what she was doing but had merely smiled and looked mysterious and murmured something about being patient. By the second house on Wednesday I was beginning to feel rather desperate about it.

But then – and perhaps the whole thing was her doing – Julie came round during the interval and invited us to a Christmas dinner Tommy was giving at the *Flying Horse*. Uncle Nick, Cissie and I, Jennings and Johnson and Ricarlo, were being invited from our show, and there would also be some people Tommy knew who were playing in the pantomime.

'I'm glad about this, Julie,' I whispered at my dressing-room door. I had a small dressing-room to myself, that week. 'But is it going to be any good to us?'

'I think it might, darling. And I'll give you a signal when I think you ought to leave. Oh – and don't eat and drink too much.' And her laugh floated back as she hurried away.

A little scene in Uncle Nick's dressing-room, later that night, made me realize once again what an unpredictable character he was. We'd been talking about putting back the *Vanishing Cyclist* for Boxing Day, when I stopped a moment and then suddenly exclaimed: 'I'm a fool – and a mean fool at that.'

'Now what is it, lad?'

'It's Sam and Ben and Barney. Y'know, uncle, unless something's going wrong, I never think of them as themselves during the act. And this week they're not dressing with me. So I've forgotten all about them. Not asked them what they're doing for Christmas. Not bought them anything. And now it's too late.'

'It might have been but for me,' said Uncle Nick dryly. 'They'll do all right at their digs. I've asked. I've also sent 'em a big hamper – everything in it they could want – and it has your name on it as well as mine. Cissie's too, of course.'

'Oh – that's wonderful. What a relief!'

'I dare say. But you should think, lad. Keep things in mind, the way I do. And now I'll trouble you for half a sovereign, Mr Herncastle, for your share of the hamper.'

'All right, Uncle Nick. Here's your ten shillings. But would you have asked for it if I'd said nothing?'

'No. Never a word.'

I laughed. 'So if I'd never mentioned Sam and Ben and Barney, I'd have saved ten shillings.'

'That's right, lad.'

'You'd have paid my share out of your own pocket—'

'I would. But you'd have gone down in my estimation, don't forget, Richard. And my esteem ought to be worth ten bob to you—'

'Yes, of course. But I must say, Uncle Nick, you're not an easy man to understand—'

'That's because I'm sensible through and through. And thoroughly sensible chaps like me are getting rare.' And he didn't say this with a smile; he meant it. 'Most of you now are more or less barmy. Well, I'm not. Oh – and watch yourself tomorrow at this dinner of Tommy's.'

'Why should I? What d'you mean?'

'Don't come it, lad. I mean Miss Julie Blane. Do you think nobody noticed you, week before last, at Sheffield? Cissie's got no sense but she has sharp eyes and ears. And I don't miss much. Now, lad, none of that tomorrow. We want a Merry Christmas, not trouble.'

'I thought you didn't believe in Merry Christmases.'

'I don't. We're mostly just kidding ourselves. But I know about trouble, and I don't want any of it. So watch where your hands go tomorrow, lad.'

I got up late on Christmas morning, had nothing but tea and a slice of toast, admired the presents that the Bentwoods had given each other, and saw them go off, laden with fancy packages and still laughing heartily, to spend the rest of the day at his brother's out Trent Bridge way. This was about noon. We'd been told to be at the *Flying Horse* at one o'clock, so I spent half-an-hour putting my presents together and then taking down the bits of holly and pink paper-chains that Mrs Bentwood had put up in my room: they didn't seem right for it, somehow. The day was cold and might soon be colder, so I left the gasfire on, but not at full, and put a saucer of water in front of it so that the room wouldn't seem too dry when I came back. I couldn't escape the feeling that something important was going to happen in that room before the day was done.

Off I went, carrying my presents and walking rather slowly because I had plenty of time, turning into North and then South Sherwood Street, on my way down to the Poultry. I was in two moods that ought to have cancelled out, but they didn't. Either they stayed on two different levels or I oscillated between them. With the first, I was sharply expectant and rather excited. After all I was on my way to what would probably be a lively and rich Christmas dinner, in a famous old pub, and Julie would be there, and anything might happen, then or afterwards. Julie glittered among these hopeful thoughts like the fairy on top of a Christmas tree. In the second mood I felt empty and sad. I may have been influenced by the Christmas morning look of the place, the blank-faced and muffled streets, the way in which the town seemed to turn its back on me, after telling me it was at home and I was homeless. All that may explain why I kept feeling empty and sad. But I believe now there was something else, nothing to do with the day and the place but entirely concerned with this Julie affair. I believe that just before I really began this affair I had a foretaste of what the end would be.

Fourteen of us sat down to dinner. Added to our eight were a Principal Boy (buxom, forty), Principal Girl (all curls and dimples), Fairy Queen (big blonde, wonderful for Ricarlo), Demon King (oldish baritone, all eyebrows and blue chin), and the Broker's Men, the comical Begby Brothers (small, any age, battered faces), all of course from the pantomime. My place at the table was between Cissie and the Fairy Queen sitting across from Tommy and Julie. I asked Julie where poor old Courtenay was, but she shook her head and frowned at me; I guessed that he was out of favour with Tommy. (So was I, but I learnt afterwards that Julie wangled my invitation by telling Tommy that after all I was Nick's nephew and that Nick wouldn't come if I couldn't.) We'd already exchanged our presents while we were drinking pink gins or sherry-and-bitters. Uncle Nick gave me a wonderful assortment of watercolours and brushes; Cissie had two ties for me; and Jennings and Johnson, in exchange for my old malt whisky, handed me a case with three fine pipes in it; but all I exchanged with Julie was a quick whisper that we'd do our present-giving later. Then we sat down to an enormous amount of food and drink. The women – except Julie, who always kept her own cool style in public – were at first immensely ladylike though determinedly winsome and eyelash-fluttering but then, as the wine and whisky went down and crackers were pulled and paper hats donned at all angles, they loosened up, read out fortunes and riddles from the crackers, screamed with laughter as the jokes of the comedians became broader and broader. Uncle Nick, his cigar alight and now into his second bottle of champagne, wrapped three little toys from crackers in coloured paper, rolled the tiny parcel between his hands, then opened it to show us that the toys had changed into a packet of cigarettes. Ricarlo, to please the Fairy Queen, juggled with a fork and a spoon and four unpulled crackers. Tommy kept putting on different paper hats and making speeches to fit them, and he was very funny until he became too noisy and incoherent. Jennings and Johnson, finding vaguely appropriate hats, did an act as a Nevada Sheriff and a Red Indian. Julie and I laughed and clapped with the rest, but every time our glances met I knew that, like me, she wasn't really there and one of them. Then Tommy, attempting a vast gesture, tipped his chair back and fell with it and had to be helped to his feet by Uncle Nick and Hank Jennings; but, glassy-eyed and babbling, he insisted upon being given another drink. By this time, everybody was leaving the table. I caught a look from Julie, and in the movement and confusion I slipped out unnoticed.

Remembering what Julie had said, I'd not eaten too much but I had drunk my share of Burgundy, and I was feeling neither empty nor sad as I walked at a smart pace back to the Bentwoods', clutching my presents. I went straight up to my room, turned up the gasfire, drew the curtains, and tried a few different lighting effects. The Bentwoods had electric lights – and in 1913 a lot of people still hadn't – and had plenty of them; my room had a ceiling cluster, draped in yellow silk, and six pink-shaded bulbs on the walls; so that it was possible to try various effects. I unpacked Uncle Nick's watercolour gear but I felt too restless to examine it and gloat over it; and anybody who wants to find a touch of symbolism there may do so. I put on my slippers, had a wash, tried on one of the ties that Cissie had given me, and didn't like it. All the time of course I was wondering if and when Julie would come. The thought that I might wait hours and hours, all for nothing in the end, was unbearable. Yet if I'd suddenly had a definite message to say she couldn't come, I could have borne it, I might even have felt relieved. If this seems inconsistent, I can't help it; that is how I felt. I padded around, picked up things and put them down without looking at them, went out to the head of the stairs several times, and generally slowed time up by not trying to pass it in some sensible way. I kept on looking at my watch, of course, though there was no point in knowing whether it was now twenty-past four or half-past, and anyhow I told myself that my watch wasn't reliable, which indeed it wasn't. And then, just as I'd almost decided she couldn't be coming, I heard the front door open and I rushed downstairs.

After we'd embraced and kissed and she began taking off her outdoor things, she said: 'Did it seem ages, darling? I left the very first moment I could. Tommy had to be carted to bed not very long after you left, but then I had to make sure he was fast asleep. And of course I had to walk here.'

'And now I can give you your present, Julie.' And I gave her the brooch.

'But it's lovely,' she cried. 'A lovely old piece.'

'Spanish Eighteenth Century,' I told her proudly.

'Darling, could you afford it?'

'No, but I did.'

'Sweet.' She kissed me. 'Now here's what I got for you. I noticed you hadn't one.' It was a wrist-watch, not common then as they became later, during the war; a fine one too; I was delighted. Then after I'd thanked and kissed her, she said: 'I hope your room's warm. It's bitter outside, and it's rather cold down here.'

'I've been warming my room for hours, Julie. You'll see.'

'I'll do that now. Give me five minutes, darling, then come up. And bring some whisky and glasses. If you haven't any whisky, take the Bentwoods' – Rose won't mind. But five minutes, please, darling.'

It was exactly six-and-a-half minutes, by my new watch, when I tapped on the door of my room with the whisky bottle, out of which I'd already had a nip, and then walked in, not quite knowing what to expect. She was standing there completely naked.

Something happened then that was never to happen again. For several moments, while she smiled and kept silent and I never spoke a word, I took in her beauty as I might have done that of a landscape or a noble picture, outside desire, without wanting to possess her. Nowadays we live in a world of nudes and semi-nudes, of tanned arms and shoulders, calves and thighs, so often exposed and browned that their skin seems like a kind of clothing; but then, when women were covered from top to toe, a nakedness like this was an extraordinary revelation, as if a living statue, pearly, opalescent, faintly glowing, had miraculously stepped out of the dark huddle of clothes. And Julie really was beautiful in her nakedness. Below the loosened dark hair and the delicate, slightly ravaged face, her body was full, almost opulent; the firm half-globes of her breasts a surprise after those hollowed cheeks; her thighs magnificent above the rounded knees, very feminine and having a kind of touching innocence, that she was keeping pressed together; and I had time even to wonder why painters could have offered us a sort of pinkish pulp instead of that dark triangle of pubic hair which gave the intricate pale rose-and-gold modelling of the body the final sharp accent it needed. And if all this seems too detached and cold-blooded for a normally sexed youth of twenty, seeing for the first time a mature woman who had just undressed herself for him, I can't help it, for that is how it was, though of course this pure seeing, this detachment belonging to the painter in me, only lasted a few moments.

Then she moved, and I moved faster, and we were kissing wildly, and my clothes were coming off, and already she was beginning to moan. This very first act of love didn't last long, and I chiefly remember being overwhelmed – almost terrified, in my fumbling inexperience, by the force and depth of her sexuality, which nothing I had known up to then had led me to expect, so that I didn't feel I was having Julie Blane but had been suddenly pulled into a huge strange world, or perhaps an ocean, of moaning and frenzied flesh, of pleasure that was also pain, and back into a time before names had been given or personality had emerged.

We sprawled in glistening exhaustion near the fire, had some whisky and smoked for a while. She wanted to tell me something and yet didn't really want to talk, so what came out was in broken bits, which I had to piece together as best I could, though I was in no mood to start doing any detective work on her intimate life. But I gathered that the man she had lived with, the one who had left her, had been a wonderful lover, and that now for months, with Tommy, she had been existing in an atmosphere of terrible sexual frustration because Tommy could neither leave sex alone nor come to any terms with it, so that she was for ever being excited and yet denied any real satisfaction. But then she told me not to move and went padding out of the room. After a few minutes she came back with a towel and sponge, and very carefully, tenderly, as if I were precious, she wiped my face and other parts of me; and then, slowly at first, with a touch here, a pressure there, until not only hands but lips and tongues went exploring, she brought me by intensely pleasurable degrees into yet another strange world, a kind of Oriental garden of deeply sexual sensuality. And then on the bed we made love again, this time more slowly and for me altogether more consciously, so that now I no longer felt overwhelmed, almost terrified, but held my own with her, reaching the climax when she did. But even so, it was still curiously impersonal, anonymous, not Richard Herncastle lying with Julie Blane, but a man having a woman.

It was now more than time for her to go, as she realized in some alarm. She was quite ready to walk back to the hotel by herself but I wouldn't have that, and I dressed quickly while she put on her clothes in the bathroom, and I was ready long before she was. On the way back to the Poultry, she held on to my arm and sometimes pressed herself close to me, but said very little beyond 'Darling, it was heaven – wasn't it?' and a few other tender *Darling* remarks. Women have often complained that it was their bodies that men loved, not them themselves, but here the situation was reversed, for I couldn't help feeling that at the moment it was the body, to which she was still trying to keep as close as possible, that held all her tender interest, and not the owner of it, me, Dick Herncastle. I felt instinctively that we ought to have been talking eagerly about ourselves, and we weren't, were hardly saying a word, and somehow I felt this was wrong. We stopped just out of sight of the hotel entrance, kissed briefly, then parted.

I was beginning to feel exhausted on my way back to the Bentwoods'. Once again, as in the morning, I seemed to be not in one state of mind but two, working on different levels. On top was the usual exultation of the predatory young male, the primordial game hunter crowing to himself, for hadn't I just had, *twice*, Julie Blane, ready to take any risk to moan and cry and shudder with ecstasy in my arms? What about Dick Herncastle now? What about Tommy Beamish, who couldn't begin to satisfy her, or Uncle Nick, perfunctorily making do with poor Cissie Mapes? Young Richard Nobody could now show these star men a thing or two, couldn't he? And a good deal more of that stuff bouncing about on that top superficial level. But when it stopped bouncing and glittering and I sank down to the lower level, I was not only conscious of my exhaustion but also of a huge vague sadness I'd had – in Uncle Nick's term – my 'greens', but down there nothing seemed to be green and growing. I wasn't more myself than I'd been twelve hours ago; somehow, for all the crowing on top, I was less. I'd suddenly discovered what it was all about – no question of that – yet now that it was over, and here I was walking alone wearily through the Christmas night, what *was* it all about?

The Bentwoods weren't back, still laughing themselves sick somewhere, and I went straight up to my room, too warm, too close, now, and smelling not only of whisky and tobacco but also of sex, a kind of fishy smell, as if we had only to tumble and grapple with each other with sufficient energy and enthusiasm to return to the ocean from which our remotest ancestors once emerged. I drew the curtains and opened a couple of windows and the door, until the bitter night air was too much for me. Then I lit a pipe and carefully and lovingly spread out the watercolours and brushes that Uncle Nick, in his unpredictable fashion, had so carefully chosen for me, and then gloated over them. Perhaps because I had last used paints and brushes in Nancy's company, and perhaps for other and more mysterious reasons, she kept popping into my mind, though I tried to keep her out and actually hadn't any clear image of her, only a strong *idea* of her as a person. Then I suddenly felt hungry, took what was left of the whisky downstairs and foraged for some food, finally eating a tongue sandwich and three mince-pies. I went to bed early and read for some time, and I had turned out my light and was just drifting off to sleep when I heard the Bentwoods come past my door, still laughing.

Next morning, after Alfred Bentwood and I had washed up and cleared away the breakfast things and I had left him to check his booze and glasses (they were giving a Boxing Day party that night), I went up to my room and found Rose just finishing making the bed. She gave me a merry look. 'I didn't want to say anything when Alf was there,' she said, 'but I think you enjoyed yourself all right yesterday, didn't you? I mean, you didn't really mind having the house to yourself, did you?'

'Well – not really – no,' I replied uncertainly, not returning her look.

'And I'll bet you didn't, you naughty boy! And don't think I can't tell what you were up to. When it comes to some things, I'm Sherlock Holmes, I am.'

Dodging this approach, I said: 'Oh – Mrs Bentwood – Rose – I took some of your whisky. I'm sorry – but I'll pay you back—'

'No, you won't, my lad. It was in a good cause.' And then she screamed with laughter. I had to laugh with her but I think I had a kind of vision – in which she was the fat shaking symbolic image – of an immense, bawdy and untiring femaleness. And 'just to show there's no ill feeling' she said, she gave me a smacking wettish kiss.

6

Up to now I've taken it all slowly and carefully, week by week, but though I have the dates and the places in the diary I kept – opening at Leicester on December 29th, Birmingham on January 5th, Bristol the 12th – now it is rather like a film that has slipped out of its sprockets and goes racing and blurring. For this is more or less how it was, once I had taken Julie. I wanted her, as she did me, and nothing else mattered at all. I did the work I had to do, and I think not badly, though both Uncle Nick and Cissie were beginning to give me some curious looks; I moved into one set of digs after another, through one stage door after another, had an occasional drink with Jennings and Johnson and smiled at their endless reminiscences, took trams or walked along strange wintry streets, put on my make-up and wiped it off again; but in a long meaningless dream. Any painting was impossible anyhow, of course, but I never even went near an art gallery, telling myself the light was not good enough. I existed only to make love to Julie, though in fact it wasn't love we were making; in a real sense we weren't lovers at all; we were fanatical conspirators and two people sharing the same fever.

The burning question that roared above a plain of dust and ashes was – how and where were we to find a place to make love in? That's all I cared about, and if anything she was more desperate than I was, more determined and ingenious, and, considering the risk she ran, more incautious. The hasty encounters we contrived, night after night backstage, always reduced to a few whispers and inflaming touches, only made us more desperate. At the end of the Nottingham week and the beginning of the one at Leicester, a sullen town we all hated, she was in no state to make love, as she frankly told me, but after that of course it was all much worse. On the Wednesday night, New Year's Eve, we took a chance that would have seemed to us sheer lunacy even a week before. She and Tommy were going to a party some of his Leicester pantomime friends were giving, and she delayed her changing, saying that she had a headache, until Tommy, who was always impatient to get to any party, went off without her. I had a little dressing-room of my own that week and I waited in there, after telling Uncle Nick and Cissie – and I was sharing digs again with them, couldn't get out of it – that I wanted to finish a sketch I'd been doing; and then she came along as soon as she was sure that Tommy had gone, and I locked the door, and we began making love of a feverish and furtive sort in that messy little place, and in the middle of it the fireman, going his rounds, knocked at the door, and when I answered him he wished me 'A Happy New Year' and seemed to hang about, probably hoping for a tip. This left us half-undressed, incapable of enjoying each other, compelled to be silent, and wondering when it would be safe for Julie to sneak out. Never again, we said.

I was just in time to bolt my supper at the digs before Uncle Nick, who could be surprisingly ceremonious on occasion, filled three glasses with champagne and asked Cissie and me to stand up and be ready to drink a toast to the New Year. Our signal would be the midnight chimes.

'Well, Cissie, Richard – here's to Nineteen-fourteen, and may it bring us at least half what we want.' Cissie, ready to cry, kissed him. I shook his hand. There were vague sounds of revelry outside; even Leicester could celebrate the arrival of 1914.

'Nick, why shouldn't we ask for everything we want?' Cissie was quite serious.

'Unreasonable,' Uncle Nick told her, not altogether facetiously. 'Ask too much and you might not get a dam' thing, girl.'

'I didn't know you were superstitious.' This was from me.

He was lighting a cigar. 'I'm not.' After a puff or two: 'But it pays to be reasonable – even when you're moving into an area where you can't make a plan and it's all unpredictable. Now you two get off to bed – and I don't mean the same bed – because I want to start the New Year by having a smoke over that two-dwarf illusion.'

On the landing above, Cissie suddenly stopped and gave me a kiss. 'Happy New Year, Dick!' Then she looked at me with narrowed eyes and spoke in a whisper. 'I know what you've been doing. I can smell her perfume. And *he* knows there's something going on, though I shan't tell him, even if he asks me. But you're a very silly boy, Dick. We've all warned you.'

They had too, of course; but then it had been too early for warnings; now it was too late. We managed better in Birmingham, where Julie knew a woman who was manageress of a shop, and we spent two afternoons, all she dared to snatch from Tommy, in this woman's back bedroom, making wild love. For Bristol I got an address from Ricarlo, who had stayed there before, and while he kept the landlady talking and laughing in the kitchen on Tuesday afternoon, I was able to smuggle Julie in and out of my room; and Friday afternoon was easier still, for Ricarlo took the landlady to the cinema. And around these events Bristol itself was just a city in a huge vague dream.

If I had been free of this fever and we had not been in the dead of winter, I might have enjoyed Bristol, with its ships in the centre of the city, their masts showing above shops and trams, and without this obsession and in more friendly weather, I could have done some good sketching there. But what with trying to satsify our appetite for each other, then letting it grow in the imagination, then wondering where we could go next and exchanging hasty whispers backstage about new plots and plans, we became more and more like feverish fanatical conspirators, with all zest gone for ordinary living, through which I passed – and here I can't speak for Julie – like a sort of zombie.

But then a talk with Uncle Nick suddenly brightened and sharpened the whole dim picture of our touring life. I'd joined him in his dressing-room between the houses on Saturday night at Bristol. 'I don't know what's happening to you, lad,' he began, with more severity in his eyes than in his voice. 'But half the time you look as if you'd found tuppence and lost a shilling. What is it?'

'It's the winter, I think, uncle – the dark days, not being able to look at things, to take out my sketchbook – having that wonderful watercolour set you gave me and not being able to use it.'

This satisfied him. Though he had no interest in painting himself, he always treated my ambition with respect; possibly because he associated it with his devotion to his own art of elaborate deception, for he saw this as an art and not just something that enabled him to earn a good living. 'I was on the telephone this morning to Joe Bosenby – you remember him – my agent – you didn't like him.'

'No, I didn't, though I'd no idea you knew I didn't.'

'I notice things, lad. Matter of fact, I don't like him myself, and he doesn't like me, though you'd never guess it to hear us talking. Anyhow, Joe's got everything lined up again. And this is how it goes. We play Plymouth next week. Devonport really, but it sounds better if you call it Plymouth. Then, Portsmouth and Southsea. Bad dates, both of 'em, in my opinion – too many sailors, half-pissed. But there it is. Then we have a week out – February 2nd.'

'You mean we're not playing anywhere?' I didn't know whether to be glad or sorry. Tommy might take Julie away with him, though of course if he didn't then we could have the week to ourselves. But what about money?

It was as if I'd asked the question aloud. 'If you're worried about money, lad, you needn't be. I'll pay you for that week out, and then the next eight weeks, when we'll be in London playing the suburban Empires, I'll raise you to seven-pound ten, because it'll cost you more to live in London.'

'Thanks, Uncle Nick. I can see it might, though I don't know anything about London—'

'You can find out during that week out. Get yourself fixed up somewhere for the next eight weeks. You change halls but not digs in London. I always stay at the same place in Brixton – old friends of mine. He's a retired illusionist, Dutchman – name of Van Daman, married to a Frenchwoman, topnotch cook – best digs in England for me. Cissie's going home for the week out, then staying there, if she can stick it, while we're in London. I'm going over to Paris during the week out. There's a French illusionist I want to see and might do some business with. Anything else I can tell you, lad?'

'Just one thing, uncle. Are we all still on the same bill in London?'

'Oh – no. Tommy Beamish doesn't want me on the bill, and I don't want him. I stay bottom of the bill, and we'll have various stars at the top. I've told Joe to try to book Jennings and Johnson with us again. Ricarlo's going home for two or three months. Joe said we might have the Colmars still with us, and I told him I didn't care one way or the other. You haven't been rogering little Nonie Colmar, have you, lad?'

'No, and I doubt if anybody else has. I think she's just a teaser, though it's all the same to me whether she is or not. She's not my sort.'

'Who is your sort?' He sounded casual, but he gave me a sharp look.

'I don't know yet.' And to keep him off the subject, I went on hurriedly: 'Where are all these Empires in London? Are there enough to keep us there eight weeks?'

'Yes, and a lot more. Holborn, Kilburn, Stratford, Hackney, Finsbury Park, Wood Green, Chiswick, Shepherd's Bush,' he rattled off. 'That's eight for a start – all Empires. And there's a few more Empires, to say nothing of Hippodromes and Palaces and whatnot, mostly in the circuit. London's a big place, lad, and needs a lot of entertainment. They're good audiences too, most of 'em, especially north of the river. You'll like this London suburban season, Richard. I know I always do.'

I said that I thought I would too, and meant it. But then I began wondering and worrying about how and where I could talk the news over with Julie, during the second house. We were having to be more and more careful because, she said, Tommy was now giving her some odd looks and seemed suspicious. And of course we still hadn't decided what we could do, next week, in Devonport or Plymouth. One thing I'd decided, though, Julie or no Julie, was that I had to see Miss Nancy Ellis, now playing in pantomime at the Theatre Royal, Plymouth.

7

Any idea I'd had about a fancy Plymouth-Hoe style of living, that week, vanished soon after we arrived on Sunday, together with a lot of big soft snowflakes. Good digs, it seemed, were hard to find, and what I got was a dreary little room in a dreary little house in a dreary little side-street in Devonport, not far from the barracks. The house belonged to a retired petty officer whose wife looked as if she'd been a petty officer too: a severe elderly couple who in five minutes, over cups of cocoa, convinced me that I'd as much chance of smuggling Julie in and out of my room as I would have a giraffe. I told Julie this. Having got through a damp and bad-tempered band call, we were sitting in the Snug of the usual pub-just-round-the-corner – and very snug it was too, a small corner room with the firelight picking out some old copper utensils and enriching the dark polished wood, while the big fairy-tale snowflakes we could just see through the window might be falling in some other place, some other time. Julie was drinking whisky and I was trying a hot rum toddy. And at first we had this Snug to ourselves.

'That's no use then, darling,' said Julie. 'And I'm no good. We're staying down at the Grand. Tommy likes to do himself proud when he's playing a date he doesn't like. When he's anywhere north of Birmingham he feels quite different – at home.'

'What about London? You're playing all those suburban Empires, aren't you?'

'Yes, darling – thank God! And he doesn't like them either. But he has some London digs he raves about – and this is what I've been longing to tell you, Dick darling – he thinks he'd be better there alone, an idea I've been trying to put into his head for the last week.'

'Perhaps he has a woman there,' I suggested hopefully.

'He can have ten women there, for all I care. Just so long as I'm let off the chain. And I've already written to several friends to see if anybody will let me rent a nice furnished flat for a couple of months. Darling, kiss me before somebody comes in.'

I did, and that was more than another hot rum toddy. But I also had another one and brought Julie another large whisky. 'Thank you, Richard my duck. If we had a bearskin or two and plenty of cushions,

I'd like to spend the whole day and most of the night just here.' She smiled slowly, her eyes like lamps. She looked beautiful and I told her so.

'I suppose you've remembered that little Nancy Ellis is here at the Theatre Royal?' She gave me a look out of the corner of her eyes. 'Are you going to see her?'

'Yes, Julie, I am,' I said firmly. 'On stage and, I hope, off.'

'Well, don't sound so aggressive about it, darling. Remember, I talked to you seriously about her, before we began. I didn't want you or anybody else to think I'd taken you away from a girl half my age if you were serious about her. You said there was nothing in it, remember? So why set your jaw and announce you're going to see her – on and off the stage? There's no reason why you shouldn't, but please tell me why, darling.'

'To be honest, Julie, I don't know. Curiosity probably. It won't make any difference to us. I shan't stop thinking about you all the time, wanting you.'

'I wonder.' She gave me a speculative look. 'What are you proposing to do?'

'I thought I'd leave a note at the theatre for her this afternoon, then go to the matinee tomorrow. They don't have one today.'

'Tommy says we're going to the Wednesday matinee. This will be the fourth pantomime we've seen – I could scream with boredom – but I can't keep Tommy away and he insists upon my going too, so that he can explain to me exactly why the comedians are so bad, which God knows they are. But if you're there tomorrow afternoon, and I'm there on Wednesday, what happens to us, even if little Nancy's pretty legs don't bewitch you all over again? Though you like mine too, don't you?'

I said I did, that I was half-barmy about them and her, as she knew very well, but also admitted that I didn't know what we could do, this week. 'Darling, I adore you. Well now – let's think. Oh – damn!' She muttered this because we no longer had the room to ourselves. 'Finish your drink and let's go. I'll explain outside.'

Among the snowflakes, but warmed by desire and hot rum, I agreed we might take the risk of going up to her dressing-room, with me letting her go ahead and not approaching her door until the corridor was clear. It worked, and within a minute of locking the door we were making too muffled and hasty but not unsatisfying love. More room and leisure, firelight and a bed, would have been better of course, but the very impudence and then the savage intensity of the act gave it a kind of edge.

The pantomime next afternoon was boring except when Nancy was on the stage. In her page's costume she looked more entrancing than ever. And she seemed gayer than ever in a special way, half a girl – and the one I remembered – and half a cheeky boy. I watched and listened to her – and I was sitting in a front stall – with feelings so confused that I can't begin to disentangle them in order to describe them. It was the same when she came down to meet me, with a long coat over her finale costume and still made-up. Other people were milling around in the small space near the stage door where we met.

'Dick, I'm so glad.' She was rather out of breath. 'After that silly quarrel I was hoping you'd write to me – or at least send me a wire for Christmas or New Year. I would have done only I stupidly didn't know where you were. Did you enjoy our panto?'

'Not much. Except you, of course, Nancy. You were worth all the rest put together.'

She did her familiar scowl. 'I hoped you wouldn't say that, Dick. You know I hate it. Besides, it isn't true.'

'Yes it is. But don't let's start quarrelling again, Nancy. Can't you change and come out so that we can talk somewhere?'

'I'd love to, but I can't today, Dick. One of the girls is giving a special tea party, and I promised to be there. In fact I'll have to go up in a minute.'

'Tomorrow then, please, Nancy.'

'All right. But I'm not free for lunch, so it'll have to be after the matinee. I'll change as quickly as I can because neither of us'll have much time. Look – I'll meet you at the Grand – what's the matter?'

'Nothing, Nancy. Go on. The Grand? They can give us tea, can they? All right – what time?'

'About twenty-past five. And now I really must go. But Dick — oh, I'm sorry.' This was to a couple of stage hands who were trying to get past.

'Don't you worry about us, Miss Ellis,' said one of them, giving her a friendly grin. She was obviously popular with the stage staff.

'What were you going to say, Nancy?'

'Oh – nothing really. Something silly, and I really must go. Just that – you seem different somehow. Are you different? No, tell me tomorrow.' And she hurried away.

A few minutes after five, on Wednesday afternoon, I was already hanging about the lounge of the Grand. At half-past, after what seemed several hours, I had taken a table and, to save the time that was running out, I had ordered tea, scones and cakes for two. By six o'clock I had mechanically drunk three cups of tea and consumed more than my fair share of scones and cakes, and of course I knew by then she wasn't coming. Then, looking across towards the head porter's desk, I saw Julie going from the stairs to post some letters at the desk. She didn't go back upstairs, but came nearer the lounge, looked around, and then spotted me.

'But, darling, have you been eating a huge tea all by yourself? In the middle of all these naval officers' wives too.'

'I've been waiting for Nancy Ellis. She never turned up.'

'Oh – but what a shame!' She hadn't sat down. I felt she wasn't really with me, mocking somewhere outside. 'I thought the pantomime was awful, but she was rather sweet. What happens now, then? Another quarrel?'

'I'll go round and see her tonight. Wait at the stage door if necessary.'

'Dick,' she began softly, leaning forward a little. And now I knew she really was with me again, not playing a society woman behind a glass wall. 'Dick dear, I don't think I'd do that.'

'Why not?'

'Well – lots of reasons. If she couldn't help it, and you meet her with that look on your face, you'll quarrel again. If she didn't turn up because she doesn't care, the last thing you ought to do is to hang around tonight waiting for her. No – listen please, darling. This is far more important. If you've any message for me in the morning, leave a note for me at the stage door. I'll be calling there just before lunch to see if there are any letters for Tommy and me. Just a short innocent note, darling.'

I changed quickly after we'd done our second show, making too much haste, for the stage-door keeper at the Theatre Royal told me I needn't expect them to be coming out for a good half hour. So I had a beer I didn't want in a neighbouring pub, kept looking at my new wrist-watch, and even then was back there ten minutes too early, even for the first comers. Two-thirds of the company must have made their way out before I caught sight of Susie Hodson and Bob, with Nancy a few paces behind them. As I didn't want to get involved with Susie and Bob I turned away as they passed me, then whipped round, plain in Nancy's sight and hearing, and cried her name eagerly. And once again – it was like the repetition of a horrible pattern – she took a stone face hurriedly past me, catching up with Susie and Bob as if to prevent any further appeal from me. I didn't try one. I was very angry, and, later, when I was pushing pieces of baked cod round my plate and pretending to listen to retired-petty-officer reminiscences of North China, I was very miserable. I realized that I'd been expecting something from Nancy – nothing to do with sex; that was all Julie – and whatever it was, now that it turned out to be nothing, I felt a leaden figure of misery.

Next morning I walked across a dingy and slushy Devonport to leave a note at the stage door, informing Miss Blane that I would be looking over some of our equipment backstage round about three o'clock that afternoon. And so I was when she called out 'Hello, Dick!' and then vanished. Ten minutes later I was locking the door of her dressing-room behind me, and she was already half-undressed. We didn't speak; we hardly looked at each other; we made love like famished soldiers eating roast meat and pudding; but when it was over and we suddenly discovered we were cold and we sipped some of her whisky, she took my face in her hands, kissed me gently, and whispered: 'You're such a dear sweet boy, Dick. And I'm sorry. I'm sorry.'

'Sorry about what, Julie?'

But she closed her eyes, shook her head, and only said I ought to be going and must be careful. But there was nobody about at that time, of course; the place, so different from what it was at night, was empty. Cold and melancholy and empty.

The only thing I did, outside routine, on our last night in Devonport was to write, between our two shows, a letter to Nancy. After tearing up several long and pompous epistles, and when time was running out, I contrived at last to be brief: *Dear Nancy, I thought and hoped once we were going to be friends, especially after that wonderful day we had on the moors. But you did not keep our engagement for tea at the Grand. Then you walked past me without speaking. Why? Write to me, please. I shall be in Portsmouth next week, then in London for the next nine weeks, and though I have no London address you could write to me care of Joe Bosenby who is your agent as well as ours.*

And I said I was hers very sincerely. I felt I had to send this letter to Nancy, though I couldn't have told anybody, couldn't even tell myself, but this feeling wouldn't leave me alone until, late on Saturday, I dropped the letter into the box.

That week in Portsmouth was really a long wait for Saturday night when it would end. Julie and I met several times to talk, almost entirely about what would happen in London, and although anything but satiated and tired of each other, we never made love once, if only because I began the week with a cold and Julie ended it with troubles of her own. Ricarlo, mad to get home now, gave a lunch party on the Saturday for ten of us, and I was able to sit next to Julie because Tommy Beamish wasn't there as he'd had to go up to London, to Ricarlo's relief as well as mine. And it was through Ricarlo that I had already found a flat in London. A friend of his lived in a block of flats – King Edward's Mansions, Walham Green – largely occupied by variety artistes, who wanted something comparatively cheap (and Walham Green was anything but a fashionable neighbourhood) because they were so often away on tour. What I got through Ricarlo's friend was a third-floor furnished flat – two rooms, kitchen and bath – for thirty-five shillings a week. It belonged to a couple called Simpson, who had just gone on tour in an act known as *Molly Rafferty and Mike*. Julie, who had of course a lot of theatrical friends in London, was taking over from one of them, also on tour, what she said was a delicious little flat in Shepherd Market, Mayfair. How often Tommy would be there, she didn't know, but she said she was hoping to ease him out of her bedroom while still keeping the part – and the money she'd need more than ever now she was to be working in London. Just because she had so many friends there, I thought perhaps she would show signs of losing interest in me, a rather raw youth even if I had, as she told me, proved myself to be a good lover; but I had to admit to myself I saw none of these signs, and if anything she was even more eager than I was to talk about what we could do in London. And with Uncle Nick thinking about Paris, Cissie and Ricarlo bound for their homes, Jennings and Johnson about to join some Americans they knew in London, Julie and I with our London plans, Portsmouth and Southsea hardly existed for us: we gave them our acts, perhaps a little perfunctorily, and then almost forgot they were there. Meanwhile, Uncle Nick had given me a list of our surburban London dates: we opened on February 9th at what he said was one of the best of them, Finsbury Park Empire; 16th at Hackney Empire; 23rd at Wood Green Empire, and so forth; and I used to stare at this list of strange-sounding Empires, wondering what this vast London so prolific in Empires had in waiting for me.

8

Though it was only early February, Tommy Beamish was spending his week out down in Brighton with some of his pub-keeping and race-going chums and hadn't insisted upon Julie going with him, so she and I had that week to ourselves, day and night, without having to worry about him. This brought us closer together – as two persons, I mean, and not just as male and female in rut – than I would have thought possible a week or two earlier, when we simply snatched at sex together and left it at that. Of course I wasn't really the man for her but just a vague young substitute for the man who had left her; and she wasn't the woman for me, except – and it was now an exception that burned in my blood – in or around the sexual act; but now, especially after we'd made love and our bodies were at ease and seemed to feel a calm tenderness each for the other, we'd time to talk, to explain ourselves, to argue and denounce and accept, we couldn't help coming closer together as persons. We weren't in love but we were friends within our mutual sexual obsession. It is true that there were times when, sexually exhausted, she would be bitterly ironical because I wasn't the man she still needed, the one she could have made a life with, and when I, suddenly feeling empty and sad, couldn't even pretend to be the tender companion and obviously went a long way from her in my mind. But even so, we were closer, two persons together.

The February weather didn't help and we had to waste good time going underground or in misty-windowed buses and trams. Julie, extravagant like most actresses, was always wanting to take taxis, but mostly, in what she called my *Save thi brass* mood, I wouldn't have it. But she enjoyed showing me London, even if she was rather a vague guide. However, she didn't want to spend much time in museums and galleries, and I didn't want to be always going to the theatre, matinees and all. Feeling a raw provincial youth here in London, I thought at first she would try to keep me away from her friends, but to my surprise – though it was after she made me buy another suit, ready-made but quite smart – she insisted upon my meeting them and took me to several theatrical lunch and supper parties (this was during the first two or three weeks, not during the very first one), until I protested. The truth was, as I told her frankly, I didn't like most of the people I met at these parties. Some of the very old actresses and some of the very young ones were all right, but the rest, especially the better-known actors, seemed to me the hollowest, pasted-together, false-faced creatures I'd ever met, and I'd nothing to say to them and didn't want to listen to them. This ought to have annoyed Julie but somehow it didn't, and perhaps she was secretly relieved when she could go alone without feeling she was leaving me out. And I wasn't jealous; we were making love too often in that Shepherd Market flat of hers.

Certainly during that first week I spent more time there than I did in my own place. Her flat was on the second floor, up a narrow wooden staircase, above a corner shop; and it was very pink and beige and knick-knackery and feminine, full of photographs inscribed *For Darling Eva*, but very comfortable, handy yet hidden away, just the place for us that Julie must have been dreaming about for weeks. Even when we started working again, Julie at one distant Empire, I at another, I was still there a lot, either in the afternoons or late at night, sometimes all night. It was trickier now, of course, when she was working with Tommy again, because there were nights when he insisted upon taking her out to supper and then going back to the flat with her. If she knew definitely she would be free, she used to telephone from her Empire to mine, leaving a guarded message for me with the stage-door keeper. I never knew exactly what went on between her and Tommy – she didn't want to tell me and I didn't want to know – but I guessed from various remarks of hers that ever since she and I had been lovers it had been harder and harder for her to pretend any sexual interest in him, to put up with whatever she had to put up with, and that he was becoming suspicious, sometimes sulkily ignoring her for several nights on end and then suddenly demanding her company and being what she merely called 'tiresome'.

And from the look in her eyes when she said that, once or twice accompanied by a shiver she wasn't even conscious of, I didn't think *tiresome* was the right word. And after one Saturday night he spent with her – it was our third Saturday in London – I found on Sunday that she had big bruise-marks on both upper arms that she tried to hide but couldn't, and she then said she'd fallen on the stairs, and I refused to say I didn't believe her because she knew I didn't. The Tommy situation was uneasy, but after the maddening frustrations on tour, now able to enjoy each other without snatching in a kind of fever, we tried to forget it.

My Walham Green flat I never really saw at first as a place to live in. It wasn't very roomy; it was downright ugly; and nearly everything seemed to be broken or badly mended, as if the Simpsons, perhaps turning after some drink into *Molly Rafferty and Mike* at home, had thrown things at each other. A tiny old woman, who looked like a defeated witch but on better acquaintance proved to be quite a cheerful character, crept in on certain mornings and gave a kind of performance of cleaning, like an actress at the beginning of a play, and, after telling me that she didn't know what I'd do without her, left the place more or less as she found it. There was no telephone in the flat – and if there had been, the Simpsons in their *Rafferty* mood would have broken it – but there was one along the landing; and I was on good terms with the porter downstairs, who would always take a message for me. And usually I was out. That flat would have driven anybody out. Whatever the opposite of a home is, that's what that flat was.

I haven't set eyes on Walham Green for about forty years and I don't know what it's like now, but in 1914 it had a character of its own, being quite different from its neighbours, Chelsea, Fulham, West Kensington. It was slatternly and down-at-heel but cheerful, ready for anything except dull gentility. It was a western outpost of the old Cockneydom. After the Stamford Bridge football ground and the Granville (not in the class of our Empires: Uncle Nick wouldn't have looked at it), Walham Green broke out into stalls and barrows, and on fine mornings fat women stood at pub doors drinking porter. It had more newsboys than any other place I have ever lived in. Along the Fulham Road, on the Chelsea side, were some vaguely foreign little restaurants where you could get five courses of grease, all different, for eighteen pence. King Edward's Mansions towered at the corner, where the Fulham Road took a bend and the buses swept on towards Parsons Green and the Bishop's Palace; and we Mansions dwellers were the aristocrats round there, whether we were one of *Ganga Dun's* assistants or Molly Rafferty and Mike, but the common people didn't regard us – or indeed anybody else – with awe, neglected to wear collars or corsets, drank ale, porter, stout, at all hours of the day, while the men brooded over Chelsea football club and racing specials and the women discussed pregnancy and female ailments.

From there I set off every Monday morning, often by bus if I could manage it, to one of our distant Empires, often passing through miles of meaningless streets that seemed to me the chief horror of London. Monday was usually a long boring day because after the band call and making sure we were all ready for the evening performance, it rarely seemed worth while going back to Walham Green or trying the West End, so if it wasn't raining hard I'd pass the afternoon exploring these featureless suburbs and having a beer or two – the pubs being open then, before so many of us fought our great battles for freedom. And though, in those early weeks, I might be thinking too often about Julie and what we might get up to next, I did try to do my best for the act, feeling that Uncle Nick, with my humble assistance, was lighting up for twenty minutes the lives of all those people trapped in these suburbs. His Indian Temple atmosphere might be cheap and silly, his clear hard brain might be devoted only to deceiving them, but he did bring them wonder and perhaps a moment or two of wild joy when the impossible, the miraculous, seemed to happen.

After three or four weeks I seemed almost fixed in a routine of suburban journeys and performances, a rather guarded, off-hand but not unfriendly relation with Uncle Nick (who was still working on his two-dwarf illusion) and Cissie, occasional mornings and afternoons looking round art galleries but never attempting any painting, hardly a sketch, and receiving telephone messages from Julie in her distant Empire and spending lolling afternoons and sometimes whole nights at the Shepherd Market flat, where we might talk now but still met really to make love. As I was soon to discover afterwards, it was this intensely sensual, sexually obsessive affair with Julie that was central and dominating, taking away rather than adding colour and tone to the London scene, so that I moved through it half in a dream. And then the roof of my new little world fell in on me. I have the exact date: it was Sunday, the First of March.

About ten in the evening we were in the bedroom of the Shepherd Market flat, pinky and satiny without a harsh surface or tone in it, a lovers' nest. Julie had already undressed and was lying on the bed looking at me with half-closed eyes. I was undressing but had stopped for a moment to admire and wonder at the great curve of her thigh, returning for the first time since that Christmas afternoon in Nottingham and, though I didn't know it, for the last time in this world, to that purely aesthetic joy in her form and colour. And I was trying to tell her what I felt and something I said made her laugh, and that must have been why neither of us heard anybody entering the flat, though no doubt they came in very quietly and carefully after finding the outer door unlocked. Then they burst into the bedroom, two of them, without hats and overcoats, as if they'd just left a waiting car. The first was Tommy Beamish, white and hot-eyed with drink and fury. The other I could only see as a big wide man.

'No, Tommy, no,' Julie screamed, turning away.

There was a swishing sound from the cane Tommy was carrying. Then he was shouting, 'Now you ranty cheating bitch, I've caught you.' And she screamed again, harder now, as the cane slashed across her back.

I jumped forward to stop him but the big wide man stood in my way. I tried to push him aside but couldn't move him, so I used my fists. Then it was as if the room had hit me, and as I went reeling back, with blood in my mouth, I knew I hadn't a hope with this chap. But I could hear Julie screaming and I was wild with anger, and I tried again, and this time he really set about me and I felt I hadn't a face left as I went back, hit the wall, and slithered to the floor.

'For Christ's sake, Tommy,' I heard the man say, a long way off, 'that's enough. This wasn't in the bargain.'

'Look, I've stopped, Ted.' I could just open one eye and could see Tommy, standing there, shaking and slavering. 'So – shut up, shut up – don't bother me. I'm enjoying myself. Oh – it's lovely.'

If either of them said anything else for a minute or two, I missed it, for I began retching. Then I heard the big man say: 'Let's get out of this, Tommy. I don't like it.' Then he must have turned to me. 'You had a good try, me laddie. But you don't have the weight and you leave yourself wide open. Come on, Tommy.'

Then, above Julie's sobbing, I heard Tommy shouting at her. 'Now I'll tell you what I've been doing all this last week while you've been bouncing on your back here. I've been rehearsing somebody else in your part, and she opens tomorrow and you're out on your bare bleeding arse, Miss Blane. Ta-ta.' As he passed me, still crumpled on the floor, he flicked at my face with his cane: 'And look what you rogered yourself into, Herncastle – half a round with an ex-heavyweight—'

'Turn it up, Tommy,' the fighter cut in savagely. 'We're going.' And they went, banging doors behind them. And time seemed almost to stop.

I had to attend to myself first, otherwise I'd have bled over everything. I raised myself slowly and shakily, tottered along to the bathroom, and sponged my face as if it were a sick baby. I rinsed the blood and bile out of my mouth but still felt sick. When I was no longer bleeding, I went back with the sponge and a clean towel, feeling almost as helpless as I'd felt against the bruiser. Julie was lying on her face, still sobbing, and across her back were several red weals.

'I don't know what I ought to do to your back, Julie,' I began, rather thickly because my mouth still wasn't right.

'Go away, go away, go away.' She didn't turn and raise her head, so it was all muffled, but she was certainly telling me to go away.

'I can't go away and leave you like this, Julie. I'd better sponge them first and then see if I can find any ointment or something—'

'No. Go away.'

There didn't seem any reply to this, so I just waited.

Now she turned her face towards me. It wasn't as bad as mine but it was all swollen and strange, so that she looked like somebody I didn't know. 'All right then. I don't know about ointment – look. But give me a drink first – a strong one.'

After she'd gulped down the half-tumbler of neat whisky, she asked for another, and then I left her with it to look for some sort of ointment. I gave her some water after the second lot of whisky and now she was hazy and hardly knew what either of us was saying while I attended to the weals on her back. 'Why did you let him do that to me?' was one question she asked.

'You weren't looking the right way, Julie,' I told her. 'He'd brought a big bruiser along with him, and he knocked hell out of me when I tried to interfere. Look at me – no, don't.'

'Tommy's mad,' she said a little later. 'I ought to have known that all along – the things he did and wanted to do. He'll end up in a lunatic asylum. You'll see. How did he know we were here tonight? Has he been having us watched?'

'I dare say. Or he just took a chance. But don't think he was simply punishing you. He was enjoying himself. He said so. This was his excuse. And even his bruiser pal was disgusted.'

'He's thrown me out, hasn't he? Didn't he say he had? And I can't stop him. I'd a contract covering the tour, but not for these London dates.'

'But you couldn't have appeared with him again, Julie.'

'I know, I know. But now I'm in London again – with no work.' She began crying. I tried to comfort her but she told me not to touch her, now she didn't want anybody touching her. However, I helped her into a nightdress and then into bed. All she wanted now was to be left alone and to go to sleep – she'd been drowsy for the last ten minutes, after all that whisky – but she begged me to lock her in safely. I said I would do that by locking the door from the outside and then putting the key through the letterbox. She was fast asleep before I left, turned away from me, just a lot of dark hair on a pillow. I still felt rather sick; my back hurt where it had hit the wall; and I knew I must be showing a red ruin of a face, even with my hat pulled well down over it. And I was, because a man on the 14 bus asked me what had happened to it, and I told him I'd been boxing. But all this doesn't mean I was thinking about myself and not about Julie. I felt more than my own sick feeling when I thought about her; I was sick at heart.

There was a telephone in the bedroom at the Shepherd Market flat, but I didn't ring her there on Monday morning, before I went off to the Chiswick Empire, because I thought she might be still asleep. But after the band call I rang her from the stage door, asked her how she felt and said I was free now to go along, but she told me she'd rather I didn't and that she was more or less staying in bed. Then when I suggested the next day, Tuesday, she said rather vaguely she didn't think that would be any good either, and finally we settled that I should go to the flat on Wednesday afternoon, at about two o'clock. It wasn't a bad day, so after a drink and a couple of sandwiches in a pub, I wandered down to the river – it had a wonderful mixed effect of mist and sparkle – and hung around Chiswick and Hammersmith Malls, wishing I had my sketchbook with me.

But even so, though I was using my eyes, I felt as miserable as hell. That night — and at a full second house too – I all but mistimed the *Vanishing Cyclist* effect and we only just made it, and Uncle Nick was furious when we came off. 'I want to talk to you, lad.'

'I'm sorry, Uncle Nick. It's the first time—'

'Not now,' he interrupted savagely. 'Let's get this make-up off. We can't talk to each other properly looking like a couple of bloody Indians. So – as soon as you've changed – in my dressing-room.'

So later, in there, I began again: 'I'm sorry, Uncle Nick. I know it was all my fault, nobody else's. It won't occur again, I promise. But – something happened.'

'And something else'll happen if you do that again, lad,' he growled. But then he really looked at me. 'Here – what have you been doing with yourself? Look at your face.'

'I had a fight, uncle.'

'I can see that, lad. Aren't you big enough to take care of yourself?'

'Not against a heavy-weight bruiser, I'm not. Hadn't a chance.'

'No doubt. But how the hell did you come to be mixed up with a heavy-weight bruiser – eh?' As I hesitated, he went on: 'I'll bet that woman Blane comes into it. Cissie swears you've been having her day and night. You wouldn't be warned, would you?' As I still hesitated, he dropped his sharp accusing tone. 'Now look, Richard lad. You came down here with me. I'm partly responsible. So just tell me straight what happened.'

So I did, and as the whole story came out, without any interruptions from him, he glared at me, his face dark with anger. 'I don't care what happened to her,' he began, when I had finished. 'She asked for it and she must have known what Tommy Beamish is like. It's notorious. But if he thinks he can have any nephew of mine knocked about like that, without anything happening to him, he's wrong. I'll hit him where it'll hurt most. You watch.'

'But what can you do, uncle?'

'Plenty. He'll soon find out. I know some funny people in this city and I can make some funny arrangements. Just leave this to me, lad. And just leave that woman alone and attend to your work properly.'

He still left me wondering what he could do, though I felt sure something would happen to Tommy Beamish fairly soon, for it wasn't like Uncle Nick to do any idle boasting. And then even by the middle of that week, rumours were flying around, then before the end of the week there were paragraphs in one or two of the morning and evening papers, and later still some longer items in the stage and variety weeklies. At the Holborn Empire, one of the best of these dates, it appeared that Tommy Beamish had been 'given the bird', and on the second night it had happened he had been foolish enough to shout back and had then been told, at the top of several voices, that he was drunk and not fit to be on the stage. 'Yes,' said Uncle Nick complacently, 'poor Tommy seems to have been running into a bit of trouble. Joe Bosenby's very worried about it. They've been talking to him at the head office. Looks as if they might cancel all his other London dates and try to fit him in up North again. Tommy didn't behave well, it seems, and the new young woman he has in the act behaved even worse – burst into tears, they say, and ran off the stage. Perhaps he ought to put one or two of his bruiser friends up in the gallery.' He gave me a wink but said nothing about any funny arrangements he might have made through some of his funny friends.

I was bursting to tell Julie about all this. But I never did. I rushed along to the Shepherd Market flat just before two on Wednesday afternoon. She wasn't in. I hung about for half an hour, expecting her every moment, and then forced myself to go for a walk around Mayfair, returning in a hurry at three o'clock, but she wasn't there. Telling myself she might have come and gone while I was walking around, I hung about again; and so it went on until half-past five, when I daren't stay any longer. I rang her from the stage door after the first house, but there was no reply. It was misery.

Next morning I rang her from my landing. She did all the talking. 'Oh, Dick dear, I'm so sorry about yesterday afternoon. No, I hadn't forgotten. I was out seeing agents – my own kind, not monsters like that man Bosenby – and I waited and waited for one, the most important, then I was told to come back immediately after lunch, and then I was kept waiting again, furious of course but what could I do? Don't forget, darling, you're still working and now I'm *not*. No, not tomorrow, Dick dear, I have to be out again. Listen, darling, come on Sunday – no, not in the afternoon, I'm lunching with some people out at Richmond – say, six o'clock and then I'm sure to be back and you won't be disappointed—'

But I was – not only at six but at seven and then eight, after which I gave it up. I rang her up a good many times the following week, and for most of them she obviously wasn't there. But twice somebody was ready to answer and when I began eagerly, 'Is that you, Julie?' or 'This is Dick,' I was quietly cut off. The third time I waited for her to speak, and a Cockney voice asked who it was, and when I said who I was, the voice said Miss Blane wasn't in, and before I could reply the line went dead. And that was the very last time I ever spoke to Julie Blane, when she was pretending to be somebody else. That kept me off the telephone and away from Shepherd Market for a whole week, but in the middle of the following week, when we were coming towards the end of our stay in London, I happened to be in that neighbourhood one afternoon and, though knowing only too well by this time I had been ditched, I called at the flat. And somebody answered the door, but it wasn't Julie Blane.

'No, she's gone, y'know,' the young woman, obviously another actress, told me. 'I don't know the details but I believe she took somebody's place at the last minute in Lewis Atkinson's Company. They went off to Cape Town or somewhere, last Saturday, I believe. I'm *so* sorry. Is she a friend of yours? Do you know her very well?'

'Not very well – no.'

9

Actually I felt a bit better when I knew definitely she'd gone, but I'd been having – was still having – a rotten bad time. I mightn't be in love with her – and I've never suggested I was – but where she'd been in this London life of mine, right in the centre, there was a huge dreary gap where nothing happened. I'd made no friends, didn't know where to start, and I'd nobody to take even a part of Julie's place, just for ordinary companionship. And of course my pride – and at that age it's a mile high and yet trembles at a touch – had been badly hurt: I'd had nothing since that horrible Sunday night but humiliation in one shape or another. And sexually I was in a real mess. I was like a plant that had been brought on and coddled in a hothouse only to be tossed out into a cold night. I was still sexually excited, but now by somebody who wasn't there. My mouth was still watering but the feast had vanished; I could see nothing but stale bread and hard cheese. I had the obsession but not the object of it. And of course I couldn't forget that I'd been warned I was now not only a chap wandering aimlessly, most of his time, through a monstrous city that didn't want him, except for twenty minutes twice a night got up as an Indian, I was also a chap who'd been warned but wouldn't be told, a bloody fool.

However, it wasn't all ache, regret or sheer dreariness. I could still delight in the wonderful comics on top of our bills during most of those London weeks. Most of the acts that shared our bills irritated or bored me: imbecile cross-talk comedians; boozy Irish tenors tearful over their mothers; 'light comedians' with their endless songs about 'girls with curly-curls' and Brown and his pals all out on a spree; the immensely popular but tedious male impersonators, who never once looked or sounded like the soldiers and sailors they were supposed to be impersonating. At least five acts out of every eight seemed to me a waste of anybody's attention; though of course we were never on the same bill with any other illusionists or conjurers. But high above this routine stuff, and paying for all, were the star comics. Watching and listening to them, as I never failed to do, night after night, took me out of misery and self-pity, just as it must have offered a lot of those trapped people in the suburbs a sense of release, perhaps even a flash of wild joy.

Twice, topping our bill, we had a comedian who I think has been under-valued. This was Harry Tate, whose Motoring, Fishing, Billiards sketches contained the sprouting germ of so much surrealist comedy, and whose glaring and bellowing sportsman, always reduced to stunned silence by the enormity of events, was a creation touched with genius, a lunatic caricature of a real and horrible type of Englishman. And once we had Little Tich, released from the Tivoli to dazzle the suburbs, Uncle Nick, who had appeared with him abroad, knew him well, and I was introduced to him, a solemn little Mr Relph, who talked to me about painting. On the stage he might be a barrister in court, a tipsy man-about-town, a regal lady encumbered with an enormous train, but always he set these miniature beings blazing with a mad energy, as if, coming from a different species, they were flaming burlesques of our own larger dim idiocies. And just once we had Grock, who hadn't been long in England then and hadn't reached the height of his fame, but even then was the best clown I ever saw except Chaplin. He was like a serious humble but hopeful visitor from another planet, endlessly defeated by alien and hostile circumstances, and like Chaplin he brought your laughter close to the beginning of tears. I was ready to pour out my admiration and gratitude to him, but off the stage he seemed aloof, rather grim, perhaps because he couldn't feel at ease and at home in England, a divided country, one part of it in love with comic genius, the other part cold and hostile to it. To this day, if my arthritis allows it, I can do a very rough imitation of Grock's act, just a poor sketch of it, that makes people laugh who never saw him in all his comic glory. And that act did me some good, when I needed a bit of help, in March 1914.

One person who knew somehow what had happened to me – though she never directly mentioned it – was Cissie Mapes. She obviously felt we were fellow sufferers and ought to come closer together. What was gnawing at her was Uncle Nick's neglect of her and the thought that he might soon be finding another girl for the act. And any week that I had a dressing-room to myself, she would be popping in and out with the slightest of excuses, nearly always to ask me questions about Uncle Nick that I couldn't answer. Though I was fond of Cissie – sorry for her, too – I began to wish she'd leave me alone. Then one night, when we were at the Shepherd's Bush Empire, I went straight back to Walham Green; I didn't want to eat out again and I'd bought some cold stuff for supper; and I'd just about finished eating when the bell on my door, one of those shrill little brutes, went off like a fire alarm. It was Cissie, looking rather bedraggled and tearful. 'I know it's late, Dick, and I'm sorry to bother you. But I must talk to you. And anyhow this is on my way home,' she added, taking away the urgency as soon as she'd suggested it, which was typical of poor Cissie.

'All right, Cissie. Come in. Are you hungry? There's some cold ham and pork pie here – and potato salad.'

'Thanks, Dick.' She was taking off her hat and big coat. 'I could have a bite. But what I'd really like is a drink.'

'I've only bottled beer.'

'I'll take some and put some gin in it. I've got a half bottle of gin in my bag.' Cissie always carried an over-size handbag, so I wasn't surprised. 'Have you ever had beer with gin in it, Dick? Well, you ought to try it. It's called Dog's Nose.'

(And years afterwards, when I'd settled down to painting in the Dales and often walked miles across the moors, my favourite drink, when at last I reached a pub, was a large gin in a pint of draught beer – Dog's Nose. It's a curiously potent drink, somehow much stronger than the gin and the beer drunk separately. And more often than not, when most of it had gone down, I remembered Cissie visiting me that night in Walham Green.)

After we'd both dipped into our Dog's Noses and she was eating pork pie, Cissie between bites said earnestly: 'What d'you think of me, Dick? I want your straight honest opinion. I don't care what you say so long as it's the truth. I really don't — honestly I don't.'

It was just like Cissie to choose this moment, when she'd done nothing to her face except put pie into it, to offer herself for a frank appraisal. But then she often looked even worse when she was trying too hard to keep up with women like Julie. And I've told already, describing her after we first met, how I felt her looks weren't bad in a rather weak style, not the kind that attracted me but not unlike those we often saw then on sentimental coloured picture-postcards. 'Looks and figure first, I suppose, Cissie?'

'I'm a girl, aren't I? I'm not asking if I'll do for a bank manager. Go on.'

Being even younger than she was, I was a bit solemn and pompous about it, not realizing that what she wanted then wasn't anybody's candid opinion but a little praise to cheer her up. I said that her face wasn't bad at all, pleasing rather than not, and her figure better still, though I did feel she didn't always make the best of herself —

'Not like Miss Julie bloody Blane, of course,' she cut in savagely. 'Not in that class at all, of course. Except when she has to take a hiding from Tommy Beamish. Oh – yes, Nick told me. He still tells me a few things —'

'Do I stop now?'

'She walked out on you then, didn't she? And can't you see why? She couldn't face you after that had happened – no bloody fear, not the grand Miss Julie Blane, not her. But if I'd been in and out of bed with you for weeks – oh – don't think I didn't know what was going on – I'd not have run away from you the way she did —'

'What are we doing now, Cissie?' I asked her, just managing to keep my temper. 'Do I go on? Do I tell you how thoughtful, kind and considerate you are? How careful you are not to say the wrong things —'

'You don't have to be sarcastic,' she flung at me. To girls like Cissie, in those days, to be *sarcastic* was about as bad as slapping their faces hard. But then, as I looked at her and said nothing, suddenly her face crumpled and she came blindly round the table to where I was standing and collapsed against me, so that I had to hold her.

'Here, let's sit down,' I said, backing towards the only armchair. I sat in it and she sat on the floor, her hands across my knees and her face, turned my way, resting on her hands.

'I know I'm silly,' she began, 'but you do like me a bit, don't you, Dick? Well, I'm so miserable. I don't know what to do. Nick hardly ever wants me here, now we aren't living together. And I thought I wouldn't mind 'cos I'd be living at home, back with my family again. But that's no good either. It's not really different, but I am. Y'know, after going round with Nick – being waited on – nice rooms – best saloon bars an' all that. There's eight of us in that bloody little house and half the time it's like a screaming pigsty. And I've only to say anything or just give 'em a wrong look, and they're on to me, as if I'd got my money off the streets. Not that they don't like the money – oh no, I can't pull it out fast enough – it's me they don't like. So home-sweet-home's a dead washout. And all I've got is Nick – and I haven't got him. And you of course, Dick dear – you know how fond of you I am, don't you? But then you don't want me.' She raised herself up.

'And a real old mess it would be if I did, wouldn't it?'

'I know, I know, I know. I understand some things a lot better than you do. But I have to have *something*. There's a fellow lives two doors from us at home – works at a grocer's and quite nice-looking and dresses smart – who used to be gone on me – still is, he says – but he seems so boring and dreary now. I know everything he's going to say next – not like Nick and you – and he always gives the same little cough first, so I could scream. Give me a kiss, Dick. No – not like that – a real kiss.'

There were a lot of good reasons why I didn't want to start kissing her, though I'll admit the deepest of them was that I didn't enjoy it, but I couldn't refuse that one, though I then disentangled us gently and held her at arms' length. However, her mind was now on something else.

'Dick dear – listen – and tell me the truth, please, dear. Has Nick ever spoken to you about engaging another girl, to take my place?'

'No, Cissie. He's worried about two dwarfs – not two girls.'

'You'd tell me if he *did* say anything, wouldn't you? Please, Dick – you must. Here – we're not drinking. The gin's here but where's some more beer, to put another nose on a dog? No, tell me, I'll do it – don't move.' Like most young men, then and now, whenever a girl or woman offered to wait upon me, I let her. So I filled and lit a pipe while Cissie mixed the gin and beer, talking all the time: 'You know what's happening soon, don't you? No? Well, that's because you haven't been taking much interest lately. And anyhow Nick knows you don't like Mr Bosenby. I don't either but if you saw me with him you wouldn't believe it, I lay it on thick just because he's the agent. But that's why you don't know what's happening, you don't listen to sweaty greasy old Bosenby when he comes round.'

'No, I keep away from Uncle Nick when Bosenby's there,' I said rather loftily. But of course I was curious. 'If you know what's happening soon, then tell me.'

'Here you are, dear. And all the best!' We drank together. She sat on the floor again, resting against my legs. 'Well, to start with, we're probably having two weeks out. And I don't care where Nick's going this time, he'll have to take me with him.'

'He won't, you know, Cissie. And I wouldn't try too hard to make him.'

'I know, Dick. I was only talking big. He'll do just what he wants to do.' She said this rather proudly, not sadly. 'Anyhow we're going round with the same bill. I mean, like last time but not the same turns. Nick's been working it out with Joe Bosenby. I don't know who we've got yet, but some of 'em might be nice and friendly. And we'll be together for months. Mostly in Lancashire at first — a place I love, I don't think – opening in Liverpool, but I don't remember the date, if there was one. Well, that's it, dearie, and it could be fun, couldn't it?'

'It could be.'

'Oh – you're a long streak of misery, you are.'

'I was thinking.'

'I know that.' She finished her drink, then gave me a lopsided smile. 'But about which one? Innocent little Nancy or wicked old Julie — which?'

'Neither. I've other things to think about, Cissie.'

'Not at this time of night you oughtn't to have. And I'm here, aren't I? I've got everything they have. And if you don't believe me, I'll show you.' She began climbing up, breathing hard. 'Can't we have some fun for once? You gave her plenty, didn't you? Making me jealous. Keep still, you silly boy.'

It was now a wrestling match I hadn't to lose or win. I felt a fool, of course, but it couldn't go on and at the same time I was really anxious not to hurt her feelings. 'Now listen – please listen – Cissie,' I said finally, holding her firmly at arms' length. 'If we started something now, we'd go on with it, then sooner or later – and it mightn't take long – Uncle Nick would find out – and then where are we?'

'I'd have to go – not you–'

'Probably both of us. But I'm thinking about you, Cissie, especially after what you said earlier, when you were feeling rather desperate. Now he's never said a word to me about any other girl taking your place. We've got months of work ready for us – you've just told me so – and I just can't see him disturbing the act. Not unless he thinks you and I are up to something—'

'And that wouldn't be because he really wants me,' she said bitterly, moving away now. 'Just pride, that's all. One of his belongings. And you don't really want me. I know—'

'No, you don't. I'm just trying to be sensible – for both of us.' As I went on along that line, nobly resisting temptation, she was sitting at the table, leaning forward with her head between her hands, her hair rather dishevelled, her eyes shuttered, her mouth a vague dark pout in the blur of her face, all the light on the Naples Yellow shoulders of the blouse she was wearing; and I remembered it afterwards as if Sickert had painted it. And I thought my noble resistance line very clever, keeping her away from me without hurting her feelings; but it would have been better for all of us, as things turned out, if I hadn't been so clever and so sensitive about her feelings but had made it quite plain she didn't attract me as a woman, which after all was the basic truth of the situation. 'Come on, Cissie,' I said finally. 'It's getting late, and you must have a long way to go. I'll take you down to the bus or the Underground. And – look – don't forget your gin. There's still some left.'

'And I know what to do with it,' she mumbled as she attended to her face. But she obviously felt better when she took my arm outside and prattled away. She felt better than I did. I couldn't imagine what would become of Cissie Mapes.

It wasn't the next day but the day after that I saw Nancy Ellis, who'd never replied to my letter so that I didn't know where she was or what she was doing. I'd been to the National Gallery in the morning, and then, after a snack and a beer at a pub near the Coliseum, I'd gone to Leicester Square tube station to take a train to Earls Court, not the best way back to my flat but I liked to do a little exploring. Going down the steps leading to the platforms and then arriving at the space between them, I hesitated a moment, though I knew to which platform I had to go. I turned to glance at the train standing at the platform I didn't want. I saw somebody sitting close to the window who looked rather like Nancy. I rushed nearer – and it *was* Nancy, absorbed in a book. I gave an idiotic shout, which obviously she didn't hear, and then before I could tap on the window or make for the door, the train was moving. In less than twenty-five seconds I had found her and lost her again. Watching the train, gathering speed, sway into darkness and vanish, carrying her in its black tube to God knows where, I cursed the luck.

However, this glimpse of her jolted me into action I ought to have taken before. I hurried out of the station and went to find Joe Bosenby's office in Charing Cross Road. I'd never been there but I knew the address because Uncle Nick had showed me one or two letters from him. I went up some very dirty stairs by the side of a music shop. In the room marked *Enquiries* about twenty people, all kinds, were sitting along the walls, which had been distempered, some years before, a sad mauve. It had a thick mixed smell of old cigarette smoke, underclothes worn too long, and some sort of antiseptic stuff that wasn't winning. At the far end of the room, next to a door marked *Private*, and behind a table, a typewriter and a telephone, sat a middle-aged woman. When I went closer I saw that she looked rather like a female Fishblick. On her wide flat bosom was pinned, under a black gunmetal knot, a watch nearly as big as a man's. I looked at her; she looked at me; we hated each other at sight.

I told her I was inquiring about a friend of mine, Miss Nancy Ellis.

Wasting no more eyesight on me, she looked at some papers. 'Nobody of that name here,' she threw at me.

'She used to be in an act called *Susie, Nancy and Three Gentlemen —'*

'Oh – *them.*' They were now in the dustbin. 'We no longer book that act.'

'But you don't know—'

'Haven't the least notion.' And she waved me away.

And I went, partly because I felt a fool and partly because there were so many people waiting. I had an idea that if I'd told her I was with Nick Ollanton and was related to him, she wouldn't have behaved like that. But I felt too shy. As I left the room rather slowly, one of the young men who'd been waiting joined me. He had black round his eyes and a rim of rouge round his collar to prove that he really was on the stage. 'With guns on her,' he began cheerfully, 'they could use her in the Navy – Dreadnought class. Asking for an audition, laddie?'

I told him I wasn't, being in work, but I wanted to trace a girl whose act wasn't booked now by Joe Bosenby.

'What's her beautiful name, laddie?'

'Nancy Ellis.'

'I've heard it. I've seen it. I know it. Wait a minute, I—' But then, after raising my hopes he brought them down with a crash. 'No, can't tell you, laddie. But you know what to do, don't you? Take a dekko at all the adverts in the pro papers. Ought to be there somewhere even if she's only under *At Liberty*.' And he rattled off the names of these theatrical and variety weeklies, of which there were four or five then. After some trouble, I bought them all, and took them to Walham Green to read through carefully. But I couldn't find Nancy Ellis, nor any mention anywhere of Susie and Bob Hodson. It was maddening. I felt like a man in a desert who'd suddenly seen a spring bubbling into the air and then vanishing.

I went to Joe Bosenby's again, though, during our last week in London, and this time I was accompanying Uncle Nick, who'd asked me the night before to meet him there, without telling me why. There were people – and they looked the same people – still waiting in that outer room. Uncle Nick, with me keeping close to him, strode past that dragon-woman without giving her a nod, even a look, straight into Joe Bosenby's private office, which was all mahogany, signed photographs, deep armchairs, and the rich mingled odours of cigars, whisky and brandy.

'Hello, Nick – and hello to you, young fellow! Have a cigar. I think old Pitter's got 'em all lined up for you along there, but I'd better make sure.' He rang a bell. 'And I'll tell you frankly, Nick old boy, I doubt if there's another agency in London that could have found so many for you to look over. And I'll also admit, while I'm at it, that I couldn't have done it myself. It's old Pitter—'

'That's no news, Joe,' said Uncle Nick dryly. 'I know about old Pitter. Though I don't know how he does it. What are you paying him now – thirty bob a week?'

'Certainly not, Nick,' said Bosenby, almost proudly. 'Two pounds.'

'How's his wife nowadays?'

'Still ailing but not failing – worse luck. That's why I raised him to two pounds.'

'I hope you can afford it, Joe,' said Uncle Nick, with one of his darkly sardonic glances. 'I don't like to think of you throwing your money about.'

There was a timid knocking at the side-door, not the one we'd used, and Pitter came in, elderly, stooping, shabby. In those days there were still old clerks or humble general assistants who seemed to have been left over from the vanished Dickens world, who still worked very long hours, always terrified of being dismissed, for just enough to keep them alive; and clearly Pitter was one of them. He trembled at the sound of Bosenby's loud if wheezy voice. 'All ready for Mr Ollanton along there, Pitter?'

'Yes, quite ready, Mr Bosenby.'

'Have you been keeping them quiet, Mr Pitter?' Uncle Nick asked, using a much friendlier tone than Bosenby had.

'I've done my best, Mr Ollanton, but you can't imagine what some of them are like when they find so many others there. They're not easy to deal with, Mr Ollanton, not easy at all. May I ask how you've been keeping, sir?'

'Can't grumble, Mr Pitter. Oh – and this is my nephew, in the act with me, Richard Herncastle.'

'A great pleasure, Mr Herncastle. I've often had the privilege—'

'No doubt,' said Bosenby, cutting in brutally, 'but let's get on with it, Pitter. Our time's valuable even if yours isn't.'

'Of course. I'm sorry, Mr Bosenby. This way, please, gentlemen.'

We went by way of the side-door into a dingy corridor. On our left, behind two closed doors, a piano was being thumped and some people seemed to be rehearsing a ragtime dance number. We went further along and Pitter opened a door on the right, holding it for us and smiling uncertainly. He might have been the humble host at a party of Dickensian clerks. But when we passed him we might have been walking into a story by the Brothers Grimm. It was a small but rather high room, with peeling yellowish wallpaper and just one picture, enormous and very dark, of an idiotic horse. And it was full of dwarfs.

'This is enough for me,' said Bosenby at the top of his voice. 'Give you the bloody creeps. So I'll leave you to it, Nick old boy. Pick where you like. See you later.'

There seemed to be scores of them when we first looked in, but after Bosenby had left us, I realized that actually there were a dozen. They had been making quite a noise, arguing and laughing, but now they were all silent, all still, their eyes staring up at ours. They all belonged to the same physical type as Barney, with big heads, small bodies, tiny legs, and two or three of them looked exactly like him. Some looked prosperous, smart manikins, ready to do business; others were very shabby and seemed either over-anxious or sulky; and one with a great overhanging forehead, rolling eyes, and a slobbering mouth, looked quite mad. But even while I noticed these differences among them, I still half-felt in some weird dream. (And occasionally they popped up in dreams, for years afterwards.) I don't believe I could have attended to anything properly in there, have gone round asking names and making notes. Even Barney sometimes still made me feel uncomfortable; and the effect here was not that of Barney multiplied by twelve but by twelve hundred. True, I felt genuinely sorry for them and, in a queer way, half-ashamed of myself for being so different; and yet – and yet – not through me, not really through them, poor little chaps – something sinister crept into the room, into the afternoon, into this life on the stage with Uncle Nick. Here, well before the next passage of this life had begun, anticipating the peculiar colouring and tone it would have, a certain note was sounded, like a horn sounding distantly in an orchestra, and *it was sinister*. But of course I didn't know then I would look back on this afternoon, would hear that sinister note repeated, when I began the next tour with Uncle Nick. We shall come to that recognition in its own place.

Meanwhile, Uncle Nick, a tallish man in any company, was busy, a stooping giant, among the dwarfs, closely regarding them and asking questions, with Pitter at his elbow occasionally supplying information. Finally they seemed to settle on one, very like Barney in appearance but giving the impression that he was far less excitable and silly. I heard his name, which was Philip Tewby. But by this time several of the odder dwarfs were becoming noisy, complaining loudly and shouting at each other in their disappointment.

'That's enough, Mr Pitter,' said Uncle Nick. 'Let's get out of this – and tell 'em they can all go home.' We left screams of rage behind us. 'I've made a note of his name – Philip Tewby.'

'I think you'll find him a responsible little chap, Mr Ollanton,' said Pitter. 'I know they were pleased with him at the Balham pantomime.

Have you any idea when you'll be wanting him, Mr Ollanton?'

'Not yet, Mt Pitter. I'll wire you as soon as I do. And I'm much obliged to you for finding me so many to choose from. Have a cigar, Mr Pitter?'

'Thank you very much, Mr Ollanton.' He was blushing with pleasure. 'It's exceedingly kind of you, I'm sure. Thank you.' He handed us back into the presence of Joe Bosenby, who was shouting down the telephone.

'I've got one who looks useful,' said Uncle Nick when Bosenby had finished. 'Pitter knows about him. He can attend to it when I wire. Now, Joe, how's our bill looking for the new tour? Any news?'

'*The Ragtime Three* are fixed. Happy with the middle of the bill though they're a big draw. Now about Lily Farris, Nick. She has to go on top, old boy. They go off their heads about her in Lancashire. It's not Lily herself that's insisting on top billing, but her pianist chap, Mergen, who's her manager – and though he looks soft he's as hard as bloody nails.'

'So am I, Joe.'

'I know, Nick – harder. But you're getting the same money she is – and why should you bother? You'll be still packing them in when she's back on the end of a pier. Let the little lady have it, old boy – eh? All right? Done.' Pleased at having settled this billing, which he knew the head office of the syndicate would accept, Bosenby gave me a smile that turned into a leer. 'Lily Farris – eh, young man? Something to look forward to there, if you can get on the right side of her, 'cos she's not too easy to please, Lily isn't. Seen her act?'

'Yes, I have. She's boring.'

'That's my lad,' said Uncle Nick. 'Can't see anything in her myself. Well, we'd better be going.'

'Just a minute, please, uncle.' I looked at Bosenby. 'I came here, the other day, to ask about Nancy Ellis, but the old girl out there neither knew nor cared.'

'No, Violet thinks they no longer exist if I don't book 'em. And they left me. Nothing to do with little Nancy, of course. It's the sister and her fool of a husband. I'll try to find out where they are and what they're doing.' He made a note on a pad. 'And next time, young fellow, don't let Violet stop you. Ask for me and don't take No for an answer. But wait a minute. If I get the information, where do I send it? Where are you going to be during your two weeks out?'

'I'll write it for you.'

Uncle Nick looked over my shoulder. 'You're not expecting to go to bed with anybody in Kettlewell, are you, lad?'

'No. I'm going there to do some painting.'

'Well, that'll be a change.' But I knew that he was pleased. Uncle Nick always liked the idea of my painting, and in the end it was through him, years later, that I was able to become a full-time professional watercolour painter.

Joe Bosenby stared at the address I had passed over to him. 'Kettlewell? I've never heard of it.'

'And it's never heard of you, Joe,' said Uncle Nick. 'You'd be as strange as a Zulu up there.'

10

I don't suppose Joe Bosenby liked me any better than I liked him, but, after all, Uncle Nick was one of the most successful performers on his list so I was worth a little trouble, even though it was probably Pitter who found the address in Hampstead at which Nancy could be reached. It arrived after I'd been several days in Kettlewell, and I didn't write until a few more days had gone by. But it was a long letter, beginning with a brief reference to her curious behaviour in Plymouth, but then going into a fairly detailed account of how I was spending my time up there – the great walks, the sketching and then sometimes something better than sketching, the huge meals to which I returned when the light was going, the odd characters I met. And I ended simply by saying that I felt she would have enjoyed most of it too and that I was always thinking about her. I don't know if it was a good letter or not; but I certainly meant it.

For the ignorant, the under-privileged, the uninitiated, I must explain that Kettlewell is in Upper Wharfedale, and from it a good walker, going in almost every direction, can reach some of the most beautiful country in the world. In 1914, before moorland tracks became motor roads, it seemed remote and wonderfully unspoilt. I had gone rather early for this country and on the tops some days my hands felt frozen, and one or two afternoons were darkened and slashed by sleet. But going up there for most of my two weeks out was the most sensible, refreshing and heartening thing I did in all that time when I was appearing with Uncle Nick. I came closer than I'd ever done before to feeling that I really was a painter, not yet a good one but at least a hopeful one; I walked in all weathers but the very worst; I returned, tired but triumphant, to smell the ham and eggs in the pan for me and then to smoke drowsily in the lamplit peace. All the variety stages, all the Empires, seemed far off and almost unbelievable. I seemed to be in another country, breathing an altogether different air. And if I pass over this intermission quickly, that is not because I have forgotten it – for some of it attached itself to the very centre of my being – but because it was entirely separate from my variety-stage life, so has no part in this account of that life.

But I knew when I had to leave them that I had found refreshment, sustenance, sanity, among the great hills. What I didn't know was how soon I might have to call upon these resources.

Book Three

1

We were opening this tour in Liverpool, and on the Sunday evening I joined Uncle Nick and Cissie there. They hadn't liked the digs they'd had before in Liverpool, so we were all three staying at a small old-fashioned hotel (*Bed and Breakfast Five Shillings*) not far from Lime Street Station. Uncle Nick and Cissie had just had a week together at Bournemouth but hadn't enjoyed it. But Uncle Nick didn't like Liverpool either, and told me why he didn't, a few minutes after I'd joined them in the hotel.

'It has some fine buildings, as you'll see, lad,' he began. 'Good art gallery too, I believe. But after you've seen Rotterdam and Amsterdam, Hamburg and Bremen, Copenhagen and Stockholm, as I have, this place makes you wonder what'll happen to us. They're clean, this is filthy. They're civilized, this isn't – except in spots. It's full of huge policemen moving on hordes of gutter rats. Where the fine buildings stop, the slums start, miles of 'em. I wouldn't keep a dog there. However, it's a good date.'

'Who have we got with us this time, uncle?'

'I can not only tell you that, lad, but I can give you the running order, which I was largely instrumental in fixing.' He produced a notebook. 'First turn – *Duffield's Dogs*—'

'They're sweet,' said Cissie.

'You keep 'em, girl, I don't want 'em. Then – *The Colmars*—'

'So you'll have Nonie rubbing herself against you, Dick.'

'I won't,' I told her. 'But I hope she'll leave Barney alone this time.'

'Next – Number Three – *Lowson Brothers*. Know the act? Well, they're a couple of ambitious but not very bright lads who do some dancing – not bad – and some of the most unfunny crosstalk in the business. I've put 'em in front of us because they're not bad enough to send the customers out to the bars and not good enough to spoil our welcome. So then we're in the same spot. By the way, I've had some new band parts copied while we were in London, and a German friend of mine, Max Forster, has worked on the score for me, improving it. So perhaps I'd better join you tomorrow at the band call, Richard – just this once, that's all.'

I told him I'd be grateful if he would. 'What about the second half of the bill, uncle?'

'It opens with *Montana* – a balancing act. He's a Swiss who does a lot of things nobody particularly wants him to do, while balancing on a ball. A dullish safe act. Next is Lottie Dean, who's modelled her act on Florrie Forde – thighs a yard wide in tights and idiot chorus songs. She's followed by Lily Farris, who doesn't mind following her because they're such a contrast. And the last turn is *The Ragtime Three*, who like being last because they can give encores, if they've any voice left, at the second house. That's the lot. I've been on better bills and I've been on worse. We oughtn't to do badly.'

'What I'm wondering is – are they nice friendly people?' Cissie said, rather wistfully.

'You'll have to make friends with Duffield's dear little doggies, girl. I'd say the rest of 'em are either dull or dam' silly.'

'I'll miss Bill Jennings and Hank Johnson,' I said.

'So will I, lad. But Joe booked them into the West End halls, and then, on the strength of that, they're going back to America in September. They're the only friends I've made in the profession for the last couple of years or so. Some of you people—' and he looked from me to Cissie as if there were a dozen of us – 'seem to think I don't want any friends. And certainly I don't want to be cluttered up with dear old pals who aren't dear or old or pals, but I like to be on the road with one or two men I can talk to, as distinct from spongers and idiots, the sort that somebody like Tommy Beamish would gather round him like wasps round a jam pot.'

'What's happened to Tommy Beamish?' I asked.

'He had a bit of a breakdown after that trouble he ran into,' Uncle Nick said grimly. 'But Joe told me he's preparing a new sketch that he'll take through the Midlands, Yorkshire, the North-East and Scotland. He won't overlap with us anywhere, I'm glad to say. Now then, lad, while I remember. As soon as you see Sam, Ben and Barney this morning, warn 'em I'm going to run through the *Vanishing Cyclist* tomorrow afternoon – we might be all a trifle rusty.'

'What about the two-dwarf illusion, uncle?'

'Haven't got to diagrams yet, lad. Now you'll have to be up early in the morning. Better get to bed.'

It was a wet Monday – as it nearly always seemed to be when I had to go down early – and though we were into spring, Liverpool appeared huge, gloomy, unfriendly. All our stuff was safely in; I warned Sam, Ben and Barney about the afternoon rehearsal; and then, after some coffee that seemed to have been dredged up from the Mersey, I hung about waiting for the band call and for Uncle Nick. As he was late I had a chance to take a look at most of the others. After all, we'd be sharing the same bill for months to come.

I didn't see either Duffield or his dogs, only a tired-looking woman who, I was told afterwards, was Duffield's sister and did all the real work. Nonie Colmar had come along with her uncle, Gustav; he gave me a nod and she put her tongue out at me. Montana and his wife, who handed him the instruments he played while balancing on his big metal ball, looked a dull Swiss couple who ought to have been running a small hotel.

Lottie Dean, probably about fifty and with dyed red hair, was a battleship of a woman, who had in anxious attendance, like a destroyer going round and round a dreadnought, a little woman, pale and thin, who was always addressed as 'Oh – for God's sake – Ethel!' The Lowson Brothers, Bert and Ted, parted their hair in the middle and had it plastered to their skulls, wore green-striped suits, pink shirts, yellow shoes, and suggested a couple of Cockney barber's assistants. But I must admit that by the time I'd accepted this suggestion I was feeling a bit depressed. Uncle Nick had now arrived, with Cissie, and I told them I wasn't finding these other people on the bill very exciting.

'They're about average, I'd say,' Uncle Nick observed. 'And they're here to entertain the audience, not you, lad.'

'Dick's thinking about his Nancy,' said Cissie. 'Or that Julie Blane. That's his trouble.'

'Well, let's get on with it.' Uncle Nick was about to take the stage, the new band parts under his arm, when to his disgust he found that *The Ragtime Three* – all three of them too – had claimed the attention of the conductor and his sixteen men. He retreated, cursing them all.

'You too, Mr Ollanton?' We'd been joined by a man who introduced himself to Cissie and me – Uncle Nick, after giving him a nod, being busy with a cigar, in defiance of all the notices about No Smoking – as Otto Mergen, Lily Farris's pianist and manager, the man I'd heard Joe Bosenby mention. 'Miss Cissie Mapes? Yes, of course. Mr Richard Herncastle? A pleasure. Mr Ollanton's nephew who wants to be a painter. Isn't that so? Yes, he mentioned you to us. Lily's up in her dressing-room, but she'll be down soon. You like Liverpool, Miss

Mapes?'

'No, she doesn't, Mergen,' said Uncle Nick, who was still out of temper. 'And neither do I. Business should be good, though.'

'I think so. Yes, I think so.' He said something else but he spoke softly and it was impossible to hear him, there was now such a blast of sound from the orchestra and the three ragtimers – all youngish Americans, a plump one playing the piano, a tall one playing the saxophone, a medium-sized one doing the singing or shouting.

'What a bloody din!' And Uncle Nick didn't say it, he shouted it, and as at that moment the noise had been sharply cut off, everybody heard it. Somebody laughed, but not on the stage, where the three of them stared in our direction. While the pianist and saxophone player argued with the conductor, the one who'd been singing came off and marched truculently up to Uncle Nick. 'Who called it a bloody din?' he demanded.

'I did,' Uncle Nick said calmly. 'I'll say it again if you like. What a bloody din!' He replaced the cigar, lowered his head slightly, and stared darkly at the young man, whose truculence was oozing away. There was always something unusually formidable about Uncle Nick.

'That's because you're out of date on these new numbers, Pop.'

'Don't call *me* Pop,' said Uncle Nick fiercely. 'And don't be all morning with that band. As for your new numbers, I shared a bill for months a year ago with Hedges Brothers and Jacobsen, who brought 'em here. And they were a bloody din then too.'

'Come on, Marcus boy,' one of them called from the stage.

'Now get a move on with it,' said Uncle Nick, waving him away.

'I don't think I'd like to quarrel with you, Mr Ollanton,' Mergen said softly. 'But hadn't we better move a little further away? Lily ought to be down any moment now.'

We left the wings and the spread of the big white working light, and we moved into a little space at the top of some steps that went down towards the stage door. This was wide open, letting in the daylight, and there was also some daylight coming in at the back of the stage, where the sets had been brought in earlier. But as well as this drift of daylight, our little space had two electric bulbs, one painted red, the other yellow. The result was a queer mixed light I never remembered seeing before, a light in which even familiar faces like Uncle Nick's and Cissie's looked odd and rather sinister. As for Mergen, I had felt there was something sinister about him, felt it right from the first; and now while we waited there and I had time to take him in, the effect was stronger still: he seemed a figure of corruption.

He was a man of no particular age, anything between an unhealthy forty-five and a fairly spry sixty-five; a fattish baggy man, hair and eyes a kind of light pewter, his face a yellow-grey, but with a thick-lipped, swollen mouth rather like the sort of mouth ventriloquists' dolls are given. He spoke slowly and softly, without any obvious foreign accent yet with that extra care which educated foreigners bring to their English. (Uncle Nick told me later that he thought Mergen came originally from some Baltic country.) There was also a certain tone in his voice, together with an obvious desire to please, that reminded me of some parsons and priests: he might have been a missionary of some remote and evil religion. And the final and most ironical fact about Otto Mergen – though I only discovered it much later – wasn't simply that he went round, year after year, accompanying an English variety star, but that, under another name, it was he who wrote and composed the naively girlish, sentimental and very English songs Lily Farris made so popular, the identical songs I was to hear being roared out in *estaminets* behind the line at Neuve Chapelle and Loos.

Lily Farris now appeared, and with her was a young man who looked like a desperate blond rabbit. His name was Alfred Dunsop, and, after being sharply prompted by Lily, he invited us all to lunch at the Adelphi Hotel. Then Lily and Mergen, Uncle Nick and I, left him with Cissie while we attended to our band call. Uncle Nick told Lily she could go first; Mergen had already distributed their band parts, and now he went to the piano recovering from the ragtimer; Lily spoke to the conductor, who was obviously well acquainted with her act; Mergen gave some cues from the piano; and he and Lily were so experienced, business-like, quick, that they were through in ten minutes. Uncle Nick, who always lost his temper with conductors, now lost it again, told me to do what I could with this conceited blockhead, and went striding off the stage. When I had finished, I found Mergen waiting for me, to tell me that the other four had gone in Alfred Dunsop's car to the Adelphi. It had stopped raining, he said, and if I didn't object, then he and I might walk to the hotel, where he and Lily were staying.

'Who's this Alfred Dunsop?' I asked him as we started off.

'Alfred is the only son of a very rich cotton man,' he replied in his soft careful way. 'I believe his father supplied many many millions of Hindoos with their loin-cloths. All your *Ganga Dun's* poorer relatives, we might say, are Dunsop Senior's customers. Not Alfred's yet. Alfred does not pay much attention to business. For some months now, he's been completely infatuated with Lily. He's her slave,'

'And what about her? She seemed to be bossing him.'

'She never stops bossing him, we might say. As far as she is concerned, Alfred is there to be bossed.' We were making our way along a crowded pavement, and then we had to cross a road, so there was no more talk for several minutes.

'I think I must tell you a little about Lily,' he began when we could talk again. 'She is the third of eight children of a cabinet maker – not a first-class man – in West Ham. She has no secrets from me, so she took me once to visit her family. It was a very good home to get away from and then stay away from. Do you know West Ham?'

I didn't, but I'd no chance to tell him so because we were now separately dodging round some men who were selling and buying noon editions of the evening papers.

'So Lily enjoys singing about love,' he began again, 'and is attracted to men, but she hasn't the least desire for marriage, domesticity, a family life. Probably because he has not succeeded in making her his mistress, Alfred would marry her at once, but she laughs at him. And of course Alfred is very easy to laugh at. He looks a fool – and he *is* a fool. He is at the opposite extreme, we might say, from your uncle, Mr Ollanton, who is a clever man and clearly a very formidable man.'

'Yes, Uncle Nick's got plenty of character.'

'And Lily and I deeply appreciate his attitude towards her top billing. Most courteous, very gracious. You won't think me intrusive, I hope, if I ask what his relations are with Miss – er – Mapes?'

'She's in the act. They share digs. He has a wife but they've separated.' I told him so much because I wondered what he was up to, for I was certain he never talked for talking's sake and was always up to something.

'From your knowledge of him, do you think he will be strongly attracted by Lily?'

'No, I don't.' And I didn't, but the reason I gave him such a curt answer was that talking like this, with a stranger in the crowded Liverpool streets, suddenly seemed idiotic.

'And why not, may I ask?'

'Oh well—' I hesitated partly because I wanted to appear reluctant but also because I didn't want to tell him that Uncle Nick didn't like Lily's act. 'I don't know – but – well, Uncle Nick's mind doesn't run much on women. He has to have one around – you know – but I really can't see him chasing Lily Farris.'

'I am very glad to hear you say so,' Mergen said emphatically. 'Very glad indeed. The young men we saw this morning seemed anything but formidable, though of course Lily didn't see them herself.'

'I'm hungry,' I told him. 'I need that lunch I've been invited to. Let's push on.'

The head waiter, who knew Alfred Dunsop, gave us a rather small rectangular table. Alfred sat at one end, with Lily on his right and Cissie on his left. Uncle Nick was next to Lily; Mergen was at the other end, facing Alfred; and I sat between Mergen and Cissie, facing Uncle Nick and Lily. While we were ordering and talking about nothing in particular, I took a good look across the table at Lily Farris. In her act, which I had seen and found boring, because I didn't enjoy very sentimental ballads sung in a sweet-young-girl soprano, she looked about eighteen. Here, without her light-brown ringlets and pink-and-white make-up, she looked about ten years older. Her chief feature was a long nose, not jutting out at all, thin and straight. Her eyes were curious, not because of their colour, a muddy hazel, but because, without being protuberant, they were the opposite of deep-set, almost in the same plane as her forehead and cheeks, rather like the eyes of some delicate animal. And she had a tight hard upper-lip but a full if narrow under-lip. She wasn't beautiful, not really even pretty, but I could imagine that if you wanted to look at that face, then, like Alfred, you might want to look at it a lot. A suggestion of the sweet-innocent-young-girl of the act hung about her; and this was even more obvious in her voice – and I mean her ordinary speaking voice that she was using now across the table – which she used very carefully, though she still had some trace of the Cockney left, and gave the impression she was a good little girl thanking teacher for a prize. In addition, she had a trick of opening her eyes wide at moments when she was listening or talking.

I'd been talking to Cissie for a few minutes about the other people on the bill when Lily held my eye, smiled, and said in her good-little-girl tone: 'I hear you're a naughty bad boy.'

'Who told you? Cissie, I'll bet.'

'Now, Dick, I didn't,' Cissie began.

But Lily, though she might not have seemed to have the voice for it, was clearly a ruthless cutter-in. 'Can I call you Dick too? If you'll call me Lily.'

'All right, Lily.' Uncle Nick and Mergen were talking, probably about the tour and business. Cissie was now in retreat, and anyhow was always ready to be happy with her food, and Alfred was staring with his mouth open.

'Tell me, Dick,' said Lily, 'do you paint people?'

'No, I don't. Only landscapes.'

'Not people at all?'

'Oh – well, I've tried a few sketches of faces, but I don't pretend to be any good at it.'

'I believe you're just being modest now.'

'He did a lovely one of me.' This was Cissie, emerging from her breast of duck.

'Well then,' said Lily, not even bothering to look at Cissie, 'you can do one of me. Alfred would buy it. Wouldn't you, Alfred?'

Alfred had a try for independence, probably his last. 'Well, I might – and then again I might not.'

I could talk like that: 'And I might do it – and then again I might not.'

It was then I felt a distinct pressure of another foot against mine. It wasn't Cissie's, I knew, and it certainly wasn't Alfred's, and Uncle Nick and Mergen, still talking hard, were on the wrong side for this pressure. Only lily could be giving me this signal, but there was no hint of it in the reproachful look she was giving me.

'I'm sorry if I said the wrong thing, Dick. But don't you think you might try?' The pressure increased, was almost urgent.

'I don't care about anybody buying the sketch, Lily. It's just that it isn't my kind of work. It needs a different kind of artist. But if you really want me to try, then I will.'

'This afternoon?'

'Hey – whoa!' Alfred cried. 'Steady the Buffs, Lily! Don't forget—'

'Oh – do shut up, Alfred. It wasn't a definite arrangement.' She looked at me. 'This afternoon?'

'Sorry – we're rehearsing.'

'Go on – I'll bet you aren't.'

'And I'll bet he is,' said Uncle Nick very firmly. 'I don't know about you, Miss Farris, but in my line of business we have to keep working at it. So we'll have to be off, soon.'

'I hear you have a wonderful act, Mr Ollanton,' said Lily, very dignified now. 'I'll sneak into the back of a box and watch it.'

We left Lily and Co. still sitting at the table and took a taxi back to the Empire. (Uncle Nick had sold his car while we were in London, and he was now brooding over buying a new one.) 'I hope one of you thanked that chap Alfred for his lunch. Because I didn't. Got a lot more money than sense, that chap has. One of the nuts, I suppose,' Uncle Nick concluded contemptuously. 'You've got a long face, Richard lad. Think you ought to be drawing Lily this afternoon, instead of riding that bike – eh?'

'No, I don't. It was her idea, not mine.'

'I oughtn't to have said anything to her about you and that Julie Blane,' said Cissie. 'Put ideas into her head, I could see that.'

'Not ideas,' Uncle Nick told her. 'One idea. The one that's always in your head.'

'No, it isn't, Nick, and well you know it. But I'll tell you one thing, both of you. I don't like that lot. I have a funny feeling about 'em – her and that Mr Mergen and that silly Alfred, who's just dotty on her and she doesn't care tuppence for him. Yes, I have a funny feeling.' She looked defiantly at Uncle Nick and then at me.

'That's all right, Cissie,' I said. 'So have I.'

'Now what's all this, you two?' Uncle Nick snorted at us.

And then I remembered what I'd felt when we'd been looking at the dwarfs, that afternoon at Joe Bosenby's. 'I know what I feel about them, though I can't tell you why. They're sinister. I know it sounds silly, Uncle Nick, but I can't help it. They're *sinister*.'

'You're getting as bad as Cissie, lad. Sinister!'

'All right, uncle, all right. I'm fanciful. But for all that,' I added slowly, 'I don't think I'm going to like this tour.'

2

One of my troubles during the first weeks of that tour was that I kept expecting a reply to my long letter to Nancy. I'd asked her to write to me care of Bosenby's office, which of course always knew where I was. But every post was a disappointment, until I forced myself to believe she would never write. Another trouble was that though I might believe there was something sinister about Lily and Mergen, they had at least some fascination for me in their different ways, whereas the rest of the people with us were a dead loss. I simply couldn't bother about them.

The three Colmar men (I'll come to Nonie later) had always been aloof, though I did see them around with the two Swiss, Montana and his wife. Duffield's sister, who did all the work, always seemed tired and rather frightened. Duffield himself, who sported a bristling moustache, had once had a commission in the militia and still liked to call himself Captain; and according to Lily and Cissie, he fancied himself with the girls. Lottie Dean and her 'Oh – for God's sake – Ethel', who fussed over her as if she were Madame Melba, meant as much to me as I did to them. Bert and Ted Lowson were harmless but not my sort. As for *The Ragtime Three*, who were called Benton, Duff and Marcus, they were the kind of Americans I didn't like then and have never liked since, just as Bill Jennings and Hank Johnson were the kind I've always taken to at once, being calm and easy, amusing and friendly. Benton was solemnly boring, Duff was loud and brash, and Marcus was both boring *and* brash. No new friends there.

The one who was really enjoying herself at last, with six new men on the same bill with her, was little Nonie Colmar. She seemed to be giggling and squirming in every possible corner. This was the life for Nonie. And it was a nuisance simply because of its effect on Barney, who now hardly saw her at all and was of course wildly jealous. The further result was that he was becoming unreliable in his work and harder to handle. I didn't really like Barney, he was too silly and excitable and too fond of showing off, but because he was a dwarf I was sorry for him. So on the first few weeks of this tour, Sam and Ben Hayes and I were always having to chase after him or cover up for him, giving ourselves extra work so that Uncle Nick wouldn't notice how unreliable Barney was becoming, wouldn't kick him out and put in his place a steady intelligent dwarf – like Philip Tewby. (I couldn't forget that name.) Of course, once Uncle Nick had passed the diagram stage of his new illusion, he would need two dwarfs; but he hadn't arrived at any diagrams yet, and because I guessed he was feeling frustrated, I didn't want to question him. He was in fact moody and irritable during these weeks, as poor Cissie complained to me more than once.

Later in the Liverpool week I tried a pen-and-wash drawing of Lily, who 'sat' for me rather grandly, as if she were minor royalty and I were an academician, in the sitting-room of her suite at the Adelphi. (Unlike Uncle Nick, a careful West Riding man, Lily liked to splash her salary as she went along. I gathered, however, that she and Mergen made plenty of extra money out of the sheet music of their songs.) Mergen wasn't around that afternoon – probably he was busy with some unimaginable wickedness of his own – but halfway through the sitting, to my annoyance, Alfred came trotting in, not looking quite as vacuous as before because his eyes were clouded with suspicion. 'Hello, hello, hello! What's going on?'

'Lily's doing the dance of the seven veils,' I told him. 'And I'm cleaning a bicycle.'

Lilly giggled. 'Don't be silly, Alfred. And go away.'

'I'm not being silly, it's him. I can look, can't I?' And to prove that he could, he stared over my shoulder. 'Well, I don't think that's very like her.'

'Neither do I.' And I got up, tore the drawing across twice, and went looking for a wastepaper basket.

Lily was furious, not with me but with Alfred. She didn't explode at all – she wasn't the explosive type – but she went over to him and said through her teeth: 'Now look what you've done, you bloody twat. Get out and stay out.'

'Half a jiff, Lily,' he protested. 'I didn't mean any harm. And who is he anyhow — just a cheeky young blighter—'

'I'm telling you. Get out and stay out.' And he had to go.

I was busy packing up my sketching gear. She came closer and watched me, not speaking until I'd finished. Then she said softly: 'I get mad with him sometimes, he's such a twerp. But he's rolling in money and doesn't mind chucking it about. You could find him useful, like I do. You didn't have to tear that drawing up, Dick. Nasty temper you're got, haven't you, dear?'

'No, I haven't, Lily.' Then I gave her a grin. 'To tell you the truth, that sketch was going wrong anyhow. Otherwise, I wouldn't have torn it up, not for a dozen Alfreds.'

'You'll try again then, won't you? Shall I order us some tea? I always have some about now.'

From the time when the waiter came for the order to the time when he left us with the tea, sandwiches and cakes, she talked about our act, which she had seen from the back of a box as she had said she would, praising Uncle Nick and asking me various impersonal questions about him. But then, not long after the waiter had gone, she gave me one of her narrow smiles, which didn't belong to her good-little-girl voice, and said: 'You heard what Alfred called you – a cheeky young blighter? Are you, Dick?'

'Not really. But I know what he meant, Lily.'

'I wish you'd tell me something,' she said softly. 'I wish you'd tell me exactly – and I mean *exactly* – what you did with that actress – what's-her-name – Julie Blane?' Her eyes, looking green now, stared expectantly; her mouth had fallen open; and – though I may have imagined this – her long nose seemed to quiver a little: she looked a bit crazy. 'Tell me *everything* you did. Go on.'

I don't know if I blushed, probably I did. I certainly shook my head and mumbled something about being able and not wanting to tell her. Remember, in spite of her little-girl act, she was about eight years older than I was and a top star, well known everywhere, singing numbers so popular that you could hear their choruses being rolled out, towards closing time, in hundreds of pubs. I might be embarrassed and a bit sickened, but I didn't feel I could tell her to shut up.

She leant forward and put a cool hand to my cheek. 'I spoke too soon, didn't I, dear? Later then, when we're really friends. I expect you think I've a lot of friends, but I haven't. Have you?'

'No, I haven't. And I don't think I'll make many on this tour. I've been feeling a bit depressed about it. We seem to have struck a poor lot this time.'

'Nothing new to me, my dear. I'm very particular,' she went on, in a false ladylike tone that reminded me of poor Cissie when she was trying to be grand, 'very particular indeed. I act friendly and don't put on too many airs – me being a star turn and all that – but as for being really friendly with most of the people on any bill – well, you ask Otto Mergen. He'll tell you how very particular I am.'

'What about him – Mergen? I'm curious about him.'

'You're not the only one, dear. Otto's a mystery man. He been with me five years now and still I don't know much about him. First time I met him, he was half a musical act, the other half being a German woman who must have weighed eighteen stone. She dropped dead one night when they were playing Collins's, Islington – and if you're going to drop dead, that's as good a place as any – so he talked me into taking him on. You've heard him. He can talk anybody into anything – very educated and all that – and lovely speaking voice, don't you think?'

'No, I don't. Too soft and oily for me.'

'That's 'cos you're North-country. Also you might be jealous. But I don't sleep with him, y'know, dear.'

'I didn't think you did, Lily.'

'A lot of people do. They don't say it straight out, but it's written all over 'em. Including your friend Cissie What's-it, but I wouldn't call her very bright, would you? I'll tell you one thing about Otto Mergen. And it's a tip worth having, dear. Whatever you do, keep on the right side of him.'

'Why? What will he do to me if I don't?'

'I don't know. I don't know how it works. But things – some of 'em very nasty things – will start happening. No, it's God's truth, Dick. I've seen it over and over again. So don't say or do anything he can take offence at. And he's very sensitive, Otto is. Just be careful, dear, that's all. Make a friend of him if you can.'

I nearly told her I'd just as soon think of making a friend of a crocodile. But what I did say was that I ought to be going. And I was just about to pick up my sketching gear when she came close to me, looked at me hard, and said in her little high voice: 'I think Otto likes you. And he knows I do. When you come to draw me next time, we won't have Alfred butting in, we'll lock the door. Now – don't move.'

I'd just time to notice that her eyes were green again and her nose perhaps quivering, though I won't swear to that, when she held my face lightly in both hands. Then she didn't kiss me, as I thought she was going to do, but crammed her tongue into my mouth and took her hands away to run her fingers down my thighs. Though I hadn't expected or wanted anything like this to happen, my arms of their own accord tried to go round her, but in a flash she was well out of reach.

'You're an artful young sod, aren't you?' And she didn't say it, she shouted it, quite angrily, and this time really did look crazy. And before I banged the door behind me, I heard her say a few other words I didn't expect to hear, at least not from one of England's sweethearts of song. When I was safely down the corridor, relieved to find I hadn't left my sketching gear behind in the hurried exit, I spent a minute or two mopping my face and telling myself it was all quite true.

And that wasn't the end of it either. I was sharing a fairly big dressing-room with Sam and Ben Hayes and Barney that week, but after our second show they changed before I did – they were meeting somebody in a pub and anyhow I was feeling a bit dreamy – so I was alone there when, after some urgent knocking, Alfred came in, flushed and watery-eyed.

'Hello – what's-it – Hernstable—'

'It's Herncastle. You've just read it on the door.'

'All right, all right, don't get shirty, old man. Look what I've brought you.' He was taking three bottles of whisky out of a brown-paper bag. 'All for you – though I'll have a mouthful if you ask me nicely. Any glasses?' He stared around and looked disgusted. 'Rough luck having to put your disguise on and then take if off in this place, isn't it? You ought to see the room that Lily has.'

'She's the star. I'm just one of the Indians.'

'Clever turn that, though. Couldn't think how you did it. But like to see you produce a clean glass, old man.'

I got up rather wearily and found the only clean glass we had. 'Help yourself. I don't want any. I need some food before I can begin drinking whisky. But thank you for the three bottles, Alfred, if they really *are* for me.'

'Course they are. I told you. All for you – except for this drop I'm having. Cheers! Let's sit down for a minute or two, talk things over – er – Jack – no, that's not it – Dick. Isn't that right – Dick? Good!'

He wasn't drunk but he'd been drinking, and now he tried to sprawl at ease on one of the hard little chairs we used, and he ended up by resting an elbow on the shelf, covered with our make-up stuff, that ran underneath the long lighted mirror. I hadn't quite finished changing, so I went on with it while he talked.

'Came to apologize, Dick,' he began, looking very solemn. 'Lily's idea really. 'You've got to apologize to that boy, Alfred,' she said to me. Those were her very words, Dick old man. You accept my apology? Let's get that settled first. You accept my apology?' He stared at me anxiously, his mouth wide open.

'Yes Alfred. So just forget about it. And thanks again for the whisky. And help yourself.' I was now busy with my tie.

'Sit down a minute, Dick old man. I want to say something very serious, and I can't say it unless you're sitting down. That's better.' But he swallowed some whisky before staring at me anxiously again, squinting a little.

'All right, Alfred.' I was beginning to feel impatient. 'What is it?'

'I'm not going to mince words, Dick old man. I'm not going to mince words.' He said this as if he were refusing to make shepherd's pie out of a dictionary. 'I love Lily Farris, and I don't care who knows it, I've loved Lily Farris ever since I first saw her – and she sang *There's a Stile by the Meadow* and *Down Honeysuckle Lane*. Marvellous! A great star turn, as we all know, but that's only the beginning, only the beginning. Now you don't really know Lily, do you?'

'No, I don't, Alfred,' I replied without any hesitation.

'Well I do, old man. I ought to, after following her all over the place. Chasing her at first, if you like – yes, chasing her. But now we're the greatest of friends. That's all, though – friends.' And here he might have been quite stern, with another kind of face and voice. 'I think she's fond of me. In fact I'm sure she is. And I've told you what I feel about her. But she's not only a pure sweet girl – everybody knows that – but, Dick old man, while she has to put on a bit of an act as a star turn – I mean, off the stage, old man – behind it all she's shy. Believe it or not, she's desperately shy – *shy*.'

He stopped there, and after waiting a few moments I felt I had to say something. 'I dare say you're right, Alfred. You really know her and I don't. But I don't understand why you're telling me all this.'

'I've a reason – a good reason.' He frowned at his glass, and I think he was wondering what this reason was. 'I'll explain later. Don't forget, Dick old man, I came to apologize. When she told me I must apologize, I said, "Certainly, certainly". So I did, didn't I? We may not be pals yet, but we could be, couldn't we? Now I can't be with her all the time. Even as it is, there'd be a hell of a row if my governor knew how much time I do spend with her. But you'll be going round with her for weeks and weeks and weeks – seeing her every day.'

'I won't, you know, Alfred. You can be on the same bill with people

231

and hardly ever see them, especially if they're in a different half of the programme. I don't expect to be seeing much of Lily Farris.'

He didn't look cunning then, but he did look like a man trying against odds to look cunning. 'What about this portrait lark?'

'I may never have another try. And even if I did, what of it?'

'Then what about Mergen – Mr Otto bloody Mergen?'

'Where does he come into it?'

He leant far forward, nearly overbalancing. 'I don't trust him, Dick old man, don't trust him a yard. Clever as the devil and has an enormous influence over her, and she's too innocent to understand the kind of putrid blighter she's dealing with. I've warned her but she just laughs – like a trusting sweet kid. Now, Dick old man, as a favour to me, a great personal favour, what about keeping an eye on Mr Otto bloody Mergen?'

'Sorry, Alfred but—'

'I'd make it worth your while. Let's say I'm not about for a few days – it might be even a week – then next time we meet – all on the Q.T. of course – you give me a little report—'

'No, Alfred, I'd be useless. I rather agree with you about Mergen – there's something sinister about him – but I don't propose to spend much time with him or Lily, so I'd be no good to you. Try somebody else.'

'Who, for instance?'

'I don't know.'

'Of course you don't, because there isn't anybody. And Lily likes you – in an innocent friendly way, of course, probably because you want to be an artist – I told you she insisted on me coming to apologize – and if she likes you, then Mergen will be coming smarming around – and then—'

'Sorry, Alfred, but I can't oblige you.' I got up and began putting the whisky back into the bag. 'And I wish you'd keep this whisky, please. I'm not much of a whisky drinker myself, and if I leave it here we'll have a drunken dwarf in the act. And I must go. I'm hungry and there won't be any supper if I don't hurry back to the hotel—'

'You can have supper with us, old man,' he said eagerly. 'Lily's at her very best when the show's over and we're having supper.' His eyes were illuminated by the thought of this coming enchantment, and at that moment I couldn't help liking him and feeling sorry for him. But I wouldn't listen to any more, made him take his whisky away, and went down the corridor to see if Uncle Nick had left. He had.

The next night, Friday, the call boy gave me a message from Mr Mergen asking me if I would be kind enough to see him in his dressing-room after the first house. So I went down to the floor below, where Mergen, in his dress shirt-sleeves and with a towel round his neck, was restoring his make-up, having just sweated at his piano.

'How very kind of you – Richard. May I follow your uncle's example and call you Richard? What would you like to drink – gin – whisky – or I have some excellent lager? Well then, we'll both drink lager.'

After he'd poured out the lager and we'd both dipped into it, he said in his soft cat-walking way: 'I believe you had quite a long talk last night with our friend, poor Alfred Dunsop. Did you find it embarrassing?'

'A bit, not much. He only told me what you'd already told me – that he's madly in love with Lily. She'd sent him to apologize—'

'Yes, yes, I know about that. And it wasn't just to prove the strength of her hold upon him – though we might say she enjoys doing that – but the truth is, you made quite an impression upon her, the other afternoon.'

'She did on me too,' I said in a flat dead tone, so that he could make what he liked out of it.

His odd pewtery eyes tried to find the meaning in my face. I dipped into the lager again, so he did too, while he was wondering what the next line of approach ought to be. 'Lily's unusual personality, which is difficult to detach from her stage character, repels some people while others – like Alfred but not always so foolish – find her fascinating. What about you, Richard?'

'She has a certain fascination – yes, Mr Mergen,' I replied, in the same manner as before. And I suddenly sounded to myself about twenty years older.

'Though she has not said anything, I believe she is feeling rather hurt that you have not suggested another afternoon for a sketch portrait—'

'Now look, Mr Mergen—' I was my own age again now – 'it was only yesterday afternoon I had my first try at her. Now I'm taking advantage of the fine weather. Today I did some sketching down near Speke, and tomorrow I'm going across to the Wirral—'

He cut in smoothly: 'Lily's giving a little supper party tomorrow – she often does on Saturday nights – and if you'll come too, she'll invite your uncle and Miss – Miss—'

'Mapes. Cissie Mapes. Well, it's very kind of Lily, and if Uncle Nick and Cissie accept her invitation, then I'll come along too. Otherwise – no, Mr Mergen.'

He regarded me in silence for a few heavy moments, his ventriloquist's doll's mouth contorted into what might have been a smile – and might not. 'Richard, I have been asking myself if you are merely naive or what some people might call "a cool young card" – if you don't find that description offensive—'

'Yesterday afternoon, I was called "an artful young sod" – and this was after I'd done nothing, said nothing, only taken what was being handed out to me. Better tell yourself I'm merely naive. That was very good lager, Mr Mergen. Thanks.'

In the end, Uncle Nick decided he didn't want to go to Lily's party – a cold buffet supper up in her sitting-room – but said I could take Cissie, who hated to miss any party even if she suspected she wouldn't enjoy it. Alfred was there, probably to sign the bill, and looking and sounding about the same as he'd done in my dressing-room: I was still 'Dick old man'. Mergen was whispering and squelching around. There were two middle-aged Liverpool men, business acquaintances of Alfred's, who had managed to leave their wives at home and were now wondering if it would be just eating, drinking, talking, or would suddenly turn into an orgy. Lily, who was in pink with some white lace and looked very much the demon good-little-girl, almost immediately planted Cissie on to these two middle-aged men. Then she took me into a corner, cluttered up with a large armchair, a standard lamp and some bulrushes, to introduce me to a nice arrangement of black curls, wide brown eyes and dimples, called Phyllis Robinson, who had been expressly summoned just to please me. This girl blushingly denied as soon as Lily had left us, to tell the waiter he needn't stay and to tell Alfred to make himself useful, though she, Phyllis, insisted upon giving me the armchair itself while she perched on one of its arms, saving herself from the standard lamp and the bulrushes by bulging over on my side.

I wouldn't bother about Phyllis Robinson if this was going to be her only appearance on this tour, but as she will turn up again, playing a stronger role, I'd better say something about her. She was eighteen and for the last five years she'd been burning with admiration and enthusiasm for Lily. And now, after some help, she had built up an act that was a frank imitation of Lily's – she was even known sometimes as the *Lancashire Lily Farris* – and after a number of local engagements, which had just kept her going, she was hoping to get a contract from a variety agent in Manchester, who was talking about booking her for the summer season on one of the Blackpool piers. She felt about Lily what I felt about Turner, Girtin and Cotman, but my men were dead and her Lily was there in the same room. And all the time she was praising Lily to me, she was worshipping her with her eyes, hoping for a little smile, even a glance, across the room. She was as innocent as a newlaid egg; quite pretty and very silly. When I went for more food and drink and came back to find Alfred in the armchair, looking exhausted after making himself useful, I felt relieved, not annoyed. Phyllis and Alfred could now sing Lily's praises together, among the bulrushes.

Seeing me leave the corner, Lily called me over and introduced me to the tallest and thinnest woman I'd ever seen. She was Lady Chernock, and Lily told me afterwards she was the widow of a rich cotton man. She had immense cheekbones gleaming above the caverns of her cheeks, and a sort of lemon-tasting mouth, though she could open it wide to laugh, and then showed great yellow teeth. She was very smartly dressed and looked rather like a member of some French decadent-aristocratic set; but she spoke with a broad Lancashire accent and didn't seem to have very much more sense than Phyllis Robinson. While we were talking to her, Lily worked herself round to stand in front of me, very close, and let one hand drift behind her back, to begin pressing and then scrabbling around, until I moved and said that Cissie and I ought to be going.

'Ah've got a dam' big 'ouse Ah don't know what to do with,' said Lady Chernock, shaking hands. 'Lily knows all about it, don't yer, love? Tell 'er to bring yer one week-end.'

Cissie was more than ready to go. She'd had more than she wanted of the two middle-aged men and Mergen. It was a fine night so we decided to walk back to our hotel. She'd had a few drinks and she took my arm and kept close to me all the way.

'I wouldn't have gone but I thought it might cheer me up. But it didn't. Not with that lot. I'm feeling miserable, Dick dear. You'll say I'm always telling you that – but this time it's different. To begin with,

I have this funny feeling. I've had it ever since we started on this tour. I hoped we'd have some nice friendly people with us – specially a woman or two I could talk to – but we haven't. That Miss Duffield who looks after the dogs – aren't they sweet? – she wouldn't be bad but she's no life in her – all worn-out and frightened of her brother – or something. As for Lily Farris and that Mergen, they're beginning to give me the creeps. Dick, you won't get mixed up with them – promise. Nick doesn't like 'em, y'know.'

'I don't know that I do, Cissie. But if I let Uncle Nick decide for me, I wouldn't be seeing much company.'

'He laughs at me when I tell him about this funny feeling. But he's been getting grumpier and grumpier ever since we came to Liverpool – and it's not the audiences and the business, they're all right.'

'He can't work out his two-dwarf trick —'

'And that's another thing. It's bad enough having *one* dwarf – Barney's such a little nuisance now; I've had to slap him hard twice this week when we're in the dark together – so what's it going to be like with *two*?'

'Better perhaps, Cissie. There are serious and sensible dwarfs. We saw one in London —'

'Look out, Dick.' She clutched me harder. There were gangs of roaring and rolling drunks about, some of them trying to sing Lily's – and Mergen's – songs. True, there were also some giant policemen. But you had to be careful and watch where you were going. Shadows came suddenly and threateningly alive.

'Do you think he found another woman in London, Dick?' she asked.

'If he did, he hasn't said anything to me about it, Cissie. But then he wouldn't. However, if I'd to make a guess, I'd say No.'

'I don't think he wants me at all now – except for the act. Oh – he's still liable to say "Come on, girl" – might do it tonight. But what's that? Anybody would do – except that lamp-post of a woman you were talking to. I think he'd draw the line there.' She giggled. Then she was serious again. 'Don't you go and get tangled up with Lily Farris the way you did with Julie Blane. I bet she's an even more peculiar bitch. What's become of that nice little Nancy Ellis – don't you know?'

'No, I don't, Cissie. I've written to her but she doesn't reply.'

'Oh – well, you know what letters are in this business. Or if you don't, I'll tell you. They get lost, *returned to sender*, or follow you around for months. So don't give up hope, dear. And anyhow, wherever she is, she's a nice kid and well out of this lot. No, Dick, honestly – I have this funny feeling all the time. Trouble's on its way.'

Cissie, though we didn't say it then, was an intuitive.

3

We played the Palace, Manchester, after Liverpool, and it was while we were there that Cissie had one very good day, I think the last before everything went sour and then rotten. The weather during the earlier part of the week was wonderful, the blue-and-gold Maytime of the old poets. One Tuesday night, Uncle Nick heard me describe how I'd been by train that day, to do some painting, down to the Peak District. He wanted to try out a 60-h.p. Napier he'd been offered, so he arranged to take it out for the day on Wednesday. We'd have a picnic lunch, champagne and all; he would drop me wherever I felt like doing some painting; he could go roaring up and down and around the Derbyshire hills; and Cissie could go along with him or stay with me, whichever she preferred. And it worked beautifully. He was happy, trying out the Napier, a sporting car but reasonably roomy and magnificent with all its shining brasswork. I was happy because I did a couple of watercolours I wasn't ashamed of – one in the morning, among the higher hills in the northern part of the country; one in the afternoon, further south, where the walls are like white veins in a green hand. And Cissie, who spent the morning roaring round with Uncle Nick and the afternoon near me, and of course was with both of us when she spread our lunch out on the grass, was perhaps the happiest of all. She was no country girl but she had the deep feminine delight in an excursion and a picnic on a beautiful day, and the even deeper joy, rising from the very depths of the heart, which most women seem to feel when they are with their men and those men are happy. (It is an argument, I suspect, for the essential superiority of Woman, able to be entranced not by pursuits but states of mind.) And if I remember and celebrate that day, it is not only for the work I did, the best I was to do for some time, but also because I like to remember Cissie as she was that day. For once I hadn't to feel sorry for her.

If the next day had been fine, I'd have gone down there again, but the weather suddenly broke and so, still feeling in a painting mood, I rang up Lily at the Midland Hotel and told her that if she was free to sit I'd have another try at her that afternoon. Neither Alfred nor Mergen was there, and I was able to work for a couple of hours without any interruption, though of course I allowed Lily to relax or move about every twenty minutes or so. I don't pretend to be a portrait man, and now it's many years since I've even attempted a head, but that afternoon the careless boldness of the immature artist, who doesn't know what he can do and what he can't do, served me well. After two hasty attempts, going wrong from the start, that I tore up, I got near to what I wanted, with a rather delicate pen-and-wash drawing that suggested the changeling, half-fascinating, half-repellent quality of her personality. It does still, for I have just been looking at it, and then returning through it to that over-furnished plushy sitting-room in the Midland Hotel, Manchester, over half a century ago, with the rain and the smoky air cutting down the light from its big windows.

When I told her I'd finished, she came over and looked. She'd been very quiet, very good. 'Is that me ?'

'It's the best I can do. But I'm not Augustus John, y'know, Lily.'

'Can I have it, Dick?'

'No, Lily, I'm sorry but you can't. I might be able to do a fairly exact copy, or I could have it photographed for you – no colour of course – and then you could have as many copies as you wanted.'

She nodded, not thinking about what I'd said, and moved away to sit down. 'You don't know what you're like outside – not really – do you? Only what you're like inside. And there I'm a bleeding mess.'

I said nothing to this but very quietly began tidying up.

'You don't like my act. Oh – I know – the news soon gets round. You think it's just a lot of horse-shit. But there's a part of me – perhaps a little part, but it's there all right – that believes in all those stiles by the meadow and honeysuckle lanes and old mill streams. Like you believe for a minute or two what you see and read on Christmas cards. I don't know where those lovers' lanes and honeymoon rose-gardens are. What I know is where they *aren't* – in a house in West Ham fit for a family of three and stuffed with ten, where your mother starts drinking because another one's on the way, where your jolly Uncle Cliff, back from the sea, takes your bloomers down when you're only twelve, where – oh, shut me up!' She waited a moment or two while I went on quietly packing up my gear. 'So there's a part of me left over that believes that somewhere it's different, and that's the part of me I sing with – at least while I'm singing softly with the piano, before the band's come in on the second chorus and I'm belting it to the back of the gallery. And I'm singing mostly to people who are in as big a bloody mess inside as I am. That's not you, Dick, or that cool clever devil of an uncle you've got. And I'll give you a tip, while I'm in the mood. Don't get mixed up with me. *Or* Mergen – especially him.'

'Who is he and where did he come from, Lily?'

'I don't know exactly. But I do know he'd a big reputation as a classical musician before he had to leave Prague. And I don't know why he had to leave in a hurry, but I can guess. Now, Dick, you're a nice clever kid – so push off before I start something I can't finish, like last time, and get angry with myself and then angry with you. We'll keep it clean and easy for once.'

For the next three weeks I don't think I exchanged a dozen words with either Lily or Mergen. What they were up to, during that time, I don't know, though Cissie told me she'd seen them both backstage and outside with the Americans, Benton, Duff and Marcus. We were playing all the larger Lancashire industrial towns, and to this day I never see one of Lowry's pictures – those with the factory chimneys, the high brick walls that might belong to a prison, the narrow streets going nowhere in particular and their dark matchstick people on their way to the same nowhere – without remembering that tour. I tried a few uncluttered street scenes, but their blacks and reds, their hard contrasts of light and shade, were too strong for the style and tone I preferred in water-colours: they needed an oils man or a savage etcher. Of course I could always get out of the towns, even in industrial Lancashire, but except when we went further north, to Preston and Blackburn and Burnley (this last quite close to my beloved Pennines), the flat half-ruined countryside, though it offered some curious effects and tones I could have captured later, depressed me so much that I would merely mooch around in the sunshine and do no real work.

However, the audiences were good, and our act went particularly well, perhaps because we seemed to them, after the mills and the narrow dark streets, to offer them more than one kind of magic. One night, a second house too, I remember, the *Rival Magicians* illusion went wrong. This depended on Barney, wearing his stilt-boots as the rival magician, jumping out of them and apparently collapsing into a mere huddle of robes as soon as Uncle Nick fired his green flash. But at this performance, after the flash went nothing happened except that the rival magician began swaying, as if he were drunk, and then of course the laughs began. It was the only time I remember when Uncle Nick lost his nerve, suddenly helpless in his surprise and disgust, and the only time I was able to rescue him. I'd been crouching, a little further upstage, the mere attendant fearful in the presence of these mighty magicians; and now realizing that something would have to be done, I sprang up and forward, shook Barney hard to free him from the boots, pushed him so that he dropped into his huddle of robes, to achieve the vanishing effect, and then, while the laughs built up to solid applause, I bent down and hurriedly pushed the invisible Barney and his robes clean off the stage into the wings. Then I hurried back and humbly bowed before the greater magician, giving Uncle Nick, now himself again, a chance to acknowledge both my adoration and the applause.

Once he had taken his final call, Uncle Nick came off to pounce upon poor Barney, trembling in the wings, and rush him up to his, Uncle Nick's, dressing-room, to give him hell. I let them go and went behind – it was now the intermission, and they were taking down our temple set – to find Sam, who was responsible for our props, asked him for the stilt-boots and then took them upstairs with me. I changed quickly, because I always felt uneasy and rather silly in my Indian rig, and carried the boots along to Uncle Nick's dressing-room. He was still in his costume and make-up and so was Barney, and an odd pair they looked in that room, no Indian temple. Uncle Nick was sitting up straight, looking hugely impressive and glaring down at the wretched Barney, who was grovelling at his feet, half-crying and screaming, 'Mis' Ollanton, Mis' Ollanton – please, please, Mis' Ollanton!' As soon as I was inside, Barney scuttled off.

I might have known I'd get no thanks from Uncle Nick for my improvisation. 'We're doing *my* act, lad,' he began. 'If you want one of your own, go and build it up, then try to get bookings for it.'

'I was wrong then, was I?'

'Well, what do *you* think?'

'It seemed to me I was saving the illusion, perhaps the whole act. But if I was wrong, then the next time we have an accident I do nothing, I just wait for you to do something – is that it?'

'That's exactly it, lad,' he replied coolly. 'Even if I seem to be making a balls of it, you've got to leave it to me. After all, it's my responsibility. But if you and the others start improving on what we've rehearsed, inventing new bits of business, in a few weeks we won't have an act at all. I'll admit that this once I wasn't bright and you were and what you did came off, but don't ever do it again, lad. It's still *my* act whether it goes right or wrong. Now what about these boots?'

As I handed them over, I told him I didn't think they were right, and though I knew Barney was apt to be careless, I also knew that he was having trouble with the boots and had complained about them several times.

'We'll take the *Rival Magicians* out and put the *Magic Ball* back in its place,' he said slowly, still looking at the boots. 'Catch Sam before he goes, and warn him. We'll run through the *Ball* at twelve tomorrow. As for these stilt-boots, I think I know a way to improve 'em so that Barney can get out of 'em quicker and also move better when he has them on. It can be done, Richard. What can't be done is to improve that silly little bugger. I don't know why I keep him on.' But what we both didn't know then was that the improved stilt-boots would help to save Barney's life.

It must have been two or three days later when I received a letter, forwarded by Bosenby's office, from Julie Blane in Cape Town:

Dear Dick,

This won't be a letter about theatre life in S. Africa because we have hardly begun, but I like the company and I have been given two good parts and it's all a welcome change from playing twice-nightly in those ghastly towns. I am sure you understand now why I didn't want to see you after that horrible Sunday night. Though I was genuinely fond of you, there was not enough that was real between us to withstand the embarrassment and feeling of humiliation that came with that night. But the real reason I am writing is to explain what happened at Plymouth and why Nancy, poor child, didn't want to speak to you. It was all my fault, Dick dear, and I behaved in the bitchiest fashion. When I went behind after the pantomime matinee with Tommy Beamish and he went to see one of his comic pals, I saw Nancy and she told me she had to change in a hurry because she was meeting you for tea. Then – and I suppose it was a kind of jealousy or

envy because she seemed so young and eager – I told her she needn't
bother and then told her about us. She was upset naturally, but if she
cares anything about you she'll come round. Perhaps by this time you
are meeting regularly or at least writing to each other. If so you won't
need this letter, but if you are not then it might be useful. And if I know
anything about girls, she is secretly devoted to you – unless of course
some other attractive and attentive boy has turned up. And I think –
this is a compliment – will have to be very attractive and very attentive
to drive you out of her mind. There!

Please keep on painting, Dick dear, and don't dream of staying in
Variety even a month longer than you feel you need to do.

Your still affectionate
JULIE.

This letter did two things. Before it arrived I might have had a lot
of feeling for Julie that I was, so to speak, hiding from myself. This
letter proved I hadn't. It released no hidden feeling at all. As far as
Julie was concerned, I read it quite coldly: she didn't seem to mean
anything to me. But the letter also proved that although I might not
have been thinking so often and hard about Nancy, I must have
accumulated, without knowing it, a store of feeling about her that this
letter now revealed. I astonished myself, which is something that
happens, more often than most of us like to admit. As soon as I read
this letter a second time, it was from a ghost about somebody who
was terribly real. The result was that although I didn't reply to Julie,
I wrote another very long letter to Nancy, explaining everything. It
was as if I was having a race with this other attractive and attentive
chap, though for all I knew, not a word coming back from Nancy, he
might have already arrived to take complete possession of her. I
couldn't see Nancy keeping two or three chaps on strings, playing one
off against the other, trying to settle for the best bet. I was sure she
was an all-or-nothing girl.

The trouble was, I was well-placed only in the nothing department,
not knowing where she was or what she was doing, writing letters to
which there never came a reply. Like an idiot, somehow I felt that this
second long letter of mine *must* compel one from her – as if it belonged
to an entirely different order of events from that which governed the
unanswered long letter I had written in Kettlewell – and for days I
made fierce demands at the stage door for a letter and then felt sick

with disappointment. Moreover, because some unknown place was charged with a magical life because Nancy was there, the last trace of any such life vanished from wherever I happened to be. The streets seemed meaner, the towns more dismal, and my existence among them stupider and more tedious, emptier of any meaning. If I'd been older, secure in the knowledge of my craft, a mature and dedicated painter, I could have met this challenge by doing more and better work, capturing in form and colour both the immediate despair and the distant tantalizing magic. But I was too young and foolish, too uncertain yet in my art. So I trapped myself in a vicious circle. Because the heart went out of my painting, I was left with nothing I wanted to do, and then, bored and restless, I saw everything even worse than it was – and much of it was bad enough – with every shape and tone made uglier by my dissatisfaction. I have sometimes imagined since then, years afterwards, that the worst horrors of our older industrialization are projections in sooty brick, rusting iron, sulphur fumes and much of their people's inner despair; just as our new industry, so clean and smooth, tedious and deadly, represents the inner world of its new people, in which there is no despair because there never was any hope, because there is in fact no deep feeling of any sort.

Finally, I still had this vague idea, which first arrived when I saw all those dwarfs, that my life had taken an invisible turning towards the unpredictably sinister. It was the equivalent, I suppose, of that 'funny feeling' upon which Cissie was always mournfully harping. On one level of experience, as I have said, I was unreasonably surprised and disappointed that no reply came from Nancy. But on a level below that, no doubt even more unreasonable, I felt obscurely that Nancy couldn't be expected to communicate with me. I felt it, I remember, when I took the trouble and went to the expense of ringing up Pitter in Bosenby's office, to beg him to find out for me where Nancy was. I suddenly felt, rather than saw, that while she was moving up one road, we were hurrying down another, where, round some corner, whatever was sinister would instantly threaten us, would stand glaring and roaring like a giant tiger. It was almost as if I felt she and I were now in two different worlds.

I don't know what other people's experience has been, but I've found that almost always after nothing much has happened for some time, then suddenly a lot happens – bang-bang-bang! And again almost always it is just when you have arrived at a time and a place that seem to promise that nothing will happen. You sit yawning and the roof falls in. This is how it went that week we played Burrington, a miserable town huddled in the tindery wastes of South Lancashire. It had a town hall that looked like a very large urinal, two hotels – one bad and the other very bad – no theatre but a Palace of Varieties. This was smaller and older than the Empires we'd been playing in – the dressing-rooms were the worst I'd ever seen – and in fact Burrington wasn't part of the circuit we were touring and our week there was a fill-in date. There was plenty of room behind – though a lot of it was crammed with rubbish from old pantomimes, creating all manner of odd corners and culs-de-sac – but the stage area was smaller than usual and Sam, Ben and I had a hell of a job getting in with our Temple set early on Monday morning. The staff behind consisted of old men who had been on too long or lads who hadn't been on long enough. The lighting equipment ought to have been in a theatrical museum. And the band call lasted over three hours and even then many of us simply gave up in disgust, not recognizing our own music, for the orchestra of the Burrington Palace of Varieties didn't offer us the usual sixteen or so players but only eight, including the musical director himself, an old man with a dyed blue-black moustache who in theory played the piano *and* conducted and in practice did neither. So perhaps, after all, I oughtn't to have been surprised when so much happened at Burrington, because right from the start we were all losing our tempers or feeling horribly depressed.

4

I had already lost my temper and was now feeling depressed, washing a leathery meat pie down with a pint of bitter at the usual pub-round-the-corner, when Mergen joined me at the bar, mopping his face and then asking for a large brandy. I'd been keeping away from him and Lily, but I could imagine what he'd gone through at the band call and saw him now as a fellow-sufferer.

'I tell you, Richard,' he began, after he had swallowed half the brandy and had given his face a final mopping, 'Joe Bosenby must have been insane when he booked us into such a place as this. I thought Lily and I had seen the last of such places years ago. What she will say tonight, I cannot imagine.'

'I know what Uncle Nick will say when he tries to work on that stage,' I told him, 'that is, if he says anything and doesn't simply blow up.'

'The hotel is equally bad. We are at the Imperial. Are you?'

'No. Uncle Nick can always find one that's worse. The Victoria. The rooms smell like old magazines in an attic. I don't like getting drunk but I don't know what else I'm going to do.'

'I can offer you something better,' he said in his careful soft way. 'In fact Lily gave me a message for you. It is about tonight, when I think we shall need *something* to make us feel life is still worth living. Her pretty and charming young admirer – the Miss Robinson you met in Manchester – has an engagement at what she calls "a smoking concert" a few miles from here, so Lily, who can be very kind, has asked her to spend the night with us at the Imperial. And you, Richard, are specially invited to join us at supper. The food and drink will not be bad because we have made our own arrangements. There will only be the four of us, and I think you will find that pretty little Phyllis will not be as shy as she was in Manchester.' He noticed that I hesitated, so he went on: 'I think we might say it will be altogether more agreeable than going back to your even worse hotel, with your uncle, not in the best of tempers, and his frightened Miss Mapes. Good food and drink – and a pretty girl – um?'

Still feeling a bit uncertain, I thanked him and said I would see how I felt after the second house. 'It's going to be hell, I know, and I might feel fit for nothing except crawling into bed.'

'You say that because you have already had a very long morning. You need a rest. But tonight, after it is all over, you will be longing for a good supper and cheerful and charming female company. I am an old performer and I know, Richard. When you have changed, go back to the hotel with your uncle, don't eat but have a drink or two – I strongly recommend two-thirds sherry and one-third brandy as an *aperitif* – then ask the hotel to lend you a key if there is no night porter, and join us about eleven o'clock. We have taken the whole of the third floor, which sounds more extravagant than it is, because there are only four rooms – Lily has had one bedroom turned into a sitting-room – but it does mean we shan't be disturbed. So all you have to do at eleven o'clock is to make your way to the third floor of the Imperial. That will not be too difficult, will it?'

I gave him a long hard look. I couldn't help feeling that by talking to me as if I were a timid child, he was trying to shame me into accepting. Then he must have realized that he'd overdone it. 'The other thing is that Lily will be so disappointed if you do not complete her little party. You stand very high in her regard, Richard. And since she has received the photographs of the portrait you made of her, she is very anxious to give you something in return. So tonight there will be good food and drink and a pretty girl who believes that Lily's slightest wish is law. Perhaps I am a little jealous. I say to myself if only I were a good-looking young man.' He tried to look wistful but those hard little pewter eyes ruined the effect.

'Yes, I'll bet you do, Mr Mergen. Well, thanks for the invitation. But I don't know now what I'll feel like doing by the time we've got through the second house tonight. It's going to be hell.'

And it was. Trying to please a first house that hardly existed – after all, it was a fine evening in early summer – I nearly broke my neck as the *Vanishing Cyclist*. Uncle Nick, who hadn't played for years on a stage as small and badly equipped as this, spent the time between our performances rearranging the act, cutting out every big effect, and composing long abusive telegrams to Joe Bosenby. He had reached boiling point in about twenty seconds, just before we went on at the first house, and he stayed there for the rest of the evening. When we went back to our hotel, all he cared about was sending his final version of the telegram and also trying to reach Joe Bosenby by telephone. Cissie was silent and seemed miserable. Mergen had been quite right; I now found myself eager to go somewhere and do something; and I even tried the drink he recommended – two parts sherry to one of brandy – but didn't care for it. The Victoria Hotel hadn't a night porter or any front door keys to lend me, and seemed to think I should either stay in or go out for the night. In the end I gave a woman in the kitchen a shilling to leave a small side-door open for me. By this time it was eleven o'clock, and I strolled down the road and then across the square to the Imperial. It was a night of stars, and the general conclusion up there, I gathered from a glance or two, was that another speck of dust had turned into an imbecile. I hope by now it's clear that I was uncertain about this Lily-Mergen party. But I was also feeling very hungry.

In that bedroom-turned-sitting-room on the third floor, where a cold supper – smoked salmon, chicken and ham, trifle – had been laid out, Lily embraced me warmly and ordered Phyllis-my-darling to do the same, which I must say she did without any awkward bashfulness. Phyllis was looking very pretty, the flush in her cheeks suiting her curls-and-dimples style. She was wearing a bright emerald evening dress, to stun them, I suppose, at the smoking concert. And I had an idea that she'd been given, either here or among the smokers, a few glasses of Cissie's favourite tipple – port-and-lemon.

We were a bit crowded at the improvised little supper table, where Mergen kept our glasses filled with hock. It was a thirsty sort of night; the smoked salmon and the ham were rather salty; there was plenty of cool hock within easy reach (Mergen must have had at least three opened bottles down beside his chair); we were talking loudly and laughing; so we drank a lot. We denounced smoking concerts; we denounced the Palace of Varieties, Burrington; we shouted 'No – really – listen' at one another, or at least Lily and Phyllis and I did, while underneath the table our legs had begun to lead an intimate life of their own. All this would have been very jolly – and I won't pretend I wasn't enjoying most of it – if I hadn't been sitting opposite Mergen and occasionally noticing a look in his eyes that didn't seem to have anything to do with his fat smiles and gurgles and funny stories. It was as if somebody else, cold and watchful and a bit mad, was looking through those eyes. However, by the time we'd finished eating I stopped noticing them, if only because Lily had introduced some caper about drinking healths that demanded she should put her arms round my neck and kiss me and also demanded that Phyllis should follow her example. But now Phyllis's arm-flinging was so wild and her kisses so wet and her giggling so persistent, she was obviously more than half-sozzled. I wasn't there to represent any temperance society, and I'd had my share of the wine and could feel I had, but after all this was a kid of eighteen, smoking concerts or no smoking concerts, a kid who hardly knew what she was doing and didn't care so long as she was doing what Lily told her to do.

So I shook my head at Mergen when he reached across to fill her glass again, but if he saw me he paid no attention, and Lily was demanding another toast. Two minutes later, laughing senselessly, Phyllis threw herself back in her chair and went over with it. She hadn't hurt herself – they never do – but was lying there, her eyes closed, making dreamy bubbling noises, obviously ready for bed and not for any return to the table. I pulled her up and then Lily, who was stronger than she looked, took hold of her, telling Mergen to open the bedroom door and then give me some brandy. This door was not outside but near the window of the room we were in, and if anybody wants to know why bedrooms should lead into each other, on the third floor of the Imperial Hotel, Burrington, I have no reply; I didn't design the place, and that's how it was. When Lily, half-leading, half-carrying Phyllis, disappeared behind this door, Mergen closed it and approached me with a bottle of brandy and a glass.

'Richard, you will have some of course.' His eyes didn't sparkle, they weren't that kind, but they seemed to shine a little, like pewter with some sun in the room.

'No, thanks.'

'My dear boy, I cannot accept your refusal. Brandy at such a moment as this is the unbeliever's benediction.'

'I dare say, but I don't want any.'

'I believe you will change your mind.' He must have noticed that I was staring in the direction of that bedroom door, for he went on: 'Phyllis is a beautiful girl, don't you think?'

'No, not beautiful – but quite pretty.'

'Ah – you speak as an artist. But at this moment in her life, we might say, she is like a peach – or a pear – perfectly ripe for picking – and enjoying.' He poured brandy into three glasses, took a sip or two from his own glass, closed his eyes and wagged his head slowly, to show what a wonderful time he was giving himself. I wasn't impressed. Also, I didn't like this peach-picking lip-smacking talk of his.

He came out of the brandy to twist his thick rubbery lips into a smile. 'I envy you. I admit it - I envy you. To be your age again – ah!'

'It's none of my business, but how old are you?'

'Older than I look, older than you think. Too old. Much too old.' He pulled an extraordinary face, somehow squeezing all his features together. When he had let them go again, he took a good swig of his brandy, without any eye-closing and head-wagging this time. It seemed to me then that he was getting a bit sozzled.

Lily came out of the bedroom, looking curiously brisk and businesslike. 'Brandy for me?' she inquired, and when Mergen had handed her a glass, she gave him a dismissing kind of nod, and without saying a word he went into the bedroom. 'Don't you want any brandy, Dick?'

'No, thanks, Lily. What I want is to know what's going on.'

'You're a lucky boy,' she said, after she'd swallowed some brandy as if it were water. No eye-closing and head-wagging with her: down it went; and then she talked. 'You could have tried for three months and you wouldn't be as close to it as you are now. I'm giving it to you on a plate, and all you can do is to stand there looking sulky and suspicious. But it suits you, and I expect you know it – you artful young sod.'

This was to be the Manchester scene in reverse, for there she'd called me that after she'd played with me, but this time, having told me what I was, green-eyed again and with her nose quivering she went into her act, her tongue going into my mouth like a parcel into a letter-box, and her hands busier than ever. And this time, though I won't pretend I felt nothing, it was I who stepped back and escaped.

'Oh – come on, you're all right,' she cried impatiently. And she grabbed me by the wrist and pulled me towards the bedroom door. 'And now – for God's sake – what more do you want? Look!'

I thought afterwards they'd have been much cleverer, with what they had in mind, if they'd left young Phyllis half-undressed on that bed instead of stripping her out of every stitch, spreading her out there completely naked. It might be because I'd attended a life class or because my mind simply worked that way, but it is a fact that I didn't see her in terms of sex at all but as a figure sharply illuminated by the light above the bed, with rosy highlights and greenish shadows, with exquisite curves of breasts and thighs; one hand covering her eyes and the other turned up at the end of an outflung arm. I was staring at Woman, not at Phyllis Robinson, stripped and helpless in a stupor.

'Here she is,' I heard Mergen saying. 'Take her, my dear boy, take her.'

'And hurry up. Give it to her.' This was Lily, breathing hard, almost in my ear. She began fiddling with my buttons and I pushed her away. I thought I heard her hiss at me.

I turned to Mergen. 'Now then, what exactly is the idea?' Not that I didn't know by that time, but I wanted to make him come out with it.

'There she is, Richard. You enjoy her. We enjoy your enjoyment.

People have different tastes, you must understand—'

But then Lily came hissing up, far gone in whatever was the matter with her, and I slapped her face – hard. Before she could do anything but let out a screech, I rushed her through the doorway and gave her a final shove that sent her cannoning into some furniture. I rushed back into the bedroom to lock that door against her. Mergen hadn't moved and looked like a huge horrible old image made of wax.

I opened the other door, the one for the corridor. 'Out,' I told him, 'or I'll set about you – by God I will. I'll knock the shit out of you, Mergen. You'd enjoy watching me rape a nice little sozzled virgin, would you? Outside – go on.'

He moved now, slowly, lumbering towards the doorway like half a defeated army. Then he turned: 'What are you going to do?' he inquired, hoarsely.

'Nothing you'd enjoy watching.' I could hear Lily at the other door now, scrabbling at it with her nails like a giant cat. 'And — listen. Tell Lily if she doesn't stop that, I'll come round and slap her till she can't see.'

As soon as he'd gone, I pulled the bedspread slowly and carefully from under Phyllis and covered her with it, pushed a pillow under her head, took the key out of the door into the corridor, turned out the light, then locked the door from the outside. This meant that Phyllis was now safely behind two locked doors, just in case Lily and Mergen thought of some other way of enjoying themselves, but I felt she ought to be able to unlock the corridor door, if only to look for a bathroom, and then I saw there was sufficient space under the door for me to push the key through with a pencil, far enough for the silly little goose to see it when she returned to her senses.

I've described exactly what I did and what I said but by leaving out what I was feeling, the rapid heartbeats, the nervous catching of breath, I realize that I've presented myself as altogether too much of a cool, determined, virtuously heroic figure. So now I'll add that about halfway between the Imperial and Victoria hotels I had to stop – and fortunately there was nobody about – because the waves of nausea were mounting higher, the cold sweat was thickening, a sour tide of bile was sweeping up my throat, so that I had to spew the splendid hospitality of Lily Farris and Otto Mergen into the gutter.

And though there were many weeks of the tour still to go, I never spoke to either of them again. They never even looked at me.

5

On the Thursday morning of that week in Burrington, I was sitting over the ruins of my breakfast, smoking a pipe at the *Manchester Guardian* and trying, not for the first time, to work up some interest in Asquith's Home Rule Bill and the Problem of Ulster, when the policeman arrived.

'Which are you?' he said.

'What are you talking about?'

He looked at a notebook. 'There's three of you here, isn't there? Ollanton, Mapes, Herncastle, I've got. So which are you?'

'I'm Herncastle. And I'd say that Ollanton and Mapes are still in bed. Why? What are we supposed to have done?'

'You'll be told. Superintendent Hill wants to see you at half-past eleven sharp on the stage of the Palace. Now do I go up and tell these other two or do you?'

'Oh – I'll go. Let's see if I've got the message right.' I repeated it. 'But I don't see Mr Ollanton parading for the police unless I give him some reason for going.'

'There's been a body found,' said the policeman. 'You'll be told all about it.' And off he went.

Uncle Nick was shaving. It was a pleasure to watch him shaving, for he kept his German hollow-ground razor beautifully sharp and he held it and moved it as if it were a feather passing over his skin. Every time I caught sight of him shaving I had to remind myself that I'd never been good with a cut-throat and was much better off with a safety razor.

'A body found?' He gave me one of his suspicious dark looks. 'Is that all he said?'

'Except that we'd be told. By the Big Chief, I suppose. Where's Cissie?'

'I can't tell you, lad. She might be sitting on the W.C. having a good cry. She's sentimental and constipated, so she spends a lot of time in there. I'll tell her. But I wish you'd told that bobby to come up here. I'd have got more out of him than that. *Body found!* That's not enough.' He lathered his chin again.

'I know. But if they're calling everybody on the bill to assemble on the stage, that must mean the body was found in the Palace.'

Uncle Nick made a kind of affirming noise as he shaved round his mouth. Then, when he was able to talk: 'Yes, I worked that one out for myself, Sherlock Holmes. Might possibly be one of the company too, though they've got stage hands down there that have been dead for years – only nobody's noticed. Well, you pop off. I'll bring Cissie along.'

Just after half-past eleven, there were more people on the stage of the Burrington Palace of Varieties than it had seen for a very long time. There were about twenty of us pro's, and another twenty or so of staff, including the eight from the miserable band. There were three police in uniform, two constables and a sergeant, then a middle-aged man and a youngish man in plain clothes, and then of course Superintendent Hill himself, who was elderly and fat and a great gasper and wheezer, rather like an old shunting locomotive. It was ironical that all Cissie's and my vague premonitions of disaster should be confirmed, the label *Sinister* firmly plastered on to this tour, by this gasping and wheezing old codger.

'Sorry – cause any inconvenience – but no option,' he began, staring indignantly at nobody in particular. 'Plain case of murder.' We all gasped with him. 'Body of young woman – discovered by theatre fireman – early this morning. Medical report confirms – death by strangulation. Body identified – young woman known as – Nonie Colmar – member of acrobatic troupe. Medical and other evidence – suggests she was strangled towards end or just after – second house last night.'

Here Gustav Colmar shouted something in very rapid and furious French and looked as if he were about to make a headlong charge at the policemen, but the young Colmars restrained him. The superintendent waited, looking patient now instead of indignant, and then went on: 'Only chance – finding person guilty of this brutal crime – have your co-operation. Certain questions – must be answered — this morning. When did you – last see – young woman, Nonie Colmar, alive? At what time – did you – leave theatre last night? Must warn you — exact truth — absolutely necessary. Inspector — word from you?'

The middle-aged man in plain clothes said severely: 'In a minute I'll tell you how we'll set about this question-and-answer business. But in case any of you think it's funny and feel like doing a turn, I just want to say that in my opinion one of you, standing here on this stage, is a callous brutal murderer, who's killed at least once and might do it again unless we catch him and hang him. So let's not be funny about it nor have any lies.'

We were then divided up between the police for questioning, and perhaps because the *Ganga Dun* Company ranked among the more important performers, it was the Inspector himself, whose name was Furness, who questioned us. Uncle Nick took charge of the situation, convincing Furness at once that he, Nick Ollanton, was the serious responsible man, on or off the stage.

'You won't have any trouble with us, Inspector,' said Uncle Nick. 'We come on at the end of the first half—'

'I know you do, Mr Ollanton,' said Furness. 'I've seen the show. Very clever. What time did you leave?'

'Miss Mapes, my nephew Richard Herncastle and I left about ten-past ten, and were in the Victoria Hotel sitting down to our supper before half-past. And you can easily check that.'

'Right. Now what about these men?' He looked at Sam and Ben, stolid as ever, and at Barney, who had his mouth wide open, kept blinking hard, and was jigging about in his usual restless fashion.

'You'll have to ask 'em,' said Uncle Nick. 'I didn't see 'em after we went up to our dressing-rooms. Ask Sam Hayes. He's been with me for years and he's a reliable steady man. And don't take any notice of little Barney. He's always like that. Most of 'em are.'

Sam looked at the Inspector. 'We'd gone by five-past ten. Stage-door keeper must have seen us. Ask him.'

'I've already asked him. But he's an oldish man, not very noticing, and, as he says, it's not his business to clock people in and out. Wait a minute. I'll bring him here.'

As we waited, Cissie said shakily: 'I know I never liked her much. But this is terrible. I can hardly believe it. I mean – who could have done it?'

'Don't look at me girl,' said Uncle Nick. 'I didn't—'

'You haven't to be silly, Nick. None of us did.'

'Somebody did.'

'Perhaps a tramp got in somehow,' said Cissie hopefully. It was very common in those days for tramps to be on top of any list of suspects.

But this wasn't good enough for Uncle Nick. 'If you'll believe that, you'll believe anything. Well, Inspector,' he said as Furness returned with the stage-door man, 'can we get on with this?'

'I'm as anxious as you are, sir, to get on with it. Now then,' he commanded the stage-door man, 'tell them what you told me.'

'I place these two,' said the stage-door man, indicating Sam and Ben, 'as going off early, not much after ten, I'd say. But not him.' He pointed to Barney, 'No, not him.'

'He never sees me,' Barney shouted. 'He never sees me. I go in and out – he never notices. He's half-blind – I'm small – he never sees me. Mis' Ollanton – Mis' Ollanton—'

'Oh – shut it, Barney,' said Uncle Nick. 'Sam, did he leave with you two last night?'

'Yes, he did,' Sam replied. 'Didn't he, Ben?'

'That's right,' said Ben. 'The three of us left together. We nearly always do.'

'If Barney was on the far side,' said Sam, 'doorman wouldn't notice him.'

'I can imagine that,' said Furness. 'And where did you go after you left?'

'Where we've been every night,' Sam told him promptly. 'Vaults of the Sun Inn. We like to have a pint or two there after we've finished.'

'And I could do with one now,' said Furness. 'All right, you three can go. You go back to the sergeant, stage-door keeper.' As they went off, he looked at Uncle Nick. 'I doubt if we'll be bothering you again, Mr Ollanton—'

'You mean she was seen alive a good time after we left?' said Uncle Nick coolly. 'No, you don't have to reply. I guessed that fairly early.'

'Ah – you're a sharp one, Mr Ollanton. And I guessed that fairly early too. If you'd wanted to get rid of that young woman, I'll bet she'd have just vanished – ha ha!' Now he lowered his voice. 'But as we're talking, Mr Ollanton, can you give me any information that might be useful?'

'I could – and so could young Richard here. Cissie, just wait for us down by the stage door – I want to spare your blushes.' He waited until, rather slowly and reluctantly, she had gone. 'This is the second time I've had these Colmars going round with me. We did a longish tour starting last September. The girl was nothing in my line – too young and flighty – but she was a ripe little piece in her stage costume – and she was very fond of pushing her tits around and waggling her arse. Ask this lad. He's the right age to know what she was up to.

Richard?'

'She didn't attract me, not after the first few times I saw her in her stage costume, and she soon stopped trying.' I waited a moment. 'My impression is – but it's only a guess – that she didn't get much chance outside to be with men, her uncle and the other two kept an eye on her. So she made the most of her chances backstage to amuse herself. She was a born teaser – if you know what I mean-'

'And she teased somebody once too often,' said Uncle Nick softly.

'And that means,' said Furness, softly too, 'we needn't waste much time on the stage staff.'

'I hate to admit it – I don't want to be travelling round with a murderer – but I'm afraid that's true. And anyhow, from what I've seen of the stage staff here, they wouldn't have anything to tease. But I don't think there's any more we can tell you, Inspector. So if you don't mind—'

'No, there's nothing else just now.'

'Then I've got to talk to the manager here.' He turned to me. 'Do you realize, lad, that the Colmars' act is out? The girl was essential to it. Either they'll have to find another girl and train her or they'll have to change the act completely. And I don't see 'em doing that for a week or two, even if they're kept under contract. And if the manager here can't find a good fill-in for tonight, we'll all have to spread our acts. So you might have to warn Sam and Ben. But I'll see what the manager's doing. You go and wait with Cissie.'

'Could I give her a drink round the corner, Uncle Nick? She probably needs one.'

'Or you do. Go on, then.'

Most of the others were still being questioned in groups on or around the stage. We'd been let off lightly, no doubt because we'd been among the earliest to leave, but also, I suspected, because Inspector Furness wasn't anxious to keep Uncle Nick hanging about. As I caught a passing glimpse of some of the other men on the bill, I couldn't help feeling glad I knew and cared so little about them on this tour. What if it had happened on the previous tour and I'd been compelled to wonder about Bill Jennings and Hank Johnson and Ricarlo?

Cissie was waiting near the stage door, looking miserable and biting her lower lip and shaking her head at two young reporters. All three of them brightened up when they saw me. 'We're going round the corner for a drink, Cissie. Uncle Nick knows. No. I can't tell you chaps anything, not because I don't want to, but because I don't know anything. Wait for Inspector Furness – he shouldn't be long.'

There was nobody from the Palace in the bar, just a couple of oldish men who didn't like the look of Cissie and probably thought she was a tart. I settled Cissie into a corner, bought myself a strong ale, and gave Cissie, who said her tummy felt queer, a concoction called 'gin and pep' recommended by all barmaids to ladies with queer tummies. Then of course we talked about the murder. She said she could guess what Uncle Nick and I had told the Inspector about poor little Nonie, but that didn't prevent her from demanding to know exactly what we *had* told him.

After ten minutes of this, she said: 'I don't understand you, Dick. I mean the way you're taking this horrible murder – 'cos that's what it is. Nick I understand. He's a hard man and so proud he'd never let on anything could upset him. Whatever happened, he'd say he'd seen something ten times worse – in Berlin or somewhere. But you're quite different – a nice boy – sensitive and artistic and all that – so you ought to be *feeling* how horrible it is. Aren't you?'

'I expect I am really, Cissie. It's still too new and strange and unreal. Now if I'd *seen* her-'

'Stop that. I can imagine – and I've read about what they look like when they've been strangled. And I tell you, Dick, I'm *frightened*. It's all right for you two men – nobody'd try to strangle you – but if they don't catch him it might be my turn next week. You don't know what it's like being a girl, Dick. You can feel so helpless. You can think you're alone with a nice man and then suddenly you see a look in his eye that makes your blood run cold. It's true, Dick, and it's not funny. And now we know we're going round with a murderer. And till they catch him I'm not going to trust any man on the bill a yard – not a single yard. If any of 'em tries to stop me in a dark corner, I'll scream my head off.'

Uncle Nick arrived, not to join us for a drink but to march us out of the pub. 'They've booked an Irish tenor from Manchester as a fill-in,' he announced. 'We'll be packed out tonight, both houses – you'll see – and this fellow'll bring the place down warbling through his adenoids about his dear old Irish mother. As soon as the English go to music halls, they love the Irish.'

He was right about the houses that night. We played to capacity at both performances. Uncle Nick was furious. 'Talent wouldn't bring them in, but a murder will. They were wondering which of us looked most like a strangler.'

'I don't blame 'em,' said Cissie sharply. 'That's what I'm wondering too.' We were now back at the hotel, having supper. 'And so far I'm divided between that Duffield and the tallest of the American boys and that nasty-looking Mr Mergen—'

'And that'll do for you, Cissie,' said Uncle Nick.

'What d'you mean, Nick?'

'I'll explain exactly what I mean, girl. Unless I stop you here and now, we're going to have that murder morning, noon and night. You'll never talk about anything else. So you stop it now. Let the police work out who killed her. That's what they're paid for, though I don't see this lot here getting very far. It's twenty to one they'll have to call in Scotland Yard. All right, let *them* do it.'

'You're not human, Nick.'

'Sometimes I wish I wasn't, girl. Now you say you're frightened – you're horror-struck—'

'And so I am.'

'I dare say. But you're also like all those bloody clowns who packed us out tonight. You're enjoying it. You've tasted blood and you're licking your lips—'

Cissie jumped up, glaring at him. 'That's a filthy dirty lie, Nick Ollanton. You ought to be ashamed of yourself, talking like that to me. I've had enough.' And she hurried out, crying as she went.

'There's something wrong with us, lad,' said Uncle Nick, ignoring Cissie's outburst and exit. 'Did I ever tell you about that old Indian who came round to see me?'

'You began telling me but then you stopped yourself.'

He nodded sombrely. 'That old Indian said he saw rivers and oceans of blood. All our own doing, he said. That's what we really wanted.'

'That's a bit steep, isn't it, uncle?'

'Maybe. Maybe not. But as soon as we have a murder backstage, they're fighting to get in and take a look at us. Talent won't pull you in if you live in a place like this. It takes something quite different. You've seen it for yourself, lad. And now I'll tell you what I told Cissie. Leave this murder to the police. If you've any ideas, keep them to yourself. I don't want to hear about 'em. The only idea I'd like from you – and this is a compliment, lad – is something new for the act until I've worked out the two-dwarf effect. We couldn't bring your painting in, could we?'

I hesitated. 'Well – I did have a vague idea—'

'Come on, let's have it. You can always leave the details to me, Richard.'

'The audience choose one of several subjects to be painted – a rustic cottage or a cornfield or a ship at sea and so on. They're shown two blank canvases. One is put on an easel and is turned away from them. I start painting on the other – working fast because the subject will be already pencilled in. When I've done, say, a third of it, the other canvas is turned round to show a third of it too. I do two-thirds; the magic canvas has done two-thirds. When I've finished, it's finished too – the identical picture. Of course I've painted the magic canvas first, but in some way it's covered with blank canvas that's on spring rollers and goes up into the frame. Of course I realize that it would be much easier if it wasn't shown in stages, so that there'd be only one big piece of blank canvas to release—'

'But not as effective,' Uncle Nick interrupted eagerly. As always he was a different man as soon as he had some trick to consider and work out. 'Y'know, lad, you've got the right feeling for this sort of work. Now let's see how we might manage it.' He brought pencils and paper out of his capacious inside pocket. For the next half-hour or so we were happily at work on various devices for the magic canvas, which, Uncle Nick insisted, we must be able to show closely to some members of the audience, even allowing them to touch it, before the trick began. Naturally I felt rather proud and pleased that Uncle Nick should take my idea so seriously. As for him, I think he was happy to be away from the dark confusion of life in Burrington and elsewhere, to be in his own little clean and lighted kingdom of elaborate but innocent deceit. And perhaps I remember this occasion so well because I doubt if I ever saw him so easy and happy again.

6

But Burrington hadn't done with us yet. Late that same Thursday night came another blow. I had a small bedroom at the end of a landing. Uncle Nick and Cissie had a much larger bedroom on the same landing, but they were not next door to me because a bathroom and some kind of sample-cum-showroom came between us. I mention this because I think the fact that I was along the same landing and yet not next door partly explains why Cissie took the chance she did. I had had the light out for some time and was more than half asleep when I felt rather than saw or heard that somebody had come into the room.

'Dick, are you awake? It's only me – Cissie.'

'What's the matter?'

'Oh – I'm so frightened, Dick dear. And *he* doesn't care. Let me stay a while – please – please. I just want you to hold me so I won't feel frightened. That's all. Just hold me and tell me it's all right. I haven't come for *that* – you know – honestly I haven't – I'm too frightened. But of course I know what it's like for a man, holding a girl, and if you want it, I don't care – just so long as you comfort me.'

'Well, I'm sorry you feel so frightened, Cissie – though really you've nothing to be frightened of. But this is a bad idea, and it just won't work, and, you'll be sorry in the morning.'

'I don't care what I feel in the morning. It's what I feel now—'

'Cissie, I'm sorry but I just don't want you here – for your own sake as well as mine. Get back to your room before we're all in trouble.'

'Dick dear, *please!* Can't you understand—?'

'He understands all right.' Cissie gave a little scream, and then Uncle Nick switched the light on. He looked almost satanic in his long red dressing-gown, glaring down at Cissie, who had flung herself half across the bed and with only a light wrap over her nightdress, had managed to uncover a lot of herself. 'He understands and so do I. Now get up and get out – go on.' As soon as she had rushed out, crying hard, he said: 'She thought I was asleep and I wasn't. So I overheard enough to know it was none of your doing, lad. Is it the first time it's happened?'

'Yes, Uncle Nick. And don't be too rough with her. She really is frightened half out of her wits—'

'She never had any. And if she's so frightened, then she ought to be glad she's going. And she *is* going.'

'Oh – no, uncle—'

'Oh – yes, nephew. I'll pay her tomorrow for this week and next, but she finishes on Saturday. And I don't want any argument. Good night, lad.'

Next morning, Friday, as soon as I saw him – Cissie stayed in bed – I begged him to keep her on, but he wouldn't listen and declared that he'd been thinking of getting rid of her for some time, that she was putting on weight and slowing up the box-and-pedestal trick. But I didn't believe this, though I didn't tell him so. The truth was of course that she'd injured him where it hurt most, in his towering pride, though it's only fair to add that, unlike many such men, he didn't pass any of his resentment on to me. He was still telling me she would have to go and talking about finding a substitute, some girl who had worked with him before, when Inspector Furness interrupted us.

'Good morning, gentlemen. Just a question or two before you're too busy—'

'I'm busy now,' said Uncle Nick. 'Have to find a girl to take Miss Mapes's place. You explain, Richard.' And off he went.

'Now what's going on?' said Furness, after staring reproachfully at Uncle Nick's back.

'He's sacking Miss Mapes. She won't be with us after Saturday. But I don't imagine she's one of your suspects.'

'Quite right, young man. We can let her go. Quite apart from your alibi here – and that's been checked – she couldn't have done it. A woman just might have done it if her hands were big enough, like a man's. But there isn't a woman in your company with hands that size. No, one of the men did this job. And if you had to make a guess, who would it be? Who seemed to be having most trouble with that girl – y'know, being led on and then told to behave himself?'

'Honestly, Inspector, I don't know. We don't see much of what's going on. We're not like people in a play. We do our acts and then go back to our dressing-rooms.'

'So I gather, so I gather,' he said gloomily. 'Though one or two have mentioned that dwarf Barney you have in your turn. Did you say something?'

'No. Barney did fool around with her now and then – he's a silly little man – but anyhow he went off early with Sam and Ben Hayes.'

'I know he did. Give a guess, then.'

'It won't be worth anything,' I said slowly. 'But I'd say – either Duffield or one of those three Americans. And if you tell me that's sheer prejudice, you're quite right – it is, Inspector. What I've been wondering is how you're going to continue your inquiries. We move to Preston on Sunday, then to Blackpool the week after.'

'We know all about that, young man. That's the chief reason we're calling in the Yard. And I can't say I'm sorry. Ten to one you'll get Inspector Crabb. Heard of him, haven't you? No? Well, he's a terror. Doesn't look like a crab but he behaves like one – moves sideways and then suddenly it's a pinch. I knew Alf Crabb when he was a sergeant up here. Always looks as if he'd found a sixpence and then lost a shilling, but he's hot as mustard, Alf Crabb is. Where's Miss Mapes? Still in bed?'

'Yes. Hiding her misery.'

'Think she could tell me anything I don't know – especially now she's going?'

'No, Inspector. She'd a lot to say about the murder yesterday, but she never told me anything I didn't know. I'd leave poor Cissie alone if I were you, Inspector. You'll probably get nothing but showers of tears.'

I was dreading these myself, but as things turned out I never saw them. In fact, to my regret, for I'd grown very fond of Cissie, I was never even able to say good-bye to her. This was her doing, not mine. She stayed in bed nearly all that day; she went through her two performances that night, without speaking to anybody; I wouldn't have thought it possible for her to remain so aloof. Then it happened that Uncle Nick, Sam Hayes and I had a technical argument about one of the effects, so that it was later than usual when we left. But there was no Cissie at or near the supper table waiting for us. 'I'm tired, lad,' said Uncle Nick. 'You nip upstairs and tell her we're here. Though if she's still sulking and doesn't want any supper, it's all the same to me. But I'm ready for *my* supper.'

When I came back, the food was on the table and Uncle Nick was beginning to help himself. 'It's taken you a long time,' he grumbled. 'If she doesn't want to come down, she needn't. I told you that. And it's never any use arguing with 'em, y'know, lad.'

'She wasn't there to be argued with,' I said as I sat down. 'And I had to look round to make sure she'd gone.'

He stared at me. 'How d'you mean – gone?'

'There isn't anything belonging to her up there, uncle. She must have packed earlier. Now she's gone. She must have caught a late train to London.'

'Well, I'll be damned. There's a vindictive little bitch for you. She got her money – an extra week too – between the houses, then off she went, without a word, deliberately leaving us in the cart tomorrow. That's a woman, lad. You can't trust 'em a bloody yard. She knew dam' well I'd arranged for Doris Tingley to join us at Preston on Sunday, and that I hadn't a hope of getting her here tomorrow, so off she goes without a word, leaving us in the cart. All bloody female spite. No loyalty to me or to the act.'

Young as I was, this righteous indignation, coming from a clever man, seemed to me ludicrous. (And I've learnt since that most righteous indignation is.) He'd told the poor girl he'd done with her at the end of this week, really because she'd hurt his pride, and now, when we'd have to play two performances without her, he was condemning her lack of loyalty as if it were an outrage. I couldn't help secretly sympathizing with this feminine realism, and Uncle Nick's humourless outburst made me understand why women so often felt that men were wooden and stupid, pompous and hypocritical. On the other hand, I also couldn't help feeling rather hurt that Cissie had gone off without a word to me. After all, we'd spent months in each other's company and had been friends.

'Well, you'll have to get hold of Sam, Ben and Barney in the morning, lad. We'll have to run through the act tomorrow afternoon, putting a lot of old stuff back to fill in without her. As soon as we've finished trying to eat this muck, I'll do a running order for the rehearsal. And you'll have to tell Sam and Ben to make sure, before we start, that some of the old effects are working all right. Whatever we do, it'll be a ragtime job, but it'll be good enough for Burrington on a Saturday night. I wish to God we'd never set eyes on the bloody place,'

'So do I, Uncle Nick,' I cried fervently. 'This week's been nothing but a disaster.'

He gave me a hard look. 'Yes, and it might be a bit worse than you think, lad. But let's get started now. First thing to do is to put down the times of the effects with the girl in them, then we can see how much time we have to fill in with the old tricks.'

It was late and I was tired when I went up to my room, and I'd undressed and was about to get into bed before I noticed the letter that Cissie had slipped between the pillow and the bed-clothes. It was such a scrawl and ill-spelt muddle that it took me several minutes to puzzle it all out. Finally I made out that she was sorry she'd gone without saying Good-bye and giving me a last kiss but she couldn't stand it any longer and had to go, though she'd nowhere to go but back home which I knew she hated, and that I was a nice dear boy and that she didn't mind my being so stand-offish with her when it came to the point because she knew all the time I was really in love with that little Nancy Ellis even if she did seem to be not bothering about me, and that she hoped we'd meet again some day and that I wouldn't forget her because she was a true friend and perhaps a bit more. And it ended with some of those crosses for kisses I came to know so well, later in the war, after I had taken a commission and had to censor the men's letters. Cissie belonged entirely to that huge inarticulate world in which words fail the feelings and crosses mean kisses.

I felt really miserable, reaching perhaps the lowest point in this disastrous tour, after I had finished reading Cissie's farewell letter. Now we had a murderer, people like Lily Farris and Mergen, and others I didn't care for, going round with us (because however brutally he might behave sometimes I couldn't exclude Uncle Nick), and no Cissie, a real friend, no matter how silly she might be at times, a person, eager and warm-hearted, and not just a dummy or somebody sinister and murderous. It was actually a hottish night, on that Friday in Burrington, but now it felt cold.

7

During the Preston week I don't know what the police were up to – perhaps they were waiting for Inspector Crabb to come and take charge of the case – but I do know that I saw nothing of them. I also know that it was a bad week for us in the *Ganga Dun* company. Not that the act itself was going badly. It was in fine shape and was well received. But, to begin with, Sam and Ben and Barney all seemed to be ill-at-ease, not at all on their usual good terms with one another, and strangely quick to resent any criticism. I don't suppose I was any better. I still hoped for a letter from Nancy, even though I kept telling myself that I didn't, that I'd done with the girl. And like everybody else on the bill – except the murderer himself and Uncle Nick, who shrugged the whole thing away and refused to discuss it – I was haunted by the murder, for ever wondering, as they looked sideways at me and I at them, which one of them could have strangled poor Nonie. And when I wasn't being haunted or wondering – and if this seems contradictory, I'm sorry, but that's how it was – I was bored. Then Uncle Nick, with whom I shared digs that week, was morose and silent, even though the act was going so well. The truth was, though he wouldn't have admitted it even under torture, he was feeling half-lost without Cissie. He might have neglected her or have been rough with her, but now that she'd gone, he missed her. It wasn't simply a question of having a girl to go to bed with – he could easily have found plenty of bedmates – for I think that what he missed was Cissie's ego-flattering, intensely feminine companionship. Even her naivety and silliness made him feel all the more experienced and wiser. And Doris Tingley, now taking Cissie's place in the act, though not in bed, was a very different kind of woman.

Doris had worked for Uncle Nick for two or three years, and had then left him to marry Archie Tingley. She had agreed to come back because Archie was always losing or changing jobs, and they needed the money. I had to admit, though I would have preferred not to, that she was a much better performer than Cissie, quicker, stronger, and more dependable, altogether a superior professional. She was about thirty, a straight wiry woman with black hair and blazingly indignant blue eyes. She was, I think, the angriest person I've ever known. She was permanently angry. There may have been moments late at night when Archie, who had a lot of charm, coaxed her into a melting mood, but I couldn't imagine the scene. She was a devoted wife but only in a furious way, as if being married to Archie was the last straw. She was both quick and conscientious in her work with us but always behaved as if we were all insulting her. It was like working with a tigress. Sam, Ben and Barney were terrified of her, and even Uncle Nick handled her very carefully. Perhaps because I was much younger than they were, a mere soft boy in her eyes, she was rather easier and friendlier with me. She was always on the alert, ready for instant mobilization, against any man making a pass at her; though this expression wasn't current then, and she called it 'trying any funny business'. And perhaps because she saw me as being too young and soft for any determined funny business, she was less on the alert, more at ease, with me. But even so, she was still angry.

Uncle Nick had suggested she might like to attend the band call with me as she didn't know the music we were using now; and when I was through, feeling relieved, I asked her if she'd like a drink.

'Who's paying?' she demanded.

'Oh – I'll pay, Mrs Tingley.'

'Don't call me that – it sounds so dam' silly. You're what's-it – Richard – Dick, and I'm Doris. But that doesn't mean I'm going to spend any money on you in these ridiculous *pro* bars. Signed photos of great artistes, I don't think. All pals of the landlord, I also don't think. Well, you can buy me just one Scotch-and-splash, but don't imagine I'm joining in any rounds. I'm here to save money, not spend it. Last night I beat that woman in my digs down to nineteen bob for the week – bed, proper breakfast, hot supper. And if I hadn't been feeling so tired I'd have got her down to seventeen-and-six – it can be done. That's Lily Farris, isn't it? I suppose you think she's a wonder.'

'No, I don't, Doris,' I said as I edged her away. 'As a matter of fact, I dislike her.'

'Good for you. So do I. On *and* off. What did she do to you? No, don't tell me if you have to blush. I don't like dirty stories.'

After we had settled in a corner of the usual bar – and they really were all uncommonly alike, as if one super-Empire had had one great litter of bars-round-the-corner – she said, in a voice that I wished not so loud and clear: 'Now what's all this about a murder? I asked Nick but he didn't seem to want to talk about it. Did it himself perhaps.' She fixed her blue glare on me. 'Well, come on – tell me.'

So I told her about Nonie and what had happened to her. 'And we seem to be waiting for an Inspector Crabb to take charge of the case.'

'Well, he can't drag me into it, can he? And if it's one of that lot I saw this morning, I'm not surprised. Two or three of 'em looked like sex maniacs. Just let any of 'em try any funny business with me, that's all. Just lay a finger on me, that's all. One night – where was it? – Sunderland, I fancy – I kicked a comedian right in the – well, where he'd feel it most. And I'll tell you what variety's full of – mostly – riff-raff, just downright common riff-raff, earning ten times as much money as they're worth.'

'Some of them, I agree.' And even if I'd violently disagreed, I wouldn't have said so. 'But after you'd left the Variety stage, didn't you ever miss it?'

'Certainly not,' she replied indignantly. 'Except the regular money, such as it was. Being married to Archie Tingley's enough variety stage for me. He's in and out of more jobs than any other man in England. When people ask me what he's doing, I have to think, and even then sometimes I'm two jobs behind him. He can get almost any job he wants. You'll soon see why when you meet him – he's coming up at the end of the week – waste of money, of course, but he swears there's a man he has to see. But as soon as he's in a job, either he can't keep it or he doesn't like it. And what do I say? Nothing. Or not much. Twists me all the time round his little finger,' she said angrily. 'I wish to God I'd married a steady man I didn't much like.'

'What's your husband doing now, Doris?'

'Have some sense, Dick. I've just told you that's the sort of question I hate. He's selling something – Turkish tobacco or electric fittings or bicycles – and he can't even ride one. But he'll tell you himself before the week's out. He'll be here on Friday.' Now she glared at me as if I'd just suggested that her Archie and I should go round all the pubs in Preston. 'But if you think I'm fool enough to let him booze all his money away in your company, you can think again. Now I'm getting out of here. You can please yourself.'

If it had not been for the Tingleys, first Doris and then Archie, that would have been a dismal week in Preston. I couldn't even go out painting because now Uncle Nick ordered me to do six bold oil paintings of simple subjects for the trick I'd first suggested. They had to be in oils because he felt that canvas was essential. He was now working with Sam and Ben on a trick frame containing spring rollers. He had decided there had to be four of these: a big one at the side that, at a touch, released a blank canvas covering everything, so that members of the audience could examine it before we began; then three smaller rollers at the top, each controlling a third of the canvas underneath, which in turn covered and then uncovered three sections of the picture itself. So I had to paint six of these: a rustic cottage, a cornfield, a wood, a seaside scene, a village street, and some factories with tall chimneys; crude daubs, all of them. In addition I had to prepare a number of identical canvases, with the various subjects lightly pencilled in, so that on the stage, painting them in view of the audience, I could work quickly and accurately. The audience apparently chose which of the six subjects it preferred, though this choice of course was faked because we had to know which of my finished pictures to place behind the two layers of canvas in the magic frame. Actually it was some weeks before Uncle Nick was satisfied with the spring rollers and the release catches hidden inside the broad elaborate frame, but when he finally introduced *The Magic Painting* into the act, he gave me twenty-five pounds and promised me a third of the proceeds if he should ever sell the trick. I never saw it from the front, of course, but from the applause and various comments I heard, it did appear to be very effective, another marvel. They saw two framed blank canvases; they chose one of the six subjects for me to paint; when I finished a third of the picture, the magic frame was turned round to show that it too had painted a third of the picture; then two-thirds, then the whole picture; and both paintings could then be compared and examined. Years afterwards, I saw an American illusionist at the Palladium working the effect very successfully, and I had a hard time persuading my wife that it was I who had first thought of it.

But it was a dismal job – because even then I was a painter first and an illusionist a long way afterwards – painting one after another of those idiotic subjects with the same quick-drying oils I would need when reproducing them on the stage. With the spring rollers and the release catches, Uncle Nick had the sort of tricky task he enjoyed; but my part of the illusion was just a bore. The weather was fine too, so I hated all the more being kept indoors grinding away at those daubs. And Uncle Nick, who ought to have been enjoying himself, was still morose and almost silent, as if he had problems far removed from spring rollers and release catches and magic canvases. No doubt he was secretly wishing he had not been so hard on Cissie, but I couldn't help wondering too if the murder, which he still refused to discuss, wasn't worrying him on the same hidden level. But when I asked him when he thought we might expect Inspector Crabb 'the terror', he merely snorted contemptuously.

So I was glad, needing some relief and a change, when between the houses on Friday night Doris Tingley looked into my dressing-room – a Hindoo maiden with furious blue eyes. 'Archie's here. If you've nothing better to do, you might as well come and have a look at him. You can exchange men's rubbish.'

Archie was as handsome as a man on a sentimental picture postcard, the one holding a girl's hand in a bower of roses. He had doggy brown eyes, wavy hair, and a beautiful moustache, and he was better dressed than any man I'd had anything to do with for months.

'It's a pleasure, my dear fellow. Your uncle doesn't like me, you know, I suppose because I stole Doris away from him.'

'That helped, but he wouldn't like you anyhow,' said Doris. 'I don't know why *I* do.'

Archie ignored that. 'But I'm sure you and I will get along nicely, Dick. Have a drink.'

'There isn't any,' said Doris fiercely.

'Well, my dear, I can easily pop out for a bottle—'

'You're not starting that—'

'Doris, Doris,' he began reproachfully, giving her a sweet sad smile, 'please remember I've come over two hundred miles—'

'To see a man – you said so—'

'No, darling, I made a mistake about him. He's in Carlisle, not Preston. And that was only an excuse. I came to see you. I'm missing you terribly already, my dear. And now when I suggest a friendly drink—'

'Oh – all right, buy a bottle. But come straight back.'

He patted her shoulder, winked at me, and hurried out.

'That man,' said Doris angrily. 'How I put up with him, I can't imagine. Not that he isn't better than most of you. He does try to please, not like most men, who think they're giving you a treat just yawning or blowing smoke in your face. It's not Turkish tobacco or bicycles but boats now,' she added in disgust. 'Boats! I ask you!'

'What kind of boats?'

'Little boats – for park lakes. And I doubt if he's ever been in one in all his life. He gets talking to some chap in an expensive saloon bar – money's no object when he's out on his own – and in half an hour they're bosom friends – then it's boats for park lakes. One time he'd have put in a bid for five-thousand rollerskates if I hadn't stopped him. Always some jolly nice chap he's met, and they always turn out to be half-barmy. If he ever met a sensible one, I've still to hear of him. Boats for park lakes!'

Later, when he was drinking the whisky he'd bought, by himself too because Doris and I remembered we'd still to give a performance, Archie said: 'What I really want to get into, my dear fellow, is the moving picture business. Films – they're the coming thing. Doris doesn't believe it—'

'I should think not,' said Doris indignantly. 'Lot of silly rubbish and always looks as if it's raining.'

'Sheer prejudice, my dear. You never look at them.'

'Well, do you? And if so, who with? Because we all know what picture palaces are for—'

'Why don't you join us, Dick my dear fellow, and we'll go out to supper?'

'No, we won't,' said his wife furiously. 'Not when I've ordered and paid for supper for us both at the digs. Besides, where d'you think you are – Paris? Next thing you'll be wanting to drink champagne out of my slipper.'

'She looks quite fetching as an Indian, don't you think, my dear fellow? Has she had any little notes yet – flowers – that sort of thing?'

'What – in Preston?' She glared at him. 'Archie Tingley, I don't think you know where you are half your time. All right, Dick, you pop off now. You've seen him and now you know what I've to put up with.'

'Doesn't mean a word of it, old man. Absolutely adores me. I adore her too. Wonderful marriage.'

'Oh – you shut up!'

'Look here,' I said to them as I was leaving, 'I've had a dreary week. Let's lunch together tomorrow – upstairs at that big corner pub, where you turn to come in the front here – you know the one. It'll be my lunch.'

'It will *not*,' said Doris indignantly. 'What – a boy your age, earning half my money! Never! It'll be our lunch. Well, say something, Archie – don't just stand there. And leave that whisky alone.'

So we arranged to meet at one in that upstairs room. I was a few minutes late and found Archie at the bar downstairs, drinking pink gin. 'Sorry I'm late,' I began.

'Not at all, my dear fellow. Have a quick one. Two pink gins, my dear,' he said to the barmaid. Then as he turned to me again, he lowered his voice. 'We went up and then I came down again. Not just for a drink. The fact is, one of those bullying middle-aged North-country waitresses tried to take command up there, and of course she'd picked the worst woman in England for that kind of hanky-panky. Doris has eaten 'em for breakfast. In fifteen seconds she was tearing into the wretched woman, and I tried to look as if I was making for the *Gents* and left 'em. Well, happy days!'

As it was a fine warm Saturday, the lunch-room upstairs was almost empty. As we passed a middle-aged waitress, pink and flustered, Archie gave me a nudge. 'Still wondering what happened to her,' he whispered. Doris was sitting at a table near the window, giving sharp directions to a younger waitress. She was wearing an angry scarlet blouse and even the bird on her hat had an indignant eye. 'I'm ordering for all of us, and if you two don't like it, you can lump it.' Then, to the waitress: 'Everything for three. And don't start any nonsense about anything being *off*. Unless you want me to go down to the kitchen myself.'

In fact we had a good lunch, which included a bottle of burgundy, for which I insisted upon paying, defying Doris's blue glare. Throughout the meal Archie became more and more expansive in spite of his wife's persistent discouragement. He was wearing a handsome light-grey suit, a pale-pink shirt, a polka-dot bowtie, and he looked like the hero of a musical comedy. I told him so.

'Delighted to hear it, my dear fellow. Though I've never had any ambitions in that direction.'

'And it's about the only one,' said Doris. 'That and deep-sea diving. And talking about musical comedy, I see that one of our dear old pals – though I could never stand him – is rehearsing for a new one, *The Girl in the Band*. Charlie Pearse, no less. Where's that copy of *The Era* we brought, Archie?'

'It's here. I have it,' he told her, and then began turning the pages. 'Ah – here we are. *The Girl in the Band*, shortly opening at the Regent. Tom Bowen, Gertie May, Nancy Ellis, Charles Pearse – yes, there he is.'

'Did you say Nancy Ellis?' My voice sounded peculiar, but then I felt peculiar.

'Nancy Ellis – yes. Know her?'

'Of course he knows her,' said Doris. 'Just look at him.'

'A-ha! A-ha – a-ha – a-ha – a-ha!'

'Oh – stop it, Archie. You sound like a billy-goat. Well, Dick, what about this wonderful Nancy Ellis? Is this love's young dream – or aren't you feeling well?'

'I'm all right, thank you, Doris,' I replied carefully. 'But she and her sister were touring with us until they went into pantomime at Plymouth. And I've been wondering what had happened to her.'

'And what about *her*? Has she been wondering too?'

'I don't know.' And something in my tone must have given me

away.

'Well, if she hasn't, she ought to have been,' said Doris indignantly. 'You're probably worth ten of her. I'll bet she's one of these peroxide blonde soubrettes who'll never see thirty-five again—'

'She's eighteen – perhaps nineteen. And if she were here – and I wish to God she was – you'd hate that bet—'

'And now change your tune, my dear,' said Archie, who had been lighting an enormous cigar. 'Dick's had enough. Where's your womanly intuition?'

'It went on strike about the time I first met you,' Doris told him. 'And who gave you that flor de cabbagio?'

Archie let that alone. He looked at me, taking out the monster cigar to do it better, and produced a kind of lightning sketch of a millionaire talking to some humble admirer. 'Dick, my dear fellow, there are one or two things you ought to understand about me.'

'We're off,' said Doris.

'My interests are wide – very wide – though not deep—'

'And you can bet your boots on that,' Doris told me.

'I try this and that and the other,' Archie continued, still ignoring his wife, who was now pulling half-furious and half-humorous faces. 'And why? Actually, for two good reasons. First, I'm accumulating a good deal of valuable experience, giving me – well, an insight—'

'Into what?' Doris again, of course.

'Secondly, I'm waiting for the proper moment to arrive. To enter the moving picture business. Not at the producing end. No, no, no, I've not the slightest desire to make films, my dear fellow. I'm quite ready to leave that to other people.'

'Very good of you, Archie dear. I ought to tell 'em.'

'No, no. I want to go in – but at the right moment, that's all-important – at the distributing or exhibiting end. I want to be in a position to meet the demand for moving pictures that is about to grow and grow and grow. Dick, I assure you, nothing can stop them. Doris doesn't understand this because in some respects she's hide-bound—'

'She's husband-bound, you mean—'

'Quiet, my dear. I'm talking to Dick, and not only because I like him, which I do, but also – to be perfectly frank – because I hope he'll pass some of this on to his uncle, Nick Ollanton, a clever man – who might be wondering now what to do with his money.' He took a pull at his cigar, then regarded me earnestly, 'It's absolutely inevitable.'

'What is, Archie?' I felt it was time I said something.

'Moving pictures will go up and up, variety down and down.'

'Never,' cried Doris. 'Who wants to watch photos instead of living people?'

'My wife,' said Archie, as if she wasn't there, 'is devoted to me of course – as I am to her – but she thinks I'm a chump because I try selling bicycles or tobacco or boats for park lakes, and she has to come here – only for the time being, of course – to earn her living. But I'm only waiting for the right moment, the real opportunity, to get into moving pictures, to sell films instead of all this other nonsense. And I tell you,' he continued, addressing us both now, 'that with any luck, in ten years' time, Doris will be riding behind a chauffeur in a big car and will hardly believe she used to escape from a box twice-nightly at Preston.'

'You daft idiot,' said Doris. 'I'll probably be keeping a lodging-house and you'll be doing the washing up and cleaning the shoes. And the only moving pictures you'll know about will be the ones you sneak off and pay ninepence to see. And that's what Dick thinks, only he's too polite to say so.'

And it was a nice thought, and what Uncle Nick thought when I mentioned Archie Tingley to him ('He's just a nicelooking flippertyflopperty, lad'); and all three of us were wrong.

Later that afternoon I wrote my last, my absolutely final, letter to Nancy Ellis – Stage Door, Regent Theatre, London, and it was short, rather curt but also a bit sad:

Dear Nancy,

I have just heard that you are rehearsing at the Regent so this ought to reach you quite soon. If you have ever sent any replies to my letters, I have never had them – not a word. I shall not write again – this is the very last time – but it would not hurt you just to send me a line, even if it is only a postcard, to tell me you are not interested. Then perhaps I could stop thinking about you. For the next three weeks I shall be at the Palace, Blackpool.

Yours very sincerely,
Dick (and in case you have
forgotten – Herncastle)

It made me feel a little better, but not much.

8

I'd been to Blackpool before, of course; nearly everybody went there from the West Riding, though not every year as so many Lancashire people did. When the Lancashire towns had their holidays or *wakes* (we called them *tides* in the West Riding), their people went swarming to Blackpool, often loaded with provisions, and many of them were so determined to spend every penny they had saved that they took care to pay their landladies in advance. It was strange to arrive there to work and not on holiday, to breathe the strong sea air and yet not be rushing across the tiers of promenades to the sands, a boy again. It was strange and melancholy. I didn't belong to the bustling and noisy crowds of holiday-makers – and the thought of helping to entertain them gave me no particular pleasure – and I didn't seem to belong to anybody or anything else. Not unnaturally I felt worse here than I had done in the grim industrial towns. I was of course at the age when you can't control your moods and so you over-indulge them, and no doubt I went striding and scowling through the crowds, which mostly appeared idiotic, like another Ishmael. But even so, my feeling of melancholy isolation was real.

(Here I must explain that what I remember best after half a century are actual sights and scenes, which I can recapture with pencil and paints but not in words; and this explains why I so rarely try. But next to what was actually visual, I best remember states of mind, recalling exactly – for myself if not for the reader – what, for example, I felt in the huge glare and bustle and cheerful idiocy of Blackpool in the earlier *wakes* weeks.)

The town was packed to its attics. But Uncle Nick, in his careful way, having appeared there several times before and knowing what to expect, had booked accommodation well in advance at a biggish boarding-house not far from the Palace. Now that Cissie wasn't with him and he didn't need a double room, there had to be a reshuffle, which nobody seemed to mind as it was early Sunday evening and there was not much else to do. He was given a fairly large single room on the first floor, and I had a much smaller one on the floor above.

The landlady was an iron-handed Scots widow, Mrs Taggart, who was assisted by a daughter, a reddish hungry-looking girl called Tessie, and by a plump and sniffling maid-of-all-work who oughtn't to have been named Violet. There were three other people sharing my floor. Two of them, Maisie Dawe and Peggy Canford, were with a concert party on one of the piers. The third, Mr Pringle, bald and rolypoly, was an astrologer. But there must have been at least twelve of us sitting down to cold roast lamb, boiled ham, potatoes and salads, on Sunday night. Uncle Nick, who disliked this boarding-house style of life, said little and looked grim. I talked to Mr Pringle and the two girls, both fairly pretty and lively, but I still felt melancholy.

The band call at the Palace, next morning, was no trouble, for this was a large, very successful, well-managed variety theatre. Even so, it was embarrassing; the management was all right but the performers were all wrong. We never had liked one another, not from the beginning, and now with the murder still hanging over us we all moved through a mist and a bog of mistrust and suspicion. For some reason I couldn't discover, the backstage atmosphere seemed worse here in Blackpool than it had been the week before in Preston. And it seemed ages — in another world – since I had looked for Nancy at band calls or had gone off with Julie for a drink. (This will seem an exaggeration only to people without imagination and unable to remember what they felt in their youth. When we are older we are able to live in – and make the best of – one continuing world, but when we are young we feel sometimes that in an unknown and sinister fashion the whole cosmos has been changed, one age ended and another begun when we were not noticing what was happening. So, little more than a year later, when I was at the front, it would seem ages – in another world – since I attended this band call in Blackpool.) And this morning I didn't propose to loiter for two seconds or to go for a drink at any usual pub-round-the-corner. I would take a look at the sea, a sharp walk along the promenade for half an hour, and then discover what Mrs Taggart and Tessie were offering us as a good hot midday dinner, Blackpool's pride.

On my way to the stage door, however, I was stopped. 'Now, let me see, what's *your* name? Mine's Crabb, by the way – Inspector Crabb. Oh – I see you've heard of me.'

'Yes, Inspector. I'm Richard Herncastle – with the *Ganga Dun* company.'

He glanced at a notebook. 'That's right, so you are. Well now—' He hesitated a moment, slipped the notebook into his pocket, then looked hard at me and said: 'You've done what you have to do here, haven't you? Good. So what do you do now?'

'Usually I have a drink, if there's anybody I want to have a drink with. But as there isn't, I was going for a walk.'

'Then I'll tell you what we'll do, Mr Herncastle, if you've no objection. You and I will take a walk *and* have a drink. What d'you say to that?'

'All right, Inspector.'

'But not very enthusiastic, eh?'

'I don't think I can conjure up any enthusiasm this morning, that's all. But so long as I'm back at my digs at one, let's have a walk and a drink.'

'We'll do that, then.'

Out we went into the hard bright sunlight. Out there he looked all wrong with his bowler hat, high collar and narrow black tie, and dingy blue suit. He was tall and thin, though wide-shouldered, and while his nose was long and sharp and he had a lot of chin, his moustache drooped shapelessly. I could hardly see his eyes because he kept them half-closed against the strong sunlight. But if he really was, as Furness had declared, 'a terror', he didn't particularly look it or sound like it.

'Wonderful air,' he said, after several sniffy pulls at it. 'But I don't like this place. Never did as soon as I had any sense. It's just one big money-trap, crammed with idiots and sharpers. But the air's wonderful. Oughtn't to be but it is. Pity we can't pipe it into Westminster. Half these people are drunk on it already. Look at 'em.'

That was unnecessary. We were now having to push our way through mobs of holiday-makers – scarlet-faced mums, dads with huge caps at the back of their heads, young men wearing comic hats, girls giggling – and nudging one another, children running and screaming, and people selling things, buying things, chewing and sucking things, and a fairground din coming from somewhere. We went down to the lower promenade, which was not so crowded, but just below us the sands were thickly carpeted with folk of all ages, sizes and shapes to the edge of the sea, immense, calm and indifferent, only a shade or two darker than the bleached blue of the high summer sky. Inspector Crabb stopped, to wave a hand downwards first to the crowded beach and then upwards to the packed main promenade above us.

'Some time since I was here,' he said. 'Do you know what all this does to me? You'll never guess. It frightens me. That's what it does – frightens me. I think I know why, but that'll keep. Let's move on.'

It was pleasant and quite easy to talk on this lower promenade, though Inspector Crabb wasn't my idea of the perfect companion for such a stroll. 'I called at your boarding-house this morning,' he told me as we went along. 'Spoke to Mr Ollanton – your uncle, isn't he? He said you'd be at the Palace. And that's about all he did say. Wouldn't express any opinion about the crime. Shut me up, shut himself up. Why? Any idea why he doesn't want to talk? It's not just me. Furness had a note about it. So why?'

I laughed. 'You don't think he's a suspicious character, do you?'

'I think everybody's a suspicious character. I've enough suspicion in me to choke a horse. I'm suspicious by trade and by nature, I am. But I've gone through Furness's notes, and I know a cast-iron alibi when I see one. You and Mr Ollanton have got one that dynamite wouldn't shift. But I still ask why he doesn't want to talk.'

'I've asked myself that, Inspector, and I think I know the answer.'

'Let's have it then, Mr Herncastle.' Crabb was one of the few people I'd known up to that time who always called me Mr Herncastle, making me feel older, heavier, more responsible.

'Uncle Nick's a very clever man,' I began rather slowly. 'He's also very proud, very vain. No, that's not right. He's more proud than vain. And he's in the mystery business. He invents tricks and illusions.'

'Yes, I've seen his turn. I've a sharp eye but he had me guessing. And the wife really believed he was some sort of Indian magician. But that's the sort of thing she wants to believe. Sorry to interrupt. Go on.'

'Well, so far this murder's a mystery bigger than any of his. This is the real thing. If he could solve it, he'd talk fast enough, but because he can't, because it baffles *him*, the great Nick Ollanton, he doesn't even want to discuss it.'

'Very neat, quite clever, Mr Herncastle,' said Crabb. 'You might be right, then again you might not. Excuse me.' He stopped to lay a hand on the shoulder of a man who was sauntering by with a plump wife and two children. 'Why, if it isn't Spider Evans!'

'Oh – hello, Inspector!' And the man motioned his wife to keep going. Fear flickered in his eyes.

'You wouldn't be working up here, would you, Spider?' Crabb inquired with a kind of sinister geniality.

'No I wouldn't. I'm having a holiday same as everybody else here.'

'Not everybody, Spider. I've only been here since last night, and I've spotted six or seven wide boys I know without even looking for 'em. So watch it, Spider. Just play on the sands.' As we moved away, he said: 'I've too good a memory for faces, and, as I told you, a very suspicious nature. But one of you at the Palace is more dangerous than Spider Evans and his pals. It's you people I'm interested in, not them. Somebody'll be doing a turn at the Palace tonight who might get his hands on another girl's throat. Nasty cases these, Mr Herncastle. Better cut up here, hadn't we? Time's getting on, and you might like a glass of beer before you have your dinner.'

He said nothing more until we found a quiet pub, on the way back to my digs, and we took our glasses of beer into an empty corner. 'Well, I'll be watching your show tonight, both houses, and maybe several other nights as well. I'll be round at the back too, because, after all, there you are, all of you, aren't you? Even Furness and his Chief didn't believe somebody slipped in from outside to strangle that girl. It was one of you.'

'It wasn't me,' I told him. 'So don't waste your time on me, Inspector.'

He drained some beer out of his moustache, then looked at me solemnly over his glass. 'I know it wasn't you, Mr Herncastle. I'd bet on that even if your alibi wasn't cast-iron. But I'd like to waste some of *your* time, if not mine. You and your uncle are one of the turns, in the company. And you're not suspects. So I can talk to you. But Mr Ollanton won't talk. Says in effect it's my job not his. Shuts up, no doubt for the reason you've given – he feels small for once. That leaves you, Mr Herncastle. And that's why I got hold of you this morning, why we're drinking this beer that's a bit too warm for my taste. You want this case solved and done with, don't you?'

'Yes, but-'

'Excuse me. Just let me finish. You're one of 'em behind the scenes, and if I'm to be careful – and I am careful – you're all I've got, the only one I can talk to, compare notes with, you might say. You might know something I need, without being aware of it. You see what I mean? But you were going to say something.'

'Just this, Inspector. Of course I'll help you if I can. But I must warn you that I don't really know all these other people on the bill. Though we've been going round together now for about a couple of months, I've seen very little of them.'

He had small greyish eyes, and now I got a sharp glance from them. 'That's not usual. Stand-offish, are you, Mr Herncastle?'

'No, I don't think so. On an earlier tour – with different people – well,' I ended rather awkwardly, 'I made several friends.'

'But not this time – eh? Well, there must be a reason. Perhaps they're different this time. Perhaps you don't take to 'em – eh?'

'Well-'

'That's the sort of thing I like to know,' he said briskly. He looked across at the clock above the bar. 'Time you were off or your dinner'll be cold – or not there. I may be looking in on you between the first house and the second.'

I was back in time to take a place at the big dining-table between Mr Pringle the astrologer and Peggy Canford, the older and less attractive of the two concert-party girls. She had rather fine eyes but her face was too long, her cheek-bones and mouth too big. She was the concert-party pianist, she told me; the other girl, Maisie Dawe, a rather plump and dimple-and-curls brunette, not unlike a more sophisticated Phyllis Robinson, was the soubrette of the troupe. She was sitting opposite, next to Uncle Nick, who wasn't bothering to talk to her and looked disgruntled, probably because he hated eating in this boarding-house style. Maisie offered me a professionally bright smile, so I smiled back, and Uncle Nick caught it and gave me a hard look. There were several other people there, but if I knew their names then, I certainly don't now, and I think they must have been holiday-makers.

Peggy Canford, I discovered, was an intelligent girl, but very cynical. She hated Blackpool and her concert-party work. 'Two long shows a day, don't forget. Your two turns a night are just a rest-cure. I'm at that piano for the best part of my five hours. I'm so bad-tempered in the afternoons, wishing I was somewhere else, anywhere, half the time I play too loud and fast, and then we have a row afterwards. But it's all the same – the kids are making such a noise. What about this murder of yours? Tessie says an Inspector from Scotland Yard called this morning. Walrus moustache, she says. Don't start taking an interest in Tessie. She's just longing to nab somebody and get out of here. A baritone on the North Pier had your room the week before last, and Tessie was in and out of it all hours. Look at poor Maisie – daren't eat her pud. I can eat anything – and do – and even then I'm hungry half the time, after pounding that dam' piano. I was playing in a ladies' trio at Harrogate before I came here, and it was misery – the other two were wrapped up in each other, and I never set eyes on a man under fifty-five, and I thought I'd go mad thumping out those foul Indian Love Lyrics. The other two loved 'em – they were each less than the dust beneath the other's chariot wheel. Come in and have a drink one night. You'll be safe with two of us. It's when Tessie looks in and wants to know if you'd like something special for breakfast, that's when you want to watch out. I must run. Can't keep the kiddies waiting.'

When I joined Uncle Nick, he said gloomily: 'We'd better go up to my room. Can't talk privately down here. I shouldn't have booked us into this monkey-house. Everything in order along at the Palace, I imagine. Yes, they know how to run a variety theatre.'

His room was full of large pieces of furniture meant for somewhere else. But there was only one easy-chair, and he dropped into it, after taking off his coat and collar, for it was a warm afternoon. I sat on the edge of the bed and felt sleepy after the sea air and the heavy meal.

'I suppose that Inspector Crabb got hold of you, didn't he, lad?'

'He did.' And I told him what had passed between the Inspector and me.

'You want to discourage that caper or he's going to be a bloody nuisance. Besides, let him do his own work. That's what he's paid to do. He's very sharp, by the way. Take no notice of that moustache. I've often seen and heard him mentioned in London. Not that we've anything to be afraid of, lad, of course. Whoever did it, we didn't.'

'But who did, uncle?'

'I don't know – and, to be honest, I don't much care.' He was smoking a cigar, and now he took it out and looked at it, as if it was either very good or very bad. 'Oh – yes, there's something else – I nearly forgot.' He was elaborately casual, so that whatever it was, I felt he hadn't nearly forgotten it. 'D'you remember that dwarf I picked out, that afternoon at Joe Bosenby's? Philip Tewby, his name was.'

'I remember him – the very serious, dignified one.'

'That's him. Well, this morning I sent Pitter a wire telling him I want Tewby up here if he's free.'

This woke me up. 'Have you worked out the two-dwarf effect,

Uncle Nick?'

He hated to admit he hadn't. 'No, give me time, lad. This is in a different class from your picture trick, y'know. Very ambitious. But I thought it might be safer to have another dwarf with us. He can take over one or two of Barney's jobs.'

'Barney'll yell his head off. He's difficult enough now—'

'I know he is,' he cut in irritably. 'You needn't tell me about Barney. I've known him a lot longer than you have, lad. But with another dwarf about – a lot more responsible than he is – Barney'll have to mind his p's and q's, won't he?'

'I suppose so,' I said doubtfully. 'But I don't quite see-'

He cut me short again. 'You're half-asleep, lad. Go and have a nap – you were up early this morning — and I don't want you yawning your head off tonight. We've got to be good here. There'll be two full houses, you'll see.'

I don't suppose I'd been lying on my bed ten minutes before I fell asleep. But I seem to remember drifting towards it through a queer phantasmagoria of Blackpool crowds and the promenades and piers, the Tower and Winter Gardens, concert-party girls and Crabb and dwarfs, all jumbled up and making no sense but somehow turning sinister...

9

About the time the first house ended, that night, Doris Tingley was sitting in my dressing-room, knitting in a sporadic angry way and talking about Archie, who had gone to Birmingham. There was a knock, and in came Inspector Crabb.

'Evening, Mr Herncastle. Now this must be the young lady who vanished out of that box—'

'And what if it is?' said Doris, looking as if she'd taken an instant dislike to him.

'This is Inspector Crabb from Scotland Yard,' I said hastily.

'You don't surprise me,' said Doris, getting up. She gave him one of her blazing looks. 'Now don't you start bothering me. I wasn't with the company when that girl was killed.'

'That's right, Mrs Tingley, you weren't. Still, we might have a chat sometime—'

'What for?'

'You might have some ideas about the rest of the turns – the men, of course—'

'Well, I haven't. So don't waste your time.' Still the Hindoo maiden, except for her eyes and tone of voice, Doris left us, banging the door behind her.

'Was that me,' said Crabb as he went towards the chair Doris had been sitting on, 'or is she always like that?'

'She's always like that. Puts you off at first, but now I like her. Have you been in front, Inspector?'

'I have, Mr Herncastle. Yours is easily the best turn. Very very clever. Now how on earth could she have got out of that box? Like to tell me?'

'No. Not allowed.'

'Quite right. Well, all I can say is that I'm glad your uncle is a law-abiding man. If we'd had him against us, we'd have been in for some trouble. Not that we aren't in for plenty, as it is. Evidence that'll stand up in court, that's our chief worry, Mr Herncastle. I could name you six murderers walking the streets of London this very minute. We *know* they're guilty, but we can't prove it. This could turn out to be one of those cases. I say, it *could*. But it's early days yet. Now I'm taking you into my confidence, Mr Herncastle—'

'I'm not sure I want you to, Inspector.'

'Well, you remember what I said this morning. I like to have a wall to bounce the ball against. Now I can't talk freely unless you give me your word it'll go no further. No – let me finish. I'm asking a favour of you. Right. I want you on my side. But don't forget – one reason is—' and he lowered his voice – 'your uncle, Mr Ollanton, has adopted what I think is a thoroughly bad attitude. Mind you, unless he's deliberately concealing evidence, he's within his rights. If he doesn't want to talk to me, I can't make him. But it's all the more reason why I feel I can ask you for a bit of co-operation. For instance, your word it won't go on further – eh?'

'All right, Inspector.'

'Well done! Duffield now – what d'you think of him?'

'I don't really know him. I don't like him because he lets his sister do all the work while he does all the showing-off.'

281

'Quite so. Though she isn't his sister. She's an old flame with the light out. Nowhere to go. Nothing to do. Loves dogs. Now if *he'd* been killed, we'd know where to look. He's been in trouble once for passing dud cheques. But he always knows where to find women – his sort always do. Why'd he want to strangle a girl?'

'I don't know. But then I don't know why anybody would.'

'Hasn't a girl ever worked you up and then laughed at you, till you felt like killing her?'

'No. I've never felt like killing anybody.'

'I believe you.'

'Thanks. By the way – and I've only just remembered them, though I know it seems silly – what about the Colmars themselves?'

Crabb shook his head regretfully. 'That would have been nice and neat. Foreigners too, her own sort. But Furness and I put them through a mincer. Cast-iron alibis – as good as yours. And no motives. The two young ones are puffs, and the older one, her uncle, was half-mad with rage and grief. He talked a lot. Accused everybody, including that dwarf of yours—'

'Barney? That's nonsense. He's just a silly little man.'

'So I gather. And he left early that night, with your two other men. Now what about Lily Farris's pianist – Mergen? Know him?'

'Yes. And I don't like him. Or her either.'

'Quite right, Mr Herncastle. I've heard some rumours about her. And we can prove Mergen's a nasty piece of work. But I don't see him strangling that girl.'

'Neither do I. He's too oily and soft.'

'*And* careful. Whoever did this suddenly went mad with rage, I'd say. Do you see Bert or Ted Lowson mad with rage? By the way, they're not brothers but cousins. And they're both engaged to be married, though that doesn't prove anything. They give each other an alibi and that doesn't prove anything either. But I don't see either of them doing this job, do you, Mr Herncastle?'

'No. I just can't imagine either of them boiling with anger. But then they bore me – on or off the stage.'

'Same here. Well now, these three young Americans—'

It was at this point that Uncle Nick looked in. 'I want you, Richard.'

'Good evening, Mr Ollanton,' said Crabb. 'Enjoyed your turn very much. Best on the bill.'

'Glad to hear it,' said Uncle Nick curtly. 'Want you now, Richard –

look sharp.' He went striding along the corridor, an impressive figure in his *Ganga Dun* make-up.

'You'll be seeing me again, Mr Herncastle,' said Crabb. 'But not tonight. Ta-ta!'

As soon as I'd followed Uncle Nick into his dressing-room and had closed the door behind me, he said: 'You don't want to encourage that chap to sit about here, lad.'

'I'm not doing. But he says he has to talk to me because you won't let him talk to you, uncle.'

'Well, if I can say no, so can you.'

'Is that a good idea?'

I expected him to say it was, Uncle Nick being fond of his own ideas, but for once he didn't. 'No, perhaps you're right. But don't encourage him, that's all.' He dropped his voice almost to a whisper. 'Open that door – quietly but quickly – jerk it open.'

I did, but there was nobody about. 'Did you think Crabb would be listening out there?' I said as I closed it again. 'He's a bit cleverer than that, I fancy.'

'I know. But I just wanted to make sure.' He waited a moment. 'Now I've had a wire from Pitter to say that dwarf, Philip Tewby, will be here tomorrow. His train gets in at four, and I want you to meet him. You can't miss him no matter how many people come off the train.'

'But where do I take him? We can't start looking for digs-'

'I know, I know, lad.' He didn't raise his voice but he made it sound very sharp, and he glared at me. 'You don't need to tell me the town's full up. Just listen, that's all. I've made arrangements with a woman I used to know. She can find a corner for him. Here's her name and address.' He handed me a slip of paper.

'All right, I take him to this address,' I said rather sulkily. 'But then what?'

Uncle Nick surprised me again. Instead of more sharp tones and more glaring, he looked thoughtful and muttered: 'That's right. Then – what? He'd better see the act a few times. But I don't want him backstage. I'll have to make some arrangement. Look – tell him where we're staying, then tell him to come and see me at half-past eleven – that's on Wednesday morning, of course. And another thing while I remember. I want you out of there by eleven o'clock, lad. Take one of those girls for a walk on the prom. Anyhow, make sure you're out of the way. And if you want to go for a walk with your friend Inspector

Crabb, that'll be all right to me. Now you know what you have to do, Richard. Isn't that the callboy?'

'Yes. I'm going. And I know what I have to do.' But I didn't move, though he was now facing the mirror, ready to attend to his make-up. 'Just one thing, uncle. What's this all about?'

'My business, not yours. I may need another dwarf, that's all. Don't get big-headed, lad. You'll be telling me how to run the act next. Now bugger off.'

I was glad that night when Peggy and Maisie, the concert-party girls, who finished later than we did, came bursting in for supper. When I felt aggrieved, in those days, I was inclined to take refuge in long sulky silences – a bad habit that I've tried to get rid of – and if that's how I wanted to behave, Uncle Nick was the last man to try to talk me out of it. We both needed some female chatter, and the girls, free at last after a long day, were as ready for talk as they were for food.

'Ham again,' said Peggy. 'There must be more ham eaten in this town than any place in the world. Perhaps it's ham that makes 'em so stupid. We'd the stupidest audience tonight I've ever known. Talk about dense! Poor Sid Baxter – he's our comedian, and he's really very clever – was down to comic postcard jokes and mothers-in-law and lodgers and kippers and drunks and W.C. gags. It must break his heart.'

'Peggy, I didn't tell you,' Maisie cried, 'but when he came off after the sketch, he coughed and coughed and there was blood on his handkerchief. Lorna – that's his wife,' she said to us, 'she's our vocalist – she was terribly upset again – and she started crying in the dressing-room.'

'I don't like life,' Peggy announced. 'It's no use. I've tried it and I don't like it.' She looked across at us defiantly.

'A couple of glasses, Richard,' said Uncle Nick. 'Then perhaps these young ladies will take a glass of champagne with me.'

'Thanks very much, Mr Ollanton,' said Maisie. 'I could just do with one.'

'So could I,' said Peggy. 'Thank you. But what about it, Mr Ollanton? You're a star turn – booked up for years – loads of money – so I suppose you think life's wonderful.'

'No, I don't.' Uncle Nick frowned and said nothing for a moment or two. 'I don't dislike life the way you seem to do. But then you may be a fish out of water. I'm not. I'm where I want to be, doing what I want to do. But even so, there's nothing wonderful about it. Most of the time it's like – let's say – living with a lion. One day you can make it jump through hoops, or even ride on its back. But get careless, make a wrong move, and it'll have you in a corner and be tearing an arm off.'

'When do you take it easy then?' This was Maisie.

'You don't.'

And I knew he meant that. I thought too how odd it was that he should be so tirelessly concerned with stage magic when, because of some deep flaw in his nature, he couldn't enjoy, couldn't even recognize, the magical element in life, all the enchantments of love and art to which, I was sure, he was blind and deaf. And perhaps it was to compensate himself for this loss that he had built up such a high fortress of pride.

But now Peggy was talking again. 'I'll tell the truth – and to hell with girlish reticence. I'm no great treat, but I can bang and rattle on a piano for hours, keep accounts, cook and sew and scrub, if I have to, and I'm not afraid to take my clothes off-'

'Darling, what's this?' cried Maisie.

'Shut up and listen. That's me, then. And I do believe that if any man I knew to be clean, sober, kind and capable of earning a steady four hundred a year, asked me to marry him, I'd nail him on the spot. How about it, Mr Ollanton?'

'Sorry, Miss Canford. To begin with, I'm married already—'

'We could live in sin—'

'And you wouldn't suit me. You're too intelligent.'

'This is *your* chance, Maisie. But don't you like intelligent women?'

'Not to live with. I like to be the one who supplies the intelligence. Now Richard here, he's different—'

'He's too young—'

'He wasn't for a certain West End actress I could name, older than you girls—'

'Oh – shut up, uncle.' I was embarrassed by the stares of the two girls, curious and speculative, and not by any memories of Julie, now a non-haunting ghost. All that intense and choking excitement, that racing and pounding of the blood, not long ago, and now – nothing! But we were interrupted here by little Mr Pringle, the astrologer, who came trotting in from the kitchen carrying a tray that held a large cup of cocoa and some biscuits.

'Good evening all,' he said. 'May I sit with you? I heard your voices and felt I needed a little company. I've been hard at work all evening up in my room.'

'Come and sit by me, Mr Pringle,' said Maisie. 'You know I love you.'

He sat beside her, nodding and smiling. Uncle Nick was staring at him. 'Do you really mean you've been hard at work all evening?' Uncle Nick asked him.

'Certainly I have, Mr Ollanton,' said Mr Pringle, solemn and dignified now. 'Why do you sound surprised?'

'Well, I imagined – that – well, you were on to something that didn't require any hard work.'

'In fact you thought I was a charlatan,' said Mr Pringle. 'Taking money for doing nothing.'

'Mr Pringle works very very hard,' said Maisie, looking reproachfully at Uncle Nick. 'And he only charges half-a-crown for giving advice, based on the stars. And only ten shillings for a full horoscope, which takes him hours and hours. You ought to see his room. It's full of shelves of star maps – and things. It's all – *scientific* – isn't it, Mr Pringle?'

'Certainly it is, my dear. Though there's philosophy and art in it as well. All very ancient.'

'I know that,' said Uncle Nick. 'But I never thought you took it seriously.'

'If I didn't, Mr Ollanton,' said Mr Pringle gravely, 'I wouldn't call myself an astrologer. I know other and easier ways of earning a living, you know. Originally, I was a jeweller and watchmaker, apprenticed to the trade. I can still repair a watch or clock if I have to.'

'Mr Pringle,' Peggy told us, 'is very clever as well as being an old sweetie. I'm not sure myself about all these stars and influences of his—'

'Peggy, you can't say that,' Maisie broke in excitedly. 'Look how right he was about – you-know-who—'

'I was right about him too,' said Peggy gloomily. 'The artful blighter.'

'Well now, Mr Pringle,' said Uncle Nick. 'I'm in the magic line myself, as you know. So I'll make a bargain with you. You come and have a look at my magic at the Palace – take a night off – and I'll have half-a-crown's worth of advice from the stars or a full ten-bob's worth of horoscope, just as you please.'

Mr Pringle nodded solemnly, looking hard at Uncle Nick over his spectacles. 'Very well, Mr Ollanton. That's a bargain. In the meantime, I'll give you a little advice for nothing. You're a Taurus, I believe. No, no, never mind about that. You come and tell me exactly when and where you were born, sometime tomorrow morning. But I can tell you now you're about to engage yourself in something that's very difficult and might be *very dangerous*. So you must be very very careful. But then you know that, Mr Ollanton. Am I right?'

'You might be,' said Uncle Nick. 'And then again – you might not, Mr Pringle.' He sounded careless and casual, just avoiding the contemptuous. But while this might do for Mr Pringle and the girls, it wouldn't do for me, who knew him so much better. I could catch behind this tone faint echoes of a shocked surprise. Uncle Nick, I could have sworn, really *was* engaged in something that was very difficult and might be very dangerous. It was fine again, the next morning, but there was a strong fresh wind ruffling up the sea and there seemed to be salt in the air as I walked at a sharp pace along the main promenade, as far as the North Shore and back. To my relief, I didn't run into Inspector Crabb, but then, when I left the promenade to return to the digs, I saw him across the road, talking to two men outside a pub. And then, as I hurried along, I had just time to see that the two men were Sam and Ben Hayes.

There were plenty of people coming off the London train that I had to meet at four, but I had no difficulty finding Philip Tewby, so like and yet so unlike Barney. He was struggling with a suitcase nearly as big as himself, and though he refused to hand it over to me, he agreed to let me share his grip on the handle. It was like walking with a magically transformed Barney. Philip Tewby was an extremely serious and dignified little man, very neatly dressed, whereas Barney always looked hopelessly shabby and slovenly, as if he had long ago given up all hope of improving his appearance. We were beaten in the rush for taxis at the station, but then, fortunately, because people were pointing and grinning at a young man and a dwarf carrying a suitcase between them, we found a taxi along the road. After I had read out the name – it was Mrs Schurer – and the address from the slip of paper Uncle Nick had given me, and we were on our way, Philip Tewby and I settled down to some solemn conversation.

'Before I forget, Mr Tewby,' I began, 'I have an urgent message to you from Mr Ollanton. You must go and see him at half-past eleven tomorrow morning.' And I gave him the address of our boarding-house. 'Don't fail to be there, because my uncle seems to think it's very important,'

'If it's important to him, Mr Herncastle,' said Philip Tewby gravely, 'then it's important to me.' And he pulled out a pocket-book and made a note of the time and the address. 'I'm looking forward to working with Mr Ollanton, who is very well known and much respected in the profession. Have you any idea what is being planned for me, Mr Herncastle?'

'No, I haven't, Mr Tewby. No doubt my uncle will explain. Have you been to Blackpool before?'

'For one season, a few years ago. At the Tower Circus. Running on and falling about, between the acts, with the clowns. To amuse the children, Mr Herncastle – of all ages. I'm fond of young children – I like to hear them laugh – but not the others, Mr Herncastle, not the others. I saw very little of the town itself – with two performances a day, Mr Herncastle, and often feeling very tired – two of the clowns were always very rough. But I am a serious man, Mr Herncastle, and I think life is a serious business, and a whole large town devoted only to frivolity and foolishness and greed – can that be a good thing for our country, Mr Herncastle?'

'Probably not. But you ought to see the places these people come from, Mr Tewby. We've been playing some of them. No wonder they come rushing here to chuck their money away.'

He turned to look up at me with his wise sad dwarf's eyes. 'I'm not blaming them, Mr Herncastle. But should all this money be thrown away here? What if they began to spend the money at home, to make those places better? We have so many dirty, ugly towns, Mr Herncastle.'

'I know we have, Mr Tewby. I've been going round some of them since I saw you last.'

'That wasn't a pleasant afternoon for me, Mr Herncastle. Not until Mr Ollanton asked me my name and what experience I'd had, and I thought it might lead to an engagement. Do you know this Mrs Schurer, Mr Herncastle?'

'No, but she must be somebody my uncle knows. The town's full up, and he must have asked her if she could find him a bed for you.'

'I appreciate that very much, Mr Herncastle. It was thoughtful of him – most thoughtful.'

I agreed that it was, and then told myself it was surprising too, because I never thought of Uncle Nick being thoughtful in this sense. But then there was something peculiar and mysterious anyhow about this sudden enlistment of Philip Tewby, when we didn't seem to need him in the act; and I remembered Uncle Nick's equally peculiar and mysterious manner. And why, for instance, had I to leave the digs, next morning, well before Tewby was due there?

Mrs Schurer lived in a newish row of houses off the North Shore. When we lugged Tewby's suitcase up to the front door, we could hear two people inside shouting at each other. Mrs Schurer answered my ring; she was an older, henna-haired Doris Tingley, and looked as if she'd just been shouting. But she seemed glad to see us; perhaps she felt she'd been shouting long enough.

'Come in, come in. You're Nick Ollanton's nephew, are you? Pleased to meet you. I used to be with Nick. And this is the—'

'Mr Tewby,' I cut in hastily.

'How d'you do? It's just a small attic room, Mr Tewby, but it's clean and comfortable.'

'It will be just what I want, thank you, Mrs Schurer.'

We were now standing in a little hallway, which immediately became too crowded when a fat man joined us. He had a scarlet moon of a face; he was wearing a shirt open at the neck and trousers that refused to meet at the top, round his great belly; and he was smoking a cigar in enraged short puffs, like an indignant locomotive.

'And this is my husband, Max. You might have overheard me having words with him. Well, I'll show you your room, Mr Tewby – leave the bag down here just now. And Max, you can let steam off, talking to this young man.'

Max Schurer's English was fluent enough, too fluent, but he spoke with a thick foreign accent that must be left to the imagination. He took me into a sitting-room that was filled with knick-knacks, stage photographs, and newspapers, all kinds of newspapers, foreign as well as English. 'You wish a glass of beer? No? Then pardon me – I am very thirsty after shouting with my wife.' And then he filled and drained in one vast gulp a glass of lager.

'We make a big argument,' he began, after picking up his cigar and looking at it suspiciously. 'I say we leave this country – not to Germany or France, no bloody fear, but to Holland, to Switzerland, to

Denmark or Sweden. I am a chef – I am here at the Metropole – so I can work any place. Holland, Switzerland, Denmark, Sweden,' he shouted, as if they were railway stations we were arriving at all at once.

I began to think he was barmy. 'Why do you want to go to those places? What's the matter with this country?'

'Sometime perhaps I tell you all that is matter with this country,' he shouted. 'But now I wish to leave, to go to one of those places, because soon there will be War. Yes, yes, yes – War, War, War, War!' He grabbed some newspapers and shook them under my nose. 'Archduke Francis Ferdinand is assassinated at Sarajevo. You have seen?'

'I read something about it.'

'I have worked in Vienna. I have worked in Belgrade – though only for three months – terrible. I think about international affairs. Austria will ask too much of the Serbs. Then there will be War.'

'I dare say. But there's always some sort of war down there—'

'Down there? It is not down there. It will be everywhere. It will be here. Why do you think I tell my wife we must go? Serbia brings in Russia. Austria brings in Germany. Russia brings in France, which brings in Britain. Then Europe is on fire. Except in the places where I wish to go. None of this can I make my wife understand. Ah – you British – with your suffragettes and votes for women and home rule for Ireland and five hundred rifles going to Ulster – when soon there will be *War – War – War*. Not a little Balkans war – but one big terrible hell of a war between the Great Powers-'

'Now stop it, Max,' said his wife, returning. 'And take poor little Mr Tewby's bag up for him – do you good, state you're in.' After he'd gone, she smiled apologetically at me. 'I heard him going on at you, just the way he does at me. You mightn't believe it, the way he's just been shouting and carrying on, but there isn't a nicer kinder man in this town than my Max, and he's a very clever chef, he can get work anywhere, and he only came to the Metropole because I wanted to be here. But he will go on and on about all this foreign politics – and what Austria said to Italy or what Germany'll say to Russia, as if they were a lot of quarrelsome people living further along the street. It's his hobby really. Do you go in for it?'

'No, I don't, Mrs Schurer. I prefer painting.'

'Isn't that nice? I wish he did – or fretwork or stamps or something.

He says it's because he comes from Alsace. He's got two pals – one from the Metropole and another from the Imperial – and some nights they argue here, top of their voices, till all hours – and I have to keep knocking on the ceiling. Well, I suppose a man has to have something – and it's not like he was gambling or going out with other women – but when he starts saying there'll be a war and we ought to go live in Sweden or somewhere, I begin to lose my patience.' She waited a moment, as if listening. 'He's taking his time coming back, isn't he? D'you think he's started an argument with poor little Mr Tewby?'

After the first house, that night, Uncle Nick asked me to bring him the stilt-boots from our prop basket below. He had worked on these with Sam and Ben, after that time when Barney nearly fell, but he hadn't put *The Rival Magicians* back into the act, and so we hadn't used them.

'And you'd better find some strong paper or a bit of cloth,' Uncle Nick went on. 'I'm taking them to the digs.'

I must have stared at him.

'Well, get on with it, lad,' he said irritably. 'I know what I'm doing, even if you don't. And there's no reason why you should have everything explained to you. Just take an order for once. Oh – and what about Philip Tewby?'

'I left him having an argument with Max Schurer about international affairs,' I replied, with a grin. 'But I'd already warned him you wanted to see him in the morning. He'll be there – he's a thoughtful responsible little man.'

'I dare say,' said Uncle Nick gloomily. 'But if I'd known what I know now, I'd have had no dwarfs in the act. They're as bad as women.'

10

Next morning, Wednesday, obeying Uncle Nick's strange instructions, I went out about quarter to eleven, with a sketchbook but no paints, not wishing to collect a Blackpool crowd. Low clouds were beginning to settle, and it looked as if rain was on its way. However, I was able to spend nearly two hours wandering about the big fairground near the South Shore, and sketching anything that caught my eye. This was a wonderful time off, a refreshing release from my growing and darkening bewilderment. I forgot about the murder and Inspector Crabb and Uncle Nick's increasingly odd behaviour. There are all manner of strange or attractive shapes in a big fairground, some fine patches of colour too – and I made notes of them. And there were not too many people about at first, so altogether I had a good morning. Whenever I could live and function, if only for an hour or so, as a painter and not as somebody on the variety stage, I felt better at once, easier and more hopeful and confident; and this explains why, when I was cut off from painting and drawing, when I felt I couldn't be anything but a young man in variety, I was so often inclined to feel darkly bewildered and rather pessimistic, as if I was about to be lost for ever in a confusing and evil world.

It began to rain in the early afternoon so I went along to the Winter Gardens, wondering what I would think about the place now, not having visited it since I was a schoolboy and dizzy with wonder at its array of amusements. There must have been at least a thousand people dancing in the enormous ballroom. I wandered round the lowest balcony, like the dress circle of a theatre, occasionally stopping to look down on the dancers, seeing myself as a detached social observer but secretly hoping, I think, to pick up some astonishingly pretty girl who – if the magic worked – would be by herself and longing to meet somebody like me. But as the magic wasn't working, the few girls who weren't dancing were either in pairs or with mothers or aunts; and anyhow not one of them was astonishingly pretty.

Then the orchestra moved into slow waltz-time, and all the partners on the floor took three steps, swinging clasped hands, and then waltzed three steps – I think that's right, but I can't be sure because it is well over forty years since I last saw this particular dance, which I believe was called 'The Veleta'. It was very popular at that time, especially in places like Blackpool, where a thousand or more could do it together, making a delightful moving pattern. The working girls in the provinces were as skilled in this slow graceful dance as their social superiors were in London, where I had seen them, in their 'bunny-hugs' and 'turkey-trots'. And as there were not enough young men, many of these girls, that afternoon, were dancing together, better off than they would have been with the newer and more fashionable dances, more highly charged with sex. I forget what Viennese waltz, by Lehar or Oscar Straus, was being played, probably something out of *The Count of Luxemburg* or *A Waltz Dream*, but I know it helped me to lose myself in the scene. And I wasn't pleased to find myself jerked out of it by Inspector Crabb.

'Very nice, Mr Herncastle,' he said, sitting down beside me and putting his wet bowler on the broad ledge of the balcony. 'Very nice indeed. But I still say it frightens me.'

'Oh – in here too, it frightens you, Inspector.'

'That's right. Outside, inside, all the same. But then I don't see what you see. I have to look a bit longer and harder. And there might be a Brinkley, a Mackay, a Stratton down there, keeping nice time—'

'Who are they?'

'Murderers, Mr Herncastle. Some of the few we caught. And since I saw you last, I've run into half-a-dozen more wide boys from London not up here for their health – or anybody else's. They're not my concern these days, of course – I've other fish to fry – but I let 'em know I spotted 'em. Now about these two men you work with, Mr Herncastle – Sam Hayes and Ben Hayes – can you tell me anything about 'em?'

'Not much. Except when we're on stage or backstage, I see nothing of them. I'd call them reliable – but dull.'

'Betting men, though, aren't they? Betting men lose oftener than they win. Right? Then they need money. That's your weakness when you're a betting man.'

'It's always seemed to me a stupid business. But Sam and Ben have never asked me to lend them any money.'

'What about Mr Ollanton? Do they ask him?'

'I'd hate to tell you what Uncle Nick would say if they tried to touch him. He's a hard man, Inspector.'

The dancers were applauding the band or themselves now; the delightful moving pattern was just a lot of people; the dance was done. And I wished they would all begin again and that Crabb would go away.

'But would you say – a ruthless man?' Crabb was giving a fairly good imitation of a person passing the time with smalltalk. 'Or would that be going too far, Mr Herncastle?'

'I think much too far, Inspector. But of course I'm prejudiced in his favour. He's treated me very well on the whole, but then, after all, he is my mother's brother.'

'Has a wife living in Brighton, I'm told,' said Crabb, still doing his small-talk act. 'They don't get on – eh? Then he was living with what's-her-name – Cissie Mapes, wasn't he? Got rid of her rather in a hurry, didn't he? Oh – it must be the Lancers now, the way they're forming up. Never cared for the Lancers myself. What about stretching our legs?'

He examined his bowler, gave it a rub with the inside of his mackintosh, was about to put it on but then changed his mind, and then we began moving round the back of the balcony. The band went into some jiggety-joggety Lancers tune, which I could hear as a background to the talk that Crabb poured into my ear.

'Had a word with this Cissie Mapes before I came up here. Not under suspicion of course, as Furness told you. But I thought she might have noticed something I could use. When they're not lying their little heads off – and most of 'em can't resist it – women often tell you something useful. They notice more than men do. They're detectives by instinct.'

'And what did you get out of poor Cissie, Inspector?'

'Ah – you say *poor Cissie*. Do you know why?'

'Well, chiefly, I think, because my uncle was rather hard on her.'

'Well, unless she's very lucky – and I don't think she's going to be – I'd say she'll be on the streets very shortly. And then the next time I see her, if ever I do, she'll be in a back bedroom, Paddington way, with her throat cut—'

'Oh – shut up!' I stopped to glare at him. 'Look – I'm sorry, Inspector, but I was fond of Cissie—'

He took my arm, really to start us moving again, but I felt almost as if he were arresting me. 'How fond? Didn't go to bed with her, did you? No, I know that. She told me. You were just friends, she said. Right. Then I offended you, didn't I, by saying she'd be going on the streets? I'm a nasty brutal chap – eh? But I don't want her to go on the streets, though I'm not her friend. You *are* – right? But what will you do to make sure she doesn't go on the streets? I'll tell you. Not a bloody thing, my boy. I just might, but you won't. Nor your uncle, who used her and then stopped using her. So how much are your delicate fine feelings worth – eh? And d'you know where you're living? On the moon. Not down here, where a lively girl, just being silly as lively girls often are, suddenly finds some fingers round her throat and gets turned into a piece of meat. And if I feel frightened in a place like this, where it's all amusement and silliness, it's because I know there are tigers loose. I live with that knowledge, young man, day and night.' This time he stopped. We were in a blank corridor, where the ballroom ended and the band could hardly be heard. 'Now is there anything you can tell me that I ought to know?'

'No, there isn't, Inspector,' I assured him earnestly.

'All right, then. Enjoy yourself. But be careful. There's enough clap round here to lay up a brigade of cavalry, horses and all. Good afternoon, Mr Herncastle.'

The five or six days that followed this encounter in the Winter Gardens were very strange indeed. To begin with, this was Blackpool in early July, the big holiday season, with the whole place crammed and roaring with mums and dads and kids and girly-girls and imitation Knuts. (*I'm Gilbert the Filbert, the Knut with the K*, Basil Hallam was singing.) Anything that could claim a few pennies or trap a sixpence was in full swing. From the rowdy-dowdy South Shore to the more genteel North Shore, the holiday money of the innocents was cascading, down into the shows, eating houses, shops that sold nothing worth having, the wine lodges and pubs, into the outstretched hands of pierrots and buskers, photographers, fake auctioneers, hoarse vendors of peppermint and pineapple *Blackpool Rock* and ice-cream and candy floss, fortune-tellers, dealers in comic hats, false noses, miniature walking-sticks, water pistols, balloons, and the things that rolled out as you blew and made rude noises. And there were mornings, when nothing seemed real except the children hurrying with their buckets and spades and the wind blowing from the sea. And above it all, an iron upraised finger by day, a narrow constellation by night, rose the Tower, not new even then and seemingly a giant toy, but really perhaps a presage of a coming murderous age of towers.

It was strange to wonder at it all during the day and then find oneself every night in the middle of it at the Palace, where the same people laughed and clapped and Oo'd and Ah'd as if they'd never been in a variety theatre before. Lily Farris, with the melodious girlish sentiment concocted by Mergen, and the Ragtime Three, who made the most noise, were their favourites. However, they were always ready to admire and applaud Uncle Nick, though he had to work harder than usual to capture the attention of such audiences, noisy and restless and unable to concentrate for long – he was at his best in front of people who were closely attentive, sceptical, defying him to bamboozle them – and I often caught a sardonic glint in his eye. But in any event, he wasn't his customary self during this Blackpool time.

But what was stranger still was to wander about in this vast idiotic holiday-carnival under the influence, as I soon was, of Inspector Crabb. I ran into him somewhere every day, and he always insisted upon talking. He had his own professional reasons, of course – I knew instinctively that really he was always hard at work – but even so I think he enjoyed emptying and darkening the scene for me, stripping it of all its silly pink flesh to show me the hard and often murderous bones. Sometimes, quite deliberately, I think, he would briefly describe some other case of murder in which he'd been involved, offering me the corpse, the scattered clues, the closing of the net, the murderer trapped. It was as if he made me see, running through the coloured paper and the gold and silver tinsel of this Blackpool holiday scene, a scarlet cord dripping with blood. He destroyed whatever innocence it had. And it was here that the sinister feeling, which I had first known, months before, when I had seen all those dwarfs at Joe Bosenby's, arrived at its climax. This was not Blackpool's fault, but I never went there again.

The only person in the act who wasn't behaving strangely was Doris Tingley, very much herself if only because Blackpool and its crowds offered her endless excuses for indignation and belligerency. But Doris hated walking, so we never met during the day. Sam and Ben, never lively at any time, now seemed fixed in a sullen withdrawn mood. I never saw Barney except on the stage, but then I'd always tried to avoid him because he irritated me. His competitor or colleague, Philip Tewby, might have been sent back to London for all I knew, and the only time I mentioned him, Uncle Nick shut me up. As for Uncle Nick, now I saw him only at night, for he rarely got up before I had gone out and then he would go off somewhere in his car. I put this down to his dislike of the mid-day boarding-house dinner, when we all sat round one table, but then I was puzzled by his silence about where he'd been and what he was doing. On the Sunday, the beginning of the second week, when I came back from my walk, Mrs Taggart told me that he must have gone off to Fleetwood, because he'd been asking her about the road there and hotels; but he never said a word about it to me when he returned, fairly late that night. It wasn't that he was unfriendly, making me feel I'd offended him in some way. But he seemed completely self-absorbed and determined not to be communicative. So I felt shut out, and now that Nancy had

had plenty of time to reply to my last, my final sad letter, and hadn't, I felt completely and finally shut out there too, and was left with the unsolved murder and Crabb and the Blackpool scene and the sinister feeling.

So one night I accepted the invitation of my neighbours, Maisie Dawe and Peggy Canford, to join them in their bedroom for a drink. They had a bottle of port and I brought some whisky, making a nasty mixture if you didn't keep to one drink – and we didn't – and we told stories and giggled a lot, and Maisie was saucy and naughty and vaguely amorous, sitting on the floor and leaning against my knees, but I knew instinctively that it was Peggy, sitting across from us, not touching anybody, just staring, her fine eyes burning, her wide mouth now a little loose, who was in the mood for deeds and not more and more silly words. So I wasn't surprised, half an hour after I'd left them, to hear her come creeping into my room. And it wasn't much good, and I was sorry because I liked Peggy though I'd no real sexual feeling for her. After Julie, she seemed inexperienced and clumsy, rather embarrassing, but the chief trouble was that she was thinking about some other man, and, before she left me, she began crying at the thought of him. I fell asleep at once when she did leave me, but an hour or two afterwards, with the port and whisky at war inside me, I woke and had to think after a fashion, though I didn't want to, and everything my mind alighted on seemed either darkly confused or altogether hateful.

11

It was on the Wednesday of the second Blackpool week that Uncle Nick looked into my dressing-room, just after we'd come up after the first house performance. And this in itself was a surprise after he'd been so aloof. 'Quite a stranger,' I told him.

'Don't try to be funny, lad. It isn't your style. Now then – did you see your friend Inspector Crabb today?'

'Yes, just for a minute or two, this afternoon. Ran into him by accident, as usual-'

'That's what *you* think. Did he say anything?'

'Yes, he said he was going up to London tomorrow.'

'You're certain?'

'I'm certain he said it, Uncle Nick.'

'Did he seem pleased with himself?'

'Hard to tell – with him. But now you ask me – yes, I think he did.'

Uncle Nick nodded. 'We can't talk here – and anyhow I may have things to do, besides amusing these blockheads for a second time. Now listen, lad. Come up to my bedroom straight after supper. If you were going to do anything else – have one of those girls, for instance – drop it. I want you up in my room, then we can talk. Take it easy during supper. Don't give anybody the impression you're excited and eager to get away – try to seem natural – but a minute or two after I've gone up, you follow me. Right? And keep your head screwed on, lad. You're going to need it.'

Five minutes after he'd left the supper table, I'd joined him in his room. He locked the door and then put two chairs as far away from it as they would go. 'Sit there, lad. And keep your voice down. And if I forget and raise mine, just remind me. Now one of two things is going to happen tomorrow. Ether Crabb is going to London, as he told you, and if he is, then he's going to tell his superior officers he's cracked the Colmar Case and to ask for a warrant. Or he's banking on you telling me he's gone to London – and he'll keep out of the way until evening – and then he'll spring the trap. And either way I'm ready to bet any money there'll be a couple of plain-clothes men outside that stage door tomorrow night. However, I've made my preparations. But I need your help, lad. So now I've got to put it to you.'

Then I understood, in a flash, what I ought to have seen days and days before. Perhaps I did, but had immediately buried the thought. 'It was Barney, wasn't it?'

'Yes, it was Barney all right. And of course Sam and Ben lied when they told the police he'd left early with them that night. They're still sticking to it, but Crabb stopped believing them, I fancy, some days ago, and I never did believe them, though I thought at first they were just saving Barney some trouble. Even now they don't know he did it. But I know, because I put it to him and he confessed. That's why I sent for Tewby, even before I knew exactly what I was going to do.'

'And what *are* you going to do, uncle?'

He gave me a long hard look. 'I'm going to ask you to give me a hand helping a murderer to escape,' he said grimly. 'That's what it'll look like, and what we'll be charged with if we're caught. This is no joke, lad. We're for it if this trick doesn't come off. But what else can I do? This poor little tormented sod isn't a murderer. He didn't want to kill her. She'd deliberately excited him, and then laughed in his face, telling him he wasn't a man. Before he knew what he was doing, he'd got his hands round her neck and was shaking her, and then she tried to scream and he felt he had to stop her. He'll never do it to anybody else. He's not a killer, not a sex maniac, just an excitable silly little man who'd the bad luck to get entangled with a stupid cruel teaser. And I can't let them arrest him, put him in dock after dock, get some prosecuting K.C. to turn him into a monster until in the end they drag him kicking and screaming to the hangman. Now, lad, either you agree with that or you don't. If you do, and if you're ready to help me, then remember you're going dead against the law and you could be in the dock yourself – accessory after the fact or whatever it is. You may like Crabb, I don't know, but for my money he's a cruel bastard, and above him there are rows and rows of 'em, with wigs and gowns and trumpets, all hard-hearted self-righteous old buggers.'

'Keep your voice down,' I told him.

'All right, lad, all right. But are you with me or with them?'

'I'm with you, of course.'

'Good for you, Richard. And I'm sorry I've seemed so stand-offish lately, not telling you anything, but I daren't till I knew how you'd take it. Besides, you were seeing too much of Crabb, who's about ten times as artful as you think he is. But some of us are artful too, and we happen to be in the vanishing-and-escape business.' Clearly feeling relieved now, he lit a cigar, produced a bottle of champagne that had a little tap fixed in its cork, filled two glasses and told me to drink to the trick of the *Vanishing Dwarf*.

'I must explain one thing, lad, before I come to details. Why have I dragged you into this? First – and more important as you'll soon see – I can't work the effect by myself. Secondly, the more it's muddled between us — you doing something you don't understand but have been told to do – me being somewhere else and not knowing what they're talking about – the less chance they'll have of convicting us of anything if we don't bring it off. It'll seem so muddled they won't know where they are. But – by God, lad – there hasn't to be any muddle on our side. You and I have to know exactly what we're doing. It's the same old thing I've told you before. On the inside we plan and time it exactly while the audience on the outside – the police now – just look on half-dazed—'

'But it's hardly the same, though, Uncle Nick,' I ventured to cut in. 'The audience comes to be entertained. It asks to be deceived. But the police–'

'Yes, yes, yes, I know. They're sharper and we'll have to be sharper. But the difference is still there – between what really happens on the inside and what seems to be happening from the outside. Now let's get on. No – wait – I'll put the stuff together first.' Then, in his quick neat fashion, he brought out an odd assortment of things from various drawers and his trunk.

After he had carefully checked these things, he went on: 'Now this lot you take to Tewby in the morning: grease paint, white beard and moustache and spirit gum, turban and long robe. He has the stilt-boots, he's been getting used to 'em for the past week. You help him to dress and make up. Don't leave him till you're satisfied with his appearance and feel sure he can do it himself. He has to look like a fairly tall and rather frail old Indian. This old Indian will pay me a call between the houses, arriving at the stage door at twenty to nine and leaving at nine o'clock. You'll bring him – and this means you'll change as soon as we've finished the act for the first house — and you'll take him away. Only of course he'll be Tewby when he comes, and Barney when he goes. Tewby takes over Barney's part for the second house—'

'Will he know what to do?'

'What d'you take me for, lad? I've coached him and he's seen the show four times from the gallery, wearing a blazer and a schoolboy cap. And he's a smart little chap – not like Barney. He'll know what to do all right.'

I accepted that, and said so. 'Barney exchanges costume and make-up with Tewby – wearing the stilt-boots, of course-'

'Of course. He'll be clumsier than Tewby but he's only to hobble downstairs, with us helping him, and then to go from the stage door to the car that'll be waiting, leaning on your arm. And don't forget that whoever's watching the stage door will have already seen this old Indian arrive. Besides, they're waiting for a dwarf, remember.'

'But when I've got Barney into the car, where do I take him?'

'To Fleetwood,' said Uncle Nick, leaning forward as he lowered his voice. 'I've already fixed that. Look – here are four fivers. That's what I've agreed to pay. There's a Dutch coaster, bound for Rotterdam, lying there – the *Flora* – Captain Freeler. All I have to do is to telephone a message to him in the morning – I've fixed all that too – telling him when to expect you. I'll tell you later exactly where to find the *Flora*. The car's all fixed too. You can leave that to me. None of these chaps knows what we're up to – I couldn't risk that – but it doesn't matter if they know it's something shady, they're not fond of the police, any of 'em.'

'Does Barney know where he's going?'

'Not yet. You'll tell him. But he's so frightened, he'll go anywhere. I've already written to a man I know in Rotterdam – I've played there and he's a kind of agent – and all I have to do in the morning is to send him a cable, which won't mean anything to anybody but him. I'll give Barney some money – ten or fifteen sovereigns he can change in Rotterdam – and then he'll do the best he can till he gets a job over there – they have plenty of circuses in Holland and Germany. However he goes on, it'll be better than hanging. But you'll have to keep a firm hand on him, he'll be gibbering with fright – poor little bugger!'

Here I ought to explain that such an escape from one country to another was much easier in 1914 than it would have been afterwards. Except in Russia and Turkey no passports were required. It was only after our great war for freedom, and to make the world safe for democracy, that we were all clamped into the passport system, thereby making it possible for totalitarian states to keep a stranglehold on their citizens. (Take away an ordinary decent man's passport, and he is helpless. Only rogues, with an ample choice of forged passports, can defy the system.) Another smaller point is that the British golden sovereign, which we used then, could be exchanged anywhere abroad because its face value was its actual value in gold. So, with no passports wanted, no visas, and with a handful of sovereigns, you could go anywhere at a moment's notice. And as Uncle Nick and I were talking, late that night, the whole easy age was sauntering towards its destruction.

'I'll be out of the act for the second house,' I told Uncle Nick.

'You're not indispensable yet, lad,' said Uncle Nick, grinning. 'We'll just have to get along without you. I've worked it out. We drop *The Vanishing Cyclist* and of course we can't put in *The Rival Magicians* without the boots, which don't forget to bring back. It'll go better with

Tewby than it ever did with Barney. But I'll have the Box and the levitation effect again – Doris is more dependable than Cissie ever was – and I'll include some of the old tricks. We'll manage. Now just run through what you have to do, lad, so we make no mistakes. That suffragette lark we worked in Leeds was just playing around compared with this. One wrong move, don't forget, and we're under arrest. Now, run through it slowly, Richard.'

Even during the morning of that Thursday the stifling feeling of excitement mixed with apprehension began to build up. Taking the things out to Philip Tewby and then helping him with the old Indian costume and make-up was easy enough, but even then there was one awkward moment. It came when we were both satisfied with his appearance and he had moved around a little wearing the stilt-boots, which added nearly two feet to his height and, with the long robe, made him look an entirely different person. He grimaced a bit as he moved around in them.

'I've done my best to get used to them, Mr Herncastle,' he said. 'But because of the angle of my feet and the straps, they are rather painful, I'm afraid.' With the beard, the turban, the robe, the added height, he was somebody quite strange, but the sad wise dwarf's eyes were still the same.

'I'm sorry, Mr Tewby, but it won't be too bad. You can take everything off now, and then be ready for me tonight at about twenty-past eight. When we get out of the car at the stage door, you can hold on to my arm, as if you're a frail old man, then it's only a matter of getting through the stage door and climbing some steps.'

'And then I change costume and make-up and take part in the act, Mr Herncastle. With some preliminary instructions from Mr Ollanton, I hope. That's understood? Very well. Then I've only one question, Mr Herncastle. Why am I doing this?'

This question was something I'd never discussed with Uncle Nick. For a moment or two I didn't know what to say. 'Mr Tewby,' I began slowly, 'you're just doing what you've been told to do. You don't know what it's all about. You can't imagine.' I looked hard at him. 'You can't possibly imagine, Mr Tewby.'

'I see, Mr Herncastle.' He took off his turban, then sat down to loosen the big boots. 'I've had some interesting discussions with Mr Schurer. He still wants to leave the country, before it's too late, he says. He doesn't understand that Mr Asquith, a man of peace, would never allow this country to be dragged into some European war. Mr Schurer and his friends are too excitable, far too excitable. Oh – one last question, Mr Herncastle. If, by chance, the police ask me how long I've been working with Mr Ollanton – what do I say?'

'Tell them the truth, Mr Tewby. Since the beginning of last week – Tuesday, wasn't it? But you don't need to tell them exactly what you've been doing. I'll pick you up here – as the old Indian scholar, Dr Ram Dass of Bombay – at twenty-past eight.'

I walked back, having taken a taxi there. During the rest of the morning and in the afternoon, when I felt so disturbed I had to take another walk, the excitement went churning around deep inside, yet at the same time, as I cut my way through the holiday crowds, now in the sun again, I felt that what we were proposing to do, with our stilt-boots and false whiskers, seemed quite unreal, just a kind of joke between Uncle Nick and me, nothing to do with policemen and prisons. But then, when the excitement refused to be kept down, quite suddenly the crowds, all the holiday sights and sounds, would seem unreal, with nothing real left except my part in Uncle Nick's latest and greatest illusion.

He had a last quick word with me as I was changing after our first house performance. 'I've told the stage-door keeper I'm expecting an Indian visitor—'

'He's Dr Ram Dass of Bombay.' And I began laughing.

'Easy, lad, easy. And don't rush things. There's plenty of time. Easy does it, Richard. Oh – and the chap who'll be driving your car is Stan Brown. I'm paying him well, and he knows what's what and doesn't give a damn for anybody.'

It was a big impressive car, and Stan Brown was wearing a chauffeur's cap and uniform. As I sat beside him and then we drove off, looking straight ahead and hardly moving his lips he said: 'As a rule I don't put on this sort o' gear, but it'll be useful tonight. Nothing like a uniform and the idea there's somebody rich and important in the caper to impress the bloody bobbies. Notice them two plain-clothes men watching the stage door? You surprise me. Stuck out a mile, silly twerps! When that's all you're up against, it's a shame to take the money. Who are we fetching?'

'Dr Ram Dass of Bombay.'

'I'll believe you but thousands wouldn't. And what would he be an expert on, in case I'm asked?'

'Indian magic.'

'That's right. There's a big run on that in Fleetwood, they tell me.'

There was nobody at the Schurers' to see Tewby as Dr Ram Dass come downstairs and then go out to the car, leaning, on my arm. Max Schurer was working, and Uncle Nick, Tewby told me, had given Mrs Schurer two tickets for some show. This time I rode at the back with my distinguished old Indian, but that didn't prevent Stan Brown from talking to me over his shoulder.

'If he's a famous old Indian, then I'm Maude Allan,' Stan told me. 'I'll admit he's a better job than the Father Christmases we have round here, but he won't stand a good close look, not while it's still daylight. I'll get in as close to the stage door as I can, then you'll have to work fast – getting him out and then inside.'

If anybody had challenged me when I was helping Tewby out, he could have heard my heart thumping. But nobody did. There are always people hanging around a stage door and I caught an 'Oo – look at him' and a giggle or two. As we passed the stage-door keeper, with Tewby on my arm, I said: 'I'm afraid there are some steps to climb, Dr Ram Dass. But we can take them slowly.' Unfortunately we'd no alternative; the stilt-boots were hard to manage going upstairs; and though Uncle Nick's dressing-room, where I was taking him, was only up one flight, I was sweating with impatience and anxiety before we arrived there. As this was between the houses, there were some people about, all performers, but they looked only mildly curious. You would need a two-headed man to excite people backstage.

Once inside the dressing-room, with the door locked behind them, and under Uncle Nick's sharp instruction, the two dwarfs quickly exchanged costumes and make-up, though I had to help Barney with the boots, which he feared and hated, and Uncle Nick added some last touches to his Ram Dass make-up. Then, when it was already about five minutes to nine, we ran into more trouble with Barney, who was shaking and almost hysterical. He'd brought a big bag with him that he wanted to take away.

'It's impossible,' I said to Uncle Nick. 'What are we supposed to be doing with a big bag? And who'll carry it? He can't – and manage the boots. I can't – if I'm to support him—'

'I know, I know. It stays here.'

'Oh – Mis' Ollanton – Mis' Herncastle,' Barney began yelling. 'All my things – my precious things—'

'Shut up, you silly little bugger,' Uncle Nick told him fiercely. 'We're trying to do the best we can for you.'

'If I may make a suggestion, Mr Ollanton,' said Tewby, now a Hindoo dwarf. 'If Barney picks out the things he really must have, then we roll them into a bundle, he could carry it under his robe.'

'Right. Get on with it, you two.' Then Uncle Nick looked at me. 'One thing, Richard. Whatever Stan wants you to do, between here and Fleetwood, just see you do it. Stan knows what he's doing. Right? And the best of luck, lad. I won't forget this. Now you understand exactly what you've got to do at Fleetwood? Hurry up with that bundle, you two. Time's getting on. And for God's sake – try to keep steady, Barney. Yes, lad, I'm coming down with you. Makes a bit more fuss and muddle.'

As we went out, Barney, who was shaking and very wobbly in the boots, had Uncle Nick, very impressive in his Indian Magician's rig, on one side of him and me on the other; and we almost carried him to the door of the car, which Stan, looking both important and respectful, was holding open.

'Been a great pleasure and a privilege, Dr Dass,' Uncle Nick cried heartily, as I pushed Barney, now nearly collapsing, further along the back seat and got in beside him. Uncle Nick was holding the door open himself now, filling the space, while Stan climbed into his driving seat. 'Hope we can meet again, Dr Dass,' he cried, and then slammed the door as Stan moved off. Fortunately for us, the light was going quickly now. If it hadn't been, I don't think we could ever have carried off the substitution, Barney being in such a state, almost gibbering. As it was, I thought, to my horror, I heard somebody shouting 'Just a minute' as we were on the move, though I wasn't certain, and anyhow Stan Brown was not the man to be halted like that.

He drove fairly fast, but not fast enough to attract any attention, not towards the North Shore, which would be on our way to Fleetwood, but towards the South Shore. 'Aren't you going the wrong way?' I called to him.

'No, not for what I'm going to do, chummy,' he called back. 'You start hurrying this up – and we'll all be in the cart. I know what I'm doing.'

Somewhere on the edge of the town, at the back of the South Shore, he drove us into a garage. It was a biggish place, badly lit, where there were perhaps half-a-dozen cars. 'All change here. Out you get,' he shouted as we stopped. Then as he got out, he called to somebody invisible to me: 'All right, Charlie, it's only me – Stan. I'll be taking the little tourer.'

I dragged rather than helped Barney out. 'Why have you brought us here, Stan?'

'We change cars, we change rigs, we're going to be different people. At least I am – and so is he – you can just wear a big cap, I've got one somewhere. There's no chauffeur now – see.' He was already taking off his uniform coat. 'And help him to look like whatever he is like. And if he's what I think he is, he's going to sit on the floor in the back. Then, instead of two nobs and a chauffeur in a big car, we're just two chaps in a little car. You mightn't think it, but I'm Careful Stan, I am. And don't forget, Fleetwood's only ten miles away, and it's getting darker every minute.'

I still had to help Barney to change and remove his make-up. I thought after I had got him out of the stilt-boots he would have to go barefoot to Holland, but he had some slippers in his bundle. I wrapped the whiskers and the turban and the boots in the robe, and stuffed them into the back of the touring car. Barney crept into the back and vanished. I sat in front and waited for Stan, who'd gone to have a talk with the invisible Charlie. It was about ten o'clock when we left the garage and after half-past ten when we came within sight of the *Flora* at Fleetwood. After Barney and I had got out of the car, Stan said he wanted to see some pal of his and that he would come back for me just after eleven.

Captain Freeler was a thick shortish chap with the broadest behind I'd ever seen on a man. He regarded Barney and his bundle with genial contempt and put a member of the crew in charge of him. I said good-bye to Barney and then followed Captain Freeler into his cabin, where I handed him the four five-pound notes that Uncle Nick had given me for him.

Captain Freeler didn't like the look of them. 'I hoped to have twenty of your fine English sovereign pieces.'

'You can get them from the bank in the morning, Captain,' I told him. 'When do you sail?'

'Not till early afternoon. So I will go to the bank, as you say.'

'And you'll keep Barney – the dwarf – out of sight tomorrow, please.'

'Of course, of course. He will not be seen. Someone meets him in

Rotterdam – um? All that has been arranged, no doubt – um? So – we have a drink.'

The Dutch schnapps or whatever it was made me shudder.

'It is too strong for you?'

'Well, the truth is, Captain Freeler, I'm tired – I've had a long day – and my stomach's empty—'

'O-ho – you have empty stomach. So we eat a little. Sit down please, young man. In five minutes we have something to eat.'

While he was gone, I tried the schnapps again, cautiously this time. I could hear Captain Freeler shouting something in Dutch. Now that we seemed to have brought off the deception, Uncle Nick's most ambitious illusion, I felt deflated, not elated.

'Dutch pea soup,' Captain Freeler announced, as he returned followed by a man carrying a large tray. 'There is nothing better – all times of day and night. So – you add as many little pieces of ham – bacon – as you wish – like so.' And a minute later I was helping myself to the tiny pieces of fried bacon and sprinkling them on to the soup, which was thick, almost solid. It was also very good, and years afterwards, when I had a painting holiday in Holland, I often ordered Dutch pea soup and remembered Captain Freeler and the night of Barney's escape.

It must have been nearer twelve o'clock than eleven when Stan brought me to within a few yards of the digs and then stopped. I told him I would get the robe and stuff out of the car. But before I could move, he had checked me. 'I'd leave it if I was you, chummy,' he told me, talking out of the side of his mouth. 'That's a police sergeant standing there, where you want to go. Pick your stuff up tomorrow. It'll be in the garage. Now you just get out quietly, take no notice of him, and look as if mother's milk is running out of your mouth.'

I saw the sergeant but pretended I hadn't, while he pretended not to have seen me. There was a light coming from under the dining-room door, so I went in there. Uncle Nick was sitting at the table, smoking a cigar and drinking champagne. On the other side of the table, looking very angry, was Inspector Crabb.

'Where have *you* been?' Crabb asked sharply.

'What's it to do with you where he's been?' said Uncle Nick. 'However, Richard, stretch a point. Tell him. Me too. I've been wondering where you'd got to. Had your supper?'

'Yes, that's where I've been. Having some supper – with a friend.

No law against it, is there, Inspector?'

'How long has that dwarf, Tewby, been working with you?'

'Well, he arrived a week last Tuesday. I know because I met him.'

'When did the other one, Barney, go?'

'A few days afterwards, I suppose, Inspector. The two dwarfs looked exactly alike in their make-up, so I never noticed when Barney left and Tewby took over from him.'

'Barney was seen going in and out of the Palace stage door right up to tonight.'

I shook my head. 'That would be Tewby.'

'They arrested poor little Tewby tonight,' said Uncle Nick, 'though of course they had to let him go.'

'Arrested him for what, uncle?'

'That's enough of the cross-talk,' said Crabb angrily. He glared at me. 'Where's Barney now?'

'I don't know, Inspector. Why should I? He wasn't a friend of mine. You should try Joe Bosenby's Agency–'

'I've told him that,' said Uncle Nick.

Crabb brought his hands down flat on the table and then got up. 'We'll find him, y'know. Don't make any mistake about that. And when we do. I'll make him talk. And then one of you – probably both of you – will be in it up to the neck, or I'll eat my hat.'

'Well, good night, Inspector,' said Uncle Nick affably.

Crabb's reply was to bang the door. Then the outer door was opened and shut violently.

'Good lad! He got no more change out of you than he did out of me. He knows damned well that we diddled him but he can't think how. The great Inspector Crabb is *baffled*. I take it everything went all right at the other end? Good. Then Crabb's stuck with the Case of the Disappearing Dwarf. Not bad – eh, lad?' It was, I think, at least in some ways, his best trick.

12

We were in Leicester again during that first week in August, when the war began. This had nothing to do with the Lancashire tour that had ended at Blackpool. We no longer shared the bill with any of those people. Uncle Nick had meant to take a holiday, but had been persuaded by Joe Bosenby – and, I believe, an extra fifty pounds a week – to accept a few dates, topping the bill in place of a very popular light comedian, Norman Bentley, who was having his appendix taken out. We had four dates definitely fixed: Leicester, Nottingham, Sheffield and Leeds. Most of the acts with us at Leicester were terrible, August being a thin time for variety in industrial towns. Only one of them, at the bottom of the bill and so next to us in grandeur, was playing the same dates that we were: it was a vocal husband-and-wife act, Iris Hampton and Philip Hall, who sang duets from operettas and were dressy, stiff and ultra-refined, and behaved backstage as if they were slumming. Uncle Nick disliked them on sight; and they disliked him because they thought they ought to be topping the bill.

As the star attraction, earning more money than ever, Uncle Nick ought to have been pleased with life. The act itself was better than I'd ever known it, chiefly because Doris Tingley and Philip Tewby were much quicker and easier to work with than Cissie and Barney had been. As a team now, we were in wonderful shape. But a good act isn't complete without a good audience. And the first houses were poorly attended all that week – so that Uncle Nick, as he confessed to me, felt he wasn't earning the extra money he'd demanded – and though the second houses were much better, the audiences were restless and silly, unable to concentrate their attention, to Uncle Nick's disgust. As soon as we were in the war – though we didn't know how far in we were or what was really happening – Uncle Nick ended the act with what he called 'children's party conjuring', pulling out of a tube of paper a lot of flags – the 'big flag finish', he called it, jeering at himself – and always concluding with a gigantic Union Jack, which brought more applause than all the clever illusions put together. 'We'll find ourselves in a madhouse soon, lad,' he muttered to me as we came off, one night. 'I can feel it coming. Bloody idiots!'

I think he damned the war, there right at the very beginning, because he saw it as another, bigger, more impressive and demanding performer, a rival top of the bill. When the newsboys came running and shouting along the streets – a sight and sound I'd almost forgotten until I made myself remember those August weeks – I would sometimes buy a paper, but Uncle Nick never did, though, if we were together, he'd always contrive to learn the latest news from me while still appearing to be aloof or contemptuous. Never an admirer of ordinary people at any time, he was now savage in his scorn.

'Just notice the way they're taking it, lad. Like a free trip to Blackpool or Margate. It's a brand-new bit of excitement at last. They lead such dreary lives in their Land of Hope and Glory – and I'll bet Iris Hampton and Philip Hall will finish their act singing that, by next week – I say they lead such dreary lives that they think a war, so long as it's somewhere else, is a treat. And they'll display their patriotism by throwing stones at German bands and looting pork-butchers' for free sausages. It's a nasty excitement too, lad. I can feel it in the audiences. They don't want to settle down, look and listen properly, enjoy themselves like civilized people. If one of us broke our bloody neck, they'd be delighted, the mood they're in now. I wish to God I'd never let Joe Bosenby talk me into this. I ought to be having a holiday now in some quiet little place – West of Ireland perhaps. But then at the moment I don't know a woman I'd like to ask. And a man needs a woman on a holiday.'

'Well, find one, Uncle Nick, and then take her on a holiday as soon as we've played these few dates.'

'You're too optimistic, lad. Not about the woman – that wouldn't be hard – but about what it's going to be like. Some of 'em seem to imagine it's going to be all Bank Holidays.'

We were talking over supper – we were sharing digs and had them to ourselves – and no sooner had Uncle Nick mentioned Bank Holidays (and we'd had three in succession that first week) than there came through the open window the sound of confused cheering, probably from the pub down the road.

'There they go,' said Uncle Nick. 'All cheering and beering. Hurray for the Navy! Hurray for Kitchener – who only knows how to beat fuzzy-wuzzies and Boer farmers! Three cheers for the red, white and blue!'

'Uncle Nick, you talk as if you weren't on our side.' But I smiled as I said it.

'No, that's not it, lad. But just wait a week or two, then I'll explain exactly what I think and feel about this war business we've got into. Now let's talk about something else, for God's sake.'

The next two weeks, first in Nottingham and then in Sheffield, I spent a lot of time with Uncle Nick, just as if I already knew, in some dark corner of my mind, that we were close to the end of our association. He still had his car, and he would run me out to where I wanted to do some sketching or painting, go roaring off somewhere, then come back to share a late picnic lunch. Two or three times we took Doris Tingley and Philip Tewby with us. These ought to have been very pleasant days, but we took that excitement with us, and I for one always felt that somewhere not far away, perhaps just the other side of the heat haze, things were happening that we didn't know about and wouldn't understand if we did. I didn't think it was all a lark, like the people Uncle Nick denounced; but on the other hand I couldn't take it quite seriously; so I felt uneasy, not firmly on the ground, a bit up in the air in the wrong way, and the work I did was no good. We'd now got *The Magic Painting* into the act, and the trick daubs I sloshed on twice-nightly – the Rustic Cottage, The Wood, and the rest of them – didn't seem much worse than the messes I was making during the day.

One afternoon, when Doris Tingley was with us, we had to stop the car at a crossroads to let a battalion of territorials, headed by a band, march past us. Doris cried, and was furious. 'Every dam' time I hear one of those bands and see all these boys marching, I can't stop myself crying. I ought to put my head in a bag. *Crying!*'

'You've hardly started yet, Doris,' said Uncle Nick. 'There's going to be plenty of crying before we're out of this. God's truth – look at all the dust they've kicked up.' When we were out of the dust and had come to streets again, we stopped near a hoarding. 'See that poster, Richard. Kitchener wants you. What d'you say to that, lad?'

I didn't say anything. Not then.

13

At the end of the Sheffield week and then all through the week at Leeds, Uncle Nick no longer asked me where I'd like him to take me in the car. I was back to trams and trains while he, so far as I could gather, spent his time between the digs, the Queen's Hotel and the General Post Office, writing letters, telephoning to London, sending telegrams and even cables. I didn't know what he was up to and took care not to ask him, even when pressed by Doris and Tewby, because obviously it was business, and Uncle Nick liked to keep negotiations to himself and then off-handedly announce the result of them. We all knew we had no immediate date after this Leeds week, and as day after day passed and Uncle Nick said nothing to us, just gave us hard looks to stop any questions, we were increasingly curious and anxious. But this was true of me – I don't know about the others – only up to Friday. However, I was as surprised – though not as disappointed – as the others were when Friday night came and went and he hadn't said anything to us. Indeed, the hard looks were harder than ever.

I didn't go out sketching on Saturday – I rarely did because there were too many people about in the afternoon – but I had a walk during the morning. We were still sharing digs, and as soon as I joined him at the dining-table I knew something important had happened and that, whatever it was, it delighted him, even though he was working hard to hide his delight.

'I know there's *something*,' I told him. 'What is it?'

'Not now, lad. I'll explain tonight, after we've done our day's work and are feeling easier. I want you all there, when we've changed after our second show, in my dressing-room. So tell the others. Oh – and see there are glasses to go round – I've three so you'll need another three. We'll be drinking champagne, but I'll look after that – a couple of bottles, I fancy. And that's all till tonight. What's the latest about Gallant Little Belgium? It must be a lot different from the Belgium I know.'

I didn't want to argue this point, so I changed the subject. 'I wonder what's happened to Barney.'

'Oh – I forgot to tell you that, lad. He's with a circus in Hanover. He didn't tell me of course – I doubt if he can write – but that Dutch agent did. The Germans are thorough, so of course Barney might be interned now – he *might* – though I doubt if even the Germans will go poking around circus dwarfs. By the way, Richard – and you can tell the others this – I want to see two bang-slap-up splendiferous performances by the *Ganga Dun* Company tonight. I have a good reason.'

So of course I passed this on to Doris and Tewby, Sam and Ben. Now as a rule a Saturday second house wasn't our sort of audience: it wanted to laugh and to sing chorus songs. And, as I've already explained, the war excitement didn't help us. Nevertheless, the performance we gave to the second house at the Leeds Empire, that Saturday night at the end of August, 1914, was the best ever. Apart from all that flag nonsense at the end, Uncle Nick's 'children's party conjuring', it had all our best illusions and effects, including the Box trick, which Doris worked much faster than Cissie, *The Rival Magicians*, where again Philip Tewby was much better than Barney had ever been, *The Vanishing Cyclist* and my *Magic Painting*. We were all, you might say, magicians and master showmen, that night. Everything we did was dead right and beautifully timed. And I'll swear that something went out from us to the audience – it is at these times that stuff in a can going on screens can't be compared with live acts – so that the people in front knew intuitively this was no ordinary performance. The applause at the end wasn't like thunder, because it never is, but it was long and hard, like a hailstorm on a wooden roof. And Uncle Nick did – something I'd never seen him do before – he made us all take a call with him. But then – it was the last performance we would ever give with him.

He was filling glasses when we arrived in his dressing-room, which was the star's room and so the largest. 'I'd like you to take a drink with me first, before I say anything. Sam and Ben, I know you two would rather have a couple of pints of Tetley's strong ale, but you must put up with this tipple of mine for once. Well – your very good health, all of you, and thanks for a great last performance. Yes, it's the last. But before I explain why, I want you to take these.' He began handing out pay envelopes. 'You'll find two weeks' money in there. And as soon as you've heard what I have to say, Sam, you and Ben and Tewby had better go down and start packing up. Not you, Richard, I want you. But make sure everything's ready to go, early Monday morning, Sam, because I've arranged for a cartage company to call for it and then send it on to a warehouse in London, ready for when I sail. Because I'm going to America. It's all fixed.'

The five of us all began talking at once, but after emptying his glass he told us to keep quiet. I can still see him now: he was wearing a light suit and a dark crimson tie; and his face, like those of most actors who have just removed their makeup, seemed pale and rather shiny, so that his fierce black eyebrows and glittering dark eyes were thrown into strong relief.

'I'm going to America not just because they want me over there and are ready to pay me very good money. You see, I don't like this war. I don't believe in it. I think it never should have happened. But now it's started, we won't be able to stop it. So I'm going to America.' He looked at me. 'What I'm going to say now, lad, doesn't apply to you, so don't interrupt me.' I nodded, and, after giving me a quick grin, he turned to the other four. 'I can't take you people with me, for various good reasons. And I hate throwing you out of work—'

'And I should think so, Nick Ollanton,' Doris blazed at him. 'At a time like this too!'

'You think it's a bad time to be out of work, Doris?'

'Of course I do. Not that I can't manage – and I want to see what Archie's up to – but I'm thinking about these three—'

'Doris, you're wrong. Now listen, all of you. This isn't going to be a bad time, it's going to be a good time – I mean, to find jobs. Kitchener's asking for a hundred thousand men. And he'll get 'em. And another hundred thousand. And another and another. And they've already called up the regular reserves and the territorials. So what does that mean? It means that in a few months they're going to be desperately short of men — and women, if they're ready to make munitions. Yes, Doris, they'll be wanting you, if Archie can spare you. As for you two, Sam, Ben, you're mechanics and you can't go wrong. Next year at this time you'll be earning three times the money I've been paying you.'

'What about me, Mr Ollanton?' said Tewby, his eyes dark with misery. 'Things were very bad before you offered me this engagement.'

'I'd forget the stage, if I were you, Tewby, unless of course you get a particularly good offer. There are lots of jobs a little man can do as well as a bigger one – perhaps better. And hundreds of thousands of men can't be taken out of civilian life without leaving vacancies behind 'em. People have got the wrong idea about this war; they think it'll be over in a few months. But I know it won't. You'll be wanted for something, Tewby, I promise you. And so will all of you. So get it out of your head I'm leaving you in the lurch, as they say. But I *am* leaving you – so this had better be good-bye.' He went round shaking hands.

'And I'd better say Good-bye too,' I said.

'That's right, Richard lad – you had. But fill the glasses first.'

I did, and then followed Uncle Nick's example. After I'd shaken hands with Sam and Ben, I said very softly: 'Inspector Crabb never made you admit that Barney didn't leave early with you that night, did he?'

'He went on at us long enough, Inspector did,' said Sam. 'Obstinate sort o' man, he was. But me and Ben's just as obstinate. Hayes family's famous for it.'

'That's right,' said Ben. It was one of the very few times I'd ever heard him say anything at all. And I never heard him say anything again.

'It's been a great pleasure, Mr Herncastle,' said Tewby gravely. 'And if I do leave the stage – and I appreciate the force of Mr Ollanton's argument – I'll carry away with me a very pleasant memory of this engagement. I still feel at times that I'm really Dr Ram Dass of Bombay.'

Then, when I grasped her hand, Doris broke out indignantly: 'Seems to me I'm crying half the time now. Must be softening of the brain. And now it's kissing as well.' And she pulled her hand away, flung her arms round me, and gave me a kind of angry Kiss.

'And remember me to Archie, Doris. I like Archie.'

'I know. He gets round everybody – except possible customers. Find yourself a nice girl, Dick. Not that it'll be easy. Most of 'em now aren't worth houseroom – idle little sluts!'

And that indignant cry was the last I heard from Doris for about eight or nine years.

Uncle Nick had his car and we drove out to the digs in silence. Champagne makes me feel lively for about ten minutes or so and then leaves me feeling empty and melancholy. Now I felt sad. I had grown fond of Doris and little Tewby, and if I didn't feel the same about Sam and Ben, after all I'd worked with them month after month, in all kinds of places. And that night, between us, we'd given people a wonderful performance, which at least a few of them might remember for years. 'Just listen to him,' one of them might say. 'Dad's always going on about that Indian magician we saw at the Empire, early in the war. Though it was a wonderful turn, I must say. You don't see anything like that now.' But I was in no position, as we shall see, to reproach Uncle Nick for breaking up the act.

We had supper alone; nobody else was staying there. We ate in a small back room – I can see it now – full of rubbed plush, some of it purple, some of it a metallic green, and dominated by an enormous bad picture – a genuine hand-painted oil, the landlady had told us, and a legacy from an uncle – of merry cardinals toasting one another in red ink. While we disposed of our cold lamb and salad and bilberry pie, we talked about Doris and Tewby, Sam and Ben, and Uncle Nick went on to describe other people who had worked for him. But then when he lit a cigar and I my pipe, this rambling talk suddenly came to a halt.

'You must have guessed why I left you out of that talk in the dressing-room. I want you to come with me, lad. I've a forty-week contract with Keith over there, then I'm booked into the Palace, New York, for a month. It'll be hard work on the road – harder than it is here – longer hours, longer journeys – but it'll be a great experience for you. It really is a New World, Richard. I don't say it's perfect. There's plenty to find fault with over there. But it'll grow and grow, get better and better, while Europe's busy cutting its own throat. I'm not quite certain yet, but I think we'll be sailing in the *Lusitania* in about ten days' time.'

'I'm sorry, Uncle Nick. You'll have to go by yourself. I'm enlisting.'

'You're *what*?'

'Enlisting. Joining Kitchener's New Army.'

He put his cigar down. 'Lad – you must be out of your bloody mind. Army? Why should you go and join any army? I'll give you a dozen good reasons why you shouldn't. Now just give me one good reason why you should.'

'It's hard to explain,' I began slowly.

'It's impossible to explain, unless you're going up the pole – barmy —'

While he replaced his cigar and pulled hard at it, I hesitated.

'Well, go on, lad,' he shouted through the cigar smoke. 'Go on. You must have something to say for yourself, however daft it is.'

I avoided meeting his dark glare, looked towards the roistering cardinals, and then spoke hesitantly. 'I don't want to be a soldier. I wish there wasn't a war. And I don't feel particularly patriotic. All this *King and Country* stuff and flag-waving doesn't make me want to cheer.'

'I should hope not,' Uncle Nick growled. 'Lot of dogshit. But go on, go on.'

'I know, though, that if I went to America, I'd be miserable. I'd never be able to take my mind off it. I'd feel I'd run away from a challenge. It's different for you – and I'm not blaming you for going–'

'Thanks very much. Bloody good of you, lad!'

'But I'm a young man – and I live here – and I feel I ought to take my chance, as so many others are doing,' I ended lamely, partly because my decision, which was now fixed and firm, wasn't entirely conscious and rational, but also because I felt I couldn't tell him that this life with him now seemed stale and sterile. I wasn't joining the army to get away from the variety stage – it wasn't as simple as that – but this wasn't my life as it was his, and I had begun to feel that any nourishment it might have offered me once, in spite of that very night's performance, had withered away.

'Now *I'll* talk,' said Uncle Nick, a triumphant gleam in his eye. 'And *I* know what I'm talking about. What you really believe, even if you don't say so, is what all these other silly buggers believe – that it's going to be a kind of picnic, a few months of marching and cheering and flag-waving, then Germany'll be done for and you'll be all back home, heroes with medals to show.'

'No, I don't think–'

'Just listen to me,' he shouted. 'And get this into your head, lad. I'm not like all these people. I've *been* to Germany. I've played Berlin, Hamburg, Munich, Frankfort – and I've kept my eyes and ears open. I *know* the Germans. They've built up a military machine that'll make you lot look like so many tin soldiers. They may take Paris – I don't know – but what I *do* know is that they're going to take a hell of a lot of beating. All over in a few months! They're all talking like school kids. This war isn't going to last months, it's going to last years and years – and every year it'll get worse. You're asking to be put into a bloody mincing machine, lad. You say you'll feel miserable in America. Well, I say it's nothing to the misery you're going to feel in a year's time – or, the year after that, if you live that long. That old Indian was right. We're in for the biggest bloody massacre of all time. And you can't even wait for them to fetch you.' He was silent a moment, then changed his tone. 'I haven't treated you badly so far, have I, lad? And I'd like to have you with me over there. Now come on, Richard, have a bit of sense.' It was much harder to resist this tone than the other, but my mind was made up. 'I'm sorry, uncle, but—'

'Oh – go to buggery!' he shouted, jumping up and striding out. He told me in the morning that I had only to say the word and I could sail with him to New York. I told him that I wished I could but I was determined to enlist. He said that if I changed my mind I could telephone Joe Bosenby. He was driving up to London and I helped him with his baggage. When all the stuff was in, we stood near the car looking at each other in silence for a few moments. The street was very quiet; it was a warm and sleepy Sunday morning. We shook hands and then I watched him drive away.

I never set eyes on him again.

14

This is an account of my life on the variety stage, which came to an end on Saturday, 29th August, 1914. So I may seem to be cheating if I go on to say that I joined the army – the West Yorks, as I happened to be in Leeds – on Monday the 31st. But I have to pass through two months of army life to arrive at the point, sharp and decisive and glittering with magic that seems to me – and I don't care if nobody agrees with me – to mark the real end of my story.

We slept for a week in a disused skating rink, along with various old tramps slipping in late, looking for a free doss, so that after a few nights there were lice about. This was my first but by no means my last acquaintance with the louse, whose pasture we were in the trenches. Then we were moved to an enormous camp in Surrey, where twelve of us shared each bell tent. (Out of our twelve, only three of us still survived, two years later.) This tent life wasn't too bad during the warm and dry September, but when we were into the second half of October, and it rained and it rained, we led a miserable existence. We were dressed in makeshift uniforms of blue serge or something similar, and wore forage caps that began to shed their blue dye as soon as they were wet. We looked – and almost felt – like convicts. They drilled us and yelled at us from early morning until dusk, after which we limped to the canteen and argued noisily about nothing and stupefied ourselves with pint after pint of beer. I had braced myself for heroism; I was ready, I felt, to face shot and shell and possible cavalry charges; what I hadn't bargained for was this convict-uniform, beer and backache existence under dripping canvas in Surrey. By the end of October I was looking back on my life with Uncle Nick, who had vanished without another word, as if it had been a series of splendid but now tantalizing dreams. By this time, just to take shelter in one of those Empires, to sit in a plush stall and smoke a pipe, would be to reach a peak of luxurious idle living.

One of the few solid buildings among our acres of canvas was a large Recreation Hall, where we occasionally watched films or tried to enjoy various entertainments that I wouldn't have been found dead at, a few months before. But then it was announced that on the evening of Sunday, 25th October, we were to be given a special treat, some West End performers coming down to entertain us. The older men, many of them former regulars, still preferred arguments, anecdotes and beer, but the rest of us, after queuing up in the rain, charged in to fill the benches behind the rows of chairs occupied by the officers. And before the performance began, there must have been two or three hundred men packed into the standing room at the back. I thought I was lucky, having a seat, though as it turned out, I wasn't. There was a stage of sorts, with a curtain, and even an attempt at an orchestra – piano, two fiddles, a double bass, a saxophone, a trumpet, and drums. They were a scratch lot but they began making music that sounded wonderful, coming out of a lost gaiety, after the bugle calls among the dripping tents and the mud. I thought it was this music, taking me back to our Empires, that was responsible for the excitement churning and foaming in me – and also thought, with a touch of self-contempt, how little it took now to make me feel almost light-headed – but afterwards I realized that this was all wrong, that on this as on other important occasions what was to happen could throw not only its shadows but also its light in advance of itself.

Our second-in-command – 'The Majah' we called him – oldish and an ex-regular officer but willowy and astoundingly elegant in our peasants' eyes – came in front of the curtain to tell us how fortunate we were and how very kind the talented West End performers were and how we were all about to enjoy a jolly good show. The officers clapped, we on the benches stamped our feet, and the packed mob at the back whistled. It's not easy to suggest a mixture of enthusiasm, scepticism and derision in whistles, but those chaps managed it. The major looked as if he was about to say something else – he often looked as if he was about to say something else, and probably always would – and then sauntered off. The band, now conducted by a young man who seemed to think he was at the Queen's Hall with the London Symphony, started up again. And if that young man was excited, I was much worse, with even less reason for it than he had.

Well, there was a baritone and 'Drake's Drum'; there was a soprano, who might have been Iris Hampton's sister, and the Waltz Song from *Tom Jones*; there was a comedian with a comedienne and one of those energetic-miming duets from a musical comedy; there was another comedian, on his own, all guffaws, patter and sweat; there was an American woman, the ragtime star of a revue, with an enormous mouth, a hoarse voice, and snapping fingers; and then there was an old-young man with wavy hair singing a catchy duet with an exceedingly pretty, rather short, fair girl. But she wasn't any pretty, rather short, fair girl. She was Nancy Ellis. And as soon as they had taken their call, I was trying to find, to push, to fight, my way out. It wasn't that I coolly made up my mind to see her, to speak to her. It was just a huge blind impulse that made me push and shove and fight to reach her. That she mightn't want to see me never occurred to me. I was far beyond any reasonable considerations, and if I hadn't been I'd never have got to her.

It was bad enough getting out of the building, but it was far worse trying to get in again, this time through the back entrance, serving as a stage door. It was raining hard now, and I was soon soaked and knew that my face must be streaked with that damnable blue dye. There were two military police round at the back there, two well-wrapped-up detestable 'redcaps', and as soon as they saw me they told me to push off. But there were some cars there too, probably waiting to take the performers back to the West End, which now, in my miserable condition, I saw as something unimaginably rich, luxurious, magnificent; and I used these cars to dodge out of sight of the police and then to watch the lighted open doorway, to see if I might have a chance of nipping in there. Time passed; the rain never stopped; but at last the two police moved away, probably to have a smoke where they wouldn't be seen. This was my chance, and I leapt at it, racing across to the open door. It led to a short corridor, which turned a corner at the end. Nobody was about but I thought I could hear voices coming from round the corner, so I ventured a quick peep and saw a good many people bustling about or loitering backstage, among them several officers. I went back to the exit, and then, noticing that the door opened inward, I got behind it. This corridor must have been recently added to the main brick building; it was made of the same kind of wood they were using for the big army huts that were just going up; and behind the door there was such a smell of wet sawdust and creosote that I kept wanting to sneeze. Rain was driving in or leaking through several knotholes. I was already soaked through; I could feel cold rivulets down my back; I began soon to be threatened by cramp. But I could see without being seen, and I knew that Nancy would have to come out this way.

Sometimes with the two military policemen within a few feet of me, I was behind that door for the longest hour there can ever have been. And I doubt if in the fifty years since then, I have ever entered a newly-built hut or been near some kinds of freshly-sawn wood without suddenly recalling, with that sharpness which smells bring, that long long hour behind the door.

Then, because the entertainment was over, everything happened almost at once. Officers came in from outside, hoping to meet the girls; officers came round the corner, escorting the performers; my corridor was suddenly filled with bodies, smoke and babble. I was feeling desperate now. Nancy, easily hidden, might come and go without my catching even a glimpse of her. I heaved, pushed, shoved myself into the corridor.

'What the devil are you doing, man?'

'Sorry, sir,' I muttered to the lieutenant. 'Urgent message for Captain Slocum.' I pushed past two or three of them, and then in front a way was cleared for the ragtime queen, a big woman, and our 'Majah', and when this impressive pair passed by, they left behind them a space into which I darted. Two captains came round the corner and between them, not smiling, looking serious, almost sad, was Nancy.

My heart went rocketing and before I knew what else was happening I heard myself crying out to her. 'Nancy – Nancy!'

'Now look here—' one of the captains began.

'Oh – be quiet.' Nancy had stopped to stare at me, the blue-dyed sodden convict.

'Nancy, it's me – Dick Herncastle-'

'Dick – Dick—' And she ran at me and then she was kissing me and trying to laugh and cry at the same time.

'Know each other obviously,' said one captain.

'Quite, but man shouldn't be here,' said the other.

'Oh – do shut up,' said Nancy. Then she looked at me, ready to laugh and cry again. 'Oh – Dick – darling – you look so awful-'

'I know I do.' And then – and to hell with the captains – 'I love you.'

'I love you too.' And she said it as if she meant it for ever. And she did and so did I.

Epilogue
by J.B.P

In spite of my protests, Herncastle had refused to add anything to round off his story – he could be very obstinate – but he did agree that we should meet one afternoon for a final discussion. This was easy because I was in London and he and his wife were staying with their daughter and granddaughter up in Hampstead. This daughter Anne, Mrs Tryford, was a widow; she had been a civil servant for many years, and was now an assistant secretary at the Board of Trade. This is all I know about her because in fact we never met. Her daughter, Meg Tryford, was a teenage art student, and, as I knew before I went to Hampstead, was Herncastle's darling. His arthritis was better than it had been when we met in Askrigg, and he was able without much trouble to let me in and show me upstairs to a first-floor sitting-room. It had a fine bow window, three rows of white bookshelves running round the walls, several coloured lithographs by Vuillard and Bonnard, which Herncastle told me he had bought in Paris, before the war, for about twenty-five shillings each (they're asking about seventy-five pounds for them now), and three of his own watercolours, which I admired before we sat down to talk.

'My wife and Meg are out shopping somewhere,' he told me. 'But they said they'd be back by teatime. I have to keep reminding myself that you've never yet set eyes on Nancy.'

'No, and that's the first point I want to make,' I said firmly. 'Because you refuse to add anything, the reader will be left up in the air, wondering why this girl who never answered your letters threw herself into your arms—'

'I know, I know. But – look – she'll be back soon, so why don't we wait to argue about that? Next point.'

'It's about what happened to people, Richard—' I stopped because he laughed. 'What's the matter?'

'Sorry, J.B., but the way you said that, calling me Richard too, you reminded me of Uncle Nick.'

'And he's very much one of the people we want to know about. You see, here and there – with Ricarlo, for example – you jump out of the past to tell us what happened to them. But with most of your people, you don't; you leave us wondering. About Uncle Nick, for instance.'

'Yes. Yes, yes. Quite so.' Herncastle was lighting his pipe. 'And we might as well have him out of the way before Nancy gets back. She never liked him. Couldn't stand him at any price. Though she's had to admit we owe him something. What he finally did made a great difference to me.' He puffed away, ruminating, and I didn't hurry him. We old buffers and puffers know how to take our time.

'Well then, Uncle Nick. He was of course disgusted with me. And not just because I was enlisting. I think he'd really looked forward to having me with him in America. So he didn't write often, and of course in the war he never knew where I was, so he'd write to me care of my Aunt Mary – his sister. He stayed out there, never came back, not even for a visit. But in 1917 he left the stage and went into business, with an American friend, at Dayton, Ohio. They manufactured some little sighting device for machine-guns in aeroplanes. He got a divorce from his wife here and then he married his partner's cousin – a widow, quite well off, I believe. He died quite suddenly – heart attack – in 1926. By that time he was a dollar millionaire. He left me twenty-five thousand dollars, which is why I said Nancy'd had to admit we owed him something. With that money, enough to live on for some years, I was able to stop teaching art and produce some of my own. It made all the difference to us. His widow paid us a visit when she was touring Europe, but she didn't think much of us – and we weren't mad about her. I saw an American illusionist at the Palladium who did the Box trick, *The Rival Magicians*, *The Vanishing Cyclist* and my *Magic Painting* – he must have bought them from Uncle Nick – but he was nothing like as impressive, at least to me he wasn't. Apart from David Devant, Uncle Nick was just about as good as anybody there was. But he wasn't a happy man, never could be. He got nothing from Woman, nothing from Art, nothing where a man's experience can be richest, most satisfying. In a sense you might say I learnt a lot in reverse from him.' He puffed away, without a word, for some moments. 'Uncle Nick – yes. I may have given an impression towards the end that we liked each other a lot less than we actually did. There was some real affection there on both sides.'

I waited, but when it was obvious he didn't want to say anything else, I said: 'By the way, there's something I forgot to tell you earlier, Richard. In the earlier 1920s, I often spent a winter afternoon, between spells of hard work, at the Coliseum. And I remember quite clearly seeing your friends, the American comics, Jennings and Johnson, at the Coliseum. They were very funny.'

'I saw them too when they were over that time. And I went behind to have a drink with them. But I don't think they ever came back again, and I've no idea what happened to them. You know, J.B., the trouble with this kind of talk – all about what happened to people – is that at our age it can turn very melancholy. You'll be asking next about Julie Blane. And she's one to get rid of before Nancy joins us. Nancy isn't narrow-minded but she thinks what I wrote about Julie is *downright disgusting*. I don't agree. I had to give an honest account of what happened and what I thought and felt at the time. Anyhow, there isn't much to be said about Julie. She came back from South Africa, after a couple of years or so, got one or two good parts in the West End, and then she died in the 'flu epidemic in 1918. I wouldn't have known if Nancy hadn't sent me a little newspaper cutting about it. She hadn't much luck, poor Julie.'

'No – and Tommy Beamish didn't have much luck, Richard. I remember him very well before the First War, and I agree with you – he was a wonderful comic. Then I forgot about him until I saw a paragraph in the *Manchester Guardian*. That was some time in the later 1920s, and he'd just died. I got the impression he'd been some years in a mental home.'

'He had – poor devil!' said Herncastle. 'He must have been about to crack up that spring in 1914, though he did some touring during the war — off and on.'

'And what about Cissie Mapes?'

'I saw her again – just once. It was in 1916. I'd come home on leave and I wasn't meeting Nancy until the next day. She was working in a hospital then, down in Hampshire, and she usually managed to get a bit of leave when I had mine. So I was on my own this first night and I decided to go to the second house at the Victoria Palace. I was early so I went for a drink to one of the big flashy pubs round there, full of tarts and chaps looking for them. Well, I was standing at the bar and there, further along, was Cissie with another woman. And they'd enough slapdash make-up on to stop a horse. So this was it. Hadn't Inspector Crabb told me that Cissie would be on the streets not so long after she'd left us? Then she saw me – stared — then recognized me and came hurrying round before I could make a move. And Crabb had been wrong and I'd just been wrong. She was in a munitions factory, somewhere in north-east London – working very hard and earning good money – and she was going to marry a sergeant in the Machine-gun Corps next time he got leave – and she and her friend were having a night out. So of course I joined them and told Cissie my news – she was delighted about Nancy – and we talked about Uncle Nick. She gave me her address but I lost it, together with a lot of stuff, next time I was up in the line. And I never saw her or heard anything about her again. I can only hope she married her sergeant and he survived.'

'Well, as another old infantryman, Richard, my experience was that the Machine-gun Corps often survived when we didn't. By the way, I don't think I told you, when we were corresponding, that I well remember Lily Farris as a boring star turn. But that was before the First War. Indeed, I'd forgotten her until you wrote about her.'

'All I know about her is that towards the end of the First War, Mergen died – he was never interned – and then she went out to Australia and never came back. But what she did out there, I don't know. And I must say, I don't care. Of course she must be dead now.'

'I'll bet everybody's dead.' The speaker had arrived before we had noticed her. Herncastle hastily introduced us. I felt at once that this brisk little elderly woman, white-haired and lined but lively-eyed and quick and decisive in her movements, could easily be the Nancy he had described, after fifty years of satisfying experience.

'You're having one of those miserable What-became-of conversations, aren't you? Well, I won't stop you – not yet. I'll make tea.'

'Where's Meg?' said Herncastle.

'I left her at the corner shop, taking a free look at some art books. She'll be back soon, though she won't want any tea. Doesn't like it. They don't like anything we've always liked, these girls. Just to show their independence.' And out she went.

'There was somebody else,' I began slowly. 'Oh – yes, the Tingleys. You wrote that you and Doris and, I think, your uncle were all wrong about Archie Tingley, then left it at that. What happened?'

'He was right and we were all wrong. Once he got into films – distributing, not producing them – there was no stopping him. He'd something vaguely wrong with him, so he was never called up, and as films became more and more popular, he shot up with them. Towards the end of my time at the Slade – I got an ex-officers' grant to go there – about 1922 it must have been, I ran into them and then they took me to the Savoy in a whacking great Rolls. He made a fortune, Archie did. But I never could help feeling that Doris would have been happier if he hadn't. They're still alive – in their eighties, living in Bermuda. And they've got several pictures of mine out there that I'd like to take another look at – and they've asked us to stay, but we can't afford the fares and I'm not going to let Archie pay them. So there it is.'

'And here this is,' said his wife, coming in behind a tea trolley. And we talked about anything and nothing, as people usually do, while plates and cups were being passed. But when we had settled down, Herncastle looked at me, with a grin somewhere behind his moustache and beard. 'Now, J.B., just tell Nancy what you said to me when we first began talking – I mean, about the reader being left up in the air – you remember?'

'I told your husband that because he refuses to add anything to that final scene, at the camp, the reader will be left in the air, wondering why you, who never answered his letters, immediately threw yourself into his arms.'

'When I heard him calling my name – and I saw him standing there, in that awful uniform, I knew – in a flash – I loved him.'

'Yes, I can understand that. And I realize you were attracted to him from the first, perhaps half in love with him—'

'More than half.'

'Yes. But what I can't understand is why you never wrote to him.'

'As a matter of fact, I did, as soon as the war began. But it miscarried somehow. That was always happening when you were on the stage. I didn't write earlier because, in those days, I was a bit too proud, a bit too hard. I felt I was falling for him too soon and too easily. He was very attractive – you wouldn't think so to look at him now, would you? – No, be quiet, Dick – and I could see all the other women were interested in him. Well, then we had that silly little quarrel, when I was leaving to go into pantomime, but I was longing and longing for him to come to Plymouth and make it up. But then his precious Julie Blane told me they were having an affair, and I thought, Oh well, he's just another of *that* sort. Then he wrote, and I began to wonder. But I wouldn't let myself write back, though I spent hours making up letters I never wrote. Then I decided I'd just wait. If he was really serious, he'd keep on writing. If he wasn't, then he wouldn't. I was testing him. Yes, I know what you're going to say—'

'Well, I don't,' I said hastily.

'It was the look in your eye. Yes, for a girl of eighteen, more than half in love with a boy, I was being very severe. But as I've already said, I was a bit too proud, a bit too hard. I'd spent too much time among people who were just the opposite. Sloppy people with no pride in themselves. Naughty sporty girls and jolly old pals. Half-plastered sentimentalists. Soakers and spongers. I don't say Susie and Bob were as bad as that – you remember them in Dick's book?'

'Yes. What became of them?'

'I'll tell you. But don't let us start that again. Bob joined up but just sat in a fort up in Scotland. They carried on after the war – concert parties, pantos, never really getting anywhere – so then, about 1930, they chucked it, and ran an hotel in South Devon. All right, Dick, don't interrupt, I *know* it was awful. Bob died during the Second War – and Susie about ten years ago. She never really forgave me for leaving the stage, which I did at the end of 1914 – in a big success too. She'd all the ambition and I'd what little talent the family had. I could always do what they wanted me to do, and do it well, but I hated doing it. I never wanted to be on the stage. And in a way—' She hesitated, then looked at her husband. 'I've never told you this, Dick, but now that J.B. is here and you're talking about the book, I'll say it.'

'If he can take it, I can, my love,' said Herncastle.

'All right then. In a way,' she said to me, scowling as Herncastle had described her doing, fifty years before, 'I may have been a bad influence on this book of his—'

'Nonsense!'

'Be quiet, Dick. You see, we hadn't talked about our stage life for years – hadn't thought about it – after all, it's ages ago and it didn't last long. But then of course Dick began remembering, and began talking it over with me. And because I'd really hated it, I think that, without meaning to, I may have influenced him to darken his picture of it. You know, everybody thinks of the old music halls being so gay and jolly, hearts of gold everywhere, all what-is-it – gusto and wonderful talent, audiences laughing and crying their heads off – even Meg believes all that – and the last time I read what Dick had written, I could see he hadn't made it like that at all, and that may have been partly my doing, and people don't like having their illusions disturbed—' She stopped to take a long breath.

'I put down as best I could exactly what I saw and thought and felt,' said Herncastle carefully to both of us. 'My belief is that by 1913, when it was organized like big business, the variety stage was already well on the decline. It wasn't any longer a kind of explosion of popular talent. That was already going into films. Like Chaplin and Stan Laurel and the rest of 'em. Even so, I wish you could have seen Nancy here as I first saw her.'

'Oh – don't start that, Dick—'

'Just a minute.' He held up his hand. We could hear from above the thumping of an implacable rhythm. 'That's Meg playing her gramophone. Let's take a quiet peep at her. It might give you some idea.'

'He means she's very like me as I was then. It's queer how resemblances jump a generation. Anne, her mother, isn't a bit like me, but I can see that Meg is.'

Very slowly and stealthily we climbed to the floor above. Some idiot pop tune came battering and booming at us. The door was half open. We crept nearer and nearer to it, and then took by turns our quiet peep. I saw a teenage girl dressed in a black sweater and bleached jeans, capering happily in front of the gramophone. She was fair, with short crisp curls, smallish with a rather square face but uncommonly attractive. She never heard us. She was capering in some other and happier place, another planet perhaps. We crept downstairs, feeling a thousand years on our backs.

'Yes,' said Herncastle when we could talk again, 'that's Nancy as she was – all over again.'

'Except that the clothes and the music are different,' said his wife, with something like a sigh.

I felt I had to say something. 'The clothes and the music are always different, aren't they?'

No doubt I could have been wiser or wittier; but let's leave it at that.

Also available from Great Northern Books:

Bright Day
by J. B. Priestley

Disillusioned writer Gregory Dawson is holed up in a Cornish hotel writing a script he must finish. A chance encounter in the bar triggers memories of the doomed world of his youth before the slaughter of The First World War and forces him to remember his time within a close-knit Yorkshire community, his days spent with the Alington family and his first, tentative steps towards becoming an author. Caught up in this lost world, he realises that to have any chance of a bright future he must first exorcise the ghosts of his past and come to terms with a tragedy that has haunted him for decades.

Jungian, semi-autobiographical and Priestley's own personal favourite, *Bright Day* is a story and a journey laced with warmth, colour and Priestley's trademark compassion and tenderness.

"Bright Day is as bright as its title, so full of youth's golden hours that one could call it a Golden Retrospective, or the Golden Book of J. B. Priestley."
Manchester Evening News

"I do not think Priestley has ever written anything better than this book."
News Chronicle

"J. B. Priestley is one of our literary icons of the 20th Century and it is time that we all became re-acquainted with his genius." **Dame Judi Dench**

"A grand writer… a great writer." **Beryl Bainbridge**

"Bright Day is good Priestley… its republication is an event to be celebrated." **Melvyn Bragg**

"A gripping and readable novel, with a powerful page-turning plot."
Margaret Drabble

www.greatnorthernbooks.co.uk

Also available from Great Northern Books:

The Good Companions
by J. B. Priestley

In the great depression between the wars, ordinary Yorkshireman, Jess Oakroyd, disreputable schoolteacher, Inigo Jollifant and Colonel's daughter, Miss Trant are all unhappy and unsure about what to do with their lives. Each seizes the opportunity to flee their current situation to seek adventure on the open road. Fate then brings them together and into the presence of a down-at-heel and fractious theatrical touring company. With Miss Trant's money, their modest talents and buckets of enthusiasm they form a travelling troupe who proceed to sing, dance, drink and argue their way through the pavilions, provincial theatres, towns, seaside lodging houses and market fairs of Twenties' England.

The winner of the James Tait Black Memorial Prize for Fiction in 1929, *The Good Companions* is a captivating, hilarious, riotous and unforgettable carnival of English life.

"Priestley is a writer whom I admire. I remember reading The Good Companions *in one fell juvenile swoop."* **Melvyn Bragg**

"A truly great novel." **The Sunday Times**

"Wonderful vitality… describes with unfailing truth and humour the rich fabric of English provincial life." **The Daily Telegraph**

"One of the great novels of the 20th Century." **Paul Johnson, The Spectator**

"A wonderful story." **Dame Judi Dench**

"Picaresque, picturesque… If you have not read it I envy you, it lies ahead…" **Barry Cryer**

www.greatnorthernbooks.co.uk

Also available from Great Northern Books:

Angel Pavement
by J. B. Priestley

Tucked away in the City of London, lies a dingy, almost forgotten side street known as Angel Pavement. Here can be found the headquarters of Twigg & Dersingham, suppliers of veneers and inlays to the cabinet-making trade. Business is bad and getting worse. The firm is fighting for its life and its staff are gripped by the fear of insolvency and redundancy. Into their midst descends the mysterious and charming Mr. Golspie and his beautiful daughter, Lena. Together they set in train a sequence of events that will transform the lives of everyone who works there.

Shot through with Priestley's trademark social conscience, Angel Pavement is one of the great London novels; a vivid evocation of the 1930s metropolis in an age of recession. It is also a brilliant and startlingly relevant examination of what happens to a group of workers when the destructive force of a rapacious financial predator is unleashed among them.

"There's a part of London no-one can take from me, because I invented it." **J. B. Priestley**

"The whole fabric of the few lives, are opened up to us with a warm and generous assiduity that is entirely convincing… Magnificent." **The Times**

"A novel by a man who thoroughly enjoys the whole spectacle of life and can communicate his enjoyment." **The Daily Telegraph**

"A marvellous writer." **David Hockney**

"A lost classic from the teeming world of Depression-era London." **DJ Taylor**

www.greatnorthernbooks.co.uk

Also available from Great Northern Books:

Priestley at Kissing Tree House: A Memoir

by Rosalie Batten – J. B. Priestley's Personal Secretary 1968-1984

With contributions from
Tom Priestley, Nicolas Hawkes and Susan Cooper

Hidden away for over 30 years and only just come to light – a unique insight into one of the most important authors of the 20th Century

A unique, warm and intimate portrait of the private, hidden life, of one of the twentieth century's most widely read authors and great public figures. The book reveals Priestley's daily routines, his writing habits, hobbies, weaknesses, eccentricities and his correspondence with a variety of organisations and people, including family, and other renowned figures of the twentieth century; a warts and all portrait, truthful, revealing, moving. A book which in the end, displays great love for its subject.

"One day I very much hope that Mrs. Batten will write a book about me because, as I have pointed out to her, she knows me better than anyone else who might want to write such a book."
J. B. Priestley, 26th June, 1979

"I have done my best and can only add the message that I put on my funeral flowers, that it comes with admiration, hope and love."
Rosalie Batten

"Priestley clearly encouraged Mrs. Batten to write a book about him. And now we find that she did, with great affection, after he died. He'd have been pleased."
Susan Cooper

www.greatnorthernbooks.co.uk